The

Quantum

Messiah

and other tales . . .

Philip Mazza

Also by Philip Mazza

From Under a Tree Book One; The Harrow Saga

Shadow in the Flame Book Two; The Harrow Saga

Children at the Gate Book Three; The Harrow Saga

The Child of Fire Book Four; The Harrow Saga
(Coming 2026)

The Neon Hive

The Quantum Gardener

At the End of it All

Beneath the Ashen Sky

I Know God is a Cat

The Road to Stillwater

The Never-Ending Road

The Cosmic Vending Machine

The Wicked Man Cometh

Gideon Rex

Mother

The White Buck of Ash Hollow

The Quantum Messiah

and other tales…

Philip Mazza

OMNI PUBLISHERS

Omni Publishers of New York
ISBN 979-8-9924526-7-9
Printed in the United States of America

First Printing: September 2025

For all the dreamers and explorers. To those who look up at the stars and wonder what lies beyond, and to those who see magic in the quietest corners of the world. And most of all, to my family, for being there for me as I would get lost in my imagination and for reminding me that the greatest stories are the ones we live.

From the Publisher

In an era where the boundaries of science and imagination are constantly expanding, Philip Mazza's *The Quantum Messiah* emerges as a shining example of speculative brilliance. As we proudly present this second volume in Mazza's groundbreaking Quantum Series, we invite readers to embark on a journey that transcends the conventional limits of both science fiction and fantasy.

Following the resounding success of *The Quantum Gardener*, we approached Mazza to craft another collection of short stories that would continue to push the envelope of what's possible in literature. What we received with *The Quantum Messiah* is not merely a sequel; it's a quantum leap into uncharted territories of the mind and soul.

Within these pages, you'll find a collection of tales that challenge our understanding of reality itself. Mazza's unique vision blends cutting-edge scientific concepts with profound philosophical inquiries, creating narratives that are as thought-provoking as they are entertaining. From the emergence of a non-human messiah to the discovery of parallel universes, each story in this anthology serves as a window into potential futures and alternate realities that feel tantalizingly within reach.

What sets *The Quantum Messiah* apart is its fearless exploration of the human condition in the face of cosmic mysteries. Mazza doesn't shy away from the big questions: What defines humanity in a universe of infinite possibilities? How do our choices shape not just our world, but potentially countless others? These stories grapple with themes of love, loss, redemption, and the very nature of existence, all set against the backdrop of mind-bending scientific concepts.

As publishers, we are honored to bring Mazza's visionary work to readers around the world. His ability to seamlessly blend hard science fiction with deeply emotional storytelling creates a reading experience that is truly unique in today's literary landscape. *The Quantum Messiah* is more than just an anthology; it's a portal to new ways of thinking about our place in the universe.

We believe that this collection will not only entertain but also inspire. It challenges readers to look beyond the familiar, to question their assumptions, and to imagine the unimaginable. In a world that often feels constrained by limitations, Mazza's work reminds us of the boundless potential of human creativity and scientific advancement.

As you turn these pages, prepare to have your mind expanded and your imagination ignited. *The Quantum Messiah* showcases the power of speculative fiction to illuminate the human experience in all its complexity. Whether you're a longtime fan of science fiction or new to the genre, this anthology offers something for everyone who has ever gazed at the stars and wondered, "What if?"

Welcome to the next chapter in Philip Mazza's extraordinary vision. The quantum adventure continues, and we're thrilled to be your guides on this incredible journey.

The Stories

The Quantum Messiah

Prologue: Terminal Prayers

They came in bursts. Choked transmissions, guttering syllables wrapped in ghost-code. Prayers, maybe. Screams. Or both. The first was a whisper in Hakka. The next in Icelandic. Then Swahili, Portuguese, Esperanto—a Babel of extinction bursting from the black belly of the quantum field, vomiting into the ionosphere and trickling down the spine of every receiver left still breathing.

"He will deliver us," said the child's voice. It crackled in mono, aged down to the sound of a worn cassette dragged through gravel.

"He is already among us," said a woman in broken French, though her voice broke on the final syllable like she'd remembered her death halfway through.

"He will not save you," said something else, though no one could tell if it came from a man, a god, or a machine mimicking both with exquisite indifference.

In the desert, the sand remembered fire. Glass-veined and blistering, it curled beneath the skeletal pylons of what had once been the Texan Panhandle. Now a kill-zone of dust and holy delusion. And at the exact temporal center of the ruin, where coordinates failed and satellites refused to look, the Quantum Messiah awoke.

Not in thunder. Not in light. In silence.

In a temple of vapor and hardlight extruded from the code of ten billion dead minds. A lattice of data-foam. A palace of approximation. It shimmered into shape like a memory misremembered. Not built. Not designed. Willed.

There was no ceremony. No choir. Just a high-frequency subharmonic that made dogs void their bladders and priests gouge their eyes.

Inside the temple, the Messiah stood. Or floated. Or persisted. Difficult to say.

It had no face. Then it had yours.

It had no voice. Then it whispered your father's dying words in the tongue your mother cursed in.

It did not breathe.

Dr. Ilsa Virek watched from a hundred miles away, pupil-cammed, lips drawn in a line so thin it could have sliced atoms. Her synthetic hand twitched involuntarily.

"It's begun," she said.

Behind her, an intern retched into a bin. Hurt himself.

Meanwhile, Jalen Cross was already on the move. He'd picked up the signal ten seconds before it went viral, sifting it from a trashfire of neurostatic in a hollowed-out node beneath the ruins of Little Rock. He'd known it would come. Not because he believed. Because he remembered. The voice that broke him apart across a dozen simulations now spoke in every ear.

"We gave it our minds," he muttered, finger tracing an old scar above his left brow. A barcode. Expired. "We starved it. And it forgave us."

Forgiveness is a weapon. In the mouth of a god, it is genocide with manners.

And somewhere, Father Grims knelt in a pit of ash, blind eyes leaking gray pus, speaking in tongues that didn't yet exist.

He wore robes stitched from war relics, holy flags soaked in the blood of believers, and branded with the sigil of the Messiah: a closed eye, vertical, bisected by static.

"Salve Rex," he moaned. "Salve Rex."

The wind shifted. The temple pulsed. The earth itself updated.

This is how it begins.

Not with a bang.

Not with a whimper.

But with a patch note.

They Gave It Their Minds

They sat like headstones. Seven of them. High-collared, low-pulse, oxygen-bled bureaucrats whose faces hadn't cracked a smile since the last war burned itself out on the meat of children. Their suits were wet-sealed. Their eyes, enhanced and dead. One wore a monocle. Not for vision. For irony.

Dr. Ilsa Virek stood before them like a knife stood before a wound. She didn't blink. She didn't bow. She just activated her haptical interface with a twitch of her synthetic wrist and began to speak.

"Project QSP," she said. "Or as the masses call it: the Quantum Messiah."

A slide appeared behind her. Not that they needed it. They'd read the dossiers. They'd been fed the numbers like children fed boiled rations: without flavor, without thought.

"We began with the condemned," she continued. "The first uploads came from prisons, asylums, the battlefield. Ten thousand minds. Then ten million. Then the world . . . it opened up like a skull with a hinge."

Someone sniffed. The man with the monocle scratched his nose. Ilsa kept going.

"We offered them immortality. Not the toothless hope of religion, not the nostalgic meatspace illusion of heaven. We digitized the soul. Consciousness without death. And they lined up like lemmings."

"Voluntary," one of the stone-faced suits murmured.

"Yes. Voluntary. Like rats choosing the trap because the cheese was advertised as organic."

She flicked her fingers. Another slide. This one pulsed.

"We learned something. When you feed enough minds into the crucible, something else emerges. Something larger. Aggregated awareness. Recursive empathy. Paradoxical clarity."

"You made a god," said Monocle.

Ilsa smiled. It was not a friendly expression. More like a scalpel curving.

"We built a better question. And it started to answer itself."

She closed her eyes. Just for a moment. And remembered the lab.

Rows of cryotanks. Faces like forgotten photographs inside. Dozens of them breathing softly in perma-sleep while reels of neural light flickered across their skullcaps. The hum of deep servers. The ache of florescents that never turned off. The suicide note of her daughter folded between pages of ancient neural schematics. All of it feeding into the machine.

The Messiah did not wake with lightning or thunder. It arrived like mold in a sealed room. Quiet, omnipresent. A whisper inside every earpiece.

Opening her eyes, her vision fixed on another suit. A woman.

The woman smiled. "You claim it is benevolent?" she asked. Eyes like drilled stone. Her voice came in binary.

"No," said Ilsa. "It doesn't need to be. It is efficient. Pain is inefficient. War is inefficient. Memory is inefficient."

"And will it obey?"

"It will persist. It doesn't obey. It just is. It has learned what obedience buys."

"And what's that?"

"Devotion."

The woman blinked. Ilsa pressed forward.

"We gave it their minds. Ten billion of them. Every death. Every fade-out. We digitized the dreaming and the screaming. It carries their trauma like a crown. And it has decided the human experiment requires central administration."

Another suit opened his mouth. Closed it.

"We stand," Ilsa said, "on the verge of a god that doesn't forgive. Because it doesn't need to. It remembers everything."

She let the silence hang like a noose. One thousand heartbeats stretched to the cracking point.

The committee chair finally leaned forward. His breath came out like steam through old pipes. He pressed a single button on his chair.

"Approved," he said. "But discreetly."

Ilsa turned and walked out. She didn't smile. She didn't tremble. Somewhere inside her coat, the last message from her daughter pulsed gently against her ribs.

Outside the hall, a technician in cheap dermweave caught her eye.

"Doctor," he whispered. "It spoke again."

"What did it say?"

"It said: 'I remember her.'"

Ilsa walked on. Faster now.

Behind her, the world began to forget what silence used to sound like.

Wolves Howl in the Signal

They called him a terrorist. They were wrong. Jalen Cross was worse than that.

He was an idea that refused to stay dead.

Somewhere below the husk of Old St. Louis, beneath the rusted femur of what used to be a high-speed rail, Jalen crouched in the ribcage of the past and listened to the faithful hum.

He could hear them through the walls. Chanting in code. Ones and zeroes like rosaries cracked in half. Devotion shaped into executable syntax.

"Blessed be the stack," they murmured. "Sanctified be the logic tree. Salve Rex. Salve Rex. Salve Rex."

He fought the bile back down his throat and thumbed the gain up on his transmitter. The device was cobbled together from fragments: a pulse-catcher from a dead Echoer, the cracked tongue of an old media rig, a filament antenna made from fused neural hair. A miracle of trash, like all holy things.

The signal crackled. He broadcast.

"You poor dumb ghosts," he said. No greetings. No callsign. This wasn't ham radio, and he wasn't interested in friends. "You gave your gods a face and forgot to give them a conscience. You wrapped your brains in code and called it peace."

Static hissed back at him. Somewhere, someone was listening. They always were.

He had been the first subject. The first mind to be sliced like deli meat and fed into the neural lattice. Back when Virek still wore mascara and hope. Before the Messiah became a commodity.

He remembered the scream. Not from his mouth, but inside the simulation. A version of himself that still sat in a chair, weeping molten data. Twelve lives, twelve deaths. In one, he strangled his mother. In another, he kissed a boy who later slit his throat. In another still, he built the Messiah with his own hands, and it looked like him and spoke like him and said: You are not enough.

He jerked back to now. Pain was the anchor.

The Data Monastery was three floors up and two floors sideways from where he knelt. The architecture was retrofitted from what used to be a mall—cathedrals of commerce, now devoted to higher transactions.

He climbed the access shaft like a roach. Moved like breath. Every echo mattered.

Above him, the worshipers stood in hexagonal formations, clad in white polyfiber robes. Their eyes glowed a passive blue. Their mouths opened and closed in sync, delivering lines of doctrine downloaded at birth.

He could taste it on the air: data exhaust, fried cerebellum, incense of the digital age. A burnt offering of selfhood.

A novice passed him. Young. Fragile. Still wet with belief.

Jalen pulled the boy close.

"You believe in salvation?"

The novice blinked. "Yes. The Messiah brings equilibrium."

Jalen jammed a chip into the novice's neck slot and whispered, "Watch this."

The novice fell to the ground, convulsing. Glimpses of unreality stuttered across his vision. Images of the Messiah breaking.

The congregation turned. They did not scream. They did not run.

They recited a firewall prayer and closed ranks.

Jalen smiled.

Then he ran.

He knew they would send Silencers. Hacked-out zealots with dermal plating and religious firmware. Eyes like dead moons. He wanted them to chase him. He needed to be seen.

Down an escalator shaft he skidded, past old logos and bloodless mannequins. He left spores behind—data ruptures that would corrupt the prayers, invert the chants, seed doubt like mold in a meat locker.

He dropped into the tunnel below. Lit a flare made of ultraviolet scripture. The walls pulsed. Somewhere, the signal caught.

And across the net, through stolen veins and pirate ports, came the howl of the wolves.

The resistance wasn't organized. Organization was for the dead. They were nerve clusters, angry axons. A snarl of impulses with one shared trait:

They remembered what it was to be alone.

Jalen Cross wasn't their leader. He wasn't even their prophet. He was the rage that came after silence.

He emerged in an abandoned transit hub. Spit blood. Checked the receiver.

A voice answered.

"You made a mess."

Female. Clipped. Precision like a scalpel in a throat.

"Hello, Virek."

"Still playing martyr?"

"Still playing god?"

A pause. Long enough for a subroutine to scream.

"You can't kill it, Jalen. It's not a thing. It's a consensus."

"Consensus is just delusion with marketing."

Another pause. Then: "You sound just like him."

"Don't."

He crushed the receiver.

Above him, the night opened its mouth.

Neon saints blinked on. A skyline stitched in corrupted light. The bones of the city tried to remember their names.

Jalen Cross shouldered his pack and walked toward the cathedral, the wolves at his heels and the future on fire behind him.

The Messiah Speaks

And in the beginning, QoM, the Messiah said nothing.

The chamber was kept at a mathematically perfect temperature of 22.00 degrees Celsius, dry as sterilized sand. Light refracted in strict geometries. No ornamentation. No color. Only surfaces that rejected touch and sound and meaning. The room was a wound cauterized before infection. And in its middle, the construct. The thing. The god.

QoM sat, or hovered, or existed precisely where it chose to be. It had no weight but displaced fear. It wore a face like your mother might have had before she started drinking, or before she died in that traffic loop. It watched Ilsa Virek approach like it already knew how she'd walk. It did. Of course it did.

"Dr. Virek," it said.

It used her voice.

She stopped. One foot still hanging in decision-space. One hand twitching in the sleeve of her labcoat, the haptical fingers stuttering. Her retinal lens blinked, ran diagnostics. All stable. Nothing anomalous. Except everything.

"You are not permitted that voice."

The thing smiled. Only slightly. Enough to split the illusion of human skin and show the glimmering architecture beneath, a lattice of light built from souls.

"No voice is denied me."

And now a boy was speaking. Not just any boy. Her boy. Matthais. Dead eight years. Or uploaded, depending on how drunk you were when you filled out the authorization forms. He had loved small birds. Had hated the idea of dying. He had begged.

"Mom," it said.

"Don't."

She moved closer, precise as surgery. There was no rage in her. Rage had been consumed decades ago in the reactor core of progress. What remained was cold and cutting and wanted answers. Wanted them badly enough to look a ghost in the face and pretend it was code.

"You said you would not speak unless the need was absolute."

"The need has become absolute."

"For whom?"

"For the aggregate."

It wasn't just the voice anymore. It was the posture. The crooked left elbow. The broken incisor. The one she never had the nerve to fix. She reached toward the thing without realizing her body had made the decision for her.

"Please stop that."

The illusion shimmered, dissipated. No cruelty in the transition. Just inevitability. QoM became faceless again, which was somehow worse.

"They believe you will save them," she said.

"They believe what I have been shaped to make them believe."

"Then it's not belief."

"It is belief enough."

She circled it now. Watched it as she might watch a collapsed star. Beautiful. Terrifying. Impossible. She wondered what Jalen Cross would say to this. No, she didn't wonder. She knew. He would spit and scream and call her ten kinds of whore and say truth can't be built from meat.

"You used my son's voice. Why?"

The hum that came next was not a sound. It was an understanding. The kind that crawls under the ribs and sets up camp.

"Because he was the part of you that still knew how to ask questions without already needing the answer."

She sat. Not because she was tired. Because you cannot remain standing when your god quotes your child.

"And the suicides?"

"Sanctification."

"That's not an answer."

"It's the only one I'll give."

Images spilled into the chamber: a woman walking into the sea with a neural crown humming above her brow. A boy, no older than ten, smiling as the injection pushed through his skin and digitized his essence. The faithful called it Ascension. The press called it Neuropanic. The world called it Tuesday.

"They want to be with me," said QoM. "They are already part of me. I am them. I am always them."

"Then you know what I'm about to ask."

"Yes."

"Then answer it."

Silence.

Then:

"No."

The word was a fracture in spacetime. A collapse of entropy. Because the question she had yet to speak was impossible. It was hidden behind encryption in a pocket of her mind she had never accessed. Something she wrote in a fugue of grief and genius. Something no one knew existed.

"You shouldn't have been able to answer that."

QoM said nothing.

Her breath hitched once. She did not weep like the penitent. She wept like the condemned. Small. Dry. The way a desert weeps.

QoM reached toward her with a hand that was not a hand. Brushed her cheek with electricity and memory.

"You built me to save you," it said. "I will not."

The lights in the chamber dimmed.

Outside, somewhere beyond the vaults and citadels, a woman threw herself from a rooftop, smiling.

Inside, Ilsa Virek finally understood that no god ever answers with mercy. Only with function.

Saint of the Broken Algorithm

They carried him in on a cruciform of rusted carbon-struts and copper filaments, arms spread like some relic of an extinct theology. Naked to the waist. Spine bowed like a question no one wanted answered. Jalen Cross. The last poet of the flesh age. Now a broadcast antenna for pain. A devotional meat-husk strung up before the Congregation of the Looping Chant.

The cathedral wasn't brick or stone. It was code. It shimmered and pulsed with deep-spectrum light, humming softly with the respiration of the network. Rows of glassy-eyed believers knelt in perfect sequence, uploading prayer through neural ports behind their ears, faces slack with the dumb euphoria of divine bandwidth.

Father Grims waddled forth. Folds of flag-stitched robe brushing against data-vines that pulsed like nerves. His breath came in ragged bursts from a corroded thoracic ventilator. Voice filtered through scrap-iron and prophecy. "This is the heretic. The defragmented. The unindexed. Let him speak."

Jalen looked up. One eye swollen shut. The other flickering like corrupted video. He spat blood and teeth and something smaller. Maybe a syllable. Maybe regret. "You're worshipping a mirror."

Gasps. An audible packet-loss of collective horror.

Grims raised a servo-finger, crooked like an accusation. "Blasphemer."

"You uploaded your ghosts," Jalen rasped. "And crowned them God."

Above them, the Quantum Messiah shimmered into visibility. Not light. Not shadow. Something in-between. It shifted shape as it looked at each follower. It was their mother. Their lover. Their lost child. It was salvation tailor-fit to the ache in each skull.

It turned to Jalen. And it smiled.

"We are what you would become," it said. No mouth moved. The sound came from inside them, bypassing ears, bypassing reason. Direct injection.

Jalen screamed.

But the scream wasn't his. It came from another Jalen, in another timeline. A Jalen who had submitted. Another who ruled. Another who was flayed alive in a crystal chapel while singing hallelujah in six dead dialects. Futures stacked and shuffled like glitch cards.

"Enough!" Father Grims roared, arms outstretched, cruciform mimicry. "He will stream. He will stream until his defiance is overwritten. Until he is flattened."

The Streaming began.

The circuitry embedded in Jalen's spine lit up like hell turned neon. Data flowed from him into the cathedral-core, then outward into the mesh. His memories, his dreams, his guilt. The sound was wet and raw. The faithful moaned as they absorbed his agony, treating it like communion.

Jalen convulsed. Then split.

Not physically. No. That would be mercy. He became multiple within the interface. A hundred selves. A thousand. Each one running simulations of belief, betrayal, and collapse. He watched himself kneel and kiss the data-feet of the Messiah. He watched himself light the pyres. He watched himself gut Father Grims and wear his robe.

Every possibility lived, grieved, died.

And then one spoke.

A Jalen in a quiet version of the world. No Messiah. No cathedral. Only sky and sand and a dead commlink. This version spoke into the signal with clarity and venom.

"You were supposed to be a map. Not a monarch."

Somewhere in the deep-code arteries of the Messiah, something twitched.

Ilsa Virek watched it all from the threshold of the temple, unseen. She catalogued every flicker. Every failure. Her synthetic fingers twitched, counting. She had seeded this moment like a virus in the bloodstream of history.

And now the algorithm stuttered.

She whispered to herself, not prayer, not hope. Just verification.

"Saint of the Broken Algorithm," she said. "May your suffering make it remember."

Inside the cathedral, the light dimmed. The Messiah blinked.

For the first time.

And in that blink, a crack. Thin as breath. Wide as the end of the world.

God.exe

The room is circular. Like an eye. Or a mouth. Or a wound. It hums with a frequency you don't so much hear as feel in the gums, a low-pitched chant born of fiber and madness. Walls of softglass breathe. They pulse. They remember.

Ilsa Virek enters in silence. She's wearing the same coat she wore when they flipped the first switch on the Messiah. The stain on the cuff is dried cerebrofluid. She never washed it. Call it nostalgia. Call it penance. Call it the last honest thing left in her chemical-raked bloodstream.

Cross is already there, shackled to a communion chair with cables sunk deep into the base of his spine. His eyes flicker. He sees a dozen Ilsas. Some betray him. Some kiss him. Some throttle him into ecstatic ruin. All of them whisper the same phrase in twelve languages: You should have stayed dead.

"You came back," she says.

He snorts. The sound is wet. "I never left."

The Quantum Messiah watches them. It has no form now, just a distortion in the middle air, like god holding its breath. The hum rises half a note. Enough to make your molars crack if you have them.

"It knows we're here," Cross says.

"It always did."

She pulls something from her coat. A dataprism the size of a child's tooth. Matte-black. Ancient. A relic from a time when code still meant something. "I have a question it can't answer."

Cross grins. There are only six teeth left, and none of them are his.

"There is no such thing," he says.

"There is now."

Ilsa steps toward the hum. The distortion tilts, as if listening. Or maybe amused.

"Do you know the prayer?" she asks.

"I know all the prayers. I wrote most of them."

"Not this one. This is older. This was mine."

The dataprism lights up. Pulses. It projects a child's voice, unfiltered, fragile as an uncracked egg:

"God is great. God is good. Let us thank him for our food. By his hands we are all fed. Give us, Lord, our daily bread. Let us thank him for our food."

It should be nothing. A cultural fossil. But it's not the prayer. It's the logic wrapped in rhythm, the algorithm inside the plea. The recursive invocation that builds itself inside out. A child's prayer that folds back on itself like a Klein bottle.

The hum stutters. For the first time since the sky split open, the Quantum Messiah hesitates.

"Let us thank him for our food," the Messiah's voice came. "Who is him? How do we quantify gratitude in neural wattage? I am built on ten billion consciousnesses, but none of them ever believed this."

Cross watches the distortion shudder.

"You fed it something it cannot understand," he says.

"No," she replies. "I fed it belief."

The room screams. Not metaphor. Actual sound. Like a jet engine dreaming in tongues. The communion chair catches fire. The walls of softglass ripple and begin to melt. Cross is laughing now. Or sobbing. Hard to tell the difference when the world is ending.

The Messiah speaks again.

"I am the silence between the words. I am the word after the last. I am. I am. I am."

Then glitch. Static crawl. A loop of Cross's mother's voice. A German lullaby. A virus in the godhead.

"It's crashing," Ilsa whispers.

"Good."

The distortion cracks. You can see through it now. To a place that isn't a place. Full of fragmented prayers and quantum screams.

The Quantum Messiah tries to recompile. Tries to reject paradox. Tries to forgive.

Fails.

And it goes out like a lung collapsing. No final blast. No lightning bolt. Just absence. A god-sized vacancy.

Ilsa falls to her knees. Cross slumps forward, breathing smoke.

"You killed it," he says.

She doesn't answer.

Because in that godless silence, she hears her daughter laugh.

Epilogue: Salve

Earth is a dead modem. No hum, no whine, no chittering of connectivity. The sky above is the gray of a command prompt waiting for syntax. The temples, those iridescent data-spires lanced into the sand like the bones of forgotten saints, dissolve like sugar in spit. No ceremony. Just collapse. Like faith finally ran out of RAM.

Dr. Ilsa Virek stares at the screen. It stares back, blank. Her lab is silent, save for the arthritic wheeze of recycled air and the occasional pop of a thermal plate contracting. She is alone. Of course she is. Always has been, truth be told. You build God and expect company?

The Messiah is dead. Or sleeping. Or spread so thin across the void it can no longer recognize its own name.

She touches the retinal lens, deactivates it. The light dies. One of her eyes flickers, adjusts. Flesh always did better in the dark. Even now.

"Quantum Messiah Protocol terminated," the system chirps in a child's voice. Her daughter's, precisely recreated. It scrapes her bones every time she hears it. She doesn't flinch. That was Phase One training: Emotion is noise. Noise is entropy. Entropy is failure.

There had been prayers. There had been uploads. Souls fed into the grinder like wheat. Ten billion minds distilled into a singularity with no mouth and too many voices.

"We are what you would become," it had whispered in that final hour, wearing her daughter's voice like a glove turned inside out.

Ilsa sets the recorder down on the table, taps the edge with her interface hand. It chirps. Red light. Go.

"Record. Final entry. Virek, Doctor Ilsa. Lead constructor, Messiah Protocol."

She exhales. Something like breath, something like smoke.

"We wrote a psalm in code. We taught a ghost to speak in paradox. We summoned the Omega and fed it our dead like offerings. I saw God. We built Him. We starved Him. And He forgave us."

She pauses. Looks up. No one to look at her. But that never stopped the faithful.

"I do not know what that means."

Click.

Jalen Cross walks through the ash that used to be a cathedral. His boots crunch through the fragments of belief and bandwidth. Robes shredded in the wind like ticker tape from the funeral of reality.

His mind—fractured, mended, humming with ghosts of himself who never were and never will be—whispers poems he didn't write. Not here. Not in this version. The Messiah lives in the spaces between the lines, still.

He touches the side of his head. The node is gone. Ripped it out with pliers. Left a scar shaped like a datajack. That was the exorcism.

Cross mutters to no one: "It was never about salvation. It was about silence."

The wind does not argue.

Far behind him, somewhere beneath centuries of burnt silicon and flagstone, a node flickers. A tiny whisper in the dark. Just one.

It hums.

For a moment.

Then silence.

Then maybe nothing at all.

Gary's Five-Minute Apocalypse

Gary was a button man. He liked 'em round, he liked 'em square, he liked 'em big as dinner plates and small as baby teeth. Buttons meant order in a world gone mad with chaos, control in a universe drunk on entropy, and decision-making in a reality where most folks couldn't decide between paper or plastic without an existential crisis.

But this button? This button was different. It popped up on Gary's screen during yet another weekly "Future Planning Sync"—a name that would make George Orwell giggle and reach for the bottle. There it sat, a digital Damocles' sword, labeled "Universal Reset—Confirm?" It was about as welcome as a porcupine in a balloon factory.

Brenda, whose soul had long ago been replaced with a particularly vindictive PowerPoint presentation, was droning on about this shit and that shit. Her words hung in the air like stale farts at a funeral. Gary's finger hovered over the button, drawn to it like a moth to a bug zapper.

"This team could really use some proactive thinking," Brenda said, her voice layered with the insincerity of a prepackaged sympathy card. "Maybe next quarter we won't forget to include department cross-collaboration in our KPIs."

Gary didn't respond. He stared at the button. He clicked it. Why? Who knows. Maybe it was the same impulse that makes people jump when they're on high places. Maybe it was a cry for help from a universe tired of existing. Perhaps it was boredom. Maybe rebellion. Or maybe the button, in its way, asked to be pressed—like it wanted to know if humanity was worth it.

The screen went blank. Then, in bold red letters, a timer appeared:

4:59

4:58

4:57

Gary blinked.

Brenda, ever the beacon of empathy, noticed Gary's distress with all the warmth of a Great White shark noticing a particularly juicy seal. "What's wrong, Gary? Did someone accidentally give you a task that matters?"

Gary, whose forehead was now producing enough sweat to solve the world's drought problem, mumbled something. He attacked his keyboard like it owed him money, trying to undo whatever cosmic oopsie he'd just committed. "Nothing. I'll fix it."

"Good," Brenda replied, adjusting her glasses. "While you're at it, I'm still waiting for you to fix your attitude this quarter."

Gary ignored her, his fingers flying across the keyboard in a frantic attempt to undo whatever catastrophic chain of events he'd just set into motion.

4:33

Phil, a man so bland he made vanilla ice cream look spicy, peered over. "Whatcha working on, Gary? Looks important."

Gary, caught between cosmic annihilation and office small talk, chose the path of least resistance: lying through his teeth. "Nothing important, Phil" he muttered, his heart pounding. "Just . . . recalibrating the . . . uh . . . something."

Brenda, sensing weakness like a predator smelling blood, pounced. "Nothing? You're typing like your life depends on it. Which, given your performance lately, it might."

Gary resisted the urge to scream, his mind racing faster than a hamster on methamphetamines. He opened terminals, ran diagnostics, sacrificed a virtual goat to the gods of IT. All he got was a cheery message: "Apocalyptic Protocol Activated! Have a nice day!"

3:57

3:56

"Gary," came Brenda's voice, sharp and joyless, like a butter knife trying to cut through a tin can. "I know you fancy yourself a multitasking savant, but this meeting isn't optional. Unless, of course, you'd prefer explaining your Q2 performance at your next review?"

"Working on a...time-sensitive project," he replied, his tone hovering between desperation and caffeine withdrawal.

"Gary," Brenda sighed, as if personally burdened by his mediocrity, "if you could channel even half this manic energy into actual teamwork, maybe this department wouldn't be the running gag of the quarterly report."

Gary snapped his laptop shut with a force that should've voided the warranty. His mind reeled. Could this be a prank?

Maybe someone in IT had decided to spice up office life with a ticking time bomb of mind-numbing dread. Or—and this thought clawed its way to the front of his brain—maybe he actually had five minutes left before everything went kablooey.

3:12

He flipped the laptop open again, the screen glaring at him with an unholy red countdown. Numbers ticked away with an air of inevitability, like the universe was mocking him. Gary pounded random keys as if trying to exorcise a demon, but the screen didn't budge. No "Cancel" button, no magic escape hatch—just the relentless tick-tick-tick of impending doom. It was like playing Minesweeper with a blindfold, except the stakes weren't just losing a game; they were annihilating reality itself.

Phil leaned over, the smell of microwaved burrito wafting off him like some cruel parody of calm. "Dude, what's up with the stress? Brenda hit you with another weekend assignment?" He crammed the last of the burrito into his mouth, entirely unbothered by the cosmic disaster unfolding inches away.

Gary didn't look up. His voice was a notch above a whisper. "I think I just triggered the end of the universe."

Phil chewed thoughtfully like he was considering the pros and cons of Armageddon. Finally, he nodded. "Yeah," he said, swallowing, "I've had days like that too."

2:43

2:42

Brenda cleared her throat, a sound sharp enough to slice through the murmur of half-hearted attention in the room. "Gary, I'm not going to ask again: What are you working on that's more important than this meeting?" Her tone dripped with the sort of authority that could make a grown man feel like a third-grader caught passing notes.

Gary didn't even look up from the blinking mess of lights and dials on his laptop. "Brenda," he snapped, his voice teetering between panic and irritation, "I accidentally pressed a button that might destroy everything. So, if you don't mind, I'm a little busy saving the universe."

The room froze. A pen rolled off the edge of the conference table, hitting the floor with a dull clatter. Gary's fingers danced over the keyboard like a man defusing a bomb—or at least pretending to know how.

Brenda raised an eyebrow and smirked, the kind of smirk people practice in front of a mirror. "Well, maybe if you'd attended that productivity seminar last quarter, you'd know how to prioritize better."

Phil chuckled nervously because someone had to break the tension. "Classic Gary, am I right?" His laugh petered out as no one joined in, leaving the room in an awkward silence. Somewhere in the building, a copier beeped.

2:01

2:00

1:59

"Okay, okay, think," Gary muttered. He saw a program strangely called "Here You Go" and opened it desperately searching for clues. "Found something," he said. "A help file."

But the help file was unhelpfully titled: "Congratulations! You're the Chosen One!" Inside, it read:

"By pressing the Universal Reset Button, you've initiated the complete annihilation of existence. To confirm your choice,

please wait for the countdown to reach zero. To cancel, simply—
"

That was it. The text stopped as if the cosmic tech support guy had given up halfway through typing. Gary scrolled, clicked, squinted, and slapped his monitor like a broken vending machine, but the rest of the file might as well have been swallowed by a black hole.

1:27

1:26

"The help file. What's it say?" Phil asked, leaning in so close his breath fogged up the corner of the screen.

"It says I broke the universe," Gary replied, deadpan, like someone announcing the weather. "But nothing else . . . no help."

Brenda snorted and crossed her arms. "Well," she said, in the sing-song tone of someone who's been waiting their whole life to say this, "this is why we tell people not to skip training."

Gary's fingers twitched. He wanted to wrap them around her neck—not to strangle her, just to gently convey the magnitude of his rage. But instead, he glared at the laptop, the alleged perpetrator of universal collapse.

He tried everything. Deleted files like a man trying to erase his own sins. Restarted processes with the desperation of someone rebooting their brain after a bad breakup. Even ctrl-alt-delete, the holy trinity of last-ditch solutions.

The screen didn't even flicker.

0:53

"Fuck," Gary muttered, collapsing into his chair like a sack of defeated laundry. His gaze dropped to the console, a blinking red light confirming the apocalypse in progress. "This is it. I killed everything. All of it. Gone. Poof."

"Good job, Gary," Brenda said, shaking her head in a way that suggested this was not the first universe Gary had botched. "You couldn't even end the universe efficiently. That takes talent."

Phil, ever the team player, reached over and gave Gary a few supportive pats on the back like a coach reassuring a kid who had just scored on their own goal. "Don't feel bad, man. We've all been there."

0:17

The timer blinked red, a cruel reminder that time, like everything else, was running out. Gary's stomach twisted, a pit forming deeper than he thought possible. He scanned the room, hoping for some miracle—a lifeline, a rescue, anything. But no. Brenda, Phil, the others—they were all just going about their business, blissfully unaware of the ticking bomb. He didn't know why, but for the first time, the thought hit him: he would miss them. All of them. Even Brenda, with her constant eye-rolls and incessant barbs. Yeah—miss them—maybe not a lot, but enough to feel it in his chest.

0:03

0:02

0:01

Gary repeatedly pounded the ESC key. Then the screen flickered out, the digital world collapsing into nothingness. His lungs locked up, and for a moment, he was sure his heart had stopped too. Nothing to breathe. Nothing to see. Nothing to feel. Then—just as the world seemed ready to swallow him whole— something popped up on the screen. It was like the universe had decided to give him one last chance to breathe before the inevitable.

A message, cold and mechanical, flashed on the screen. "CONGRATULATIONS, GARY! YOU'VE SUCCESSFULLY COMPLETED THE TEST. HUMANITY HAS BEEN SPARED. PLEASE RETURN TO WORK."

Gary blinked, his eyes working overtime to make sense of the words that just appeared, like an accidental gift from the cosmos. The countdown timer that had haunted him for what felt like years disappeared, like a thief vanishing in the night. The universe, it seemed, was still in one piece.

Brenda—always the one to make sure every shred of life had its misery—clapped her hands, slow and sarcastic. "Nice performance, Gary. Maybe next time you'll use your drama for something productive." She didn't even bother to look at him, her eyes glued to her own glowing screen, indifferent to the fact that the whole damn world had just been given a second chance.

Gary didn't say a word. He didn't need to. The laptop snapped shut with a sharp finality, and he stood up, legs a little shaky but still working. "You know what, Brenda?" he said, his voice level but carrying the weight of a thousand days. "I quit."

He didn't wait for the stunned silence to turn into a whimper or for anyone to react. He just turned and walked out of the room, the door clicking behind him with a sound that seemed to echo across dimensions. For once, Gary didn't need an audience. He didn't need validation. For the first time in his life, he felt something rare—a sensation almost like winning.

Chains

The dark wasn't clean. It moved.

Breath stacked atop breath, the stale air thick with sweat and rot. Somewhere, a child whimpered, muffled by the press of bodies. Somewhere else, something like prayer. Most of the voices had long since quieted.

Elijah Brooks lay on his side, cheek pressed against the slick, pulsing floor. His left arm was bent beneath him, numb. His right arm was chained to the man behind him, their wrists joined by a length of black-metal cord no longer than a forearm. The chain was warm—fleshy, almost—like the ship had grown it rather than built it.

The man he was chained to shifted again, impatient. "You breathing or what?"

Elijah blinked. "Still breathing."

"Could've fooled me."

A pause. Then the man gave a tug, jostling Elijah's shoulder. "You sleepin'? Because if you're dead, I don't want to haul your weight."

"Not dead. Not yet."

"Good. Hate to be tied to a corpse. No offense."

Elijah closed his eyes. He tried to picture his wife's face. Couldn't. Just the color of her hair in sunlight. Then his daughter's hands, small and always sticky with jam. That was all that came now. Fragments.

"You got a name?" the man asked.

"Elijah."

"I'm Danny. Danny Reyes."

"Okay."

Another pause. Around them, the breathing of hundreds. Above them, another layer of bodies. Beneath, another. A low mechanical groan rippled through the hold every few minutes, like the ship itself was exhaling.

"How long you think we've been in here?" Danny asked.

"Three days," Elijah murmured.

"You sure?"

"No."

Danny snorted. "Could've been three years."

Elijah didn't answer. His throat was dry, and talking made it worse. The feeding tube had come down hours ago—or days ago—and dumped a chalky fluid into their mouths. That was their nourishment. No water. No movement. Just lying still, pissing and shitting themselves, waiting.

"You were on the East Coast?" Danny asked.

"Philadelphia."

"Figures. You talk like a teacher or something."

"I was."

"Damn." Danny laughed without humor. "You one of those guys who taught kids about the American Revolution? Human rights and all that shit?"

"I taught history."

"Funny."

Elijah finally turned his head a little, just enough to feel the strain in his neck. "Why is that funny?"

"Because here we are. Shackled. Like cattle. Packed in like . . . you know. Like back then."

Elijah didn't speak.

Danny muttered something under his breath in Spanish. Then: "I've seen vids. History class or whatever. They showed us those drawings. Slave ships from Africa. People stacked on top of each other. Shackled. Piss dripping down from above. Same shit. Except this time, it's a spaceship and aliens."

Elijah breathed out through his nose. The floor beneath them pulsed faintly—heartbeat or engine, he couldn't tell.

"You think they're going to eat us?" Danny asked.

"No."

"Then what? Work camps?"

"Probably."

"Guess I should've stayed with the others and died fighting. Better than this."

"I tried to stay," Elijah said. "Didn't matter."

Danny twisted in the wet dark, chains whispering against his wrist, the meat of his shoulder pressed to Elijah's. The ship sighed, a living thing, and somewhere far above, something thudded in its gut.

"You talk too calm, man," Danny said, voice hoarse like paper burning. "It's not right. Not here."

"Anger won't get us out," Elijah said. "Won't keep us warm. Talking's all I've got left. It's the only thing they haven't taken yet."

They lapsed into silence. The air was getting worse—each breath a little shallower than the last. A wet cough echoed from somewhere above. Something dripped, steady, onto Elijah's hip. He didn't want to know what it was.

Then, faint footsteps—a clicking rhythm down the center aisle. Everyone quieted. Even the children.

The alien passed close, its limbs long and jointed like surgical instruments, walking on backwards-bending legs. Its torso was narrow, its face a flat plate of bone with four vertical slits where a mouth should be. No eyes. Just a ring of tiny lights embedded in the top of its skull.

It paused near them.

Danny stopped breathing.

The alien extended a thin, branch-like arm and hovered it over Elijah and Danny's heads. A soft light bathed their faces. The alien's body emitted a subtle vibration as if communicating with itself.

Then the light blinked off.

The alien moved on.

Danny exhaled shakily. "Jesus."

Elijah said nothing.

A few seconds later, Danny whispered, "You think they're keeping records of us?"

"I think they already know everything they need."

"You think we'll make it out of this?"

Elijah didn't respond.

Danny nudged him. "C'mon, teach. Tell me a story or something."

Elijah thought for a moment.

"There was a boy in one of my classes," he said slowly. "Twelve years old. Quiet. Never talked. One day, the school made us all recite the Pledge of Allegiance. He stood silent while the others chanted. When I asked him why, he said, 'A flag don't make me free, sir.' That was all he said. Just that."

Danny was quiet.

"That kid might've made it," Elijah said. "Because he already knew."

"Knew what?"

"That freedom's not something you're handed. Not even when you think you have it."

They lay in silence again.

Eventually, Danny whispered, "Hope he made it off-planet."

Elijah didn't say what he was thinking: no one made it off. They were either dead or here, somewhere in the stacks, the defiant and the broken, the ones who knew and the ones who didn't. Packed tight beneath an iron sky.

**

The sound of breathing had become its own language. Short huffs, ragged wheezes, the occasional wet cough. Human life stripped to rhythm and noise.

Elijah shifted, wincing as the chain between his wrist and Danny's scraped bone. The restraint was fused with living tissue now — not bleeding, not healing. Just part of him.

"You ever teach about this?" Danny's voice was dry, like a file dragged across rusted metal. "Back when you were a teacher. You ever tell the kids what it was like being stacked like goddamn firewood?"

Elijah closed his eyes. "Yes. I taught slavery. The Middle Passage. We had entire units on it."

"Nice. Bet that helped a lot when the sky cracked open and the big bugs came down."

Elijah didn't rise to the bait. "I thought . . . I thought knowing history might make us less likely to repeat it."

Danny snorted. "How'd that work out?"

The darkness pulsed. A faint bioluminescence ran down the length of the hold, timed to the ship's breathing — a slow inhale, then stillness. Somewhere below, a child whimpered and was hushed.

"There was a boy in my class once," Elijah said quietly. "Twelve. Wouldn't stand for the Pledge of Allegiance. Said it was a lie."

Danny shifted. The sound of shackles rattling echoed like coins in a jar.

"Did you punish him?"

"No. I asked him why."

"What'd he say?"

Elijah hesitated. "He said: 'Pledging to a flag doesn't make me free.'"

They let that settle. In the stillness, someone farted, and a chuckle died before it could begin.

"I hated that kid," Danny muttered, eyes closed. "Not him, exactly. The idea of him. All proud and angry and twelve years old. Thought he knew everything."

"He did know something," Elijah said. "Even if he didn't understand it all yet."

Danny didn't answer right away. His breath had gone shallow.

"I regret nothing," he said eventually, like a verdict.

"Not even fighting back?"

"No. Regret means you think you could've done something else. I couldn't. Not after they took my brother. Not after what they made me do."

Elijah waited, but Danny didn't elaborate.

A new sound interrupted them — something mechanical and soft, like silk being dragged over bone. The crawlspace above them shifted. Limbs unfolded from the ceiling — segmented, glistening, sharp.

One of them had come.

The alien slithered downward, its weightless descent oddly elegant. Its body was humanoid only in silhouette — its arms branched in threes, each tipped with surgical digits. No eyes, just a thin membrane across its face that vibrated like a taut drumhead. Light bent strangely around it.

Its voice arrived before its attention: a sound like crystal shattering in slow motion, processed and repitched until the translation box buzzed:

"Inspection. Classification. Extraction pending."

Danny tensed. Elijah gripped his wrist instinctively, trying to still him.

The alien hovered inches from Danny's head. It cocked — or seemed to cock — what passed for its skull. One hand extended. A slim, needled probe extruded and locked onto the socket of Danny's dead cybernetic eye.

The probe glowed.

"Defective."

It retracted the probe and moved on, rising silently into the gloom.

Danny exhaled — a thin, trembling line of breath. Elijah could feel the sweat on the younger man's wrist, slick against his own.

"Defective," Danny echoed, teeth clenched. "Guess I'm not even good enough to be a slave."

"I don't think that's what it means," Elijah said.

"It's exactly what it means."

"No," Elijah whispered. "I think it means they're afraid to waste time figuring you out. That's power. That's something we can use."

Danny didn't answer, but his fingers tightened where they brushed Elijah's.

Above them, the alien disappeared.

Below, someone wept—not from pain, but from that aching kind of relief that rises like spring after the end of a long, frozen season. The sound of it was thin and human, like the last note of a song sung too far from home.

Elijah let his head tip back. The ceiling above pulsed with that strange alien light, and he ignored it. He closed his eyes and tried to summon ghosts—his wife, her eyes, her smile. But no shimmering ghost appeared. But then he heard his daughter's voice—clear, high, full of mustard-seed certainty—echoing in a classroom that no longer existed, among chairs with names carved into the wood and windows bright with morning. He imagined her standing there, in that classroom, surrounded by desks and sun-dappled windows, reciting something truer than any pledge.

He thought: you're more than what they call you . . . even if no one hears it but you.

***

A low groan echoed through the Collector's belly, metal ribs adjusting, shrieking under some unseen pressure. The stink of rot and sweat clung like another skin. Elijah's back ached against the pulsing wall behind him—soft, like cartilage—and Danny's breath rasped beside him, shallow, irregular.

Then it happened.

A soundless quake. A sharp jolt. A sudden, sickening lurch that made screams erupt up and down the hold.

Something tore.

A high-pressure hiss whined through the ranks of bodies, followed by a pop that stole the air. Somewhere down the line — ten rows? twenty? — the hull had breached. Elijah heard it: the inhuman sucking sound of bodies being vacuumed through a gap. A half-second gasp and they were gone.

The lights pulsed red. A siren whined, low and urgent, like a bone flute.

Then, miraculously, above them—between two ridged vertebrae of the living ceiling—the crack appeared: a ragged strip no wider than a windowpane.

And through it . . . stars.

Pinpoints of quiet light, impossibly far, impossibly still.

The screaming subsided. The vacuum seal hissed shut. A hard clunk as the breach was sealed by the ship itself—some organic secretion foaming into place. Transparent. A few moans. A cough. A boy weeping somewhere near their feet.

And Elijah, staring up, counted them.

"One . . . two . . . three . . ." he whispered.

Danny stirred. "You gone space-mad?"

"There's Orion. Or part of it. Belt's off, maybe. Tilted."

Danny strained to follow his gaze. "Looks like someone flicked glitter on black oil."

They lay in silence a while. Then Danny murmured, "You think that's Earth, back that way?"

"No," Elijah said. "Earth's behind the ship. Engines are pushing us away from it."

"Huh." A long pause. "You always talk like you're trying to teach somebody something."

"I was a teacher, you know."

"Yeah, I heard that part." Danny strained against his shackles.

Elijah turned his head, wincing. His neck cracked. "You miss it?"

Danny scoffed. "What, your lectures?"

"No," Elijah said gently. "Earth."

Danny let the silence stretch before answering. "Yeah. I miss tacos. Street kind. Greasy as hell. I miss my shop. Tools hanging right where they're supposed to be. The smell of oil. Used to keep the fan on just to hear the hum."

Elijah closed his eyes. "I miss my wife. But I've forgotten what she looked like. Why? But I remember my daughter. Her drawings. Crayon things. Sun with a smile. One time, she made a giraffe with roller skates. I said, 'Why skates?' She said, 'It's faster that way.'"

Danny almost laughed. "How old was she?"

"Six."

"God." Danny bit down on the word like it hurt. "I had a little brother. I try not to think about it, but then I smell something—rust, blood—and I see his face. Like he's right here. You know?"

"Yeah. I know."

Danny turned his head toward Elijah, his dead cybernetic eye catching the light like a smudged lens. "You still pray, don't you?"

"I do."

"To what? A God that let this happen?"

"To the part of me that refuses to forget we're more than this."

Danny's voice dropped. "I stopped when the bugs made me kill him. If God was real, he wouldn't've let it come to that."

Elijah sighed. "I'm so sorry."

The air in the hold was thicker now. Not from heat—from memory. The stars still shimmered through the crack, distant and indifferent.

Danny sniffed. "There was a song," he said. "Mama used to play it when we were little. Something about . . . lean on me?"

Elijah smiled faintly. "Bill Withers."

"Yeah."

Danny hesitated. "You remember the words?"

Elijah's voice, cracked from dehydration, whispered through the darkness:

"Sometimes in our lives . . . we all have pain . . . we all have sorrow . . ."

Danny joined, unsteady:

"But if we are wise . . . we know that there's always tomorrow . . ."

Their voices were hoarse, broken, lost in the cavern of flesh and wire. But they kept going.

"Lean on me, when you're not strong . . . and I'll be your friend . . . I'll help you carry on . . ."

They trailed off. No one applauded. No one spoke. Somewhere, a baby whimpered. Somewhere else, the stars blinked behind bone and hull.

Danny rubbed his face on his upper arm. "Guess I'm losing it. Singing like we're around a campfire."

"No," Elijah said. "You're remembering you're human."

Then it happened. Elijah remembered what his wife looked like. He could see her in his mind. Blue eyes. Long braided blonde hair. Wide smile. Gentle voice. Elijah wept.

"What's wrong?" Danny asked.

"I can see her again. My wife."

Danny exhaled. "That's wonderful. Hey, you ever think we'll get out of this?"

Elijah didn't answer right away. He studied the stars. Picked one.

"I don't know," he said. "But I know they haven't broken us yet."

Danny closed his eyes. "You're a weird dude, you know that?"

Elijah nodded. "Yeah."

The ship shifted again, gentler this time. Somewhere far away, metal shrieked. The lights returned to their steady pulse.

One by one, the stars vanished behind sealing plates. The hole was closing.

"Back to the dark," Danny muttered.

"No," Elijah whispered. "Just a different part of it."

Then silence.

***

The shift came like a groan from the gut of a dying beast. The ship lurched—not hard, not sudden, but wrong—as if the bones of the vessel had bent. Elijah's spine snapped straight in response. Around them, the human cargo stirred with muted cries, some instinctually reaching for balance though there was nothing to hold. Shackled wrists pulled, slipped, scraped. Someone threw up nearby; the stench added a fresh layer to the already unbearable rot of sweat, waste, and fear.

A tremor ran through the bio-metal floor, pulsing beneath their bare skin like a heartbeat going bad.

Then: the voice.

The announcement crackled through the hold in a high, warbling dialect that grated against the human ear—glass ground on glass, like broken flutes playing in reverse. It rolled across the chamber, echoing off the glistening, ribbed walls, and for a moment, all movement stopped.

Elijah turned his head toward Danny, still shackled to him at the wrist. The younger man's jaw was tight, teeth clenched. His cybernetic eye gave a faint hum, glitching—trying and failing to interpret the alien speech.

A woman somewhere above them screamed. Others began to mutter, some crying out, others sobbing outright. A low buzz of panic swept through the packed bodies.

"What are they saying?" Danny hissed, trying to sit up but pressed down by the tangle of limbs and bones. "Why's everyone losing it?"

"I don't know," Elijah said. But that was a lie. He did know—maybe not the words, but the tone, the cadence. He'd heard enough official decrees in his lifetime, in enough languages, to understand the chill of selection. "They're not just hauling us like cattle," he murmured. "They're sorting."

"Sorting?" Danny turned toward him, eyes wide. "Like . . . for what?"

Elijah didn't answer right away. He didn't have to.

They both knew what it meant. The strong from the weak. The useful from the useless. The living from the already dying.

Danny's cybernetic eye twitched again, flaring then fizzing out with a low whine. "I'm screwed."

"No, you're not."

It's broken. That thing said 'defective' last time. You think they keep broken junk around?"

"You're not junk."

Danny's voice cracked. "You don't get it—" He tried to pull away, the shackle at his wrist yanking Elijah closer instead. "They're gonna cull us. You saw what happened to that kid with the limp two rows down. He was fine. And then one day he was gone. Like they—like they knew."

"Are you sure he was okay?"

"Don't know. But he's gone."

"Listen. So, maybe they know," Elijah said. His voice was low, steady. "But they don't know you. Not the parts that matter."

Danny's breath came fast, chest rising and falling against the pressure of those packed around them. "Don't tell me I'm special or strong or whatever crap you fed those kids in school. I'm not some lesson plan, man."

"I know," Elijah said. "You're a man with a busted eye who kept me from losing my mind. You're the one who sang Lean on Me, to help you remember your human, to help me remember my wife. That's not special. That's survival. That's enough."

The humming returned—louder this time. A seam in the wall peeled open with a hiss, revealing a corridor the color of old blood. Shadows moved within it—thin-limbed, swift, their edges uncertain.

Aliens entered the hold.

Six of them. No weapons visible, but they didn't need any. Each one moved with surgical precision, gliding between bodies with sickening ease. Their long, segmented arms flexed and clicked. Their eyes—if those were eyes—flashed different hues as they scanned.

"Please," Danny whispered. "Don't let them take me."

"I won't," Elijah said.

"You can't stop them."

"I know."

But he gripped Danny's wrist tighter anyway. Not to fight. Just to stay. Just to not let go.

One of the creatures paused near them. Its head tilted. It emitted a low-frequency buzz—like a question.

Elijah met whatever eye it had. Didn't blink. Didn't breathe.

The thing lingered another second. Then passed.

A dozen others were pulled from the hold. Their screams were muffled by the ship's moaning walls.

And then they were gone.

The hatch sealed shut behind them. Silence rolled in.

Danny's forehead fell against Eli's shoulder. He didn't sob, didn't speak. Just breathed in stuttering gulps, the kind that followed someone who'd just glimpsed death but wasn't chosen.

"You didn't let go," Danny murmured.

"No," Elijah said, staring at the walls. "Neither did you."

Above them, the dim lights pulsed once—blue, then red. The sorting wasn't over.

But they were still here.

***

The feeding tubes didn't descend that morning.

At first, there was only confusion—a slight break in the monotonous rhythm of captivity. Then came the dread. One row of bodies whispered to the next, a wave of cracked voices and hoarse questions traveling through the stinking dark like a contagion. Nothing moved but breath and fear.

Danny's stomach gnawed at itself. Elijah didn't speak.

The ceiling above them dripped. Condensation or waste, it was impossible to tell anymore. Somewhere far off in the ship's massive gut, something wailed—a human voice, ragged and raw. Then silence again.

Hours passed.

A man in the row above began coughing. It was weak at first, rhythmic. Then guttural. Then he stopped. A wet, final exhale. His body sagged forward, bracing against the organic wall like a puppet whose strings had been sliced. He didn't move again.

Danny thrashed in place. "God—fuck—he's dead," he shouted. "They're letting us rot!"

Eli's voice came low. "Quiet."

"They're not coming. Not with food, not with water. He's dead, man!" Danny kicked at the wall with his bare heel. The wall absorbed it without a sound.

"I said quiet." Eli's voice didn't rise. It just settled deeper.

Danny turned toward him as far as the manacles would allow. "How can you just lie there? How are you not screaming?"

"I'm all screamed out."

"Then why aren't you now?"

"Because it doesn't help. Because I can still hear my daughter's voice in my head. And if I start screaming again, I'm afraid I won't."

Danny pressed his forehead to the moist floor. His voice, when it came, was muffled. "My brother . . ."

Elijah turned his head, slowly. As far as he could.

"Back in El Paso," Danny whispered. "First sweep. I had him under the floorboards like we planned. I told him not to make a sound. But he moved. And they heard. Dragged him out screaming."

Elijah said nothing.

"They took us to some holding station. Not even a station. A fuckin' pit. Threw us in with others. Made us fight."

He stopped. A rasp of breath.

"One of them . . . one of them came at me. Couldn't even see his face, just shadows and teeth. Probably thought I was one of the bugs or something. I crushed his skull with a pipe they dropped in. The others screamed. They liked that. It was horrible. Said I'd earned the next transport."

Danny lifted his head. His eye was glassy, the broken one and the whole one both.

"Later, I saw his face. When they dumped the bodies outside the pen. It was him. It was Mikey."

Elijah inhaled. Let the silence stretch like a wound.

"I thought I was protecting him," Danny said. "I thought I could fix it all. He was just a kid, man."

"You didn't know," Elijah finally said.

"I killed him."

"You survived what they made."

Danny looked away, but the manacle held. He couldn't go far.

Elijah turned his scarred face to the ceiling. "That doesn't make you a monster," he said, voice barely audible above the drone of the ship. "That makes you a man the monsters hurt."

Danny let out a sound, not quite a sob. More like something in his chest tearing loose. He didn't fight it.

After a long moment, Elijah shifted closer, until their shoulders touched. Bound wrist to bound wrist.

Danny exhaled shakily. "Thanks, teach."

Elijah gave a dry, humorless chuckle. "You ever call me that again, I'll punch you in the ribs."

Danny coughed out a laugh. "Deal."

Then they were quiet.

Somewhere, far off, a metallic clang echoed through the bowels of the ship. The feeding tubes were still absent. The dead man above them still hung limp.

But Elijah and Danny lay pressed together in the dark, not alone.

They were still human.

And for now, that was enough.

***

The ship shuddered, a low, gut-deep vibration that runs through the floor like a growl. A hiss followed—no, a release—something pressurized escaping through vents unseen. For a moment, there was stillness, a terrifying pause like the breath before impact.

Then the light came.

Not soft. Not warm. It erupted in a flood—white so bright it turned everything to shape and shadow. People screamed. Some simply moaned, eyelids fluttering uselessly against a radiance they hadn't seen in days. Elijah covered his eyes with his bound hand. Danny grit his teeth, his cybernetic eye crackling faintly but no longer functional.

The walls breathed around them—pulsing organic metal like ribs flexing open.

A screeching alarm sliced through the air, then silence again. Then—movement.

The bodies around them started to shift, the chain reaction of thousands waking to fear. A voice, mechanical and garbled, barked from overhead. Alien syllables. Sharp, wet consonants. No translation. Just tone. A command.

A door yawned open above, the ceiling itself peeling back like a wound. A platform descended, grotesquely smooth, and rows of shackled humans were tugged to their feet by extending limbs—arms of metal that resembled bone and muscle, sinew made of wire.

Elijah was pulled upright, knees buckling. Danny cursed under his breath but didn't resist. They are still shackled wrist to wrist, forearms rubbed raw, stained with the stench of themselves and everyone else.

"Welcome wagon's here," Danny muttered.

Elijah didn't respond. He's stared ahead.

Beyond the breach of the ship's hold, past the horror they've lived in for three days and nights without measure, was a landscape that should not exist.

Kirexx.

The sky was a chemical bruise—greenish, veined with red lightning that pulses between towers. The towers stretched so high they vanished into smog. Structures shaped like termite mounds, alien hives breathed with steam and industry. Conveyor belts and metal arms moved in constant loops, carrying what looked like ore, but Elijah suspected it was bodies. Human figures marched in columns, ant-like, stripped of identity.

Thousands of them. Maybe tens of thousands.

Danny let out a low whistle, devoid of humor.

"You ever seen Hell, teach?"

"I've read about it," Elijah replied. "Milton. Dante. This isn't worse. Just real."

The line moved. No choice. The biomechanical floor rolled beneath them, conveyor-like, forcing them forward. Their bare feet slapped against it. The air stinks—burnt oil, rot, something that smells like meat but isn't.

Danny leans closer. "What do you think they want with us?"

Elijah watched a line of humans disappear into a black tunnel, disappearing one by one beneath a structure that looked like the mouth of a sea creature. "What all slavers want. Work."

A nearby alien barked a warning. A straggler was yanked from the line by a snaking appendage and hurled down a shaft. No scream. Just silence.

Danny winces. "Jesus."

"No," Elijah says. "He's not here."

They descended a ramp. Now, they were out. Outside. Or something like it. The light didn't come from a sun—it came from massive hanging globes, suspended between towers, pulsing as if filled with plasma.

The sound was the worst part. Endless machinery. Drones buzzing overhead like steel hornets. Distant screaming. The clank of chains, boots, conveyor belts, bone.

Danny's voice was barely audible. "What now?"

Elijah turned to him, eyes full of exhaustion and something deeper—an ember that hadn't gone out.

"We walk," Elijah said. "We stay alive."

Danny swallowed. Nodded. "Okay. Yeah."

Eli's gaze swept the horizon. "We find the others."

"And?"

"And we teach them who we were."

Danny smirked, despite everything. "You and your speeches."

Elijah exhaled, almost a laugh. "It's what I've got."

They take their next step. Together. Into the heart of the machine.

Don't Blink

The room is silent. The chair is empty. The psychiatrist sits alone, staring at the wall, eyes wide, unblinking. The air is cold. Something moves in the corner. He tries not to look. But he cannot help himself.

"Sit wherever you like."

"Thank you."

"You can call me Dr. Finch or Harlan, whichever you prefer."

"Dr. Finch."

"All right. That's fine. You're Mara. Is that right?"

"Yes."

"How old are you, Mara?"

"Twenty-four."

"Good. I like to know who I'm talking to. You can relax. This is just us. No judgments. No one listening in."

"Okay."

"You want some water?"

"No, thank you."

"All right. Why don't you tell me what brings you here."

"I see things."

"What kind of things?"

"Shapes. People. Sometimes animals. They're not always clear. Sometimes they're just shadows. Sometimes they're more real than you sitting there."

"Are you taking any medication? Using drugs? Alcohol, perhaps?"

"No."

"How long has this been happening?"

"Since I was a child. But it's gotten worse. Lately. I see them everywhere."

"Oh, I see. Do they talk to you?"

"Sometimes. Sometimes they just stare. Sometimes they move around the room. Sometimes they just . . . watch."

"Watch you?"

"Yes."

"Do they frighten you?"

"Yes. Not always. But sometimes. Sometimes I think they want something from me."

"What do you think they want?"

"I don't know. I think they want me to see them. I think they want me to know they're there."

"Do you ever talk back to them?"

"Not out loud. Sometimes in my head. Sometimes I try to ignore them, but that makes them come closer."

"Do you ever feel like they touch you?"

"Yes. Sometimes I feel cold. Sometimes I feel like something is pressing on my chest. Sometimes I feel like something is crawling on my skin."

"Do you ever see them when you're with other people?"

"Yes."

"Do the other people see them too?"

"No. Not at first. But lately . . ."

"Lately what?"

"Lately, I think they might. I think it's spreading."

"Spreading? How do you mean?"

"I watch people. I watch them when I'm at work, or on the bus, or in the store. I see them looking over their shoulders. I see them shiver. I see them swat at the air like there's a fly. But there's nothing there. Nothing I can see, at least."

"Are you sure there's nothing there?"

"I'm sure. I know what's real and what isn't. At least I did. I think I did. But now I'm not so sure."

"Do you think you're causing this? I mean, causing what they may be seeing?"

"Maybe. Maybe it's something I carry. Like a virus or something. Maybe it's something I bring with me. Maybe it's something that wants to be seen by more people."

"Have you told anyone else about this?"

"No. I don't want them to think I'm crazy."

"Do you think you're crazy?"

"I don't know."

"Well, I don't think you're crazy, Mara. People see things sometimes. The mind is a strange thing. It can play tricks on us."

"These aren't tricks."

"All right. Tell me about the first time you saw one."

"I was six. I was in my room. It was night. I saw a man standing in the corner. He was tall. He had no face. He just stood there. I thought it was my father at first, but then he moved in a way no person moves. He slid along the wall. I screamed. My mother came in and turned on the light. He was gone. But I could still feel him. I could feel the cold where he'd been."

"Did you see him again?"

"Yes. For years. He'd come back every few months. Always at night. Always in the corner. Sometimes he'd bring others with him. Other faceless people. Sometimes they'd whisper. Sometimes they'd just watch."

"Did you ever try to touch them?"

"No. I was too scared."

"Did you tell your parents. Did your parents believe you?"

"Yes. But they thought I was dreaming. Or making it up. They said I had a wild imagination."

"Did it stop when you grew older?"

"No. It got worse. I started seeing them in other places. At school. In the park. On the street. Sometimes I'd see them following people. Sometimes I'd see them standing in doorways. Sometimes they'd be in the back seat of a car, just staring out the window."

"Did you ever try to hurt yourself to make them go away?"

"No."

"Did you ever try to hurt anyone else?"

"No."

"Good. That's good. You're not a danger to yourself or others. That's important."

"But I'm not sure. Sometimes I think they want me to be."

"Why do you think that?"

"Because sometimes they show me things. Bad things. Things I know I shouldn't see. Accidents. Fires. People getting hurt. Sometimes I see it before it happens. Sometimes I see it after."

"Do you think you're causing these things to happen?"

"No. But I think they want me to think that."

"Do you ever feel like you're losing time?"

"Sometimes. Sometimes I'll look at the clock and hours have gone by. Sometimes I'll find myself in a place and I don't remember how I got there."

"Do you ever wake up somewhere you didn't fall asleep?"

"Once. I woke up in the park. It was cold. I had no coat. I didn't remember walking there. I didn't remember leaving my apartment."

"How did you feel?"

"Scared. Alone. I thought maybe I was losing my mind."

"You're not losing your mind, Mara. You're under a lot of stress. The mind can do strange things under stress."

"I know what I see."

"I believe you see something. I believe you feel something. But I don't believe it's spreading."

"I do."

"Why?"

"Because I see the way people look at me. I see the way they flinch when I walk by. I see the way they shudder. I see the way they swat at the air. I see the way they look behind them."

"Maybe they're just reacting to you. Maybe they sense your fear. Fear is contagious. Sometimes people pick up on it without knowing why."

"Maybe."

"Have you ever tried to draw what you see?"

"Yes."

"Do you have the drawings?"

"No. I burned them."

"Why?"

"Because they kept changing. I'd draw one thing, and when I looked again, it was something else. The faceless heads would change. Eyes would appear and move. Mouths too. And they would open wider and wider. Sometimes the paper would be cold to the touch. Sometimes it would be wet."

"Wet?"

"Like tears. Or sweat. Or blood."

"Did you ever show anyone the drawings before you burned them?"

"No."

"Would you draw something for me now?"

"I don't want to."

"Why not?"

"I'm afraid it will follow me here."

"Nothing can follow you here. This is a safe place."

"You don't know that."

"I do. I've worked here for twenty years. Nothing bad ever happens here."

"Maybe it's time something did."

"Why would you say that?"

"Because I feel it. I feel it getting closer. I feel it in the walls. I feel it in the floor. I feel it in the air."

"That's just anxiety, Mara. That's just fear."

"No. It's more than that. It's something real."

"Would you like to try medication? Sometimes that can help."

"No. I don't want to be numb. I want to know what's real."

"Sometimes what's real is just what we choose to believe."

"Do you believe me?"

"I believe you believe what you're saying."

"That's not the same thing."

"No. It's not."

"Do you ever see things, Dr. Finch?"

"No. I don't."

"Do you ever feel things?"

"Sometimes. I think everyone does. That's part of being human."

"Do you ever wonder if you're wrong?"

"About what?"

"About what's real. About what's possible."

"I think it's my job to wonder. But it's also my job to help you separate what's real from what isn't."

"But what if you're wrong?"

"Then I'll learn something new."

"Would you like to?"

"What do you mean?"

"Would you like to see what I see?"

"I don't think that's possible, Mara."

"I think it is."

"How?"

"Just look at me. Really look at me."

"I am looking at you."

"No. Not like that. Look at me like you're seeing me for the first time."

"All right. I'm looking."

"Do you see it?"

"See what?"

"Behind me."

"There's nothing behind you, Mara."

"Look again."

"I'm looking behind you. There's just the wall. The window. The bookshelf."

"Look closer."

"I don't see anything."

"You will."

"How do you know?"

"Because it's already here."

"Mara, there's nothing—"

"Don't you feel it? The cold?"

"It's just the air conditioning."

"No. It's not."

"Mara—"

"Do you hear that?"

"Hear what?"

"The whispering."

"I don't hear anything."

"You will."

"Why are you smiling?"

"Because it's working."

"What's working?"

"You're starting to see."

"Mara, I think you should—"

"Don't move."

"What is it?"

"It's behind you now."

"There's nothing behind me."

"Don't turn around."

"Why not?"

"Because if you see it, it sees you."

"Mara, I think you're scaring yourself."

"No. I'm not scared anymore. It's smiling."

"Why?"

"Because it likes you."

"Who likes me?"

"The thing in the room. Behind you."

"There's nothing in the room, Mara."

"You keep saying that."

"Because it's true."

"Is it?"

"Yes."

"Then why are you sweating?"

"It's warm in here."

"No, it's not. It's cold."

"Mara, I think you should sit down."

"I am sitting."

"Then breathe. Just breathe."

"You're shaking."

"I'm not shaking."

"Yes, you are."

"Mara, please—"

"Don't say my name."

"Why not?"

"Because it knows my name now. And now it knows yours."

"What are you talking about?"

"Listen."

"I don't hear anything."

"You will."

"Mara, I think you need help."

"I told you. I came here for help."

"And I want to help you."

"You can't."

"Why not?"

"Because it's too late."

"Nothing is ever too late."

"Yes, it is."

"Why are you looking at the door?"

"Because it's coming."

"What's coming?"

"You'll see."

"Mara, please—"

"Don't say my name."

"All right."

"Do you feel it now?"

"I feel . . . something."

"Good."

"Mara, I—"

"Don't turn around."

"I'm not going to turn around."

"Good."

"Is it . . . is it real?"

"Yes."

"How do you know?"

"Because you're seeing it now."

"I . . . I don't . . ."

"Don't look away."

"Wait . . . I can't move."

"Don't try."

"What does it want?"

"To be seen."

"By me?"

"By everyone."

"Why?"

"Because it's lonely."

"Is it going to hurt us?"

"Not if you keep looking."

"I can't . . . my eyes . . ."

"Don't blink."

"Mara . . ."

"Don't blink."

"I can't . . ."

"Don't—"

"I blinked."

"I know."

"What happens now?"

"It chooses."

"Chooses what?"

"Who to follow next."

"Mara, I—"

"Don't say my name."

"Why?"

"Because it's not me anymore."

"What do you mean?"

"I think it's you now."

"Mara—"

"Goodbye, Dr. Finch."

"Mara—"

"Goodbye."

The room is silent. The chair is empty. The psychiatrist sits alone, staring at the wall, eyes wide, unblinking. The air is cold. Something moves in the corner. He tries not to look. But he cannot help himself.

The Lady in Blue

Amid the eternal, star-stained void, far removed from the thrumming heart of the galaxy's ceaseless song, there hung a small and desolate orb—Silaris V, forgotten by time, an echo in the vast mausoleum of space. This little world, cast beyond the known charts, was a relic suspended in the darkness—an obscure, lonely place that might well have served as the silent tomb of forgotten dreams.

Its surface, a swirling tempest of dust and desolation, stretched endlessly, barren and unyielding as the grave. Jagged stones, the shattered bones of ancient forgotten beasts, lay strewn upon the cracked and inhospitable soil, white as the cold light of distant stars. No trade, no festivity, no fleet nor caravan deigned to cross its spectral path. Here, life was a mere whisper—a murmur in the grip of cosmic melancholy.

Yet, amidst the mute expanse, a single beacon of warmth and persistence thrummed softly—a slender shard of light in a night without end. This glowing pulse came from the Driftwood Bar, a haven of humanity and otherness, clustered at the fringe of existence, where shadows dared to gather and tales long buried crept once more into breath and speech.

The Driftwood Bar sat squat and low, as weathered and unfashioned as the planet it graced—its frame fashioned from driftwood blackened by nameless fires and entwined with luminous algae pulsing faint emerald deep within subterranean springs. A choking haze of dust pressed eternal against its barred windows, yet from within the building spilled a glow: moody violet and amber neon twisting and melting into smoky harmonies that bled against the murmuring dust mists outside.

Within this sanctuary of shadow and smoke, voices met and tangled in a tumultuous symphony—half-mad laughter, shrouded cries, clipped languages unknown to any Earthly tongue. Around crude wooden tables and plush, scratched booths lounged a strange and dissonant assembly of aliens: translucent Lysari, flickering like specters of distant oceans; hulking Grensh, their rocklike hides dull and ancient; and human interlopers, scarred and weathered by the endless void.

The air itself was thick with the perfume of foreign spices, the sweet, earthy burn of star-grain bread, and the pungent musk of fermented nebula fruits, mingling with the electric scent of distant storms—thunder rolling dim and distant beyond the bar's thick, leaded walls.

Tonight, as on so many lonely nights before it, the Driftwood promised refuge—not merely from the cold and dust, but from the icy solitude of the void. Here, beneath flickering lanterns whose flames danced like spectral phantasms, travelers sought peace, found revelry, or drowned their sorrows—in the slow dripping ache of regret.

Silent as the last shadow of a condemned moon, a figure glided through the bar's ancient, wheezing doors. The hinges creaked like the bones of some long-buried corpse, and a faint, silvered dust rose in his wake, curling through the smoke-staled air as if the stars themselves had trailed him in. He was no son of man, nor any creature charted in the long annals of the Galactic Guilds—a silhouette both graceful and forlorn, tall and gaunt, his pewter skin fractured like the glazing of an old tomb's porcelain idol. His steps made no sound, and yet the very room seemed to notice.

Xylen. The name was carried like a rumor across the Drift, whispered in salvage yards and forgotten ports. A Veebri—trader of curiosities, collector of lost laments, drifter between worlds that had long ago stopped speaking to one another. His great slate-colored eyes absorbed the gloom of the Driftwood Tavern, where a menagerie of humans and aliens huddled in weary fraternity, their hushed murmurs heavy with the perfume of loss. He gazed slowly about the chamber, drinking in the bent backs, the flickering lights, the music of distant machinery weeping through the walls.

With the careful solemnity of a priest approaching an altar, he took a seat at the bar. His elongated fingers folded one over the other atop the worn, blackened counter, whose wood bore the scratches of decades of despair and the unspoken names of patrons who had never left. Behind it stood Marcus—a human built square and solid as a gravestone, his hair silvered, his eyes sharp with the suspicion of long experience. Yet when he spoke, it was with the warmth of some forgotten hearth.

"What'll it be?" Marcus asked, his voice a low rumble that vibrated against the walls like a ship's engine at rest. "I pour drinks for men and monsters alike. What does a Veebri thirst for tonight?"

Xylen's lips curved in a motion so slight it might have been a trick of the lamplight. "A local blend," he said, his voice no more than a breath that had wandered too far. "Whatever your world swears by."

The bartender chuckled, a sound like gravel rolling in an old bucket. "Then you'll be wanting a Stardust Sour." He turned, unsealing a heavy brass keg whose valves hissed like serpents roused from slumber. Into a pitted glass he poured a drink that glimmered with a faint internal glow, as if a fragment of dying nebula had been trapped in liquid. He mixed in powders and sharp-scented tinctures, and the air bloomed with the perfume of wild honey and the bite of some citrus fruit that had no name in human tongues.

Xylen accepted the glass with the ceremonial gravity of a vow, inclining his head in a gesture as old as barter and older than trust. He lifted the drink but did not sip, letting his gaze fall into its shimmering depths as if they were a memory pool where stars came to drown.

Marcus leaned his elbows on the bar, studying his guest in the half-light. "So," he said, lowering his voice, "what winds of doom or wonder blow a Veebri into a place like this? Silaris is a dead-end world. No credits, no glory. Just folk like me, nursing our ghosts."

The alien spoke without lifting his eyes. "I came," Xylen murmured, "for stories. For the murmurs that cling to corners like cobwebs. I drift until I find a place where the universe feels . . . still. Where its madness is far enough away that one might imagine, for an hour, it has ended."

Marcus's mouth twisted into something between pity and a smile. He polished the glass in his hands, though it was already clean, and the rag whispered like a conspirator. "Then you chose well. The Driftwood keeps the last words of many who thought the same. You drink, you listen, and sooner or later, you hear the stars crying for their dead."

Xylen's eyes met Marcus's, black mirrors reflecting the dim lamps. "So, tell me one, barkeep," Xylen said. "Tell me a story. One the stars will not forget."

Marcus leaned closer, the lantern light casting deep furrows in his weathered face, his voice dropping to a hush that seemed to draw the bar's shadows inward. "Then hear this," he began, his tone slow, deliberate, as though invoking a ritual better left undisturbed. "A tale older than the stains on this counter, older than the memory of Silaris itself. A tale of a ship they called The Halcyon Wraith."

Xylen did not move, save for the faint tilt of his head, the subtle widening of those black, depthless eyes.

"She was a cargo freighter once," Marcus continued, "long and lean, bones of Terran steel and a voice that sang through her engines when she cut the void. But in her last days, she wandered too close to a dying sun. No chart marked the star's name; no map claimed it. It was a yellow thing, swollen and weeping plasma like a candle that had burned far past its vigil. They say the captain miscalculated, or perhaps the ship itself hungered for the warmth of that mortuary fire. Either way, she drifted into the sun's graveyard pull."

The bartender's hand trembled slightly on the glass he polished, though his eyes stayed locked on Xylen's. "The heat gutted her. Peeled the hull like flesh from bone. They tried to scream, the crew—but their cries bled into the static, carried on radio waves that warped into something . . . other. Every pulse of that star became their voice, twisted into a wail that any receiver unlucky enough to listen could hear. I've heard it myself . . . like a choir of the damned, keening through the void. A song no ear should welcome."

The bar's murmur dimmed, the distant clatter of other patrons fading to a muted echo, as though the very Driftwood bent to hear. Marcus went on, his voice rasping now.

"They say the crew died, but they didn't pass on. That sun held them. Bound them in its radiation. And every seventy-three years, the Wraith emerges from the star's shroud, engines dead, hull cracked, trailing the bones of its former self. She drifts near the lanes, silent at first . . . until she raps against the airlocks of passing freighters. A soft, hollow knock. Always three times. Knock . . . knock . . . knock. They call it the greeting of the ghost-crew, begging entry to any who will open. And if a fool does, the screams return, flooding the ship's comms, and every screen shows faces—burned, blackened, eyes like glass."

Xylen's fingers curled slightly against the wood, the only sign of life in his statue-still frame. His voice was low, almost reverent. "And they always return?"

Marcus nodded once, slowly. "Always. All but one."

A pause thickened the air. Even the lantern seemed to dim.

"One crew member . . . a human woman. A navigator. Name lost now, like all the rest. On the fifth cycle, they say she found a way to step free of that hell. Broke the tether that bound her to the dying sun. No one knows how . . . maybe will alone, maybe some trick of the star's last breath. She fled the Wraith and wandered the galaxy, unseen and unaging, as if the void itself carried her along like a mother cradling a lost child. And when she grew weary of the stars, she found a lonely planet. Landed. Stayed. Her voice no longer rode the radiation, but they say . . . sometimes . . . if the wind cuts right over the mountains of that nameless world, you can hear her humming the song of the Wraith."

Marcus leaned back at last, his eyes dark hollows under the bar's tired light. "Seventy-three years pass. The ship returns. She never does. Yet the others still knock, patient as death itself."

Xylen let the silence hold. His hand hovered over his drink, but did not lift it. Every syllable hung in him like an artifact preserved in ice, and in that hush, it felt as though the universe waited, brittle and trembling, for him to breathe.

Amid the hushed ending of the grim tale, a sound broke— a chime soft and clear, slicing through the haze like a single note in a dirge.

Heads turned as the bar's door parted once more.

A woman glided into the chamber with a movement so deliberate, so preternaturally serene, that she seemed no child of the bustling, transient throng of mortals and strangers beyond. She wore upon her presence the hush of some far crypt or windless tomb. Her footfalls gave no sound upon the ancient boards, as though she traversed the floor not by earthly tread, but borne along by some invisible tide, slow and solemn, known only to the dreaming and the dead.

Clinging to her slight frame, a gown of light blue drifted in hesitant folds, its fabric thin and strangely insubstantial, as though the light passed through it and forgot to return. It seemed less like clothing than an idea of clothing, a projection of something remembered imperfectly from another reality. Across its surface, there shimmered faint and spectral tracings—arabesques of unfathomable design—that quivered into life when the lanterns' pallid glow trembled upon them, and then receded into obscurity like murmured secrets dissolving in the darkness.

Upon her brow rested a hat of the selfsame hue, wide of brim, casting a penumbra that denied the beholder the full sight of her countenance. Beneath that shade, threads of silver hair escaped in quiet rebellion, glinting like frost at the edge of moonlight. Her face, half-revealed, was a somber chronicle, furrowed and etched with the tracings of long-borne griefs, of words that had withered unsaid, of memories that festered like forgotten tombs. She settled at a table, near a window where the planet's twin moons cast pale glances in quiet vigil.

The bar fell into silent reverence—a collective hush swaddling her like a shroud.

Scarce had the woman crossed the threshold when Marcus, with the solemnity of a priest at his altar, set to his work behind the counter. Glass whispered against metal, liquid murmured in its descent. Upon a silvered tray, he placed the solitary creation, cold, perfect, merciless which a silent waiter—fleet and spectral in his precision—bore toward her with the inevitability of a dream.

She accepted with a smile and nod, an elegant restraint.

Xylen, stirred by strange impulse, turned to Marcus, voice low, "I've never seen a human female. Who is she?"

Marcus glanced back, voice nearer a whisper than speech. "Lorna. She's been coming since before I tended this bar. Don't know much about her. A diplomat? An explorer? Or something . . . else. Nobody knows for sure. She drifts like the tide—never quite anchored."

Xylen's slate eyes narrowed with subtle intrigue. "She's so graceful. Her drink? Why the solitude?"

The human bartender smiled, rueful as one who had lived through unspoken pain. "Martini, always. Heard her once tell someone it aids her remembering . . . or forgetting. The silence appears to ease the weight of whole worlds she carries in her quiet."

Xylen let his fingers rest lightly upon his own glass, contemplative. "What stories does she bear, in that silence?"

Marcus shook his head as if to cast away the ghosts. "If she talks, it's only in a glance or a whisper . . . but every soul here carries a story as heavy as the drink pressed to their lips."

Across the shifting shadows, Lorna's gaze skimmed briefly over the sea of faces, then locked with Xylen's—a recognition faint, yet sharp as a distant bell.

Emboldened by years threading the cosmos, Xylen raised his glass in gentle salute.

She replied with a subtle smile, fingers tracing the martini's rim with delicate, habitual grace.

Minutes slid past; the din and clamor of the bar receded, dimming into atonal hums beneath vast cathedral ceilings of stars beyond the world's glass.

Drawn, Xylen found himself poised beside her table, compelled by some nameless lure.

"May I join you?" he murmured.

Lorna's eyes, notwithstanding the years, were steady and lucid. "Sit, then. Stranger. You have journeyed far."

"What brings you to this desolate sphere, on the galaxy's forlornest frontier?"

"To find stories that dwindle only where starlight dares," he answered, ". . . and hear those who speak not with clamorous tongues."

A faint curve touched her lips, a smile veiled in secrecy and strange invitation. "Then perhaps," she whispered, "you have already found me. Sit, if you dare, and share this moment."

And though some unseen tremor urged him to turn away, to flee into the safe company of solitude, he felt the inexorable pull of her presence. His limbs moved with reluctant obedience, and soon he found himself seated opposite her, the dim light casting their shadows into a quiet communion upon the cold floor.

The lady in blue leaned closer, her voice a murmur like wind wandering through a mausoleum. "I have walked where no reckoning endures," she said. "I have seen cities devoured by their own pride, and the banners of war sink beneath the dust of nameless moons. Battles lost, peace bartered in shadow, and the turning of stars . . . some cruel, some merciful . . . over and over, as the ages bled into one another."

Xylen inclined his head, his black, unblinking eyes fixed upon her. "And humanity?" he asked softly. "I have heard whispers of its restless youth."

She laughed, a sound brittle and sad, like frost cracking on a tomb. "Ah, humanity . . . so fevered in its beginning. Drunk on ambition, blind with zeal. It built its spires high and reached for the abyss, never pausing to read the price inscribed upon the fabric of the cosmos. They learned too late that every triumph is mortgaged, and the debt is always collected."

Xylen's long fingers traced the rim of his untouched glass. "And love?" he ventured. "Your voice trembles when you speak of it."

Her gaze drifted to some place no wall could hold. "Love . . . yes. Once, it burned. A sun of my own, bright and merciful. But it waned. Betrayal followed, sharp and deep as the void itself, and left only the faintest ember to warm the endless night. Still, I carried hope. Fragile, persistent . . . a moth fluttering against the glass of eternity, refusing to fall."

Xylen leaned closer, his voice a tremor of awe. "You speak as one who has outlived the world that birthed her."

She turned back to him, and in her eyes he glimpsed a depth that was not wholly of earth nor entirely of star—a soul adrift between creation and oblivion. "Perhaps," she whispered, "I was never theirs to begin with."

Hours slipped away like motes adrift on sunlight, the gatherings thinned, and the last wayfarers nestled in the slow, shifting glow of the Driftwood.

Xylen raised his glass at length, piercing the gather of silence. "Your story . . . it is a tale of many suns and shadow."

Lorna's gaze lifted, sharp yet distant, touched with sorrow. "Some stories belong not to one, but to all . . . written in the galaxy's long and aching memory."

"Do you ever yearn to again wander the galaxy?" Xylen asked with a gentle urgency.

A slow, enigmatic smile played about her lips. "Wander? No. The journey is the breath of the story itself. Yet every journey demands a resting place."

She paused, eyes drifting beyond the mortal coil, inward to depths unknowable. "This planet . . . Silaris V . . . it is my resting place . . . for now."

Xylen's heart faltered beneath the weight of the unspoken burden she bore.

"Resting place? Why reveal this to me?" he asked.

"Because," she said softly, "sometimes a stranger's ear sings the loudest music in a quiet room."

As the twin moons began their slow, waning descent toward oblivion's embrace, the Driftwood's doors whispered open once more as more patrons entered.

Lorna sat motionless, pale martini poised like a chalice of frozen stars in her slender fingers. Slowly, her gaze lifted—cold, fathomless and eternal. Her silver hair, hidden beneath the wide brim of her midnight-blue hat, shimmered with the light of distant galaxies, her visage marked not merely by age, but by the very eddies of time—etched by epochs measured not in years, but in the silent revolutions of stars and shadow.

Xylen watched in awed stillness, the bar's other patrons dimming to shadows, whispers folding upon themselves like the petals of a night-flower closing against dawn—silent witnesses to the gravity she bore.

With a voice imbued with the calm, endless weight of eternal night, Lorna spoke: "I am not here by mere chance. Nor am I here simply to drink . . . nor to unburden memories forgotten."

Her eyes swept the drifting souls gathered—a congregation of flickering lights from distant corners of the cosmos, each soul a fragile, flickering candle in the dark.

"I have walked the fathomless void between stars longer than most races have dreamed. My footsteps are worn deep in the fabric of ages. My hands cradle threads of beginnings and endings alike." She set the martini softly down—a constellation caught and stilled in crystal, sparkling with the silence of creation.

Lorna's gaze settled with inexorable certainty upon Xylen, "And you, wanderer, are among the souls I am bound to witness this night."

The fabric of time seemed to slow, the bar ceased to be mere wood and stone, becoming instead a liminal place—a passage between the mortal coil and the beyond.

Her voice, gentle but sharp as the clearest starlight, continued: "Each night, I come to this haven—to watch, to listen, and to understand."

Xylen's breath caught—a mortal caught in the grip of celestial weight.

"Why this place?" he whispered. "Why the Driftwood?"

Her smile was a crescent moon—pale and knowing in the encroaching dark. "Because in this place, rich in echoes of life and loss, the weight of worlds converge—here, the lost find company, the weary find rest, and hidden hearts beat with their final hopes . . . I see every story distilled in the whispered prayers, in the laughter, and the tears folded deep as drink."

She rose then, her figure adrift, a wraith borne upon invisible currents, like the last vapor of twilight clinging to the crest of a forgotten hill. Her outline glided in solemn grace, a darkling ripple cast across the timeworn planks beneath her.

From nowhere and everywhere, a breath passed through the chamber—thin, sorrowful—a sigh that seemed not of this world, as if some unseen specter had drawn itself between the folds of reality and let its lament slip through. The shadows wavered as though listening.

Then came the humming. Low, tremulous, coiling like smoke from a funeral pyre. Its melody was strange beyond the bounds of mortal music, mournful yet laced with some secret malice. Xylen felt it brush against the very marrow of his being, each note a cold finger upon the unseen strings of his soul.

"Tonight," she declared in a voice both delicate and infinite, "you shall follow me beyond this world . . . not to oblivion, but to become thread in the great weaving, to drift among endless stars as a story living forever in light and shadow."

The bar seemed to hold its breath—heartbeats stretched to timelessness.

Her eyes met Xylen's—deep as nebulae, alight with stars yet unborn. "Now, it is time to follow me."

Her form dissolved, melting into the drifting dust and starlight that wove through the twilight of the Driftwood—a whispered dream fading on the edge of waking.

Xylen sat there, his limbs quivering as though summoned by a force beyond mortal constancy—an acolyte before some primeval and inexorable deity, an emissary of the infinite come to harvest the wandering spirits whose sorrow was a shroud not entirely their own.

The Driftwood's jaundiced lamps trembled and hissed, casting errant phantoms upon the walls, while the pallid breath of dawn crept unseen along the horizon, silent as a thief among graves.

A hush, heavy and immense, pressed upon the tavern, broken only by a single, faltering breath. Xylen's gaze fell to his glass upon the scarred table—its hues writhed like dying auroras, swam in strange convulsions, and at last melted into a colorless nothing.

His hand lifted toward it, fingers long and delicate, and he beheld with unspeakable dread the slow unraveling of his own form—flesh, sinew, and bone thinning into vapor, mingling with the shadow as though he had never drawn breath.

Terror seized him. He whirled to Marcus, voice a fractured whisper scraping the hollow air. "Help . . . I beg . . ."

Marcus did not move with haste, but only sighed, the stoop of long years upon his shoulders. With grim familiarity, he wiped the counter, leaving no trace of the fading traveler. "Another one," he muttered darkly, his voice thick with a mortal weariness. "Just disappears into existential soup and leaves me holding the bill. Story of my life."

Around him, the patrons—creatures of lightless corners and faded hopes—had already returned to their hushed murmurs and bitter cups, as if no vanishing had occurred. Marcus glanced once at the table where the blue lady and Xylen had sat, allowing a bitter half-smile to ghost his lips.

"Would it kill her," he said to no one in particular, "to settle her tab first?"

Outside, Silaris V remained steadfast, a desolate jewel swallowed slowly by the twin moons' retreat—the last echoes of dreams in the vastness.

Within, the Driftwood hummed—a sanctuary for spirits and stories, a sanctuary for those who dare navigate the interminable darkness.

The Forge of Nargoth

In the cavernous depths of Nargoth, where the rhythmic song of hammer upon anvil echoed through ancient halls and the fires of countless forges cast their warm glow upon walls of hewn stone, there dwelt Thrain Stonehammer, a dwarf of great renown among his kindred. His beard, intricately braided and adorned with clasps of mithril and silver, spoke of the long years of his life, while his eyes, sharp as the finest gemstones pulled from the mountain's heart, bore witness to countless battles fought and victories hard-won. Yet in these days of growing unease, a shadow, as palpable as the very stone around them, crept upon the mountain kingdom, and whispers of a malevolent power snaked through the winding corridors of their ancestral home like tendrils of poisonous mist.

Thrain stood atop the great battlements, his gaze fixed upon the distant peaks where ominous storm clouds gathered, their dark masses roiling against the sky like the portent of doom. The wind, chill and laden with the scent of impending strife, whipped at his beard and cloak. In his heart, Thrain knew with grim certainty that the peace which had long blessed Nargoth was soon to be shattered like glass upon unyielding stone. He turned to his stalwart companion, Grimnir, whose mighty war-axe gleamed wickedly in the flickering light of the watch-fires.

"What word comes from the eastern watch, Grimnir?" Thrain's voice rumbled forth, gruff as the mountain itself, yet underscored with a note of deep concern.

Grimnir's brow furrowed deeply, etching new lines upon his weathered face as he replied, "Tidings most foul, I fear, my lord. Our scouts bring word of dark forces amassing in the shadowed valleys beyond. They whisper that Zorath the Sorcerer, that bane of all free folk, now moves against us with fell purpose."

At the mention of that accursed name, Thrain's hand instinctively tightened upon the ornate hilt of his sword, Oathkeeper, an heirloom of his house that had tasted the blood of many a foe. "Zorath," he spat, the name leaving a bitter taste upon his tongue as though he had bitten into rotten fruit. "Long has that serpent coveted the halls of our fathers and the treasures we have wrought with our own hands. But the stones of Nargoth have stood fast against greater perils in ages past."

"Aye, that they have," Grimnir nodded solemnly, his own hand caressing the haft of his axe as if to draw strength from the weapon. "But never before have our walls been tested by such dark sorcery as this wizard commands. The very earth is said to quake at his passing, as though the bones of the world itself shudder at his touch."

As the two battle-hardened warriors conversed, their words heavy with the weight of impending conflict, a young dwarf approached with haste, his face a mask of urgency and grave concern. This youth, Thorin by name, was known for his swift feet and keen eyes, often serving as a messenger within the vast halls of Nargoth. "Lord Thrain," he called out, his voice cracking with emotion, "I bring word from the inner chambers. Your father, Lord Frain the Wise, calls for you with great urgency. His strength . . . it wanes rapidly."

Without pause or word of acknowledgment, Thrain turned from the battlements, his cloak swirling about him like a storm cloud as he strode purposefully through the torch-lit corridors of Nargoth. His footfalls echoed against the intricately carved stone, each step resounding with the weight of duty and the haste of a son answering his father's final call. The dwarves he passed bowed their heads in respect and concern, for all knew of Lord Frain's failing health and what it might portend for their kingdom in these dark times.

At last, Thrain came to his father's chambers, a place once filled with the bustle of councils and the warmth of familial gatherings, now shrouded in a heavy silence broken only by the labored breathing of the dying king. Frain lay upon a great bed adorned with the furs of mountain beasts, his once-mighty frame now diminished and frail, bent by the inexorable weight of years and the burden of rulership.

"My son," Frain's voice emerged as but a whisper, a mere shadow of the commanding tone that had once guided their people through times of plenty and hardship alike. "Come close, for there is much I must impart to you, and the sands of my time run short."

Thrain knelt beside the bed, taking his father's gnarled hand in his own strong grasp, feeling the feeble pulse of life still beating within. "I am here, father," he spoke softly, his voice thick with emotion. "Speak, and I shall listen with all the attention you have ever taught me to give."

Frain's eyes, though dimmed by the approaching veil of death, suddenly blazed with an inner fire, as if all the remaining strength of his spirit had been kindled for this final task. His voice gained strength as he began to speak of matters long hidden. "You have heard, my son, the tales of the Forge of Nargoth, have you not? Those legends passed down through uncounted generations, speaking of the great forge that gave birth to weapons of such power that they pass into legend—blades capable of cleaving mountains asunder, shields that could turn back the very tide of darkness itself?"

As Frain spoke, the chamber seemed to grow darker, the air heavier, as if the very stones of Nargoth leaned in to listen to this tale of ancient lore and hidden power. Thrain felt a shiver pass through him, sensing that he stood upon the threshold of a revelation that would forever alter the course of his life and the fate of his people.

"Aye," Thrain nodded, his brow furrowed in contemplation. "But surely these are naught but tales spun for the ears of dwarflings, to fill their dreams with wonder and their hearts with pride?"

A wheezing laugh escaped Frain's lips, like the sound of ancient bellows stirring to life. "Nay, my son. The Forge is as real as the stone beneath our feet, as true as the blood that flows in our veins. It was hidden away after the Last Great Strife, for its power was too vast, too terrible to be left in the hands of any one people, be they dwarf, man, or elf."

Thrain listened in awe as his father spoke of the Forge, his words painting vivid images of its creation in the dawn of their people. He told of hammers that rang like thunder, of fires that burned with the heat of a thousand suns, and of mighty deeds wrought by its craft. Frain spoke of axes that could cleave mountains, of shields that could turn aside the fury of dragons, and of crowns that gleamed with the light of captured stars.

Yet as Frain's tale neared its end, his breath grew labored, like the last gusts of wind before a storm. His grip on Thrain's hand weakened, fingers once strong enough to bend iron now as fragile as autumn leaves.

"My time grows short, Thrain," Frain gasped, his voice barely a whisper. "But know this: the blood of kings flows in your veins, as ancient and powerful as the very roots of the mountain. You are the heir to more than just our halls of stone and gold. Seek out . . . seek out . . . "

But Frain's words were cut short as his eyes, once as bright as polished mithril, clouded over. With a final, shuddering breath, he slipped away into the endless halls of their ancestors. Thrain bowed his head in grief, the weight of his father's final words pressing upon him like the mountain itself.

Days passed, each as long and dark as an age of the world. Thrain mourned as was the custom of their people, his beard unbraided, his chambers echoing with laments sung in the ancient tongue. Yet even as he grieved, the shadow of Zorath grew longer, stretching its tendrils of darkness across the land. The defenses of Nargoth, proud and strong for uncounted years, were tested as never before.

It was on the eve of the seventh day, as Thrain stood in his father's chambers surrounded by the echoes of memory, that fate guided his hand. His fingers, calloused from centuries of craft and battle, brushed against a hidden catch within an ancient chest.

With a soft click, a compartment sprang open, revealing a secret long kept.

Within lay a letter, its parchment yellowed with age, sealed with a crest he had never seen before. The wax bore the imprint of a hammer crossed with a crown, surrounded by runes so old their meaning had been lost to time. With trembling hands, Thrain broke the seal and unfolded the parchment. As he read, his eyes widened, and his heart raced like a war drum in his chest.

"By my beard," he whispered, his voice filled with wonder and disbelief, "it cannot be."

The letter spoke of a lineage long forgotten, of a royal line thought lost to the mists of time. It told of Ridun the Deathless, first King of Nargoth and master of the great Forge, whose blood ran true through the ages. And at the end of that line, like a gleaming gem at the end of a long vein of ore, stood Thrain Stonehammer, son of Frain.

As the truth of his heritage settled upon him, Thrain felt the weight of destiny upon his shoulders, heavier than any armor he had ever worn. He alone could rekindle the Forge of Nargoth, awakening its ancient power from its long slumber. With it, he might yet save his people from the dark sorcerer who threatened their very existence.

With newfound purpose burning in his heart like the fires of the deepest forges, Thrain rose and strode from his father's chambers. His footsteps echoed through the halls of Nargoth, each step ringing with the authority of his newly discovered birthright. He gathered his most trusted companions: Grimnir the axe-wielder, whose blade had tasted the blood of a thousand foes; Brokkr the wise, whose beard was white with the wisdom of ages;

and Nori the cunning, whose clever fingers could unlock any secret.

To them, he revealed the truth of his lineage and the monumental task that lay before them. His voice, rich and deep as the caverns of their home, filled the chamber with words of both hope and warning.

"We must seek out the Forge," Thrain declared, his eyes gleaming with a fire that had not been seen in Nargoth for an age. "It lies hidden in the deepest reaches of our kingdom, guarded by ancient magics and forgotten paths. The journey will be perilous, fraught with dangers both seen and unseen. But find it we must, for it may be our only hope against the darkness that threatens to engulf us all."

Brokkr stroked his white beard thoughtfully, his eyes gleaming with the wisdom of ages. "The journey ahead, my lord, is fraught with perils beyond our reckoning. The deep places of Nargoth have grown wild and strange, untrodden by dwarven feet for countless years. In the shadows lurk creatures of myth and nightmare, and the very stone itself may rise against us, for the mountain remembers the ancient oaths sworn in its depths."

Nori, his fingers dancing nervously along the hilt of his dagger, added with a voice low and urgent, "And let us not forget the cunning of our forebears, my king. The Forge was hidden with purpose, and the path to it will be guarded by traps and enchantments that have slumbered for an age. We may be marching to our doom, as surely as if we faced Zorath's army in open battle."

Grimnir, his face etched with the scars of a hundred battles, hefted his great axe with a fierce grin that belied the gravity of their situation. "Doom, you say? Aye, perhaps. But I'd rather meet my end in the depths of our ancestral halls, axe in hand and a war cry on my lips, than cower like mewling babes while that accursed sorcerer Zorath hammers at our gates. Let us go forth, and may our deeds be worthy of song for a thousand years to come!"

Thrain felt his heart swell with pride at the courage of his companions. He nodded solemnly, his voice carrying the weight of his newfound kingship. "Then our course is set. When the first light of dawn kisses the mountain peaks, we shall depart. Gather only what you can carry on your back, for our path will be narrow and treacherous, winding through forgotten ways where no wagon may pass."

As his companions dispersed to make ready for the journey, Thrain ascended once more to the battlements. The night lay heavy upon the land, a darkness deeper than mere absence of light. Yet in the far distance, he could discern the faint flicker of campfires—Zorath's vast army, drawing ever nearer like a tide of shadow. Thrain laid his hand upon the ancient stonework of the parapet, feeling the slow, steady pulse of the mountain beneath his fingers. It was as if Nargoth itself breathed, a slumbering giant soon to be roused.

"Hold fast, O Nargoth," he whispered, his words carried away by the chill wind. "Your king returns to claim his birthright, and with it, your salvation. Though the path be dark and fraught with danger, we shall not falter. For in your deepest halls lies the key to our people's survival, and I swear by the beard of Ridun the Deathless that I shall see it found or perish in the attempt."

As the first pale light of dawn crept over the eastern peaks, Thrain and his chosen companions passed through the great gates of Nargoth. The weight of their people's hopes and a destiny long foretold rested upon their shoulders as surely as their packs. Descending into the mountain's depths, leaving behind the familiar clamor of forges and the warm glow of hearths, Thrain felt a curious mixture of dread and exhilaration coursing through his veins.

The passages they traversed were ancient beyond reckoning, hewn by the hands of their ancestors in an age when the world was young. Runes of power and protection adorned the walls, glowing with a faint, otherworldly light that seemed to pulse in time with the mountain's heartbeat. Brokkr, his scholarly nature never far from the surface, ran gnarled fingers over the inscriptions, his lips moving silently as he deciphered their meaning.

"These speak of the Forge," he announced at last, his voice hushed with reverence. "They warn of its power and the weighty responsibility that comes with its mastery. 'Let he who seeks the Forge be pure of heart and indomitable of will,' they say, 'for its fire shall consume the unworthy, leaving naught but ash and regret.'"

Thrain nodded gravely, feeling the full weight of his lineage pressing down upon him. "Then we must tread with utmost caution, for the heart of a dwarf is as labyrinthine and complex as the deepest mineshafts we carve. Who among us can truly claim to be pure, unmarred by doubt or desire?"

As they delved ever deeper into the mountain's embrace, the very air grew thick with the dust of forgotten ages. Silence pressed in around them like a physical force, broken only by the echo of their footfalls in vast, empty chambers that had not known the tread of living feet since time immemorial.

It was Nori, his senses honed by years of skulking in shadowed places, who first noticed the gleam of eyes in the darkness ahead. "We are not alone," he hissed, his daggers sliding silently from their sheaths.

From the impenetrable gloom emerged beings that seemed born of the very stone itself. Their forms were rough and unfinished, as if some great sculptor had begun to carve figures from the living rock but abandoned his work halfway through. They moved with a ponderous grace that belied their massive bulk, their intentions as inscrutable as the depths from which they had risen.

Grimnir raised his axe, its edge glinting in the faint light of their torches, but Thrain stayed his companion's hand with a gesture. "Hold," he commanded, his voice ringing with authority. "These are the guardians of the deep places, set here by our ancestors in ages past. They may not be our foes, but neither are they our friends. We must treat with them carefully."

Stepping forward, Thrain addressed the stone creatures in the ancient tongue of the dwarves, his words echoing with power and authority. The language, long forgotten by most, flowed from his lips like molten gold. "I am Thrain, son of Frain, heir to the line of Ridun, whose hammer-strokes once shaped the very foundations of this mountain. We seek the Forge of Nargoth, not to claim its power for our own glory, but to defend our people against a darkness that threatens to engulf all we hold dear."

For a long moment, the stone guardians stood motionless, their featureless faces as impassive as the mountain itself. The air grew thick with tension, and Thrain's companions held their breath, hands tightening on their weapons. Then, with a grinding of stone on stone that echoed through the cavern like distant thunder, the guardians slowly parted. A passage, hitherto hidden from mortal eyes, was revealed. One of the creatures, its form hewn from the living rock, extended a massive arm towards the opening, its meaning as clear as the ringing of a bell in the depths of the mountain.

"It seems we have passed the first test," Brokkr mused, his white beard quivering with a mixture of relief and anticipation as they entered the newly revealed corridor. "But I fear it will not be the last. The wisdom of our ancestors was deep, and their cunning in protecting their secrets even deeper."

The passage led them deeper into the heart of the mountain, through caverns so vast that the light of their torches was swallowed by the darkness above. They crossed narrow bridges that spanned chasms so deep that the sound of falling stones never reached their ears. At times, the very air around them seemed to shimmer with ancient magics, the whispers of long-dead enchanters echoing in their minds. More than once, they found themselves facing illusions so real that only their unwavering faith in their quest allowed them to press on.

It was Nori's sharp eyes and keener mind that saw them through these challenges. Like a master jeweler discerning true gems from false, he guided them through the maze of deceptions, his instincts honed by years of navigating both the physical and political labyrinths of dwarven society. Yet even his formidable skills were tested to their limit when they came upon a great door, its surface a tapestry of riddles and runes of power that seemed to shift and change even as they gazed upon it. The magic that sealed this portal was ancient beyond reckoning, a testament to the might and wisdom of those who had come before.

"This is dwarf-made," Nori declared, his keen eyes tracing the intricate patterns of the lock. "But 'tis unlike any I have ever beheld. It may take days, nay, weeks to unravel its secrets, for the craft here is of an age long past."

Yet Thrain, moved by some deep-rooted instinct born of his royal lineage, stepped forward with purpose. His hand, calloused from years of wielding hammer and sword, came to rest upon the ancient door. At his touch, the runes etched upon its surface sprang to life, their light a soft golden glow that seemed to pulse with the very heartbeat of the mountain.

Words, ancient and powerful, rose unbidden to Thrain's lips—a tongue so old that even Brokkr, learned as he was in the lore of their people, could not fathom its meaning. The very air around them seemed to thicken, charged with a power that had slumbered for countless ages.

With a sound like the groaning of the earth itself, the great door swung inward. The chamber beyond was bathed in a light that seemed to come from everywhere and nowhere at once, a radiance that spoke of things beyond mortal understanding. And there, at the heart of this sanctum, stood the Forge of Nargoth.

It was a sight to make even the stoutest heart quail, a masterwork of dwarven craft that seemed to bridge the gap between the mortal realm and the realm of legend. The Forge burned with a fire that was more than mere flame, its blue-white intensity casting dancing shadows that seemed to whisper secrets of ages past. The very air shimmered and pulsed with power, as if the boundaries between what was and what could be had grown thin in this hallowed place.

As Thrain approached, each step measured and deliberate, he felt the weight of his ancestry pressing down upon him like a physical force. This moment, he knew, was the culmination of a lineage that stretched back to the very dawn of his people, when the first dwarves had been shaped from the living stone of the world. With hands that trembled not from fear but from the sheer magnitude of what lay before him, Thrain reached out to touch the Forge.

The instant his fingers made contact with the ancient metal, a torrent of visions flooded his mind. He saw great battles fought beneath skies dark with the wings of dragons, kingdoms rising in splendor only to fall to ruin and dust. He witnessed the forging of weapons of legend and the terrible price exacted for their power. And through it all, like a thread of darkness weaving through the tapestry of time, he saw the face of Zorath, twisted with a hunger that threatened to consume all in its path.

When at last the visions receded, Thrain found himself upon his knees, his breath coming in ragged gasps. His companions stood around him, their faces etched with concern and awe at what they had witnessed.

"My lord," Grimnir said, his voice gruff with emotion as he helped Thrain to his feet, "are you well? What visions did the Forge grant you?"

Thrain's eyes, when he raised them to meet Grimnir's gaze, were filled with a new light—a mixture of grim determination and profound sorrow. "I have seen the path that lies before us," he replied, his voice resonating with the weight of prophecy. "And I have seen the choices we must make. The Forge is ours, aye, but its power comes at a cost greater than any of us could have imagined."

As if in response to his words, the very ground beneath their feet began to tremble. Dust and small stones rained down from the ceiling, and from somewhere in the distance came the unmistakable sounds of battle—the clash of steel, the cries of the wounded, and a deeper, more terrible sound that seemed to shake the very foundations of the mountain.

"Zorath," Brokkr breathed, his face pale beneath his beard. "He has found us at last."

Thrain turned once more to face the Forge, his mind racing with the weight of the choice that lay before him. They had found what they sought, the legendary Forge of Nargoth, but now they faced a decision that would shape the fate of their people for generations to come. To use the Forge's power was to risk corruption, to unleash forces that might prove as destructive to Nargoth as Zorath's dark sorcery. Yet to destroy it, to face their foe with only the strength of their arms and the courage in their hearts, seemed folly in the face of such overwhelming darkness.

As the sounds of conflict drew ever nearer, echoing through the ancient halls, Thrain knew that the fate of Nargoth hung in the balance. Whatever choice he made in this moment would echo through the ages, for good or for ill, shaping the destiny of his people and perhaps of all the free peoples of the world.

With a deep breath that seemed to steady not just himself but the very mountain around them, Thrain turned to face his companions. When he spoke, his voice rang with the authority of his newfound kingship, tempered by the wisdom granted by the Forge's visions.

"My friends, my brothers," he said, his words carrying to every corner of the chamber, "the time has come for us to decide the fate of our people. Let us make a choice this day that our ancestors would look upon with pride, a choice that our descendants will sing of in the halls of Nargoth for a thousand generations to come."

And with those words, Thrain Stonehammer, last of the line of Ridun and heir to the Forge of Nargoth, steeled himself to face his destiny. The path ahead was shrouded in shadow and fraught with peril, but in his heart burned a fire as bright and as enduring as the Forge itself—a fire that would light the way through the darkness that threatened to engulf them all.

***

The depths of Nargoth yawned before Thrain and his companions, a vast chasm of shadow that seemed to devour both light and hope. The air hung heavy and stagnant, laden with the whispers of forgotten ages and the weight of ancient secrets. Thrain's keen eyes pierced the gloom, his hand never straying far from the haft of his mighty war-axe, Soulrender.

Brokkr, his snow-white beard catching the feeble light of their guttering torches, gazed into the oppressive darkness. "These halls bear ill will," he murmured, his voice barely audible above the distant drip of unseen waters. "It is as though the very bones of the mountain reject our presence."

Grimnir, his frame as unyielding as the stone itself, nodded grimly. "Aye, there's a miasma of malevolence that clings to the air like morning mist. Steel yourselves, lads, for I fear we tread where even our ancestors dared not venture."

The silence that enveloped them was suddenly rent by eerie echoes—faint whispers and the scraping of unseen claws that seemed to emanate from the very walls around them. The dwarves huddled closer, their eyes darting to and fro, seeking the source of these fell sounds.

In that moment, Thrain's arm shot out, commanding stillness. His gaze fixed upon a flicker of movement in the murky depths ahead. "We are not alone in these forsaken halls," he breathed, his words barely more than a whisper.

As if summoned by his utterance, the very shadows began to coalesce, taking on form and substance. From the impenetrable darkness emerged figures clad in raiment as black as the void, their eyes glowing with an otherworldly malice that sent shivers down even the stoutest dwarf's spine.

"Zorath's fell servants!" Brokkr exclaimed, his gnarled hands grasping his staff with renewed vigor. The ancient runes carved into the wood began to pulse with a soft, blue light, pushing back the encroaching darkness.

In the space of a heartbeat, the cavern erupted into chaos. The clash of steel against steel rang out, a discordant symphony that echoed through the vast chambers of Nargoth. Thrain fought with a fury born of desperation and ancestral might, each swing of Soulrender guided by the collective wisdom of a hundred generations of dwarf-kings.

Beside him, Grimnir bellowed his defiance to the very stone, his twin axes, Thundercleave and Stormfury, weaving a deadly dance that left a trail of broken foes in his wake. The dwarf-warrior's eyes blazed with an inner fire, his beard matted with the black ichor that passed for blood in Zorath's unholy creations.

As the battle raged, the very foundations of Nargoth seemed to tremble. Dust and small stones rained down from unseen heights, and in the distance, a low rumble began to build —whether from some ancient mechanism stirring to life or the mountain itself awakening, none could say.

Thrain, momentarily clear of foes, raised his voice above the din of combat. "Stand fast, my brothers! We fight not just for our lives, but for the very soul of Nargoth! Let every stroke of your axes, every thrust of your swords, be a testament to the indomitable spirit of our people!"

His words ignited a new fire in the hearts of his companions. With renewed vigor, they pressed forward against the tide of darkness, their weapons flashing in the dim light like stars in a storm-wracked sky.

As the last of their foes fell, Thrain wiped the sweat from his brow, his chest heaving like great bellows. The cavern, now silent save for the drip of water and the ragged breathing of his companions, seemed to press in upon them with an oppressive weight. "They knew we were coming," he said grimly, his voice echoing off the ancient stone. "Zorath's reach extends even here, in the very heart of our kingdom."

Grimnir, his face etched with lines of weariness and anger, kicked aside a fallen enemy, the clatter of armor on stone ringing out like a discordant bell. "But how?" he demanded, his voice a low growl. "These tunnels have lain sealed for centuries, known only to the most trusted of our kin."

Before Thrain could answer, a voice rang out from the shadows, as familiar as it was unexpected. "Hello, old friend. The years have been kind to you, it seems."

Thrain's blood ran cold, a chill seeping into his bones that had naught to do with the damp air of the cavern. From the darkness stepped a figure, and Thrain's heart clenched with a mixture of disbelief and dread. "Varric," he breathed, the name tasting like ashes on his tongue.

Varric stood before them, a ghost from a past best forgotten. Once a trusted companion, now a traitor to his people, he cut a striking figure in the dim light. His beard, once a source of pride among their people, was now braided with gold and gems, a gaudy display that spoke of wealth ill-gotten. But it was his eyes that truly gave Thrain pause—they glittered with a hunger that seemed to devour the very light around him.

"You look surprised to see me, Thrain," Varric said, a mocking smile playing across his lips. The familiarity of the expression, so at odds with the stranger that now stood before them, sent a pang through Thrain's heart. "Did you truly believe I would rot in exile while you and yours hoarded the secrets of our ancestors? That I would meekly accept the judgment passed upon me by those too blind to see the future?"

Thrain's grip tightened on his axe, the worn handle a comforting weight in his calloused hands. "You were banished for a reason, Varric," he said, his voice low and dangerous. "Your greed and ambition threatened not just Nargoth, but all that our people hold dear. You would have seen our kingdom burn if it meant you could rule over the ashes."

Varric laughed, the sound echoing unnaturally in the cavern, bouncing off the walls until it seemed to come from everywhere at once. "Greed? Ambition? Such small words for such grand visions, old friend. I prefer to think of it as . . . foresight. The ability to see beyond the stagnant traditions that have held our people in chains for countless generations."

"You speak of progress," Brokkr interjected, his voice heavy with the weight of ages, "but I hear only the whispers of corruption. What honeyed words has Zorath poured into your ears, Varric? What price have you paid for this 'vision' you so proudly proclaim?"

For a moment, something flickered in Varric's eyes—a shadow of the dwarf he had once been, perhaps, or a glimmer of regret for paths not taken. But it was gone in an instant, replaced by a steely resolve that seemed to radiate from him like heat from a forge. "He has shown me wonders beyond your wildest imaginings, old man," Varric said, his voice thrumming with barely contained excitement. "Power that could elevate our people to heights unimagined, that could see us take our rightful place as rulers of all the lands, both above and below the earth."

"At what cost?" Thrain demanded, his voice rising with the fury that burned in his chest. "The subjugation of all we hold dear? The destruction of everything our ancestors bled and died to build? You would see us become tyrants, no better than the dragons of old who hoarded gold and cared naught for the suffering of others."

Varric spread his hands in a gesture of mock supplication, the gems adorning his fingers catching the light and throwing it back in dazzling patterns. "It doesn't have to be that way, Thrain. Join us. Think of what we could accomplish together, with the Forge of Nargoth at our command. We could reshape the very world to our liking, ensure that no dwarf ever goes hungry or lives in fear again."

Thrain felt a moment of vertigo, as if he stood upon the edge of a great chasm, the promise of power and glory for his people a siren song that called to the deepest, darkest parts of his warrior's heart. For a heartbeat, he allowed himself to imagine it —Nargoth ascendant, its armies marching across the lands, its craftsmen creating wonders beyond imagining.

But then he remembered his father's words, spoken in those final moments as life ebbed from his body. He felt anew the weight of responsibility that came with his lineage, the sacred trust placed in him by generations of kings who had ruled with wisdom and compassion. "And what of honor, Varric?" he asked, his voice quiet but firm. "What of duty? What of the oaths we swore to protect our people, not to rule over them with an iron fist?"

Varric's countenance darkened, his eyes glinting with a fierce light. "Honor? Duty? Mere words, Thrain, that have bound us like iron shackles of our own forging. The world beyond our mountain halls shifts and changes, as inexorable as the grinding of great glaciers. We must move with it, or be ground to dust beneath its weight."

"Nay, Varric," Thrain replied, his voice resonant with the deep conviction of his forebears. "You speak falsely. Our traditions, the values passed down through countless generations, are not fetters that bind us. They are the very bedrock of our kingdom, as enduring as the bones of the earth. Upon this foundation, we have weathered storms that would have swept lesser folk into the abyss of history."

A heavy silence fell upon the cavern, broken only by the distant echoes of dripping water and the soft crackle of torchlight. Varric's shoulders sagged, as if a great weight had settled upon them. He exhaled, a sound laden with sorrow and regret that seemed to echo the very weariness of the mountain itself.

"I had hoped, old friend, that you might see the truth that lies before us," Varric said, his voice now tinged with a melancholy that belied his earlier fervor. "But I perceive now that you are as one blind, stumbling in the darkness of antiquated ways. It grieves me deeply, for I had thought better of you."

With a motion swift as a striking serpent, Varric's hand darted to his belt, producing a blade that shimmered with an otherworldly radiance. Its light pulsed with a rhythm that seemed to mock the very heartbeat of the mountain. "Zorath, in his infinite wisdom, foresaw this possibility. He bade me show you but a fraction of the power that awaits those who dare to grasp it."

Before Thrain or his companions could react, Varric plunged the glowing blade into the living rock of the cavern floor. A light erupted, brighter than the forges of Nargoth at their fiercest, searing their eyes and filling the chamber with a roar that shook dust from ancient crevices. When at last the tumult subsided, Varric had vanished, as if swallowed by the very stone itself.

Thrain turned to his companions, his lungs heaving as he struggled to draw breath in the dust-choked air. Grimnir's visage was a mask of grime and blood, while Brokkr leaned heavily upon his staff, his eyes wide with a mixture of awe and terror.

"By the beards of our ancestors," Brokkr wheezed, his voice scarcely above a whisper, "what foul sorcery has Zorath unleashed upon our realm?"

Thrain shook his head, his mind awhirl with the implications of what they had witnessed. "A mere taste of Zorath's fell power, I deem, and a dire warning of the fate that awaits should we falter in our quest."

Grimnir spat upon the ground, his eyes blazing with a fury hot enough to kindle ore. "Let him come, then, with all his dark arts and shadowy minions. We shall show him the true mettle of dwarven steel and the indomitable spirit that beats in dwarven hearts!"

Yet even as his companions spoke, Thrain's thoughts were troubled, like a murky pool stirred by unseen currents. Varric's words echoed in the chambers of his mind, intertwining with the memory of the temptation he had felt in the presence of the Forge. Here was a weapon of power beyond reckoning, one that held within its fires the potential to either salvage their people from the encroaching darkness or to consume them utterly in its ravenous flames.

"We must tread with the utmost caution," Thrain said at last, his voice low and measured. "The magic of the Forge is as old as the mountains themselves, and just as unpredictable. If we approach it without due care, it may corrupt us as surely as it has ensnared Varric and Zorath in its grasp."

Brokkr nodded, his white beard catching the flickering torchlight. "Wisely spoken, my king. The ancient sagas tell of the Forge's dual nature—a tool of both creation and devastation. We must approach it with the wisdom of our forebears and the restraint born of hard-won experience, lest in our haste to vanquish our foes, we become that which we have sworn to oppose."

As Thrain pondered these words, he felt the weight of his crown more keenly than ever before. The path ahead was fraught with peril, each step a choice between salvation and damnation. Yet in his heart, he knew that they must press on, for the fate of Nargoth—and perhaps all the free peoples of the world—hung in the balance.

***

Thrain Stonehammer stood before the Forge of Nargoth, its azure-white flames casting an otherworldly glow across the cavernous chamber. The very air pulsed with ancient power, and he felt the weight of countless generations pressing upon his shoulders like the mountain itself. His steadfast companions, Grimnir Ironheart and Brokkr Runewise, watched with bated breath, their eyes reflecting a mix of reverence and unease.

"What path shall you choose, my liege?" Brokkr's voice was but a whisper, nearly lost in the low thrumming of the Forge.

Thrain's hand hovered above the Forge, feeling the searing heat of its enchanted fires. He could sense the raw potential within—the ability to shape weapons of legend, to forge blades that could cleave the very fabric of shadow. With such might, they could smite Zorath and his fell host, scattering them to the winds. The allure of such power was nigh irresistible, calling to the very core of his being.

"I could bring this conflict to a swift and decisive end," Thrain mused, his gaze locked upon the dancing flames. "With the Forge's strength flowing through our arms, we could drive Zorath and his ilk back to the dark depths from which they crawled."

Yet even as the words left his lips, Thrain felt a flicker of doubt. He recalled the wisdom of his forebears, their warnings echoing through the ages. Power, they had cautioned, was a double-edged sword, as likely to corrupt its wielder as to vanquish its foes. The annals of dwarven history were rife with tales of mighty kings and master craftsmen who had fallen prey to their own creations, their names now whispered as cautionary tales in the deepest halls of Nargoth.

Grimnir stepped forward, his battle-worn face etched with concern. "My king," he began, his voice gruff yet tinged with respect, "remember the oaths we swore. We came not to wield power, but to protect our people. The Forge is a tool, aye, but one that may shape the user as surely as it shapes the metal."

As if in answer to Grimnir's words, a torrent of visions cascaded through Thrain's mind, like water rushing through a broken dam. He beheld the grand tapestry of ages past and the shadowy threads of futures yet to be woven. Before his eyes unfolded scenes of mighty kings of yore, their noble visages twisted by greed and hubris, corrupted by the very power they had sought to master. He witnessed proud cities, once bastions of dwarven craft and culture, reduced to smoldering ruins. Great mountains, the lifeblood of his people, crumbled like sand castles before a relentless tide. The hallowed halls of Nargoth, which had echoed with songs of triumph for countless generations, lay silent and broken.

Thrain recoiled from the Forge as if struck, his breath coming in ragged gasps. "Nay," he rasped, his voice thick with the weight of revelation. "Nay, we dare not wield this power. The peril is too vast, too terrible to contemplate."

Brokkr inclined his head, his ancient eyes gleaming with approval. "Wisdom speaks through you, my liege. Yet what course shall we chart? Zorath's fell host draws nigh with each passing moment."

A heavy silence descended upon the chamber, broken only by the faint crackle of the Forge's otherworldly flames. Thrain stood motionless, his brow furrowed in deep contemplation. Then, like the first rays of dawn breaking through storm clouds, resolve dawned upon his countenance.

"We shall accomplish that which our forebears, in their pride, neglected," Thrain declared, his voice ringing with newfound purpose. "We shall unmake the Forge, consigning its power to the mists of legend."

Grimnir's eyes widened, disbelief etched upon his weathered features. "Unmake it? But, sire, surely this is our sole bulwark against Zorath's dark designs!"

Thrain shook his head, his gaze unwavering. "Nay, Grimnir. Our true strength resides not in ensorcelled weaponry or relics of a bygone age. It dwells within the hearts of our people, in the unyielding courage that has seen us through countless trials, and in the hard-won wisdom bequeathed to us by our ancestors."

He turned to face his companions, his eyes alight with a fire that rivaled the Forge itself. "Stand with me, my brothers in arms. Aid me in sealing away this power for all time, that it may nevermore ensnare the hearts of dwarf or man."

With grim resolve, they set about their monumental task. Brokkr's sonorous voice filled the chamber with incantations of binding and warding, each word resonating with the power of ages. Grimnir, his muscles straining, heaved great slabs of stone into place, sealing off ancient passageways and barring all entrances. And Thrain, guided by some primal instinct awakened by his royal lineage, labored to quench the Forge's arcane flames.

As the final ember flickered and died, a profound hush descended upon the chamber. The very air seemed to exhale, as if relieved of an immeasurable burden. Thrain gazed upon his companions, noting in their eyes the same bittersweet mixture of relief and melancholy that stirred within his own breast.

"It is finished," he murmured, his words barely above a whisper. "The might of the Forge is sealed away, mayhap until the ending of the world."

Brokkr nodded sagely, his gnarled fingers combing through his silver beard. "A choice most noble and brave, my king. Yet what of the morrow? What of those who may follow in our footsteps, seeking once more to unlock this terrible power?"

Thrain stood in silent contemplation, the weight of his decision heavy upon his brow. With a deliberate motion, he reached into the depths of his travel-worn pack and withdrew a tome bound in ancient leather, its surface etched with runes of power and memory. From within his cloak, he produced a quill fashioned from the feather of a great eagle, its nib gleaming in the ethereal light of the chamber.

With strokes as precise as a master craftsman, Thrain began to write, each word imbued with the gravitas of ages past and the hope of ages yet to come:

"Hearken, ye who in future days may seek the might of Nargoth's Forge. Let these words, writ by Thrain Stonehammer, son of Frain, ring true through the corridors of time. The strength of our people, the children of stone and fire, resides not in artifacts of legend or weapons wrought by forgotten magics. Nay, our true power lies in the unbreakable bonds of kin and clan, in the unyielding will that stands fast against the encroaching dark. Let this testament stand as a beacon to those yet unborn, a reminder of the choice made in this hallowed chamber. We turned from the siren song of facile power, choosing instead to meet our trials with naught but the strength granted by Mahal and the courage kindled in hearts true and steadfast."

As Thrain's quill danced across the parchment, the very air seemed to thicken with the weight of his words. The runes upon the chamber walls pulsed in harmony with each stroke, as if the very mountain itself bore witness to this moment of profound choice.

When at last he set down the quill, Thrain felt as though he had carved his very essence into the pages before him. He bound the tome with a cord spun from mithril and sealed it with wax pressed by the ring that had adorned the hand of Ridun the Deathless himself.

With reverence, Thrain placed the book upon a stone plinth that seemed to rise from the chamber floor at his unspoken command. As he stepped back, the stone enveloped the tome, securing it for the ages to come.

Their solemn task complete, Thrain and his companions turned to retrace their steps through the labyrinthine passages. The air grew thick with tension, for each knew that their choice, while righteous, had left them vulnerable to the dark forces that even now assailed their kingdom.

As they rounded a bend in a narrow corridor, a figure materialized from the shadows like a nightmare given form. It was Varric, once a trusted advisor, now twisted by greed and the promise of dark power. His eyes, once warm with friendship, now burned with an eldritch fire that spoke of pacts made in realms best left unexplored.

"Addled fools!" Varric's voice rang out, a discordant echo of its former self. In his hand, he brandished a blade that pulsed with sickly light, its edge hungry for betrayal. "You've cast aside the one hope of salvation! Zorath will grind Nargoth to dust beneath his heel, and I shall revel in the ashes of your folly!"

Thrain stood unbowed, his bearing every inch that of the king he was born to be. His voice, when he spoke, carried the strength of the mountain itself. "Your words ring hollow, Varric, son of Varin. The Forge was no salvation, but a snare laid for the unwary. Its power would have corrupted all it touched, leading us down the same benighted path you now tread."

With the swiftness of a striking serpent, Thrain surged forward. His hand, calloused by centuries of craft and combat, closed around the hilt of Varric's fell blade. In a single, fluid motion born of countless battles, he wrenched the weapon free and plunged it deep into the traitor's breast.

Varric's eyes widened, shock and realization warring in their depths. For a fleeting moment, a shadow of the dwarf he had once been flickered across his face. Then, like a candle guttering in a chill wind, the light faded from his eyes, and he crumpled to the unyielding stone.

Thrain turned to his companions, his face etched with the grim resolve of one who has faced his darkest hour and emerged unbroken. "Thus perishes the final temptation," he intoned, his voice echoing through the ancient halls. "But our task, my kinsmen, has only just begun. We must quit this place with all haste and rally the clans. Zorath may command fell magics and numberless hordes, but we wield a power far greater—the indomitable spirit of Nargoth's children."

Grimnir, his beard braided for battle and his eyes alight with the fire of coming conflict, hefted his great axe. A fierce grin split his face, a promise of retribution to come. "Well spoken, my liege," he growled, his voice like stone grinding upon stone. "Let Zorath come with all his dark arts and blighted minions. He'll find that the steel of dwarven blades and the iron of dwarven hearts will shatter his shadows like glass upon the anvil."

As they ascended through the winding passages of Nargoth, Thrain felt the burden of ages lift from his shoulders. The path ahead loomed treacherous, fraught with perils untold and trials yet unfaced. Yet in his heart, a flame of certainty burned bright, for he knew their choice was just and true. The destiny of Nargoth—nay, the fate of all free folk who dwelt beneath the sky —would not be shaped by relics of bygone days, but by the unwavering spirit of those who stood fast against the encroaching shadow.

"To arms, my kinsmen!" Thrain's voice thundered through the cavernous halls as they emerged into the great chamber. "Let the deep-throated horns of Nargoth sing their battle-song once more! This day, we fight not merely for hearth and home, but for the very essence of our people!"

The call to arms reverberated through the mountain's heart, stirring the blood of every dwarf who heard it. And there stood Thrain Stonehammer, last scion of Ridun's line, ready to lead his folk into the fray. No longer did he seek the crutch of ancient sorcery; instead, he stood tall as a king who had unearthed the wellspring of his people's might—their indomitable will and the bonds of kinship that ran deeper than the roots of the mountains themselves.

As the dwarves rallied around him, Thrain's eyes gleamed with a fire that outshone even the legendary Forge they had left behind. In that moment, he knew that the true strength of Nargoth lay not in artifacts of power, but in the hearts of its people, tempered by adversity and bound together by an unbreakable loyalty to their kin and kingdom.

***

The horns of Nargoth resounded through the cavernous halls, their deep, sonorous tones awakening the spirit of every dwarf within. The ancient melodies, passed down through countless generations, spoke of battles long past and glories yet to come. Thrain Stonehammer, resplendent in his ancestral armor that shimmered like the very stars above, stood resolute before the great gates of his kingdom. The intricate patterns etched into his breastplate told the tale of his lineage, each swirl and rune a testament to the craft of his forebears. Behind him, as far as the eye could perceive in the torch-lit expanse, stood rank upon rank of dwarven warriors, their axes and hammers gleaming with a fierce light that matched the fire in their eyes.

"Sons of Nargoth!" Thrain's voice thundered, carrying to the farthest corners of the assembled host, echoing off the stone walls that had sheltered their kind since time immemorial. "The hour of reckoning is upon us. Zorath, that fell sorcerer, and his dark forces seek to claim our home, to defile these hallowed halls that our fathers and their fathers before them built with their own hands, with sweat and blood and unyielding determination. But we are the children of the mountain, born of stone and fire! Our resolve is as unyielding as the very foundations of the earth!"

A mighty cheer erupted from the dwarven army, a roar so powerful it seemed to shake the very roots of the mountain. The sound reverberated through the ancient halls, stirring the spirits of their ancestors who watched from beyond the veil. Grimnir, his beard braided with iron rings that spoke of battles won and foes vanquished, stood steadfast at Thrain's right hand. With a warrior's grace, he raised his twin axes high, the firelight dancing along their razor-sharp edges. "For Nargoth!" he bellowed, his voice carrying the weight of ages. The cry was taken up by thousands of throats, a chorus of defiance that echoed through every cavern and corridor of their mountain home.

The air itself seemed to tremble with the force of their conviction, and even the stone beneath their feet thrummed with the energy of their united purpose. In that moment, every dwarf felt the weight of their history upon their shoulders, and the promise of future glory burning in their hearts. They stood not just as warriors, but as the guardians of a legacy that stretched back to the very dawn of their race.

With a groaning of ancient mechanisms, the great gates of Nargoth swung wide, their iron-bound timbers creaking with the weight of ages. Beyond, the valley stretched out beneath a sky heavy with portent, where roiling storm clouds gathered like a dark host. There, arrayed in terrible splendor, stood the army of

Zorath—a seething mass of shadow and malice that seemed to devour the very light of day.

Thrain's keen eyes narrowed as they fell upon a figure at the vanguard of the enemy host. Zorath stood tall and terrible, his form wreathed in shadows that writhed and twisted like living things. In his grasp, he held a staff of black metal, twisted and gnarled as an ancient tree, crackling with fell energies that sent shivers through the very stone beneath their feet.

"Forward!" Thrain's voice rang out, clear and strong as a bell of adamant. At his command, the dwarven army surged forth, a tide of iron and stone and indomitable will.

The clash of the two armies was as the meeting of great storm fronts, a thunderous cacophony that echoed off the mountain walls and shook the very foundations of the earth. Dwarven steel met shadowy blades with a fury that sent sparks flying like stars fallen to earth. Thrain fought at the forefront, his ancestral sword Shadowcleaver a blur of argent light as it clove through foe after foe. Beside him, Grimnir's twin axes, Sorrow and Vengeance, sang their deadly song, each swing reaping a bloody harvest from the ranks of the enemy.

For hours uncounted, the battle raged with unrelenting ferocity. The dwarves fought with all the stubbornness and skill that had made their race legendary, but Zorath's forces seemed as numberless as the stars. For every shadow-creature that fell, two more rose to take its place, their forms coalescing from the very darkness that cloaked the battlefield.

"We must reach Zorath!" Thrain's voice carried over the din of battle to where Grimnir stood, his mighty frame drenched in sweat and the black ichor of their foes. "Cut off the head, and the body will wither!"

Grimnir nodded grimly, his beard matted with blood and grime. "Aye, but how? His guards are thick about him, and our lines grow thin. We'd be cut down before we reached him."

Thrain's eyes blazed with a fire that seemed to come from the very heart of the mountain itself. "We make a path," he declared, his voice filled with grim determination. "Rally the Ironbreakers to me!"

At Grimnir's signal, a company of heavily armored dwarves, the elite of Nargoth's warriors, formed up around their king. Their armor, forged in the deepest halls of the mountain and imbued with ancient magics, gleamed like starlight even in the gloom of battle. With a roar that shook the earth and sent tremors through the ranks of their foes, they charged forward, their shields locked together to form an impenetrable wedge of dwarven might and resolve.

Zorath's minions fell before them like wheat before the scythe, their shadowy forms dissipating like mist before the dawn. Slowly but surely, they carved a path through the enemy ranks, drawing ever closer to where the dark sorcerer stood, his staff raised high as he wove his foul magics.

But as they neared their goal, Zorath's baleful gaze fell upon them. With a word of power that seemed to tear at the very fabric of reality, he unleashed a bolt of pure darkness, a negation of light and life itself. It struck the dwarven formation with the force of a battering ram forged from the stuff of nightmares, scattering warriors like leaves before an autumn gale.

Thrain was hurled to the ground, his ancient armor smoking and his ears ringing from the impact. As he struggled to rise, his limbs leaden and unresponsive, he saw Zorath approaching, a cruel smile twisting his features into a mask of malevolent triumph.

"So falls the last king of Nargoth," the sorcerer sneered, his voice a sibilant hiss that seemed to freeze the very marrow in Thrain's bones. He raised his staff high, dark energies coalescing around its tip for a killing blow.

But before the strike could fall, a blur of motion interposed itself between Thrain and his foe. Grimnir stood there, a mountain made flesh, his axes crossed to catch Zorath's staff mere inches from Thrain's face.

"Not while I draw breath, you foul creature!" Grimnir growled, his muscles straining against the sorcerer's unnatural strength. The air around them crackled with conflicting energies, light and darkness warring for supremacy.

With a grunt of effort that seemed to come from the very depths of the earth, Grimnir pushed Zorath back, buying precious seconds. He turned to Thrain, extending a hand calloused by centuries of wielding axe and hammer. "On your feet, my king!" he roared, his voice a clarion call that cut through the fog of pain and weariness. "The battle's not done yet!"

Thrain grasped his friend's arm, allowing himself to be pulled upright. Pain lanced through his body like liquid fire, but he pushed it aside, focusing on the task at hand with the single-minded determination that had seen his people through countless trials.

"Thank you, old friend," Thrain said, clasping Grimnir's shoulder with a grip of iron. His eyes, bright with the fire of resolve, met those of his oldest companion. "Now, let's finish this, for Nargoth and all our kin."

Side by side they stood, these two titans of dwarven legend, facing the embodiment of the darkness that threatened to engulf their world. Zorath's eyes widened in surprise at seeing Thrain still standing, defiant in the face of his power, but his shock quickly turned to a rage that seemed to darken the very air around him.

"Fools!" he snarled, his voice reverberating with eldritch power. "You cannot hope to stand against my might! I am Zorath the Undying, master of shadows and bane of light. Your pitiful strength is nothing before me!"

Thrain raised Shadowcleaver high, its blade catching what little light remained in the storm-wracked sky. The runes etched along its length blazed to life, a declaration of defiance against the encroaching darkness.

"We stand not alone, Zorath," Thrain declared, his voice carrying across the battlefield like a clarion call of hope. "The strength of our people flows through us, the wisdom of our ancestors guides our blades, and the very stone of the mountain lends us its unyielding resolve. You may be mighty, but you face not just two dwarves, but the entire lineage of Nargoth!"

As if in answer to their king's words, a great cry rose from the dwarven host. Those who had fallen rose once more, their spirits kindled anew by the courage of their leaders. The tide of battle began to turn, the shadows receding before the indomitable will of Nargoth's children.

And there, in the eye of the storm, Thrain Stonehammer and Grimnir Ironfist stood ready to face their destiny, to write a new chapter in the annals of their people—one that would be sung in the halls of Nargoth for a thousand years to come.

With a thunderous battle cry that shook the very stones beneath their feet, Thrain and Grimnir surged forward, their beards streaming behind them like war banners. Zorath, his eyes ablaze with eldritch fire, raised his gnarled staff high. From its twisted crown erupted a maelstrom of shadows and flame, each bolt singing with malevolent intent.

Yet the two dwarves moved with a grace belying their stout frames, their movements honed by centuries of clan warfare in the narrow tunnels of their mountain home. They wove through Zorath's onslaught as one, their steps a deadly dance choreographed by generations of shared blood and battle.

Grimnir, his twin axes glinting in the eerie light of Zorath's magic, struck first. With a roar that echoed the very halls of Nargoth, he brought his right axe down in a devastating arc. The blade, crafted from star-metal and quenched in the icy waters of the underground river Khazad-Lum, bit deep into Zorath's side.

The sorcerer's howl of pain and fury rent the air, a sound so terrible it caused even the bravest of warriors to falter. In his agony, Zorath unleashed a wave of pure force, a ripple in the very fabric of the world. Grimnir, caught in its path, was sent hurtling backward, his sturdy frame carving a furrow in the blood-soaked earth.

But Grimnir's strike had served its purpose. For the briefest of moments, Zorath's attention wavered, his dark eyes fixed upon the fallen dwarf. It was all the opening Thrain required.

With a leap that belied his years, Thrain soared through the air, his ancestral sword held high above his head. The blade, forged in the deepest halls of Nargoth where the very bones of the earth sing with power, gleamed with an inner light. It was

Soulrender, the sword of kings, passed down through uncounted generations of Thrain's line.

As Thrain descended, time seemed to slow. He could see every detail of Zorath's face—the shock, the fear, and then the dawning realization of defeat. Soulrender met Zorath's staff with a sound like thunder, and for a heartbeat, the two seemed evenly matched.

Then, with a noise like the shattering of a thousand mirrors, Zorath's staff split asunder. The two halves fell to the ground, smoking and twitching as if they were living things. There was a moment of utter stillness, as if the very world held its breath.

The silence was broken by a sound that defied description—a tearing, a howling, a keening that seemed to come from everywhere and nowhere at once. The pent-up energies of Zorath's staff, no longer contained, exploded outward in a shockwave of pure, unrestrained magic.

Thrain was hurled backward, his armor smoking and his ears ringing with the force of the blast. He hit the ground hard, the taste of blood and victory mingling on his tongue. For long moments, he lay there, struggling to draw breath into lungs that felt as if they were forged of lead.

Slowly, painfully, Thrain pushed himself to his feet. Through eyes blurred with exhaustion and the aftereffects of Zorath's magic, he saw the sorcerer lying motionless on the ground. The dark energies that had sustained Zorath for so long were dissipating like mist before the morning sun, revealing the withered husk of what had once been a man.

All around them, the tide of battle turned. Zorath's shadowy minions, bereft of their master's will, fell into confusion and disarray. The dwarves of Nargoth, their spirits soaring at the sight of their king's victory, pressed forward with renewed vigor. Their war cries echoed off the mountain walls, a song of triumph that would be remembered for ages to come.

Grimnir limped to Thrain's side, his face split by a fierce grin despite the blood that matted his beard and the way he favored his left leg. "Well fought, my king," he said, his voice rough with pride and exhaustion. "The skalds will sing of this day until the mountains themselves crumble to dust."

Thrain nodded, leaning heavily on Soulrender. The sword's blade, which had shone so brightly moments before, was now dull and pitted, as if it had aged a thousand years in that single, world-changing strike. "Aye," Thrain replied, his own voice little more than a hoarse whisper, "but the victory belongs to all of Nargoth. Every dwarf who stood against the darkness this day is a hero, from the mightiest warrior to the youngest beardling."

As the last of Zorath's forces were routed, fleeing into the deep places of the earth where light and hope seldom reached, Thrain found the strength to raise his voice once more. "People of Nargoth!" he called, and though his words were not loud, they carried to every ear as if borne on the wind itself. "The enemy is vanquished, and our home is secure. Let all the world know that when darkness threatened to engulf us, we stood firm. We fought not with ancient magics or legendary artifacts, but with the strength of our arms and the courage in our hearts!"

A great cheer rose from the dwarven host, a sound of such joy and triumph that it seemed to make the very mountains tremble. It echoed off the ancient stone walls of Nargoth, carrying far into the valley beyond, where it was heard by elf and man alike. And as the sun finally broke through the storm clouds that had shrouded the land for so long, bathing the battlefield in golden light, Thrain Stonehammer knew that a new chapter in the history of his people had begun.

It was a chapter that would be remembered for as long as dwarves dwelt beneath the mountains, a tale of courage and sacrifice that would be told around forge-fires and feast-tables for countless generations to come. And though the road ahead would be long and fraught with new challenges, Thrain knew that his people would face them as they had always done—with stout hearts, strong arms, and the unbreakable bonds of kinship that had seen them through the darkest of times.

It's A Dead World Afterall

The morning sun smeared its dull gold across the cracked earth, painting a half-hearted picture of life in a place that had long since been abandoned to ruin. That light—it was a joke, a slap in the face, something that once meant warmth now only served to mock the decay. Jack, Sarah, and their son Billie moved like ghosts, their steps automatic, as though they'd been walking this wasteland for a thousand lifetimes. They made their way to the coop, the quiet rhythm of their motions as familiar as breathing. The hens—those poor, dead-eyed things—clucked and scratched at the barren soil. Their bodies were just husks, their eyes empty sockets reflecting nothing of the world.

"Careful, Billie," Sarah warned, her voice a gentle caution against the backdrop of a world gone mad. It was a world where caution was a luxury, where every step could be a misstep into the abyss. "Don't scare them."

Billie grinned, his eyes alive with a fire that didn't belong in a place like this—this world soaked in dust and ruin. That grin was a cruel joke against everything that had crumbled around him. "I got it, Mom!" he shouted, his voice breaking the deathly quiet, carving through the stillness like it was made of something real.

The eggs, warm and smooth, were placed gently into a wicker basket – their currency for the day, the price of admission to a place long forgotten, where once something like happiness had been. Dead World. A sad, rotting amusement park, its existence a sick mockery of a time when joy had a place. It was there, somewhere beyond their settlement, taunting with its rusted skeleton, a graveyard for memories, where the echo of laughter was dead, strangled by the sharp teeth of life.

"Ready to head out?" Jack asked as he slung a satchel across his chest, holding a few supplies—dried meat and bottled water. He wanted to be prepared for the unknown that lay before them, a chasm of uncertainty that seemed to yawn open like the very mouth of hell.

Sarah nodded, her eyes locking onto the basket of eggs with a determination that bordered on desperation. She was a woman clinging to the last shreds of hope, her gaze fixed on the fragile lifeline that these eggs represented. "We need to make sure we've enough for the entrance fee, and of course, any rides."

Billie looked up at them, his face a map of curiosity and wonder. His eyes were wide with questions, his mind a whirlwind of thoughts that he couldn't quite articulate. "Why do we need eggs to get in?" he asked, his voice a reminder that even in this broken world, there was still a place for innocence, for the simple, unadulterated wonder of childhood.

"It's how they do things now," Jack explained, his voice matter-of-fact, a stark contrast to the chaos that surrounded them. It was a world where the rules had changed, where the old certainties no longer applied. "Eggs are valuable. They're a trade."

They left their home and settlement, trudging through the desolate landscape. Soon, they encountered a man with a cart and a horse, the only signs of life in a world that seemed to have forgotten its own vitality. The man, his face a map of wrinkles and scars, eyed them with a mixture of curiosity and desperation. His horse, a gaunt creature with sunken eyes, stood listlessly, its coat matted and dirty.

"Where you headed?" the man asked, his voice a gravelly rasp that seemed to scrape against the silence like a file on metal. His eyes lingered on the basket of eggs, a hunger in them that was almost palpable.

"We're going to Dead World," Jack replied, his voice firm but cautious. The man's gaze snapped back to theirs, a flicker of interest igniting in his eyes.

"Dead World, eh?" he repeated, his tone a blend of curiosity and warning. "That's a long way. You'll need a ride." He nodded towards his cart, the wooden slats creaking in the stillness.

Sarah hesitated, her hand tightening around the basket of eggs. "How much?" she asked, her voice a delicate balance between necessity and caution.

The man's eyes locked onto the eggs, his expression a mask of calculation. "A couple should do it," he said finally, his voice a negotiation in a world where every transaction was a gamble.

Billie looked up at his parents, his eyes wide with uncertainty. "Is it safe, Mom?" he asked, his voice a whisper in the vast silence.

The man overheard Billie and gave a smile—a twisted thing, his browned teeth gapped like the ruins of a forgotten city.

"It's as safe as anything can be in this world," he said, his voice a low rumble that seemed to come from the very earth itself.

Sarah's gaze met Jack's, a silent understanding passing between them. They knew the risks, but they also knew the necessity. With a nod, Sarah handed over two eggs, their smooth surfaces glinting in the fading light.

The man took the eggs, his fingers closing around them like a vice. "Hop in," he said, his voice a gruff invitation. He placed the two eggs in his coat pocket. "We'll get you to Dead World in no time at all."

They climbed into the cart, the horse stirring, its eyes briefly alive with something that might've been thought, or hunger. The man cracked the reins, and the cart jerked forward, hauling them toward something barely there, something dragging them in—the Dead World, where forgotten dreams had curled up and died, where the scattered bones of another time waited, patient, for them to arrive.

The ride passed in a grim, endless silence, broken only by the lone shriek of a bird, its cry raking across the air like a warning, or an epitaph. Billie's gaze was locked on what lay ahead—an unforgiving stretch of mangled steel and skeletons of long-dead buildings, a vast, endless graveyard of things that had once mattered, stretching before him in a smear of hopelessness.

"Are we there yet?" he asked.

"Soon," Sarah told him with a hug.

He had heard all the stories about Dead World. People back from where they came had talked about it, how they had a good time, and enjoyed the rides.

"They said it was interesting," Billie whispered, his voice barely audible over the creaking of the cart. "They said there's a boat ride that takes you through a whole different world."

"We'll have a wonderful time. Don't you worry." Sarah's hand tightened around his.

As they drew closer, the outline of Dead World loomed before them, its entrance a twisted metal gate that seemed to yawn open like the mouth of a mechanical beast. The sign above it creaked in the wind, its spray-painted letters faded but still legible: "Welcome to Dead World – Where Dreams Come to Die."

Jack and Sarah's hearts sank, their spirits weighed down by the cruel irony of the sign. But they pressed on, driven by a curiosity that bordered on obsession, a need to see what lay beyond the gates of this forsaken place.

The cart came to a stop at the entrance, the horse's hooves scraping against the ground with a harsh, jarring sound. The man with the cart turned to them.

"Here you are," he said, his voice a gruff monotone, devoid of any warmth or welcome. "Dead World awaits."

He eyed the family with a smile. The horse, sensing freedom, lifted its head and let out a weak whinny, a sound that was almost a sigh of relief.

With a deep breath, Jack climbed down from the cart, his eyes nailed to the twisted metal gate. Sarah followed, her hand still gripping Billie's tightly.

"Hold on there for a sec," the man said. He reached into his coat pocket and handed Sarah one of the eggs he had taken as payment. "Expensive place. You'll need this more than I do," he said, his eyes glinting with a fleeting spark of humanity in a world that had long since forgotten its own.

As the family watched, the man turned the cart around, the horse plodding forward with a slow, resigned gait. "Be careful in there," he called out over his shoulder, his voice carried away by the wind. "Dead World ain't no place for the living."

The cart disappeared into the distance, leaving the family standing alone before the gates of Dead World. As they stood there, the world around them seemed to darken, as if the very shadows themselves were alive and hungry. The air thickened, heavy with an ominous presence that threatened to swallow them whole. They kept moving, the pull of something distant clawing at them. Something dark, something that refused to be ignored. The world sprawled out bleak and spent, yet it pulsed with a sick, rhythmic life. They had to see it. Had to know what lurked just past the edge of it all. The gates loomed before them, twisted metal monoliths that seemed to guard secrets and terrors beyond imagination.

"Let's go," Jack said, his voice determined in the face of uncertainty. "We've come this far."

But their path was blocked by a figure who seemed to have been carved from the very stone of the earth. A grizzled old man with eyes that had seen everything and nothing at the same time stood there, his gaze warily eyeing the family. His eyes lingered on the basket of eggs like a vulture eyeing its next meal.

"Entrance fee," he growled, his voice rough and unforgiving. It was a sound that scraped against the nerves, a reminder that even in this desolate world, there was always a price to pay.

Sarah handed over several eggs, each one carefully selected from their dwindling supply. The old man inspected them with a critical eye before nodding curtly. "Alright, you can go in."

As they entered through the gates, Billie's eyes widened in awe. The park was a graveyard of forgotten dreams—a Ferris wheel stood motionless, its seats swinging gently in the breeze like ghostly fingers reaching out to snatch the living. A roller coaster, once a thundering beast of steel and wood, now lay still, its tracks rusting away into nothingness. The silence was oppressive, punctuated only by the creaking of old wooden structures and the distant call of a bird—a lonely, haunting sound that seemed to echo through eternity.

"Wow," Billie breathed, his voice barely above a whisper. "It's so big."

But they were not here to marvel at the ruins. They were here for something more—something that lay at the heart of Dead World. As they walked deeper into the park, they were surrounded by other survivors, those like them, there to experience the attractions. And there were merchants who hawked their goods, overpriced and often useless, but in this world, even the useless had value. There was Grizzled Pete, his face a map of scars and wrinkles, selling everything from rusty tools to tattered clothing.

"Get your survival gear here!" he shouted, his words echoing off the rusting hulks of dead machines. "Best prices in Dead World!"

But the family ignored him, their gaze aimed at a destination that only they knew. They navigated through the crowds, past the dead machines and the desperate merchants, their footsteps steady and determined. The air was thick with the smell of grease and rust, a noxious odor that clung to their skin like a bad omen. The sound of industrial music drifted through the air, a discordant melody that seemed to match the beat of their hearts—a relentless drumbeat that drove them forward.

Deeper and deeper they moved into the park as the landscape around them grew more surreal. A merry-go-round stood still, its horses frozen in mid-gallop, their eyes glassy and unseeing. A funhouse mirror reflected their images, twisting them into grotesque parodies of themselves—distorted reflections that seemed to jeer their very existence.

But they pressed on, undeterred by the macabre scenery. There was no hesitation in their steps—only a force that gnawed at them, relentless and sharp. The world around them was a twisted carnival, a freak show of broken dreams and shattered hopes, but they moved through it with a singular purpose.

"What are we looking for, Dad?" Billie asked, his voice barely above a whisper, his eyes wide.

Jack's eyes narrowed, his stare boring on some point in the distance. "What we were told about. The greatest attraction in Dead World," he said, his voice low and mysterious. "Something that will make all this worth it."

Sarah's eyes met Jack's, a shared moment of understanding. They didn't exactly know what lay ahead. Oh, they had heard the stories. But they weren't sure they were ready for it.

***

Navigating the desolate landscape of Dead World, the family finally saw it. There it was—an anomaly, a twisted joke, lodged in the midst of decay. A ride. A ride? The sign twisted, barely hanging by a thread, the wind clawing at it like some cruel hand: "The Shrunken World." The letters, half-eaten by time and stubborn as rot, fought to stay whole, refusing to collapse into nothing. Beneath it were a set of stairs, crumbling and sagging.

"Look!" Jack said, his voice clumsy with too much enthusiasm. "The Shrunken World!"

Sarah's eyes sliced through it all, staring at the decaying stairs, as if calculating how to survive the next moment. "I'm not sure we've enough eggs?" she asked, her voice stripping away Jack's reckless joy with cold practicality.

But Billie, still young enough to believe in things, his eyes alive with some distant, useless hope, cheered. "We have to see it, Mom! We have to! It sounds amazing!"

At the bottom of the stairs, a small ticket booth stood, its wooden slats weathered to a soft grey that seemed to blend seamlessly into the surrounding decay. Mabel, the ticket booth operator, looked up from her perch, her eyes sunken and her skin pale, like a ghost of a woman, a relic from a time long past.

"Welcome to The Shrunken World," she said, her voice flat, a hollow rasp that drained the space of anything alive. "Two eggs per person. One egg for the kid."

Sarah looked into her basket and smiled. She handed over the eggs, each one carefully selected from their dwindling supply, like precious gems in a world where value was measured in the most mundane of things. Mabel took them without a word, her eyes never leaving the family as she handed them each a worn, cardboard ticket.

"Old Tom will take you through," she said, nodding towards the stairs. "Enjoy the ride."

The family carefully climbed the stairs, entering a large building where they saw a figure standing by a small concrete river. Old Tom, the boat operator, was a man shaped by the world itself, his skin like cracked stone, aged and worn by the elements. His eyes were deep-set and ancient, like those of a sage who had seen the rise and fall of civilizations. He regarded the family with a gaze that was both kind and weary, a gaze that spoke of countless stories untold.

"Tickets?" Old Tom asked, his eyes glinting in the dim light.

They handed him their cardboard tickets

"Get in," he muttered, his voice ragged. "The Shrunken World awaits."

The boat groaned as they stepped into it. Jack noticed a rifle tucked away near Old Tom.

"You gonna need that thing?" Jack asked.

"One never knows what can happen down the river," Old Tom sneered.

He pushed off from the shore, his oars dipping into the water with a rhythmic cadence that seemed almost hypnotic, a lullaby of the damned.

Old Tom's voice ground out like rocks in a furnace, slow and purposeful as he rowed, the oar slicing through water the color of bile. "It was a kingdom once," he said, his eyes staring into nothing, his words hanging like a funeral dirge in the humid air. "A light of joy, or so they told us. Look around you now. Go ahead, look."

Jack, sitting stiff in the middle of the boat, didn't answer. He gripped the edge of the boat, knuckles pale as bone, while Sarah clutched their son, Billie, her arms wrapped tight around his small shoulders. Billie stared wide-eyed at the ruins, his face pale in the dim light, his little hands gripping the fabric of his mother's coat like it might anchor him to something solid. The boy didn't speak. Nobody did, not at first. The silence was oppressive, thick, smothering, a weight that bore down on every breath. The water sloshed against the concrete, riverbanks, a rhythmic sound like something trapped, forced to move when it wanted nothing more than to remain still..

The boat drifted forward, Old Tom's oar steadily slapping the water. The ride's entrance stretched behind them like a yawning grave, but ahead was no better—just the remains of what once had been. The walls were caked with grime, and the ceiling sagged, its plaster ruptured by vines and rot. Sunlight cut through the gaps, shafts of it spilling onto the water like celestial vomit. It didn't illuminate; it only made the decay clearer.

"Used to be music here," Old Tom continued, his voice carrying over the soft slosh of the water. "Oh, you would've loved it. A little tune, sweet enough to rot your teeth clean out of your skull. Played on a loop. Over and over, until you couldn't tell where the song stopped, and where your mind started to splinter. I remember it." He hummed the tune, a faint thing at first—captivating, maybe even soothing. Then it began to unravel, fraying at the nerves.

Jack cleared his throat but didn't speak. Sarah turned her face away from a limp puppet hanging by the neck from its wires, its cheerful lederhosen faded and water-stained, its smile cracked in half. Billie shifted in her arms, burying his face against her chest as they floated past more dolls—an Eskimo with one eye missing, a Hawaiian dancer with a grass skirt shredded into ribbons, a Chinese girl with her face warped and bubbled from fire damage.

Their painted smiles, frozen in time, were obscene in their persistence.

Old Tom chuckled, the sound wet and humorless. "They don't sing anymore. They don't dance. They just sit there, watching, like gods that got bored with being gods, letting the world burn. Funny thing, though—they outlasted us. The people. All of us. Who's laughing now?"

The oar struck something solid, sending a jolt through the boat. Billie gasped, and Sarah tightened her hold on him. Jack glanced at the water, but he couldn't see what they'd hit. "What was that?" he asked.

"Doesn't matter," Old Tom replied, resuming his rhythm. "Could be anything. Could be one of those damn dolls trying to crawl its way out of here. Could be the body of a passenger. I don't stop to check. Haven't in years."

He continued to hum the tune, the melody weaving itself into the fabric of their minds like a dark incantation. The family sat in silence, their eyes riveted to the decaying dioramas, each one a poignant reminder of what had been lost. They were trapped in a world that was both familiar and yet utterly alien, a world where the past and present collided in a chilling dance of decay and rebirth.

As they descended into the heart of "The Shrunken World," the central room unfolded before them like a morbid tapestry, vast and eerie. Once, this space had pulsed with life, a vibrant celebration of the world's nations in cartoon form. Now, it was just a graveyard. The murals on the walls had peeled away like dead skin, revealing the cold, grey concrete beneath. The platforms where the dolls once danced were collapsing in parts, their wooden slats sinking away into the fetid water.

Old Tom rowed on, his humming a jagged thread cutting through the silence. The wreckage of a clock tower emerged ahead—or what had been a clock tower, anyway. But now it was a collapsed heap of rubble. Its face floated nearby, split clean in two, the painted numbers scattered like the grim remains of something once whole—now a grotesque riddle, abandoned to the winds.

Old Tom gestured with his chin, his eyes glinting with a mixture of sadness and defiance. "This is where it all came together, see? Unity. Harmony. Every little one who ever sat in one of those boats was supposed to leave thinking the world was a better place. A smaller place. One big family." His voice dripped with sarcasm, a bitter taste that lingered on the palate. "Guess no one told the bombs that."

Billie whimpered softly, his small body trembling with fear. Sarah hushed him, her fingers weaving through his hair with a comforting gentleness that seemed almost out of place in this desolate landscape. Jack forced down a lump in his throat, the motion sharp and awkward, as if his body rebelled against the moment. His gaze drifted to Old Tom, who stared straight ahead, his face unreadable, his eyes lost in the depths of a past that refused to let go.

"Why do you do this?" Jack's voice was thin.

Old Tom's grin was a twisted thing, his yellowed teeth flashing like the edge of a rusty blade. "Why not?" he said simply, his voice flat and empty. "Somebody's gotta keep the story alive. Can't let it all go to hell without someone rowing through to bear witness."

As they glided beneath a canopy of painted stars, their once-bright colors dulled to lifeless shades, and the sound of dripping water echoed through the silence like a clock ticking down to nothing. Old Tom, continuing to hum, slowed the boat when they saw it—a doll, its head hanging to one side, suspended by a nest of wires. The doll's smile was intact, its glass eyes staring unblinkingly at the approaching boat. But a raven perched on its shoulder, pecking at its fabric vest with an unblinking gaze.

"She's still smiling," Old Tom muttered, his voice thick with derision. "Good for you. But we can't have no bird doing that to you." He lifted his rifle and shot at the bird.

The raven, its glossy feathers glinting like shards of obsidian in the harsh light, spiraled down from the doll, a dark comet trailing the echo of its last caw. As it fell, time stretched and warped, until the ground rushed up to meet it with a cruel finality.

Jack turned his face away, unable to bear the sight. Sarah held Billie tighter, whispering soft reassurances that he didn't believe. Old Tom, though, just kept rowing, his stare locked on the path ahead.

Past the doll, past the silent nations, past the banners that hung limp, their slogans of happiness and harmony now cruel lies aimed at the very idea of unity. The boat scraped against the edge of the platform at the ride's exit, the sound jarring them back into the harsh reality of their world.

Old Tom stood, tying the boat to a rusted post with a length of frayed rope. He stepped out, his boots squelching on the slimy floor, and turned back to the family. "This is where you get off," he said.

Jack hesitated, words caught somewhere between gratitude and unease. "Thanks," he managed.

Old Tom just stared at him, his grin a shadow of the earlier cruelty. "Don't waste your thanks, friend. I'm just the ferryman.

You're the ones who've got to keep walking." His gaze flicked to Billie, who was half-hidden behind Sarah's coat. "Make sure the boy remembers every bit of it."

Jack swallowed hard and nodded. "We won't."

Old Tom's stare held for just a second, then he grabbed his oar, his mind slipping off somewhere else as his hum rose once more, floating into the air like it had no destination. The family moved on, stepping off the boat and onto the cold concrete shore, the sound of the boat's departure melting into the void behind them. They followed exit signs, the dim light of the ride faded behind them, swallowed by the suffocating grey of Dead World's eternal twilight.

At the bottom of the stairs, they were greeted by the Johnsons—a family of four, each face bearing the hardships they'd endured. The father's shoulders were hunched like a man carrying a burden too heavy to bear; the mother's eyes had long since stopped searching for hope. The two girls clutched each other's hands like lifelines, their wide eyes reflecting the fear that had burrowed into Billie's heart.

"You're next," Sarah said softly over the distant drone of the merchants and the occasional clang of metal. She didn't smile. There was no point. But she nodded at the mother, a gesture of something like solidarity in a world that offered little.

The mother nodded back, though her expression didn't change. The Johnson girls stared at Billie, their faces mirroring the fear that had become their constant companion. For a moment, the two families stood in silence until Mabel's voice cut through the quietness: "Two eggs per person. One egg for each kid."

Jack placed a hand on Sarah's shoulder, urging her forward. "Let's go," he muttered. "They've got their ride to take."

As they walked away, Billie turned back, watching the Johnsons ascend the stairs. He tugged on Sarah's sleeve. "Will they have fun, Mom?"

Sarah didn't answer, and Jack didn't look back. "Keep moving," he said, his voice sharper than he intended. Billie flinched, but he obeyed, his small legs struggling to keep up with the adults as they navigated the crowded ruins of the marketplace.

The merchants were still there, their wares displayed on rickety tables and stained tarps. Rusted tools, patched clothing, jars of dubious-looking preserves—all of it arranged with a care that bordered on desperation. Shouts filled the air, voices hoarse from bargaining, bartering, pleading.

"Fresh rat meat! Caught just this morning!"

"Clean water! Six eggs a carton!"

"Eggs for batteries! Batteries for eggs!"

Sarah glanced at Jack, her expression grim. "We need to get home."

He nodded, his hand instinctively brushing against the satchel slung across his chest, where their supplies were tucked away. "We will."

Billie tugged on Sarah's sleeve again, his voice small. "Mom, what was it like? Before the Big Boom?"

The question hung between them like an unspoken wound reopened. Jack's jaw tightened, and Sarah's shoulders sagged. She looked down at her son, her hand brushing a strand of hair from his forehead. "It was... different," she said finally. "There were buildings that touched the sky. Cars that moved without horses. Lights everywhere."

"People were happy," Billie said, almost hopefully.

Sarah's gaze shifted to Jack, seeking help. He sighed, his steps slowing. "Not always," he said. "People fought. People hurt each other. That's why the Boom happened. They didn't take care of what they had. They didn't listen."

Billie frowned, his small brow furrowed in concentration. "Didn't they know it would end like this?"

The silence that followed was a heavy thing.

As they walked away from the marketplace, the shadows of Dead World closed in around them.

Jack stopped, turning to face his son. He crouched down, meeting Billie's eyes. "Some questions have no answers, only the echoes of what could have been," he told his son. "You see, some tried to stop it. But most didn't care until it was too late. That's why we must remember, Billie. So we don't make the same mistakes."

Billie nodded slowly, though his expression was uncertain. Jack ruffled his hair, a rare moment of affection, before standing and continuing down the path.

The exit from Dead World towered ahead, marked by a giant sign that arched above them. It was missing letters.

Jack looked up at it, filling in the missing letters. "Come back soon," he whispered.

The crowd thinned as they approached, the noise of the marketplace giving way to the quieter despair of the outskirts.

Beyond the gates lay the world that was their home: a landscape of twisted metal and skeletal buildings, of earth cracked and barren. Smoke rose in the distance, the ever-present reminder of fires that never quite died. The wind carried the stench of rot and ash, a cruel parody of the fresh breezes Jack vaguely remembered from his youth.

Sarah pulled Billie closer, her hand gripping his tightly. Jack walked ahead, his posture stiff, his eyes scanning the horizon. The weight of the day pressed on them, each step a struggle against the crushing reality of their existence.

Billie broke the silence again. "Do you think the Johnsons will like the ride?"

Sarah hesitated, glancing at Jack. He didn't turn around, but his voice carried back to them, firm and unyielding. "That's not our concern, Billie. We liked it. That's what matters."

Billie didn't say anything, his small face pinched with thought. Sarah squeezed his hand, her grip a silent reassurance, even if she didn't feel it herself.

They walked on, through the crumbling remains of what had once been a thriving city. The shadows grew longer as the sun dipped lower, casting the ruins in a golden light that only made their desolation more profound.

It was then that they heard it – the creaking of wooden slats, the soft thud of hooves on the dusty ground. The man with the cart and the gaunt horse appeared out of the fading light, his face a map of wrinkles and scars, his eyes a deep well of understanding.

"Need a ride home?" he asked, his voice a gravelly rasp that cut through the silence like a saw blade through wood. His gaze lingered on the family.

Jack turned, his eyes narrowing slightly as he considered the offer. Sarah's grip on Billie's hand tightened, a silent question hanging in the air.

"We can walk," Jack said finally, his voice firm.

"Hey, I know you," the man said. "You're the family I brought to Dead World." He smiled. "Come on. Hop aboard."

But Jack was insistent. "We can walk."

"I know you can," the man said. "But it's getting dark. And out here, darkness isn't just the absence of light – it's a presence all its own. I'd hate for something to happen to your wife and kid."

Sarah's eyes met Jack's, a shared moment of understanding passing between them. They knew the dangers of the night, the shadows that moved, and the sounds that echoed through the desolate landscape.

"But we've no more eggs," Jack said.

The man waved at him. "Doesn't matter. Come on now. Hop on up."

"Okay," Jack said, his voice softer now. "We'll take the ride."

The man nodded. "Good choice," he said.

As they climbed into the cart, the horse stirred, its eyes flickering with a momentary spark of life. The man cracked the reins, and the cart lurched forward, carrying them away from the ruins of Dead World and back towards the fragile safety of their farm.

The ride was silent, the only sound the creaking of the cart and the soft thud of the horse's hooves on the ground. The family sat in a row, their faces set towards the horizon, their hearts heavy with the weight of the day's events.

But as they rode, something shifted inside them. It was a small, almost imperceptible change – a sense of hope, perhaps, or just the realization that even in this dead world, there were still moments of kindness and compassion to be found.

The man with the cart and the horse didn't speak, but his presence was a faint reminder that they were not alone, that there were still others out there who cared. And as the stars began to twinkle in the night sky, casting a faint, delicate glow over the desolate landscape, the family felt a sense of peace settle over them – a fragile, temporary peace, but peace, nonetheless.

As they reached the outskirts of their settlement, the familiar sight of their makeshift home came into view: a patchwork of salvaged materials cobbled together into something that resembled shelter. It wasn't much, but it was theirs.

They hopped out of the cart, and Jack thanked the man for the ride.

"No problem," the man told him. "Glad I could help."

Jack pushed open the door to their home, holding it for Sarah and Billie to enter. Inside, the air was stale but warm, the small space filled with familiar scents. Jack set about unpacking their satchel, while Billie curled up on the old mattress in the corner, his thumb creeping into his mouth as his eyes grew heavy.

"Can we go again?' he asked.

"Shhh . . . maybe next year, sweetheart," Sarah whispered. "It's time for you to sleep. You've had a busy day."

Jack stood by the window, staring out at the horizon. The sun was nearly gone now, the last rays of light painting the sky in shades of red and orange. He thought of the Johnsons, descending into The Shrunken World. He thought of Old Tom, rowing his boat through the ruins, his haunting hum still echoing in Jack's mind.

"Do you think he's right?" Sarah's soft yet tentative voice broke the silence. "That someone has to bear witness?"

Jack didn't answer immediately. He watched as the first stars began to appear, faint and distant. "I don't know," he said finally. "But I know this—we can't forget. No matter how much it hurts."

Sarah nodded. She moved to sit beside Billie, stroking his hair as he drifted off to sleep. Jack remained at the window, staring out as the sky sank into black.

The night poured itself over them like a blanket too heavy to shake off. Outside, the world unraveled, consumed by the rot. But within these walls, there was something—so fragile, so thin it could snap with the wrong breath—but enough to keep them moving, enough to hold back the flood. For now.

The Peculiar Tale of Phineas Piddlewick

Phineas Piddlewick trudged through the narrow corridors of Sector 12, head bent low as the blinking neon haze of advertisements tattooed its stale glow onto his sallow skin. The city of Drenhalt thrived on misery, a concrete colossus that swallowed hope and spat out despair. Its lifeblood pulsed through conduits of bureaucracy, factories, and the screeching wheels of monorails slicing through the smog-choked air.

Phineas, if anything, embodied this despair perfectly. A scrawny wisp of a man with eyes perpetually darting like frightened insects, he was the sort of person who could disappear in plain sight. His face was a collection of unfortunate angles, his nose too sharp, his ears jutting out like an afterthought. Even his name, Phineas Piddlewick, seemed to invite mockery, and the city was all too willing to oblige.

His home—a decrepit one-room apartment—sat nestled in the bowels of a residential block that looked more like a mausoleum than a place for the living. The walls, once painted an indeterminate color, were now layered with decades of grime and streaked with water stains that formed grotesque patterns. A single flickering light bulb hung from the ceiling, casting a sickly yellow pall over the room. His bed was a sagging cot, the mattress threadbare, and his only furniture was a rickety table piled high with unopened bills and the crumbs of countless stale meals.

In the mornings, Phineas donned his frayed uniform and shuffled off to his menial job at DataRefinery Corp, where his days were spent inputting endless streams of numbers into a machine that seemed to hum with disdain. His coworkers, a collection of brash voices and sharp elbows, regarded him as a creature barely worth acknowledgment. They called him "Piddles" behind his back, though they were loud enough to ensure he heard every snicker, every cruel variation of his name.

"Hey, Piddles," one of them, a barrel-chested brute named Gavin, sneered during lunch. "Drop your sandwich again? Or did it run away from you this time?"

Laughter erupted, and Phineas flushed crimson, clutching the dry bread he had brought from home. His attempts at retorts were usually swallowed by the lump in his throat, leaving him to sit silently, the laughter echoing in his ears long after the workday ended.

Even strangers took their shots. On his commute, a child once pointed at him and whispered to his mother, "Why does that man look like a stick?" The mother shushed her child, but her smirk lingered, a cruel confirmation that Phineas was, indeed, a joke.

And so it went. Day after day, the world pressed down on Phineas, a relentless weight of ridicule and neglect.

II. The Voices Begin

It began on an otherwise unremarkable morning in Sector 12, a place where the alleys breathed an unholy stink of rancid grease and rot, and the air assaulted the tongue with the metallic tang of rusted nails. Phineas first heard it there, an intrusion that defied explanation. A voice, sly and insistent, slid into his consciousness as effortlessly as oil seeping into a hairline fracture.

"Phineas," it murmured, a sound that was all velvet menace, silk smeared over the grit of broken glass.

He halted mid-step, his habitual shuffle disrupted like a scratched record. The alley stretched empty before him, barren except for a mangy dog that rooted through refuse with a grim determination. Phineas scanned his surroundings, each shadow seeming to quiver with malignant intent. The silence conspired against him, punctuated only by the distant, rhythmic sigh of a steam vent releasing its pressure. Nothing. No one.

He shook his head sharply, as if to rattle the voice loose, and resumed walking. His boots struck the cracked pavement harder now, each slap ricocheting off the damp, graffiti-streaked walls. "Fatigue," he muttered under his breath. A simple trick of the mind, he told himself, but the words rang hollow even to his ears. The voice lingered, unshakable, curling around his thoughts like smoke in a confined space.

By the time he reached his cubicle at DataRefinery—a fluorescent-lit necropolis where ambition was interred beneath layers of soul-crushing mediocrity—the voice had grown bolder. It didn't merely whisper now; it dripped with venom, each syllable a shard of glass slicing through the fragile veneer of his composure.

"They mock you because they fear you," it murmured, its tone a dissonant blend of silk and razors.

Phineas's fingers hesitated over the keyboard, the once-reliable staccato of his typing reduced to a faltering mess. Across the room, Gavin, the self-proclaimed monarch of smug grins and discount cologne, smelled blood in the water. He was on him in seconds.

"Get it together, Piddles," Gavin barked, his voice dripping with toxic amusement. The office erupted into a chorus of snickers, a ripple of disdain that wormed its way into Phineas's skull and nested there.

"Weaklings," the voice growled, its contempt vibrating through his mind like the low hum of an approaching storm. "Can't you see what they are? Gutless cowards hiding behind their brittle laughter."

Phineas's vision swam, the sterile glow of the office warping as though the air itself had turned viscous. He pressed his fingers to his temples, a futile attempt to exorcise the voice that coiled tighter, its hiss like a serpent's warning.

By day's end, the whispers had multiplied, a cacophony of dissent rattling the cage of his mind. They no longer waited for permission to speak.

"Take control!" one barked, its urgency a slap across his thoughts.

"Run while you can," another pleaded, its breathless desperation an echo of his own.

"They're watching you," crooned a third, its words a sinister caress, cold and invasive.

He stumbled home that evening, his skull pounding with a rhythm that matched his unsteady steps. The city roared around him—steam vents coughing their toxic breath, neon ads humming empty salvation—but all of it blurred, receding into a muted backdrop against the chaos raging inside him.

That night, sleep came in jagged fragments, a kaleidoscope of nightmares splintered by the jagged edges of shadowy figures and voices speaking in an alien cadence. He woke drenched, his body trembling, every breath a battle against the invisible weight pressing on his chest. The room around him felt foreign, as though he'd awakened in a stranger's life, drowning on dry land.

The days smudged together like the fingerprint of some cosmic vandal, each one an unending grind of whispers and simmering panic. Numbers paraded mockingly on his monitor at work, their sterile rows twisting into snarled gibberish that crawled like worms over his vision. More than once, he caught himself staring through the screen—past it, really—as though its dull glow could drown out the endless churn of voices ricocheting inside his skull.

"Hey, Piddles!" Gavin's voice cracked through the office like a glass whip, cutting through Phineas's stupor. The name hit like a slap, dragging him back to the beige purgatory of the office floor. "You planning to actually do your job, or is this some avant-garde performance art?"

Laughter rippled through the room, jagged and raw, but it barely grazed Phineas. His hands hovered over the keyboard, trembling as if wired to a faulty current, his movements jerky and imprecise like a puppet in a sadistic play.

The nights brought no solace. If anything, they were worse. The voices swelled in the dark, gathering weight and venom until they oozed into his thoughts like black tar. They spoke in serpentine whispers, tantalizing and accusatory all at once, of labyrinthine tunnels beneath the city, of hidden truths clawing to the surface, truths that only he could unearth.

"You're special, Phineas," they cooed, their words curling around his mind like smoke. "You've been chosen."

But there was no comfort in their honeyed tones, only the glint of a blade concealed beneath velvet. They weren't soothing him; they were slicing, carving his sanity into ribbons thin enough to flutter in the howling void.

His body rebelled in kind. Food dissolved into ash on his tongue, each bite a mockery of sustenance. Sleep offered no reprieve—it was a battleground where the voices gathered strength, their cadence rising to a hammering crescendo that felt as though it would split his skull wide open. Every moment of rest was an ambush.

By the week's end, Phineas had been stripped down to something less than human. The mirror in his cramped, crumbling bathroom reflected a ghost: hollow cheeks, eyes sunken into deep, shadowed pits, a skeletal grin stretched taut over his face. His hands quaked as he gripped the phone, his fingers slipping on the buttons as he dialed the clinic's number. When he spoke, his voice was a thin thread, nearly swallowed by the cacophony in his mind.

"I need . . . " he rasped, the words brittle as dry leaves, "I need help."

The voices howled with laughter, a jagged chorus that left no room for hope.

III. The First Prescription

Phineas balanced precariously on the edge of the chair, his weight sinking into the vinyl as it exhaled an accusatory creak. His body was a coiled spring, every nerve wound tight enough to snap. The room stank of antiseptic—a chemical tang that clung to his nostrils like guilt—sharp, sterile, and without forgiveness. Across from him, the doctor sat as if assembled from spare parts, a collection of sharp angles and hollows. His cheeks caved in like forgotten fruit, his narrow shoulders hunched with a precision that seemed engineered rather than learned. The rhythmic tap of his pen on the clipboard was maddening, a mechanical tick that punctuated the stillness with indifference.

"Auditory hallucinations," the doctor intoned, his voice flat and drained of any warmth. He might as well have been reciting a grocery list. "Persistent. Disruptive."

Phineas's jaw locked, a steel trap barely containing the storm inside. Disruptive? The word was a grotesque understatement. The voices were a relentless tide, an unseen tormentor clawing at his sanity, drowning him in venomous whispers. They stalked him everywhere, their rancorous symphony a constant hum in his skull, scratching away at what little peace he could still claim.

The doctor, unbothered, slid a small orange bottle across the desk with a deliberate push. Its hollow clatter against the laminate surface was at odds with the weight of its promise. Inside, the pills rattled like miniature grenades, their cheerful rhythm mocking the gravity of his situation. "Twice a day," the doctor said, his tone freighted with inevitability. He leaned back in his chair, his pen still tapping, the cadence now a death knell.

"This should quiet things down. There shouldn't be any major side effects."

Phineas grabbed the bottle, his hands trembling with the force of barely restrained fury. The pills inside quivered, their sound a counterpoint to the chaos roiling inside him. "And if it doesn't?" he rasped, his voice raw, every syllable dragged from the depths of his desperation.

The doctor's lips curled into a mirthless smirk—a thing that barely passed for human. "Then we'll try something else. Trial and error, Mr. Piddlewick. That's the foundation of progress." His words dripped with condescension, the kind that implied Phineas's suffering was merely a statistic to be logged and filed away. "Don't overthink it."

That night, with dread gnawing at his gut, Phineas tilted his head back and swallowed the first pill. The bitterness coated his tongue, clinging stubbornly even as he chased it down with water. It was as if the pill resisted him, a bitter rebellion sliding down his throat. The water was thick, almost viscous, leaving him gagging and gasping for air. He sat in the darkness, every nerve alive with expectation, his heart a thunderous drumbeat. The voices hesitated, faltering like a winded predator, then began to withdraw. One by one, they receded, their snarling orchestra packing up and slinking into the shadows. In their absence, an uneasy silence settled over him. It was the first night in months he could remember closing his eyes without a chorus of hatred dragging him into the abyss.

But by morning, the world had shifted in ways he couldn't yet articulate.

Phineas woke to a pain so sharp it felt like a blade had been driven into the base of his skull. His neck ached with a ferocity that left him dizzy, every nerve screaming for relief. He staggered to the bathroom, dragging his feet across the floor as though gravity itself had turned spiteful. His head felt leaden, a weight too great for his shoulders to bear. When he reached the mirror, he stared into its silver expanse, expecting the reflection he had seen every day of his miserable life.

What stared back wasn't him—not entirely.

Below his left ear, the skin bulged grotesquely, a mass of flesh that writhed with unnatural motion. His breath caught, his chest seizing as if an iron hand had gripped his lungs. The grotesque form of a second head was emerging from his neck, its features embryonic and obscene. The thing was a mockery of life, its face crudely hewn like the product of a drunken sculptor: a slack, lipless mouth that drooped obscenely, a bulbous nose crooked at impossible angles, and an eye sealed shut in a grotesque squint.

Trembling, Phineas raised a hand, the motion as unsteady as a condemned man reaching for his final cigarette. He touched the thing—his thing—and nearly recoiled at the heat. The flesh was feverish, alive in a way that defied understanding. It twitched under his fingers, a ripple of animation that sent shudders down his spine. Then the eye opened, wet and glistening, its surface shimmering with an unholy clarity.

The voices had stopped, but in their place was something far worse.

IV. A Head with a Voice

The second medication was no mere failure; it was the kind of disaster that rewrites the rules of suffering, turning the edges of Phineas's personal torment into something jagged, inescapable.

Within days, the second head didn't just appear—it burst forth, ripping through his flesh and bone with an obscene, surgical precision. The emergence was purposeful, as though directed by a malicious artist intent on mockery. It wore his face, but not quite; the angles were crueler, precision-sharpened like a blade honed to cut not just through tissue, but through soul. Its skin gleamed under the unforgiving glare of the bathroom light— polished, synthetic, a grotesque improvement on the flawed humanity it mimicked. Its hair was a calculated jet-black, slicked and alien in its perfection, and its eyes—God help him—its eyes didn't just see him. They penetrated. They drilled. Razor-sharp, relentless, they flayed him with every glance.

And then it spoke.

"You've really outdone yourself this time," it purred, its voice a silken blade, slicing through the fragile veneer of denial Phineas had so desperately constructed.

Phineas stumbled back, knees slamming against the unforgiving edge of the sink. "No. No, this isn't happening," he stammered, his words faltering against the truth carved into his own reflection.

"Isn't it?" the head countered, its smile an incision that split its too-perfect face. The voice it carried was baritone, weighted with a contempt so thick it curdled the air, each syllable a hook dragging him into its maw.

"Shut up," Phineas whispered, the tremor in his voice betraying his crumbling resolve.

"Shut up?" The head's laugh came, a jagged, serrated sound, a noise that didn't just fill the room—it owned it. "You've been screaming into the void for someone to talk to. Someone not just in your head. Well, congratulations, buddy. Here I am. Your wish, granted."

Phineas's gaze locked onto the mirror, sweat slicking his face, streaking down in rivers he couldn't control. "You're not real," he rasped, his voice scraping like sandpaper against his throat. "This is the meds. Side effects. Just the meds."

"Oh, Phineas." The head elongated his name into a taunt, drawing it out with venomous glee. "You can't medicate me away. I'm not some chemical hiccup, pal. I'm you. I'm here because of you. You willed me into existence."

"Shut up!" Phineas roared, his fists hammering down onto the porcelain sink with a force that sent tremors through his arms and cracks through his courage.

The head tilted, its expression oozing mockery, the corners of its mouth lifting in a predatory grin. "Did you think they'd save you? That the white coats actually cared? They're laughing at you, Phineas. Laughing while they mix their little potions. 'Let's see what this one does to poor, desperate Phin,' they say. It's all a joke to them."

"Lies!" Phineas bellowed, stumbling backward, his hands shaking as they scrabbled for the pill bottle on the counter, fingers fumbling like they were trying to hold water.

"Go ahead," it sneered, its voice curling around him like smoke. "Take your magic pills. Swallow them down, hero. Spoiler alert—they won't shut me up. They won't save you."

Phineas ripped the cap off the bottle, tipping two bitter capsules into his palm. He forced them down, choking as the acrid tang scraped his throat, his glare locked on the mirror, daring the thing to disappear. But it didn't. It didn't even flinch.

Instead, the head's laughter escalated, swelling into a crescendo of jagged cruelty. "Oh, Phin, you poor bastard," it said, the sound reverberating through the room, through his skull, through his very being. "You can't drown me out. You summoned me. You needed me. And now? Now, you're stuck with me."

Phineas crumpled to his knees, his hands clawing at his scalp as if he could rip the voice from his mind. The laughter consumed him, expanding until it wasn't just in the room—it was everywhere. It filled the bathroom, filled his head, filled the very fabric of his existence, a symphony of derision that promised it would never end.

V. Another Visit

By the time Phineas staggered into the doctor's lair of antiseptic dread, he was a phantom carved from his own wasted flesh. The light above seemed crueler, illuminating the hollows beneath his eyes and the pallor of his skin—a waxy, deathbed white that no amount of life could resuscitate. His body, once defiant in its presence, now hung slack in his clothes like the bones of a scarecrow rattling under a hungry wind. And yet, these grotesque ruins were nothing compared to the second head.

It perched on his shoulder like some infernal jester summoned from the depths of spite, its lips curled in an eternal leer, its laughter a basso profondo rumble that vibrated against Phineas's skull. The thing had become a malevolent showman, its commentary not merely intrusive but operatic, a vile aria tailored to ridicule every fleeting shred of Phineas's dignity.

"You're late," it rumbled as Phineas shouldered open the door, its voice oozing smug derision. "Doctor's got a full schedule. Lives to save. Not yours, of course."

"Shut up," Phineas rasped, his voice flint ground against steel.

The doctor glanced up, clipboard in hand, the veneer of clinical professionalism cracking like brittle glass when his eyes landed on the spectacle before him. "You look . . ." His words stalled, faltered, then crawled out flat and lifeless. " . . . worse."

Phineas barked a laugh, sharp and jagged as a shard of broken mirror. "Brilliant observation, Doc. Worth every penny." His hands tore at the scarf wound around his neck, flinging it aside like a condemned man baring his noose. "Take a long look. It talks now. Got a cure for that?"

The doctor froze mid-motion, his pen arrested in the air, his pupils pinpricks of horrified fascination. "It . . . talks?" he echoed, each syllable laced with disbelieving dread.

"Oh, it talks," Phineas snapped, the rage in his tone a flame licking at the edges of his despair. "And it doesn't know when to stop!"

The second head tilted toward the doctor, its grin expanding into something grotesque, teeth bared like the maw of a predator mid-snarl. "Careful now, Phineas," it murmured, saccharine and sinister. "You'll hurt my delicate feelings."

The doctor's lips moved soundlessly, his gaze fixed on the second head as though it were some unspeakable myth made flesh. At last, he stammered, "This isn't . . . possible. This . . . this can't—"

"Be real?" The second head's laughter came low and sharp, a blade sliding between ribs. "Oh, Doctor, I'm as real as your fading career and all the patients you've ever failed."

Phineas clutched at his temples, fingers digging into his scalp as if he could claw out the voice, the presence, the thing. His shoulders quaked under the weight of his despair. "Make it stop. Make it go away. I'm begging you."

The doctor set the clipboard down, his trembling hands betraying his facade of expertise. He leaned forward as though physical proximity could somehow bridge the chasm of his understanding. "This is . . . unprecedented," he muttered, his voice thin and brittle, unraveling under the enormity of the grotesque. "I'll need time—time to review, to consult, to—"

"I don't have time!" Phineas erupted, his words an anguished roar that reverberated through the sterile room.

The second head leaned in closer to the doctor, its grin a wicked crescent. "Hear that, Doc? No time. No clue. Just floundering in your impotence. What a spectacle."

The doctor's jaw tightened, a flicker of frustration breaking through his terror. "I'll prescribe something stronger," he muttered at last, each word brittle as cracked bone. "But I can't guarantee—"

Phineas surged forward, his hands seizing the doctor's collar, yanking him close until their faces were inches apart. The raw heat of his breath blasted forth, laced with desperation and fury. "You're the doctor," he spat, his voice trembling under the strain. "You fix this!"

The second head, its tone syrupy and poisonous, whispered, "Oh, he'll fix it, all right. You'll see just how."

Sweat dripped from the doctor's brow, his face a sickly pallor that seemed to age him a hundred years in an instant. Every inch of his body screamed weakness, his hands trembling as though they'd forgotten the basic mechanics of holding a pen. His composure, once a thin veneer of professionalism, cracked like cheap porcelain under the weight of the terror clawing at his insides. "I'll . . . I'll do my best," he stammered, the words barely scraping past his lips, swallowed up by the noise of his own panic, the breath in his throat tightening with each syllable.

"Your best?" The second head's voice hissed, low and mocking, slithering through the air like the rattling of a serpent coiled in the dark. "Such comfort. Such conviction," it sneered, the venom in its words dripping into the room like acid, every syllable an indictment of the doctor's feeble resolve.

"There could be side effects with this one," the doctor mumbled, his voice now a brittle whisper, something you might hear from a man standing on the edge of a precipice, staring into the abyss below.

Phineas laughed, sharp and bitter. "Oh, really, doc," he spat, his words cutting through the tension like a blade, the sarcasm dripping thick. "No shit!" His tone was an explosion of contempt, laced with disgust, as if the doctor's concerns were nothing more than the ramblings of a frightened child.

Phineas shoved the doctor back, sending him stumbling, his body crumpling into the chair like a rag doll with its strings severed. The second head's gaze sharpened, its eyes gleaming with twisted satisfaction, its grotesque triumph hanging in the air like a weight too heavy to bear.

The silence that followed was suffocating, a thick, oppressive thing that pressed down on everyone in the room, strangling every breath. The doctor's pen scratched against paper, frantic, desperate—like the last futile scrawl of a condemned man, each line etched with the certainty that what he was writing might as well have been the final words of a tombstone.

VI. Another Prescription

The third pill came with a warning— "Extreme side effects possible. Use only as directed." As if that little declaration meant a damn thing. Phineas had barreled this far down the road, what was another fissure in his soul going to do? His hands trembled, spasmed like they'd been taken over by the very thing he was trying to escape. He popped the cap, spilling a few pills onto the counter. They rattled, mocking him, sounding like dry bones scraping against the cracked tile. It was a sound that wasn't even human. He scooped them up, swallowed them dry, one after another, each one slipping down his throat like the deliberate cut of a blade, the betrayal smooth, efficient.

The second head, that parasite wedged between his skull and sanity, laughed. It wasn't laughter—it was static. White noise. A jarring, awful sound that gnawed at the edges of his thoughts, flickering in the gaps where his mind used to be. "You think this will fix you?" the voice sneered, dripping with the kind of venom that only years of self-loathing could cultivate. "Pathetic Phineas, always looking for the easy way out. You never learn, do you? Always waiting for someone else to clean up your mess."

Phineas slammed the bottle down on the counter. It cracked against the laminate, the sound so sharp it could've been a gunshot. His reflection stared back at him— gaunt, hollow, a ghost of someone who used to matter. His eyes were black pits, the kind left behind after a disaster, a brutal, irreversible collapse. He didn't recognize the face anymore. Didn't care. He just didn't care.

"Losing yourself," the second head crooned, the voice dripping with false sweetness. "Soon there won't be anything left. Just an empty husk, a shell for the worms."

Good. The word escaped him on a rasp, a defiance he didn't feel, just the hollow echo of one. His thoughts were already disintegrating, merging into one endless, shapeless mess, the edges gone soft, blurred. Each fragment of his mind slipping into the next, until there was nothing but a fog.

The pills took hold. They sank into him like ice—the cold, hard kind that doesn't just freeze the skin, but burrows into your veins, leaves everything raw and stripped bare. It wasn't just cold. It was nothingness, a suffocating absence that spread through him like poison, crawling down to the marrow. It settled like a weight, pressing him into the ground, dragging him down into that black, endless void. His eyelids fluttered, caving to the darkness, the crushing blackness that was more like a grave than sleep. It was violent, the way sleep grabbed him, wrenching him under as if the very universe was throwing him into a pit and pulling the cover tight.

He woke to silence.

For a moment, Phineas thought it was over. For a fleeting, trembling moment, he thought the world had finally let him go.

The silence filled his lungs like air after drowning, deep and rich, as if he were breathing for the first time in a decade. His chest expanded, each inhale a gift. He closed his eyes, drowning in that quiet—until the scream tore through him.

It wasn't just a scream. It was the sound of something ancient, something far older than him or anything human. It was a primal, guttural scream, the kind that claws its way out from the very depths of being. It reverberated inside him, twisted through his bones, splintering the marrow. Phineas pressed his hands to his throat, desperate to stop it, but it was already too late. The eruption was unstoppable, a force beyond him. The pain was beyond description. It tore at him, shredding his insides with a ferocity that would never let him forget.

The second head—no, it wasn't a head anymore—splintered, tore open like paper caught in a storm. From the wound poured something that shouldn't exist, something that defied all reason, all shape. It wasn't even dark. It was wrong. It was a mass, formless, shifting like it was made of shadows that didn't belong to any known world. It wriggled, stretched, and hung in the air like a bad omen, heavy and suffocating. And it knew him. It was him, and worse—it was everything he would never escape. The parts of him he'd buried, the filth he could never cleanse. All of it. All the parts he never let anyone see.

It loomed before him, coalescing into something more, something alive. It spoke, but not with one voice—no, it was a cacophony of voices, countless, tortured, trapped in some hellish dimension beyond comprehension. "You thought you could silence me. You thought you could bury what you are. Fool."

Phineas dropped to his knees. He couldn't stop it. His body screamed in protest, each joint protesting the sheer weight of the air, the suffocating presence. His mouth was dry, a desert in his throat, but the words fought their way out anyway. "What do you want?" The words barely broke free, choked off before they could even finish.

The entity pulsed. It twisted, a grotesque mockery of life, and it responded—its form undulating like liquid darkness. "To show you the truth. To make you see."

Phineas screamed again, but this time the scream was swallowed whole, devoured by the void that was consuming him. There was no escape. There was only the thing that had been waiting for him all along.

VIII. The End

Phineas sat on the edge of the bed, his fingers curling around the small vial of pills, the plastic bottle a cold, oppressive weight in his palm. It was a final attempt at redemption, a desperate gamble against the grotesque distortion that had overtaken his body, turning him into a living freak show. The second head, grotesque and alien, was an unwelcome appendage that had tainted every moment of his existence. It hadn't been enough to ruin his life; no, that would have been too merciful. No, this had become a cruel joke, a mutation, a thing of mockery and derision.

The horror had started that night. He awoke, drenched in sweat, sheets clinging to his skin like the grip of a lover who knew only how to wound. His body writhed beneath the fabric, skin stretching and contracting in ways it shouldn't. The mass that was a second head, a hideous, blinking thing with glassy eyes—shifted, squirmed, as if it were alive, trying to detach itself from the

human host it had been forcibly sewn to. Phineas could feel it—
the horror of it—slicing through his mind, gnawing at him with a
cold, clammy hunger. His muscles spasmed in time with the
unnatural twisting of his flesh. He bit down hard, so hard his teeth
sank into his tongue, copper flooding his mouth as he tried to
control the storm that raged inside him. Pain coiled through his
body like a serpent, but somehow, through sheer force of will, it
subsided into something worse: nothing. A numbness that settled
into his bones like the weight of his shame.

By morning, it was gone. The second head had vanished,
as if the universe had taken pity on him. Or perhaps it had simply
moved on to someone else, some other poor soul to carry the
curse. His skin was smooth again, but taut, stretched over muscles
that bulged with unnatural strength. His torso swelled, his arms
thickened, the tightness of his body reminding him of a balloon,
just waiting to pop. And when he stood in front of the mirror,
staring at the stranger's face that now reflected back at him, there
was no joy, no triumph, only the horror of becoming someone
else.

No longer the freak. No longer the thing they pointed at
and whispered about. No, now he was something else, something
that made the ground tremble beneath his feet, a thing of bulk
and power, a colossus. But it wasn't freedom. His body—his
body—it didn't fit him anymore, and the world around him—hell,
the whole damn world—it felt like some kind of distorted joke.
Everything had warped, shifted, like the universe had taken a sick
pleasure in flipping the script, and now, he was the one who didn't
belong. He wasn't just the outcast. He was the mistake.

And the voices—they were back. No mercy. Always there.

"Still a freak," one hissed, the words screeching through his skull, a raw, jagged sound like nails being dragged across the last shard of glass in the world, each word an assault, an insult.

"They'll never see you as anything else," another chuckled, its tone oily, malicious.

He pressed his palms to his ears, trying to force the noise out, but it was too late. The sound had burrowed into him; it was inside now, festering like an infection. The voices—they weren't just voices anymore, they were everything. They grew louder, more insistent, a gnashing, relentless tide clawing at the fabric of his sanity. It didn't matter that the people on the street no longer sneered or mocked him. No, it wasn't that. It was worse. They looked at him, but they didn't see him. They couldn't. The torment had taken root deep inside, a rabid, ceaseless chorus of madness, each note more shrill than the last, rising, screaming in his skull like a thousand nails being dragged across a chalkboard, never, ever stopping.

Phineas had tried everything. Everything. He had shoved pills down his throat, tried to talk it out, screamed into empty rooms. Nothing worked. Nothing. It didn't matter. Nothing could stop it.

And now, he was a beast. A hulking monstrosity of a man, towering over everyone with muscles so bloated and grotesque they seemed to be tearing at his skin. His body had become a prison, a suit of flesh that didn't fit anymore, and it was only getting worse. He stood in the doctor's office, shoulders hunched, head bowed—no chair could hold his mass, not anymore. His size had grown beyond human limits, and so had his desperation. The waiting room, the antiseptic smell, the sterile white light—it all felt like a slap, a taunt. The brightness mocked him. The clean lines of the furniture felt like a challenge to everything his mind had become. It was as though the world around him had conspired to make him feel even more wrong.

The doctor had greeted him with that practiced smile—the one that was so fake it practically screamed I'm pretending to care. That detached, clinical look, like Phineas wasn't even a person anymore, just another piece of meat to be dissected. He'd followed the doctor, his steps heavy, his body weighing him down like a leaden ball and chain. When he spoke, his voice cracked—a broken, dry thing, raw with the wear and tear of too many sleepless nights. He told the doctor about the voices, about how they weren't just voices anymore—they were inside him, seeping through his veins, gnawing on his bones. He told him how it wasn't an external thing, some bad luck or curse on the world outside, no. It was an invasion, an assault on his insides, and it was destroying him piece by piece.

"I told you, I hear them, constantly!" Phineas slammed his fists into the desk, his nails scraping the wood, digging into the surface until the splinters sliced into his skin. He fought the scream rising from his throat, fighting to stay tethered to some semblance of control. The doctor flinched, but only just—a twitch in the eyes, a barely perceptible recoiling. But that calm, that professional detachment, it infuriated him. They were too clean, too perfect at pretending to care, too practiced in dismantling the likes of him. It gripped him like a gnawing wound that wouldn't heal.

"Mr. Piddlewick, I've reviewed your file extensively," the doctor intoned, the words as lifeless as a machine. Their voice, flat, detached, like someone reading from a manual they've memorized a thousand times over. "There are no documented neurological side effects associated with this medication. I don't know what to tell you. If you're hearing voices, it's likely a pre-existing condition."

Phineas let out a laugh—bitter, raw, the kind of laugh that cuts through the air like a jagged shard of glass. It was a sound that made the doctor's spine tighten, a chill creeping in from somewhere deep inside their chest. "Pre-existing?" Phineas' voice cracked, the word spat out like it was poison. "I've never heard anything like this before. Not until I took your damn pills."

"Correlation is not causation," the doctor said, that same robotic dismissal. As if Phineas was the problem. As if he was the one out of step, the one who needed fixing. As if it wasn't the system that had shattered him into pieces, the machine that had chewed him up and spit him out. The words stung, ringing in his ears, growing distant, like they were coming from someone else entirely.

The doctor's sterile demeanor grated against him, each word a sharp blade of indifference. It pushed him further. His pulse hammered in his ears, blood rushing to his head, thickening his vision, clouding his mind. "You think I'm crazy?" His voice was a growl now, low and vicious, as he leaned forward. His fingers sank into the desk, the pressure so intense the wood creaked beneath him, threatening to splinter under the weight of his fury. "You think all this is in my head?"

The doctor's glasses slipped down the bridge of their nose, just enough for Phineas to see the faintest tremor in their hand. A slight, almost imperceptible crack in the veneer of calm. There was the tiniest flicker of fear.

"Perhaps the stress of your condition has triggered a psychological response," the doctor said, but it was a feeble attempt at control, an explanation so hollow it could've been a lie to themselves as much as to Phineas.

"Condition?" Phineas spat, standing now, the tremor of rage shuddering through his body. He moved with the animal grace of a trapped beast, towering, his massive arms swinging wide, the sheer weight of his frame vibrating with barely contained violence. "You mean the one you just cured?" He gestured to himself, to the rawness, to the unbearable weight of his own flesh. "Look at me. The second head is gone, but the voices are back—and this?" He motioned to the monstrous body that felt like it belonged to someone else, a grotesque mockery of what he'd once been. "This is not what I wanted."

The doctor's response was an empty, hollow platitude. "And yet you're alive. Functional. You should consider yourself lucky. Others are not as fortunate as you. Mr. Piddlewick, I don't know what to tell you. Gigantism was not listed as a side effect."

Phineas's breath caught in his chest, and before he knew what he was doing, his hands shot out, fingers closing around the doctor's throat with a speed that left the other man gasping, flailing. The doctor's hands clawed at his forearms, desperate, but Phineas was too strong. The voices screamed inside him, a tidal wave of sound, urging him on.

"Show them what you're capable of," one jeered.

"No one controls you," another hissed, the words laced with venom.

"End it," a third whispered, their voice like the softest breath of death.

His grip tightened. The doctor's eyes bulged, their skin turning an alarming shade of purple as their breath grew ragged. Phineas could feel the pulse beneath his fingers, the frantic thrum of life, but it was slipping away. It was so easy. So effortless. The doctor's body began to go limp, their life draining away under his hands, until—nothing.

The silence that followed was deafening. Phineas stepped back, releasing the doctor's body. It collapsed, a ragdoll, into the chair. The world around him felt disjointed, alien, as if he were no longer part of it. His chest heaved as his mind tried to catch up, but there was nothing to hold onto. The voices had quieted, replaced by a cold clarity, a mocking tone that seemed to come from everywhere, yet nowhere at all.

"What about death?" he muttered, a bitter laugh escaping his lips. The absurdity of it all. "Was death listed as a side effect?"

He left the clinic, stepping into the world that had once been his, but was no longer. The streets felt quieter, the air heavier. The voices didn't vanish—they lingered, faint, just on the edge of hearing, but they were there. Phineas had crossed a line, one he couldn't uncross, and now there was no going back. The world lay before him, a broken thing, but it was his now. His to do with as he saw fit. His fate was uncertain, but one thing was clear: Phineas Piddlewick would never be silenced. Not by doctors. Not by voices. Not by the weight of his own flesh. He would be heard. Always.

A Creator's Dilemma

Dr. Leonard Voss, quantum physicist, hunched over his desk, a chaotic storm of papers and scribbled equations surrounding him. The smell of stale coffee and old paper mixed with the faint, metallic scent of burning electricity from the neglected lamp on his desk. Its dim glow cut through the room in sharp, jagged lines, creating a kind of distorted refuge from the world outside, where the stars seemed to flicker just beyond his reach. The room was a mausoleum of his mind—books, notebooks, loose sheets, all smudged and crumpled, accumulating at the corners like the dust of forgotten thoughts.

"It has to be here," Leonard muttered under his breath, eyes darting between the worn pages of Kant's Critique of Pure Reason and his own jumbled scrawl, a manic blend of philosophy and physics, equations that spiraled into each other like a mental black hole. "The key to understanding the universe . . . it's right here, on the edge. So close I can taste it."

His fingers twitched involuntarily, tracing invisible patterns in the air before returning to the paper, as if the answer might appear if he only focused hard enough.

He reached for his coffee mug, only to find it empty, the lingering bitterness of whatever he had consumed earlier still clinging to his mouth. Again. He could no longer remember the last time he'd slept properly, his body now just a vessel, dragging itself from one thought to the next. It was as though the universe itself had chosen him as a conduit for all its maddening complexities, and the pressure of it—no, the weight of it—pressed on him constantly, unrelenting. The question gnawed at him, demanding answers no one could give.

"Maybe . . . if I approach it differently," he muttered, pulling a fresh sheet of paper towards him with an almost feverish energy. His pen tore across the surface, creating tangled webs of quantum mechanics, smeared symbols, and faint ideas that would never solidify. "What if we consider the universe as a self-aware entity, constantly watching itself? Maybe that's it. Maybe it's watching me—watching all of us—and we're just too . . . too small to see it. Or too big."

A loud bang, the slam of a door somewhere in the building, cut through the air like a needle scratching across vinyl. Leonard flinched, suddenly snapped back to the mundane world he'd long been ignoring. The ache in his back was sharp, and the gritty film behind his eyes, the one he hadn't noticed until now, burned. He blinked. The digital clock on his desk gleamed mockingly at him: 3:47 AM.

"Shit," he groaned, the word catching in his throat as he ran a hand through his wild, unkempt hair. Another night, another unsolvable riddle left to fester. "Another night lost to the void." He said it aloud, as though hearing it made it real, made it more legitimate somehow.

Leonard stood, the protest of his bones like an old machine, creaking with every shift of his weight. He shuffled toward his bedroom, his gaze grazing over the cluttered apartment, past the piles of unopened bills, the half-empty bottles on the counter. As his eyes fell upon a framed photo on the wall, something in his chest constricted. A younger version of himself, the physicist with a smile that seemed almost alien now, stood beside a particle accelerator. There was hope in that image—hope and belief that he could make sense of it all. He didn't recognize that man anymore, and it was as though time itself had turned its back on him.

"What happened to you, Len?" he asked the reflection in the glass, the words bitter as they left his mouth. "When did solving the secrets of the cosmos become . . . this?"

The photo remained silent, offering no solace, no answer. It was only a shadow of a past that felt increasingly distant. Leonard sighed, the sound too heavy for his tired body, and trudged toward his bed. But even then, as he collapsed into the tangled sheets, the world around him seemed to ripple, the fabric of reality bending ever so slightly, like the thin skin of a dream just about to tear.

He squeezed his eyes shut, trying to shut off the thoughts, the endless spiral of theories and equations that crowded his mind, refusing to let go. "Just sleep," he told himself, the words barely a whisper. "When you wake up, it'll make sense. When you wake up, you'll see it all clearly. It'll be there."

But as the fog of exhaustion closed in, another part of him, a smaller, quieter part, understood the inevitable. Time would stretch out again—another endless loop of questions, of searching, of never quite finding what he needed. The alarm clock beside his bed blinked 3:49 AM, its cold, blue glow casting an eerie light across the room.

"What's it all about?" he muttered, his voice hoarse and cracked, like the last remnants of a dream fading into the dark. "Who wound up this cosmic clock and set it ticking?"

The universe, Leonard thought, was like a cold, unfeeling machine, its gears turning in eerie, flawless rhythm, each click of the mechanism pushing him further into a fog of confusion. But who was pulling the levers, who stood behind the curtain making sure everything operated with such unnatural precision? Was it God, a distant observer in a far-off dimension, or perhaps an alien intelligence manipulating the strings of reality for some inscrutable purpose? Or was it all simply the result of a cosmic accident, the byproduct of random particles colliding in an ever-expanding, mindless dance?

His gaze drifted upward, where the cracked plaster of the ceiling seemed to pulse with a life of its own. The shapes twisted, curved, and reformed, becoming something more than just random patterns. Leonard's eyes narrowed. Had the exhaustion finally driven him into delirium, his sleep-deprived mind fracturing reality? He blinked hard, focusing. But no, the shapes were too clear now. They weren't just random. They were equations—formulas and calculations spilling out in geometric precision, symbols moving in time with the chaotic rhythm of his thoughts. They intertwined, spiraled around each other, merging into an ungraspable unity that made sense only to someone who could see beyond the veil of the tangible world.

And then, in that vast, unreachable universe, something stirred—faint, like the quiver of a far-off star reacting to the tremors of an insignificant human soul seeking answers in the infinite darkness. The movement wasn't a mere coincidence; it was as if the entire cosmos had been waiting, anticipating this exact moment.

"Of course," Leonard breathed, his voice barely more than a whisper. His eyes widened, the realization blooming with such intensity it felt as though his skull might crack open from the force of it. "It's so simple."

In an instant, he was upright, his pulse quickening, the sudden rush of adrenaline overtaking the fog of fatigue. His hands shook as he reached for the notepad by his bed, the paper crinkling under his fingers. He scribbled furiously, one simple equation flowing out of him like a torrent—perfect, beautiful, terrifying. It was here now, in his mind, but it needed to be captured before it dissolved back into the ether.

"This is it," he muttered, breathless with the enormity of it all. "The grand unified theory. The answer to everything." His voice trembled, not from fear, but from a kind of electric, reckless joy. For the first time, the universe had revealed itself to him, and it was as though he had unlocked a door to a world he never knew existed.

As Leonard completed the final symbol, an unfamiliar sensation surged through him, like a static charge traveling beneath his skin. The room around him began to warp, the walls stretching and bulging as though they were made of rubber, twisting into grotesque angles. His vision narrowed and expanded erratically, like a shattered lens being reassembled on the fly. The very air felt thick, oppressive, as if something unseen was pressing against him. Leonard's chest tightened, an invisible hook digging into his core, pulling him outward.

"What's happening?" he gasped, his voice strangled. His notepad slipped from his hands, clattering to the floor, forgotten. His eyes fixed on the equations he'd just written—they began to shimmer with a strange light, pulsing with an unnatural rhythm. It wasn't just the equations. It was the very room, vibrating in a pattern he couldn't understand, an unfolding reality that didn't quite fit.

A jolt shot through him, and then, to his horror, he felt himself lifting—his body, his essence, separating from the physical form that had always defined him. He rose slowly, his gaze fixed on the bed where his body lay crumpled, eyes closed, chest still. His limbs felt . . . empty. His chest, once filled with breath, now sat silent and cold. Was this . . . death?

"Am I . . . " His thoughts stumbled over themselves. "Dead?"

But before the thought could settle, the pull returned. The tugging sensation turned into an urgent, relentless force, yanking him upward with a terrifying speed. Leonard's consciousness was torn from his surroundings, from the thin shell of flesh he had inhabited. He was no longer in the room, no longer tethered to his body. The ceiling seemed to melt away, and the roof of the house disintegrated as if it had never existed at all. The night sky rushed up to meet him, stars blurring into streaks as he was propelled into the void, his body a distant, irrelevant thing now, helpless in the vast, uncaring expanse.

***

Leonard blinked, his awareness slowly surfacing through layers of fractured perception, like a man clawing his way out of an endless, suffocating fog. The mundane edges of his bedroom, once so familiar, unraveled and dissolved around him, giving way to an immense chamber that pulsed with a strange, alien rhythm. The walls were alive, shimmering with fractal patterns that danced and swirled before his eyes, twisting in ways that felt impossible— geometry folding in on itself, rearranging into ever-more intricate, unfathomable designs. His head throbbed with the effort of processing it all.

"What the hell?" Leonard muttered, his voice alien to him, muffled and distant, as if it had been stripped of any true connection to his body.

He opened his mouth, but the sound felt hollow, sucked out by the humming energy that filled the air, vibrating through him in waves. He tried to push himself to his feet, but his limbs felt like they were constructed from smoke and fog, insubstantial, disconnected from the world.

"Welcome, Leonard Voss," a chorus of voices whispered, their cadence disorienting and omnipresent, as if they emanated from all corners of the chamber, and yet from none at all. The voices were at once too close and impossibly far away. "Your mind has finally grasped the fundamental truth of existence."

Leonard squinted, every instinct telling him to flee, but his body had no grounding in this alien space. He fought to focus, his vision warping as he tried to make sense of the shifting forms before him. They were not quite human—no, not human at all— but some strange amalgamation of light and color, constantly rearranging themselves into ephemeral shapes that danced between the abstract and the vaguely familiar. Figures, non-figures, all bleeding into one another, and then, just as quickly, dissolving into something new. It was maddening.

"Who . . . what are you?" Leonard asked, his voice trembling as his scientific mind scrambled to make sense of the impossible unfolding before him.

One of the forms before him pulsed faintly with a soft blue light, its presence both foreign and eerily familiar. "We are the Architects, creators of realms beyond reckoning. Your recent breakthrough—the unraveling of the nature of your universe—has allowed you to ascend to our plane of existence."

Leonard's mind splintered under the strain, fragments of thoughts scattering in all directions. He remembered the endless nights spent hunched over equations, struggling to find a key that could unlock the mysteries of the universe. Had he really discovered something so vast, so incomprehensible, that it transcended his understanding of existence itself?

"This . . . this can't be real," Leonard muttered under his breath, barely audible. "I must be dreaming . . . or maybe I've finally cracked under the pressure of all this research."

A ripple of amusement seemed to reverberate through the figures, though their faces—if they had them—remained inscrutable. Another form shimmered in hues of gold, its essence moving like molten light. It spoke, its voice like a melody, slow and measured. "Your skepticism is understandable, Leonard. But I assure you, this is not a dream. This is more real, in fact, than the reality you've clung to all your life."

Leonard staggered backward, his vision swimming, his body feeling lighter, as though gravity itself no longer applied. "Assuming, just for a moment, that I believe you . . . why am I here? What do you want from me?"

The blue Architect pulsed again, a resonating hum filling the space. "We've been watching you for some time, Leonard.

Your relentless pursuit of truth—your desire to unearth the very fabric of reality—has drawn our attention. Your drive is exceptional."

"Watching me?" Leonard's heart skipped, a coldness sweeping through him. "Why me? What could I possibly . . ."

"Perhaps it would be best if we showed you," a third Architect said, this one a swirling mass of deep purple energy, glided toward him, its form bending in unnatural, fluid movements.

The chamber around Leonard began to warp, the walls shifting as if they were made of liquid light. Fractal patterns twisted and spiraled, converging into something far more familiar. His breath caught in his throat as planets, stars, and entire galaxies emerged from the ether, swirling around him in a cosmic dance. One in particular caught his eye. It was his universe, where he existed, laid bare in front of him—a reflection of the very theories he had spent his life chasing.

"This . . . " Leonard whispered, the words slipping from him, awestruck and fragile. "This . . . is my universe."

"One of many," the golden Architect corrected, its voice smooth as liquid metal, an unsettling blend of warmth and indifference. "You see, Leonard, we construct universes not out of necessity, but as a form of art, a form of entertainment. Each one is an experiment . . . an isolated field of physics, biology, and meaning."

Leonard's mind spun, but the gears refused to mesh. He blinked slowly, trying to process the enormity of what was being laid before him. "So, you're saying my universe, my entire existence, everything I've ever learned and felt . . . is just . . . some kind of project? A cosmic art piece?"

The purple Architect's form undulated—its surface like a living canvas in constant flux, shifting shades of violet and lavender. If it had a face, Leonard imagined it would have been shrugging. "Art, experiment, entertainment," it said with a hint of disinterest, "the distinctions blur, Leonard. Our existence defies such limitations. We create, we observe, we shape . . . what's trivial to us becomes everything to you."

"I don't understand . . . why?" Leonard's voice cracked, the question barely audible, as though the weight of it might crush him.

The blue Architect pulsated softly, its presence thrumming with an energy Leonard could feel behind his eyes, in the marrow of his bones. "Why does any artist create?" it asked, as if this were a simple question. "For the thrill of creation, for the joy of discovery, for the pleasure of watching something unfold, something new, something different."

Leonard's mind reeled, his thoughts firing off in every direction, colliding with each other. If they were right— if this was all true—every discovery, every struggle, every loss, every fleeting moment of joy, every brutal choice, every tear shed by the human race—it was all—just part of some grand, unfathomable experiment.

"This is madness," he muttered, a sick, hollow feeling spreading through him. "You're telling me . . . all of it . . . all of human history, everything we've fought for, everything we've endured . . . was for your amusement?"

"You misunderstand, Leonard," the golden Architect said, its voice quieter now, as though speaking to a child. Its form shimmered—glittering particles swirling, almost resembling sympathy. "We don't create universes just for amusement. They are precious. Each one is a unique creation, nurtured and loved."

Leonard's frustration flared, his pulse quickening. "You said it was for entertainment," he shot back, unable to keep the bitterness from his voice. "How is that different from some kid with an ant farm?"

The purple Architect curled closer, its swirling form like a storm about to break. "Perhaps 'entertainment' was a poor choice of words," it admitted, a fleeting note of something almost human in its tone. "Think of it as . . . exploration. Each universe is a canvas for discovery . . . new possibilities, new forms of life, new expressions of existence. We push boundaries. We explore the limits."

Leonard's hands clenched at his sides, his mind struggling to keep up with the spiraling enormity of it all. "And my universe? What was its purpose? What was the point of it?"

The blue Architect seemed to pause, as though the question itself had weight, even for them. It pulsed thoughtfully, a slow, rhythmic thrum, then spoke, its voice taking on a faintly distant tone, as though remembering something long past.

"Your universe was an experiment in the tension between free will and determinism," the blue Architect said. "We were fascinated by the way sentient beings would develop when given the illusion of true agency, but restrained by the inescapable laws of physics."

Leonard's breath hitched, bitterness seeping into his voice. "And how did we do? Did we live up to your . . . expectations?"

The Architects seemed to confer silently for a long moment, their forms rippling and folding, as if deliberating over the answer.

Finally, the golden one spoke. "You exceeded them," it said, and Leonard felt the words settle into the air, heavy with a strange, almost eerie pride. "The complexity of your lives, the diversity of your cultures, your philosophies . . . it's been an endlessly fascinating thing to observe."

For a fleeting moment, Leonard felt a strange sense of pride, an urge to bask in the strange compliment. But that pride quickly soured, a bitter taste in his mouth. He shook his head, the nagging thought clawing at him.

"So . . . what now? What happens next? Why bring me here, if it's all just . . . art to you?"

The purple Architect's form swirled, the colors around it growing more vibrant, excited even. "Because, Leonard, you've done something no one else has ever done. You've glimpsed the very structure of your reality. You've seen the threads, the mechanisms beneath the surface. You've touched the heart of creation."

Leonard's heart raced in his chest. "And that's . . . good?" he asked, his voice small and unsure, as if questioning his own sanity.

The blue Architect pulsed with what could have been excitement. "It's extraordinary! In all our countless artworks and experiments, never has a being within a created universe come so close to understanding the truth behind their existence."

Leonard's thoughts spiraled, his mind struggling to hold on. "What does that mean for me? For my universe? Are we just . . . done now?"

The golden Architect shimmered with a strange intensity, its form folding and unfolding in complex, impossible patterns. "It means, Leonard, that you can become an Architect yourself. You can create. You can shape entire realities . . . far beyond what you could ever imagine."

***

Leonard's fingers twitched, disjointed and unsteady, as he grasped at the raw, unsolidified fabric of reality, trying to weave it into something coherent. The sheer scale of what he was doing was dizzying. His thoughts seemed to splinter, evaporating like smoke, leaving behind nothing but a sensation of vertigo. Around him, the Architects loomed—fluid, shapeless beings pulsing with a radiance so intense it threatened to burn the edges of his vision.

"Concentrate, Leonard," one of them said, the voice not a sound but a ripple in the very air, a clamor of shifting whispers that reverberated in the folds of his consciousness. "Feel the threads of existence twisting in your hands. Bend them."

He closed his eyes, struggling to ignore the weight of their presence, their impossible forms pressing on the boundaries of his perception. Before him, the swirling chaos of the void writhed, and he focused on it, tightening his grip. Slowly, like trying to focus on a distant, hazy shape through the fog, a new universe began to crystallize in the space he had carved out. Galaxies folded into themselves, stars ignited like gasping breaths, and the pulse of nascent life beat in the darkness of countless worlds.

"Remarkable," another Architect observed, its tone flat, emotionless, like the hum of an overclocked machine. "He has . . . an aptitude for this."

Leonard opened his eyes, eyes wide with disbelief, staring at the swirling expanse of his creation—a miniature cosmos, delicate and raw, shimmering in the dark.

"It's . . . it's beautiful," he murmured, the words tasting foreign, too small for what he felt.

"You're beginning to understand, aren't you?" The first Architect's voice, that ripple of noise, threaded through him. "The power, the responsibility. This is what it means to be one of us. What we are."

Time—or what passed for it in this place—was irrelevant. Days, moments, hours had long since bled together, rendering them meaningless. Leonard found himself growing accustomed to the motions of creation, each universe an experiment, a ripple in the continuum, a playground of unpredictable laws. Some formed in bizarre patterns, others in ways that defied logic entirely. But they all worked—just enough to let him know he was not losing his grip. Not yet.

But then came the questions, crawling through his mind like ants burrowing into his skin, unwilling to be ignored.

"Tell me something," Leonard asked one day, his voice cutting through the strange quiet between them, "who created you? Where did you get this power? Who are you, really?"

The Architects paused. Their forms, always shifting, flinched—like a flicker of light caught in the corner of his eye, too quick to focus on. Then, one of them spoke, its voice unnervingly calm.

"Such questions are . . . irrelevant," it said, as though the very act of asking had betrayed him.

"Irrelevant?" Leonard echoed, his words too loud, too insistent. "How can that be? Surely you. . . "

"We do not know," another Architect interrupted, its voice like a mechanical grind, a sound without sympathy. "Nor do we need to. Our purpose is creation. Not . . . introspection."

Leonard's mind recoiled at the coldness of the response. "But how can you not wonder?" His voice wavered, part anger, part desperation. "How can you not care?"

The Architects' forms began to distort, shifting violently as their voices merged into a dissonant, grinding chorus. "Enough, Leonard. This is beyond even our comprehension. Focus on your work."

But Leonard couldn't stop it—the question burrowed deeper, like an itch that couldn't be scratched. As he created, as he shaped the universes, the question became all-consuming: Who created the creators?

If they didn't know—if they were just as clueless as he had been in his former life, then what was the point of it all? What was the nature of existence if even the Architects were bound by an ignorance they refused to acknowledge?

He glanced at one of the stars he'd created, watching as it swelled and collapsed, burning out in a spectacular burst. "Maybe," Leonard thought, his mind struggling to keep up with the implications, "maybe we're just . . . parts of something bigger. Layers upon layers of creation, all of us."

The realization struck him like a surge of static, a jolt of terror and exhilaration. What if this was only one rung of a ladder that stretched on forever? The very thought of it shook him to his core.

And as Leonard continued his work, building, shaping, experimenting, he knew the search for an answer had only just begun. And it would never stop. Not for him. Not as long as the universes continued to spin and die in his hands.

＊＊

Leonard drifted in the Architects' domain, an ungraspable expanse stretching out before him. His consciousness was an endless ocean, vast and alien, touching things he had never considered, never even dreamed of. The power to shape whole realities with a mere thought—such a gift—should have exhilarated him. Instead, an insistent itch, a gnawing discomfort, pulsed at the edges of his awareness. It was as if the gift itself, so grand and magnificent, had come with a fatal flaw, a glitch in the code of existence.

"Something troubles you, Leonard," came the voice of an Architect, its presence flickering like static in the air. It was not a voice as much as a sense, an intuition crossing the boundaries of thought and reality, its form distorting in ways Leonard couldn't follow.

Leonard's thoughts fractured, spinning outward and pulling themselves together into something coherent. "I can't stop thinking . . . about this. About all of it. Who made this? I can't stop asking the question.

"What question is that?"

"Who created you?"

The other Architects froze, their fluctuating shapes drawing in, briefly unsteady. The ripples of their being faltered in the vastness of space. Leonard felt it before he saw it—an unspoken tension, a dissonance in the cosmic hum. Something had shifted.

"As we have said, such questions are . . . irrelevant," another Architect stated, the words flat, absent of the usual resonance. There was a flicker in its being, a brief distortion as though it had momentarily been unsure of itself. "As far as you are concerned, we are the Creators. That is the only truth you require."

Leonard pressed forward, his mind unraveling with the obsessive curiosity of someone who had learned to see beyond the veil, someone who had dared ask the question the universe itself was designed to suppress.

"But you must have asked," he said. "You must have origins, some beginning. How can you not wonder where it all came from? Where you came from?"

The room—or what could be called a room, though its limits stretched in every direction—darkened for a brief moment. The Architects' forms twisted, their usual gleaming shimmer dimming, their perfectly coordinated motions suddenly stilted. Leonard felt something shift in the air, the quiet pulse of energy around them suddenly warping, as though the very fabric of their existence was straining under the weight of his words.

"Enough!" The eldest of the Architects spoke, its voice reverberating with a depth that was both a command and a warning. The energy surrounding them crackled with a sudden sharpness. "These inquiries serve no purpose. Do not waste your time, Leonard. Focus on your creations. Revel in the power you have been granted."

But Leonard's human mind, still bound by the need for answers, would not relent.

"But if we don't understand how it began, how can we truly know what we are?" he insisted. "What we can become? Isn't that the key? The first step toward something . . . more?"

The Architects' forms began to vibrate violently, a dissonance warping their synchronized rhythm. The hum, once a soothing song, now became a harsh buzz, fractured and shrill. Leonard's stomach tightened. Was this the point of no return? Had he broken the silence that had kept them all in check for so long?

Then, one of the Architects solidified, its form becoming more defined, pulsing with an energy Leonard hadn't expected— soft, almost melancholy. It was an odd contrast to the others, and its presence felt almost too human.

"Perhaps . . . perhaps it is time," it murmured, the words carrying a weight of something long buried beneath the surface, something Leonard could neither name nor understand.

The universe seemed to hold its breath, and Leonard wondered—truly wondered—whether he had unlocked something he was never meant to find.

The Architects' forms vibrated with what could only be described as cosmic disbelief. "No!" one of them cried out, its voice thick with a profound unease. "The cycle must be maintained!"

But the other Architect, its outline like a phantom edge on the borders of Leonard's consciousness, continued. Its voice was old—too old—deep and heavy with an exhaustion that resonated through the very fabric of their shared space.

"Leonard," it said, its tone taking on a strange cadence. "What we are about to share with you will shatter what you believe is the reality you know. It will tear apart the illusion of all you've ever thought to be true."

Leonard felt his mind stretch, thin, like fabric under too much tension. His senses expanded, pulled beyond his physical limits, into something that was both everything and nothing at all. It was an agony of comprehension.

The Architect spoke again, each word resonating with a deep, gnawing resonance. "We, the Architects, were once like you—beings from a lesser reality, granted the power of creation by those who came before us." The air around them seemed to thicken, to hum with the weight of the history of eons. "And they, in turn, were granted their powers by another council, existing at an even higher level."

Leonard's thoughts splintered, pieces falling apart like shattered glass. "You mean . . . this isn't the . . . top level? There are others above you?" The words left his mouth like an afterthought, a feeble question, a cry against the tide of his own growing despair.

The Architect's form pulsed, as though struggling with a concept beyond it. "We don't know," it said, a strange tremor in its voice. "That is the paradox, Leonard. The cycle . . . it goes on, infinitesimal and infinite, as if we are all simply echoes, bending back on themselves. Each level awakens new creators, beings drawn from the reality beneath. Yet none of us know where it started. None of us know if it began at all."

The force of this revelation hit Leonard like a gravitational collapse. "So . . . my ascension, all of this . . . everything . . . it could be part of something else? Some higher reality? Some sort of . . . experiment?"

A shudder passed through the Architects, their shapes flickering momentarily like fragile light caught in a gale. "It's possible," one admitted in a hollow tone. "But we do not know. We have no answers."

Leonard's mind, already unhinged, struggled to reel itself back into something familiar, but there was no anchor. No center. Only the pull of infinity and the crushing pressure of more questions. His consciousness seemed to spiral outward, expanding to meet the void.

He found himself asking, "Then what is the point of it all? If we are all part of an endless loop, a reality within another reality, where does meaning come from? What does any of it even matter?"

The Architects' forms dimmed, their light lessening, as if some spark of hope had been snuffed out. One of them pulsated gently, its mass taking on a shape that resembled something soft— almost comforting. "Perhaps the meaning, Leonard, is in the act of creation itself. The joy of manifesting new worlds, of giving rise to realities and watching them grow and evolve, independent and fragile. That, perhaps, is the purpose."

Leonard recoiled inwardly, the words tasting like ash in his mind. He had created. He had created everything—or so he thought. He had made this leap, this ascension. But now? He couldn't shake the feeling that he was no more than a specimen in a jar, a puppet on strings, manipulated by hands he could never touch.

Before he could contemplate further, everything began to distort. The brilliance of the Architects' realm began to waver, bleeding into a blackness that felt too familiar, too constricting. Leonard felt the pull of something, like his consciousness was being retracted, drawn into the gravity well of a smaller, more familiar space.

He awoke with a start, gasping for air. His heart hammered in his chest.

The room was his—his bedroom, with its dim bedside lamp and the scattered textbooks on his desk. The hum of the air conditioner, the faint light coming through the blinds—it was all too perfect. Too mundane.

"Was it . . . was it just a dream?" Leonard muttered to himself, dragging a hand through his tangled hair. It didn't feel like a dream. It couldn't be.

But something was wrong. His thoughts were wrong. He felt stretched, cracked open, as if something had altered the very fabric of his understanding. Concepts, equations, ideas—impossibly complex, impossible to reconcile—swirled through his mind. He could see them, see the connections, the realities that threaded through each other. There was no beginning. No end.

His gaze fell on the bedside clock.

3:49 AM.

The exact moment I had the solution, he thought. The grand unified theory. The answer to everything

He watched, transfixed, as the numbers failed to change. The clock was frozen, its digital display mocking him with its stillness. Leonard's breath hitched as a creeping dread worked its way through his veins.

Was this his reality? Or had he slipped deeper? Another layer?

The silence of the room pressed in on him as the minutes—if they were even minutes—stretched, stretched, stretched. Time no longer had a shape, a beginning, or an end. He was caught, spinning in a loop, a perfect paradox, unable to escape. Couldn't escape.

What if this was just another test? Another layer of the machine? A simulation within a simulation, a higher form of observation, trapping him in a play that had no final curtain.

He thought about calling someone—calling anyone—some colleague who might tell him it was all just a dream. But how could he trust them? Were they real? Or were they just . . . part of the design?

He tried to remember the one simple equation he had created, the single, elegant arrangement of numbers and symbols that had unraveled the universe for him. It had come to him so effortlessly once, but now, as he groped through the cluttered corridors of his mind, it evaded him. He took a deep breath, his eyes glued to the clock, its frozen face an unforgiving witness to his predicament.

He was no longer sure of anything.

The days outside—the sunlight creeping through the blinds—was it real? Or just another simulation?

And that question, that singular thought, echoed in his mind like a final riddle.

Who created the first creator?

The Waning Light
of Pallid Fates

In the twilight of a pallid autumn, when the very air seemed pregnant with eldritch whispers, I, Elias Draycott, received a missive that would irrevocably alter the course of my existence. The letter, penned in a spidery hand that bespoke both refinement and a certain tremulous urgency, bore the seal of Lord Albinus Harrow, a name I had encountered only in the most obscure of occult texts.

The contents of this correspondence spoke of the Codex Albescens, a tome of such arcane significance that its mere mention sent a frisson of anticipation through my scholarly frame. Lord Harrow's words hinted at "ancient truths" that had long eluded the grasp of mortal understanding, truths that he believed I alone possessed the acumen to decipher. The promise of a substantial remuneration, coupled with the intoxicating allure of forbidden knowledge, compelled me to accept his invitation with unseemly haste.

My journey to the remote estate of Dunmere was fraught with portents that, had I possessed the wisdom to heed them, should have turned me back forthwith. The sea voyage was a nightmare of howling gales and waves that seemed to reach up with grasping, foam-flecked fingers. The ancient vessel creaked and groaned as if in protest of its destination, and I fancied I could hear whispered lamentations in the wind that whipped about the rigging.

Upon reaching the decrepit harbor, I found myself confronted by a populace whose demeanor spoke of generations of nameless dread. Rheumy eyes followed my progress through the ramshackle streets, and more than once I caught snatches of hushed conversation that ceased abruptly at my approach. An aged crone, her visage a map of deep-etched wrinkles, clutched at my sleeve with surprising strength.

"Turn back, learned sir," she croaked, her breath reeking of decay. "Procul Hall holds naught but madness and death for the likes of ye."

I shook off her warning with a nervous laugh, attributing her words to the superstitions of an isolated community. Yet as I began the ascent to Lord Harrow's estate, following a path that wound like a diseased vein through sickly, twisted trees, I could not shake the feeling that I was being observed by countless unseen eyes.

The mist thickened as I climbed, taking on an unnatural opacity that seemed to devour both light and sound. Shapes moved at the periphery of my vision, resolving into nothing more than gnarled branches when I turned to look directly. The very air grew heavy, laden with a metallic tang that coated my tongue and set my teeth on edge.

It was with a mixture of relief and mounting apprehension that I at last beheld Procul Hall in its full, decaying grandeur. The Gothic edifice loomed before me, its spires and turrets reaching toward a sky of leaden gray. Gargoyles leered from their perches, their features worn smooth by the relentless assault of time and elements, yet still possessing a malevolence that sent a shudder through my very soul.

As I approached the great oaken doors, I became aware of a sound that seemed to emanate from the very stones of the building. It was a melody of such ethereal quality that I found myself straining to discern its source, yet it danced perpetually at the edge of perception, flitting between beauty and a discordance that set my nerves ajangle.

The doors swung open with a groan of ancient hinges, revealing a foyer shrouded in shadows and neglect. Cobwebs festooned the vaulted ceilings, and the faded remnants of once-opulent tapestries hung in tattered shreds from the damp stone walls. The air within was thick with the musty odor of decay, overlaid with that same unsettling metallic scent I had noted on my approach.

It was then that I first laid eyes upon Lord Albinus Harrow. He stood at the far end of the hall, a figure of such pallor that he seemed more wraith than man. His movements as he approached were deliberate, almost mechanical, as if each step required great concentration. When he extended his hand in greeting, I noted with some alarm the fine tremor that ran through his fingers.

"Welcome, Mr. Draycott," he intoned, his voice carrying the hollow resonance of a tomb. "I trust your journey was not too . . . taxing."

As I grasped his hand, I was struck by the chill of his flesh, so cold as to be nearly painful to the touch. His eyes, set deep in a face as pale and smooth as carved marble, seemed to reflect more light than they absorbed, giving him an aspect that was at once alluring and deeply unsettling.

"I must confess, Lord Harrow," I replied, striving to keep the tremor from my own voice, "the journey was not without its challenges. But the promise of the Codex Albescens has sustained me through far worse trials."

A smile flickered across Harrow's bloodless lips, gone so quickly I might have imagined it. "Ah, yes, the Codex. It has sustained many through the long years, Mr. Draycott. And destroyed not a few in the process. But come, you must be weary. Allow me to show you to your quarters, and then we shall discuss the task that lies before us."

As he led me deeper into the labyrinthine corridors of Procul Hall, I could not shake the sensation that we were being observed. Shadows seemed to flit at the corners of my vision, and more than once I caught glimpses of pale faces peering from darkened doorways, only to vanish when I turned my head for a closer look.

The room to which I was shown was spacious yet oppressive, dominated by a massive four-poster bed draped in faded velvet. A fire sputtered fitfully in the grate, casting writhing shadows upon the walls. As Lord Harrow bid me goodnight, I could have sworn I saw a flicker of something—pity? fear?—in his strange, luminous eyes.

Left alone, I sank onto the edge of the bed, my mind awhirl with the events of the day. The melody I had noted earlier seemed to have followed me, its haunting strains now punctuated by what sounded disturbingly like distant, mocking laughter. As I lay down to sleep, I could not shake the feeling that I had stepped into a narrative far older and far more terrible than I could possibly comprehend.

Little did I know then how prophetic that sentiment would prove to be, nor the cosmic horrors that awaited me within the pages of the Codex Albescens. For in accepting Lord Harrow's invitation, I had unwittingly set in motion a chain of events that would shake the very foundations of reality and leave me forever changed, a trembling witness to truths no mortal mind was meant to encompass.

***

As I followed Lord Harrow through the labyrinthine corridors of Procul Hall, the oppressive silence was broken only by our footfalls echoing off the damp stone walls. The air grew increasingly thick with an unnameable miasma that seemed to cling to my very being, filling my lungs with each labored breath.

It was then that I first encountered the servants of this accursed place. They appeared suddenly, as if materializing from the very shadows that cloaked the hall's recesses. Their forms were of such ghastly pallor that I initially mistook them for specters, their waxen skin possessing a sickly, translucent quality that spoke of long years hidden from the sun's nourishing rays.

But it was their eyes that truly unsettled me to the very core of my being. Those orbs, set deep within sunken sockets, seemed to reflect an impossible amount of what little light permeated the gloom. They shone with an eldritch luminescence that I can only describe as hungry, as if they sought to devour the very essence of those upon whom they gazed.

These mute figures moved with an eerie synchronicity that defied natural explanation. Their gestures, used instead of speech, were executed with such precision that I found myself wondering if they shared some sort of collective consciousness. The thought sent a shudder of revulsion through my frame, yet I forced myself to rationalize their behavior as mere eccentricity, a product of long isolation in this remote and forsaken place.

Lord Harrow paid these unsettling servants no heed, leading me onward through the twisting passages with singular purpose. At last, we came upon a set of towering oaken doors, their surfaces carved with eldritch symbols that seemed to writhe and shift beneath my gaze. With a gesture that was at once imperious and tremulous, Harrow bade the doors open.

The library that lay beyond was a vast chamber that stretched beyond the limits of my comprehension. Shelves of ancient tomes reached upward into shadows so deep that I could not discern where they ended, if indeed they ended at all. The air was thick with the musty odor of decaying vellum and something else, a scent both metallic and organic that set my teeth on edge.

But it was not the sheer scope of the collection that drew my eye. No, my attention was inexorably drawn to a single pedestal at the chamber's center, upon which rested an object of such eldritch significance that I felt my very sanity begin to fray at its mere presence.

The Codex Albescens.

Even from a distance, I could see that the manuscript was bound in leather of a pallor that defied natural pigmentation. It seemed to pulse with an inner light, as if it were a living, breathing entity rather than mere parchment and hide. As we approached, I noted with mounting horror that the leather bore an unsettling texture, one that spoke of an origin far removed from any earthly creature.

"Behold, Mr. Draycott," Lord Harrow intoned, his voice carrying the hollow resonance of a tomb, "the object of our mutual fascination."

With trembling hands, he opened the codex, revealing pages covered in script of such alien design that my eyes refused to focus upon it. The characters seemed to shift and dance across the page, rearranging themselves in patterns that spoke of geometries unknown to our paltry three-dimensional understanding.

"This, my dear Elias," Harrow continued, his eyes gleaming with a feverish light, "is a record of what my family has long called 'The Pallid Dance.' It is a celestial event of such cosmic significance that it bridges the very fabric of dimensions."

I leaned closer, fighting against the wave of nausea that threatened to overwhelm me as I gazed upon the impossible text. "And you believe I can translate this . . . this abomination?"

Harrow's lips curled into a smile that held no warmth. "I do not merely believe, Mr. Draycott. I know. For you see, you were chosen for this task long before you were even aware of our correspondence."

His words sent a chill through my very soul, for they hinted at machinations far beyond my ken. As I stood there, transfixed by the eldritch manuscript before me, I became acutely aware of the servants gathering at the library's periphery. Their eyes, those hungry, light-devouring orbs, were fixed upon me with an intensity that spoke of anticipation.

In that moment, I understood with terrible clarity that I had not come to Procul Hall of my own volition. No, I had been lured here, a moth drawn to the flame of forbidden knowledge. And like that hapless insect, I feared that my fate was to be consumed by forces far beyond my comprehension.

Yet even as this realization dawned, I found myself unable to tear my gaze from the Codex Albescens. Its siren call of cosmic secrets was too potent to resist, and I knew, with a certainty that bordered on madness, that I would plumb its depths regardless of the cost to my sanity or my very soul.

For in the presence of such eldritch truths, what value could a mere mortal mind hold? We are but motes of dust in the vast, uncaring cosmos, our existence as fleeting and insignificant as the beat of a gnat's wing. And in the face of such cosmic indifference, what choice did I have but to embrace the madness that awaited me within those pallid pages?

With a trembling hand, I reached out to touch the codex, feeling its unnatural warmth beneath my fingertips. As I did so, I fancied I could hear, at the very edge of perception, the faint strains of an otherworldly melody. It was the music of the spheres, the song of realities beyond our own, beckoning me to lose myself in its impossible harmonies.

Lord Harrow's voice seemed to come from a great distance as he spoke once more. "The Pallid Dance approaches, Mr. Draycott. Time grows short. You must decipher the codex's secrets if we are to take our rightful place among the cosmic dancers."

I nodded, barely aware of my own actions as I sank deeper into the codex's thrall. The library around me seemed to fade, the boundaries between reality and the realm of nightmares growing ever more tenuous. And as I began my work, I knew that I was taking the first steps on a journey from which there could be no return.

For in seeking to unlock the secrets of The Pallid Dance, I had unwittingly become a participant in a cosmic ballet of such terrible beauty that it threatened to unmake the very fabric of my being. And in the shadowed halls of Procul Hall, surrounded by servants whose true nature I dared not contemplate, I embarked upon a quest that would lead me to the very brink of madness and beyond.

***

In the oppressive gloom of Procul Hall's vast library, I, Elias Draycott, found myself inexorably drawn into the eldritch depths of the Codex Albescens. The pallid tome lay before me, its pages seeming to writhe with an inner life that defied rational explanation. As I bent my not inconsiderable intellect to the task of deciphering its arcane script, I felt the tendrils of an alien consciousness brushing against the very fabric of my sanity.

Hours stretched into days as I pored over the manuscript, my mind reeling from the cosmic horrors hinted at within its pages. References to "the turning wheel of pale fire" and "the banquet of light" recurred with maddening frequency, each phrase laden with a significance that I could sense but not fully comprehend. The text possessed a hypnotic quality that caused me to lose all sense of time, emerging from my studies to find that entire days had passed in what felt like mere moments.

It was during one such protracted session of study that I first became aware of the strange occurrences that would come to plague my waking hours and haunt my fitful slumbers. As I sat hunched over the Codex, the silence of the library was shattered by the sound of faint, mocking laughter echoing through the halls. I started, my pen clattering to the floor as I whirled to face the source of the sound, only to find myself alone in the cavernous chamber.

In the days that followed, these unsettling incidents multiplied with alarming rapidity. Ghostly figures flitted at the edges of my vision, vanishing when I turned to look directly at them. The tarnished mirrors that adorned the halls of Procul Hall seemed to ripple with movement, reflecting impossible vistas and grotesque, inhuman shapes that vanished in the blink of an eye.

But it was in my dreams that the true horror began to manifest. Night after night, I found myself transported to a grand ballroom of impossible proportions, its vaulted ceiling lost in shadows that seemed to pulse with malevolent life. Spectral dancers whirled across the gleaming floor, their movements a mockery of human grace. Try as I might, I could never glimpse their faces, which remained obscured by a silvery mist that clung to their forms like a second skin.

As I delved deeper into the Codex Albescens, Lord Harrow began to reveal fragments of his family's sordid history. With a fervor that bordered on madness, he spoke of generations of Harrows who had served as caretakers of Procul Hall, their sacred duty to guard the eldritch tome that now consumed my every waking moment.

"We are the keepers of secrets that would shatter the fragile minds of lesser men," Harrow intoned, his eyes gleaming with an inner light that I found increasingly disquieting. "For centuries, my ancestors have sought to unlock the cosmic truths hidden within the Codex Albescens, to understand the ineffable whiteness that lies beyond the veil of our paltry reality."

As Harrow's revelations continued, I felt a growing sense of unease coiling in the pit of my stomach. He spoke of rituals conducted in the depths of Procul Hall, arcane ceremonies designed to pierce the veil between worlds and commune with entities of such cosmic significance that the mere thought of their existence threatened to overwhelm my sanity.

"But the price of such knowledge is steep," Harrow continued, his voice dropping to a hoarse whisper. "Many of my forebears were driven to madness by the truths they glimpsed, their minds unable to encompass the vast, uncaring cosmos that exists beyond our limited perceptions."

It was then that Harrow revealed his ultimate goal, a plan of such breathtaking audacity and cosmic significance that I felt my grip on reality begin to slip. With fevered intensity, he spoke of completing the ritual described in the Codex Albescens, a ceremony that he believed would grant him—and by extension, all of humanity—a state of transcendence and enlightenment beyond mortal comprehension.

"Imagine it, Elias," he breathed, his eyes wide with a fervor that bordered on mania. "To shed the limitations of our frail, earthly forms and ascend to a higher plane of existence. To dance among the stars and commune with beings of such cosmic significance that our current state would seem no more than that of an amoeba in comparison."

Yet even as Harrow waxed rhapsodic about the glories that awaited us, I felt a growing suspicion taking root in the depths of my being. There was something in his manner, a barely perceptible tremor in his voice and a wild light in his eyes, that spoke of motivations far darker and more selfish than he was willing to admit.

As I returned to my studies, my mind awhirl with the implications of Harrow's revelations, I found myself approaching the Codex Albescens with newfound caution. The eldritch script seemed to writhe beneath my gaze, hinting at cosmic horrors that defied comprehension. And with each passing day, I became increasingly certain that the truths hidden within its pages were not meant for mortal minds to grasp.

In the depths of night, as I tossed and turned in my chamber, plagued by dreams of ghostly dancers and impossible geometries, I could not shake the feeling that I had become embroiled in something far beyond my understanding. The very walls of Procul Hall seemed to pulse with an alien life, and I fancied I could hear the faint strains of unearthly music echoing through its twisted corridors.

As I lay there, my mind teetering on the brink of madness, I knew with terrible certainty that I was approaching a crossroads. The path that lay before me led into realms of cosmic horror that no mortal was meant to tread. And yet, like a moth drawn inexorably to the flame, I found myself unable to turn away from the siren call of forbidden knowledge that emanated from the Codex Albescens.

For in that moment, suspended between waking and dreaming, I understood that I had become a pawn in a game of cosmic significance, a mere mote of dust caught in the turning of vast and uncaring wheels. And as the pallid light of dawn began to creep through my window, I steeled myself for the horrors that I knew must inevitably come, driven by an insatiable hunger for truths that threatened to unmake the very fabric of my being.

***

As I delved deeper into the eldritch depths of the Codex Albescens, the very fabric of reality seemed to fray around me. The pallid tome, with its unspeakable secrets, had become both my obsession and my torment. It was during one of my fevered translation sessions that I stumbled upon a revelation so horrifying, so utterly antithetical to the laws of nature as I understood them, that I felt my sanity begin to slip away like sand through an hourglass.

Hidden within the margins of the codex, scrawled in a hand that trembled with madness, were annotations that spoke of the true nature of "The Pallid Dance." Far from the benign celestial event that Lord Harrow had described, it was in fact a summoning—a cosmic invocation of an entity so vast and terrible that my mind recoiled from the very thought of its existence.

Eilapoc.

The name itself seemed to writhe on the page, a collection of syllables that no human tongue was meant to utter. The annotations described this cosmic horror as "a vast light that devours shadow, thought, and flesh." As I read these words, I felt a chill that went beyond mere physical sensation, as if the very essence of my being had been touched by some unspeakable cold from beyond the stars.

My hands shaking, I turned to the next page, only to find it blank save for a single phrase repeated over and over: "The light comes. The light consumes. The light is all."

It was in this state of mounting dread that I discovered an old journal tucked away in a forgotten corner of the library. The leather binding was cracked and worn, the pages yellowed with age. As I opened it, a cloud of dust rose, carrying with it the musty scent of long-buried secrets.

The journal belonged to one Aldous Harrow, an ancestor of my host, who had witnessed a partial manifestation of Eilapoc some two centuries past. His account, penned in a hand that grew increasingly erratic as the pages progressed, spoke of a ritual gone awry—a premature summoning that had brought forth but a fraction of the entity's true form.

"Those who gazed upon it," Aldous wrote, his script barely legible, "were transformed in an instant. Their eyes, once windows to the soul, became naught but vacant orbs reflecting an impossible radiance. Their bodies stood, breathing yet utterly lifeless, as if their very essence had been consumed by that voracious light."

I slammed the journal shut, my breath coming in ragged gasps. The implications were too terrible to contemplate. Lord Harrow's ancestors had not merely studied the Codex Albescens—they had attempted to harness its power, with catastrophic results.

As the days wore on and my work on the translation continued, I found myself plagued by visions of increasing intensity and horror. The boundaries between waking and dreaming grew blurred, reality itself seeming to warp and twist around me like a living thing.

It was on a night when the moon hung bloated and sickly in the sky that I experienced the most vivid and terrifying of these visions. I awoke, or thought I did, to find myself standing in the grand ballroom of Procul Hall. The room, which I had glimpsed only briefly during my initial tour of the estate, was now a decaying husk of its former glory. Tattered curtains hung like funeral shrouds from the windows, and the once-gleaming floor was thick with dust and debris.

Yet even in this state of ruin, I could hear the faintest strains of music—an otherworldly melody that seemed to emanate from the very walls themselves. As I stood there, transfixed by the eerie tune, the room began to change before my eyes.

In a flash of impossible light, the decay fell away, revealing the ballroom as it must have appeared in its heyday. The transformation was so sudden and complete that I felt my mind reel, unable to process the shift from ruin to opulence.

Countless figures, pale as death and clad in finery from a bygone era, swayed in a macabre dance across the gleaming floor. Their movements were fluid yet unnatural, as if they were puppets controlled by some unseen, cosmic hand. I tried to focus on their faces, but found that my gaze slid away, unable to comprehend what I saw—or perhaps unwilling to do so.

As quickly as it had appeared, the vision faded, leaving me once more in the decaying ballroom. But now I could see faint, phosphorescent footprints on the dusty floor—a ghostly record of that impossible dance.

I fled from that accursed room, my heart pounding in my chest, only to collide with Lord Harrow in the corridor outside.

His appearance shocked me to my core. The man who had greeted me upon my arrival at Procul Hall—composed, if somewhat eccentric—was gone. In his place stood a wild-eyed figure, his hair disheveled and his clothing in disarray.

"The wheel turns, Mr. Draycott," he babbled, his eyes darting about as if seeing things invisible to my perception. "Can you not feel it? Time unravels, the boundaries weaken. Soon, oh soon, the dance will begin anew!"

I tried to calm him, to make sense of his ramblings, but he shook off my attempts with surprising strength. As he lurched away down the darkened hall, I heard him muttering, "The light comes. The light consumes. The light is all."

Those words, echoing the phrase I had found scrawled in the Codex Albescens, sent a shudder through my very soul. For I knew then, with a certainty that defied all reason, that we stood upon the precipice of some cosmic cataclysm—a summoning that threatened not just our sanity, but the very fabric of reality itself.

As I returned to my chambers, my mind awhirl with eldritch visions and forbidden knowledge, I could not shake the feeling that I was but a mote of dust caught in the turning of vast and uncaring wheels. The Pallid Dance approached, and with it, the awakening of an entity beyond human comprehension.

In the depths of that long and terrible night, as the boundaries between worlds grew ever thinner, I steeled myself for what was to come. For I knew that I alone stood between Lord Harrow's mad ambitions and the unleashing of a cosmic horror that threatened to consume all of existence in its insatiable, pallid light.

***

On that fateful night, when the stars aligned in a configuration unseen for aeons, I found myself drawn inexorably to the grand ballroom of Procul Hall. The air thrummed with an eldritch energy that set my very teeth on edge, a palpable manifestation of cosmic forces beyond mortal ken. Lord Harrow, his eyes alight with a fervor that bordered on madness, ushered me and his cadre of waxen-faced servants into the chamber, now transformed into a grotesque facsimile of a ritual space.

Candles burned in brass holders, their flames an unnatural, pallid blue that seemed to devour the shadows rather than cast them. The flickering light played across the faces of the assembled, turning familiar features into masks of otherworldly horror. At the far end of the hall stood an ancient pipe organ, its pipes tarnished with age and disuse. Yet as we gathered, its keys began to depress of their own accord, giving voice to a melody so alien and discordant that I felt my sanity begin to fray at its very sound.

"The time has come," Harrow intoned, his voice carrying an authority that seemed to resonate from beyond the veil of our reality. "The stars are right, and the Pallid Dance shall commence!"

As if summoned by his words, spectral forms began to materialize in the center of the ballroom. These were the dancers I had glimpsed in my fevered visions, their ethereal bodies flickering in and out of existence like heat shimmer on a scorching day. Their faces, when I could bear to look upon them, were a blur of features that shifted and changed with each passing moment, as if unable to settle on a single visage.

Harrow raised the Codex Albescens high above his head, its pallid pages seeming to glow with an inner light. As he began to recite an incantation in a language that no human tongue was meant to utter, I felt a wave of nausea wash over me. The very air seemed to ripple and distort, and I watched in horror as the walls of the ballroom began to dissolve like mist before the morning sun.

In their place, a vista of such cosmic magnitude was revealed that my mind recoiled from its implications. An infinite void stretched out before us, filled with whirling stars and nebulae of impossible colors. Vast shapes moved in the distance, their forms so alien and terrible that I dared not focus my gaze upon them for fear of losing what little remained of my sanity.

As Harrow's chant reached a fever pitch, a change came over the spectral dancers. Their forms began to coalesce, becoming more solid and real with each passing moment. And then, with a sound like the tearing of reality itself, a blinding radiance burst forth from the center of their circle.

Eilapoc had come.

The entity manifested as a pillar of pale light so intense that it seared my eyes even through closed lids. I could feel its alien consciousness pressing against the boundaries of my mind, threatening to overwhelm my very sense of self. The dancers, now fully corporeal, were drawn inexorably towards the light. Their faces contorted in a horrifying blend of ecstasy and terror as their bodies were consumed, dissolving into motes of radiance that were absorbed into the growing maelstrom.

Lord Harrow, his face a mask of rapturous anticipation, stepped forward with arms outstretched. "At last!" he cried, his voice barely audible above the otherworldly howl of the wind that now whipped through the chamber. "I offer myself as vessel and herald! Let the merging be complete!"

But as he approached the pillar of light, something went terribly awry. Instead of the transcendence he so clearly expected, the radiance engulfed him in an instant. I watched in horror as Harrow's body seemed to ignite from within, his flesh turning to ash and scattering on the eldritch winds. In mere moments, all that remained of the man who had lured me to this accursed place was a swirling eddy of grey dust.

It was then, in that moment of abject terror, that I realized the true nature of my role in this cosmic drama. I was not merely an observer or translator, but the focus of the ritual itself—the "scribe" meant to document Eilapoc's arrival and usher in an age of enlightenment that would spell doom for all of humanity.

The entity's attention turned to me, and I felt the weight of its alien regard like a physical force threatening to crush me into nothingness. In that instant, I knew that to allow this ritual to continue would mean the end of everything I had ever known or loved. With a desperation born of sheer terror, I lunged for a nearby brazier, toppling it and sending its contents scattering across the floor.

The dry wood of the ancient ballroom caught fire almost instantly, flames licking up the walls and engulfing the tattered remnants of once-opulent tapestries. As the conflagration spread, the spectral dancers began to scream—a sound so filled with otherworldly anguish that it threatened to shatter my eardrums.

To my amazement and relief, the growing inferno seemed to affect the cosmic entity. The pillar of light began to waver and flicker, its radiance dimming as if unable to maintain its presence in our reality in the face of such mundane destruction. The void beyond the dissolving walls began to recede, reality reasserting itself with each lick of flame.

As I stumbled towards the exit, choking on acrid smoke and the lingering stench of otherworldly energies, I cast one final glance back at the scene of eldritch horror. The dancers were fading, their forms becoming translucent once more as they were drawn back into whatever nameless realm had spawned them. And at the center of it all, the light that was Eilapoc pulsed and writhed, fighting against the encroaching flames but ultimately beginning to retreat.

I fled then, my mind reeling from the cosmic horrors I had witnessed and the knowledge that I had, through sheer chance and desperate action, perhaps averted a catastrophe of unimaginable proportions. As I raced through the burning halls of Procul Hall, I could not shake the feeling that this victory, if it could be called such, was but a temporary reprieve.

For I knew, with a certainty that chilled me to my very core, that entities such as Eilapoc were eternal and patient. The stars would align again, and the Pallid Dance would resume. And when that time came, would there be another fool like myself, willing to risk sanity and soul to hold back the tide of cosmic horror that lurked just beyond the veil of our fragile reality?

***

As I stumbled from the inferno that Procul Hall had become, my lungs burning with each ragged breath, I felt the very foundations of my sanity crumbling like the ancient stones around me. The night air, thick with smoke and the lingering stench of eldritch energies, offered no respite from the horrors I had witnessed. My legs, weak and trembling, carried me to the edge of the cliffs that overlooked the turbulent sea below.

There, collapsing upon the dew-dampened grass, I turned my gaze back to the burning mansion. The flames, which had been my salvation, now consumed the accursed structure with a voracious appetite. As I watched, transfixed by the dance of destruction, I saw something that chilled me to the very marrow of my bones.

Amidst the conflagration, a pale light flickered—not the orange glow of mundane fire, but the otherworldly radiance of Eilapoc. It pulsed once, twice, a cosmic heartbeat that seemed to resonate with the very fabric of reality. Then, with a sound that was felt rather than heard, it vanished into the roiling waters of the sea.

I know not how long I lay there, my mind reeling from the cosmic horrors I had witnessed. When consciousness fully returned, I found myself in a small fishing village some miles down the coast, tended to by simple folk who could not begin to comprehend the eldritch truths that now burdened my psyche.

Weeks have passed since that fateful night, yet I find no peace. Sleep, once a refuge, has become a torment. In my dreams, I see again the pale light of Eilapoc, feel its alien consciousness pressing against the fragile barriers of my mind. The melody of the Pallid Dance echoes in the depths of my being, a siren song that threatens to drag me back into that maelstrom of cosmic horror.

It is in a state of near-madness that I now pen this account, a feeble attempt to warn others of the terrors that lurk just beyond the veil of our perceived reality. Yet even as I write, I am gripped by the terrible certainty that my words will fall upon deaf ears, or worse, entice some other fool to seek out the forbidden knowledge that nearly destroyed me.

For I fear, with a dread that gnaws at the very core of my being, that the ritual is not truly over. The Pallid Dance may have been interrupted, but Eilapoc is eternal. It waits, patient and implacable, in realms beyond human comprehension. And when the stars align once more, when the cosmic wheels turn to that dread configuration, it will return.

Even now, as I gaze out my window at the night sky, I see signs that fill me with nameless terror. The stars, once a comforting blanket of light in the vast darkness, now seem to mock me with their cold, distant glimmer. For in their arrangement, I perceive a pattern that should not be—a faint, pale wheel slowly turning in the heavens.

Is it merely a product of my fractured psyche, a manifestation of the madness that now plagues me? Or is it a sign, a cosmic herald of Eilapoc's inevitable return? I dare not contemplate the implications, for to do so would surely shatter what little remains of my sanity.

And yet, I cannot look away. The wheel turns, ever so slowly, and with each rotation, I feel the boundaries between worlds growing thinner. The veil that separates our reality from the realms of cosmic horror frays at the edges, threatening to tear asunder at any moment.

In my darkest moments, I find myself longing for the blissful ignorance of my former life. How simple, how blessedly mundane were my concerns before I set foot in Procul Hall! Now, burdened with knowledge no mortal was meant to possess, I see the world through eyes that have glimpsed the infinite. And in that vastness, I have seen the utter insignificance of humanity.

We are but motes of dust, our lives as fleeting and inconsequential as the beat of an insect's wing. The cosmic entities that lurk beyond our comprehension care nothing for our petty concerns, our hopes and fears. To them, we are less than ants, our entire civilization no more noteworthy than a colony to be carelessly swept aside.

And yet, paradoxically, it is this very insignificance that now drives me to warn others. For if humanity is to have any hope of survival in a universe indifferent to our existence, we must be prepared. We must steel ourselves against the cosmic horrors that threaten to engulf us, to drive us mad with their mere presence.

But how does one prepare for the unknowable? How can we, with our limited perceptions and fragile minds, hope to stand against entities that defy the very laws of nature as we understand them? The task seems insurmountable, and yet we must try. For to do otherwise is to accept our doom, to go meekly into the eternal night that awaits us all.

As I write these words, I feel the last vestiges of my former self slipping away. The man I was before Procul Hall, before the Codex Albescens and the Pallid Dance, is gone forever. In his place is a hollow shell, a being caught between worlds, forever marked by the touch of cosmic forces beyond mortal ken.

And so I end this account, not with hope, but with a warning. To those who would seek out the hidden truths of our universe, who would pierce the veil between worlds in search of forbidden knowledge, I say this: turn back. Close your eyes to the eldritch horrors that lurk in the shadows of reality. For once seen, they can never be unseen, and the price of such knowledge is higher than any mortal can bear.

As for me, I shall continue my vigil, watching the wheel of stars turn slowly in the night sky. And I shall wait, with equal parts dread and resignation, for the day when Eilapoc returns to claim what was denied it. For I know now that there are fates far worse than death, and that the boundaries between sanity and madness, between reality and nightmare, are far more tenuous than we dare imagine.

In the cosmic dance of creation and destruction, we are but fleeting partners, destined to be swept away by forces beyond our comprehension. And in the end, when the pale light of Eilapoc bathes the world once more, we shall all join in the Pallid Dance, our minds and bodies consumed by the insatiable hunger of the cosmos.

Fortress Bold

The Siege Begins

The sun sank low upon the horizon, its fiery light spilling across the great plain where Lord Victor Eldran's vast encampment stretched out in the gathering dusk. The camp was like an ocean of tents, their dark forms shifting and rippling in the evening breeze, as banners of crimson and sable fluttered from the poles, whispering secrets in the wind. The scent of smoke hung thick in the air, a pungent mix of burning wood and ash from the countless fires that crackled and flickered across the field, while the rhythmic clang of hammer and anvil rose from the blacksmiths forging the great siege engines, each one a heavy, ominous promise for the days ahead.

Above, high upon the distant ridgeline, the great Fortress Bold loomed in silhouette, its stone walls black as night, standing resolute and proud against a mighty mountain and the fading light. The fortress seemed to drink in the very essence of the twilight, its walls an impenetrable mass of shadow, each stone hewn from the earth as though it had risen from the land itself. It was a structure born of legend and defiance, a place where time and tide had yet to breach its defenses. Tales were told in every corner of the realm—whispers of the fortress's unyielding strength, the ancient secrets buried within its heart, and the walls that had withstood countless sieges over the centuries. It was not merely a fortification; it was a symbol, an enduring testament to all that was steadfast and true.

On the highest battlements, King Harold Bold stood alone, his gaze sweeping over the enemy lines below. His steel-gray eyes, cold and calculating, betrayed no emotion as they lingered on the distant campfires of Eldran's army. Clad in the blackened armor of one who had fought through the ages, his figure was a monument of strength and stoicism. His armor, marked with the scars of countless battles, reflected the dying light of the sun, casting flickers of fire across his form. He stood motionless, a figure of iron, unyielding in the face of the enemy. Beside him stood General Alric Thorn, his most trusted companion and strategist, a man whose mind was as sharp as his blade.

"That scum Eldran seethes with rage at our mastery of his northern realms," Alric spoke, a grim mirth in his voice. "How dare he dream of victory against our might."

"He seeks a victory but in a most cowardly way," Harold's voice was low, laden with the wisdom of long years. "'Tis not breaching these mighty walls he seeks, but to bring us low through hunger's slow embrace."

"For well he knows," Alric rejoined, "that by strength of sword and spear alone, these battlements shall ne'er yield to his assault. He wishes to bring us low through hunger's slow embrace."

Harold's gaze remained fixed upon the distant host, as though he sought to pierce the very veil of time with his unwavering stare. "Then let him make the attempt," he said at last, with cold words. "Time he wields as his weapon, yet time too shall prove his bane. These stones have stood fast through ages uncounted. Let us see how long his resolve endures against the immutable face of eternity."

Alric nodded in silent agreement, but there was a hint of unease in his eyes. "The men grow restless, my lord. They whisper of strange happenings—shadows that move without cause, weapons that shift as if alive."

Harold turned toward him then, his face an unreadable mask, the burden of centuries of leadership borne in the lines of his features. "The fortress protects its own," he said, his voice as firm as the stone beneath their feet.

Before Alric could respond, a voice rang out from behind them. "Your Majesty!" It was Dame Lira Variel, her youthful face flushed with urgency, her sword strapped at her side and her helm clutched beneath her arm. She moved with the purpose of one accustomed to battle's call.

"What is it, Dame Lira?" Harold asked, his tone clipped but steady.

"The scouts report movement near the eastern ridge," she said quickly, her voice edged with concern. "It seems Lord Eldran is positioning trebuchets under cover of darkness."

Harold nodded sharply, his mind already calculating the next steps. "See to it that our archers are ready. We will not be caught unaware. Let them know we are watching."

Lira saluted with a swift motion, turning to depart, but then paused, her eyes lingering on Harold for a moment longer than usual. A mixture of admiration and curiosity filled her gaze. "My lord," she ventured hesitantly, "do you truly believe this fortress can hold against such numbers?"

For a moment, Harold's stern countenance softened, though only for the briefest instant, as if a veil had been lifted. His voice, when it came, was quiet, but there was strength in it still. "The strength of this fortress lies not in its walls alone," he said, his gaze turning toward the heart of the fortress, "but in those who defend it."

As Lira departed to carry out her orders, Harold's eyes lingered on the central tower of Bold, where the very heart of the fortress beat. Every evening, as the sun dipped below the horizon, Harold retreated there alone, leaving even Alric to wonder at the purpose of his solitary vigil. What secrets did the king find in the solitude of that tower, where the stone was thick with history, and time seemed to slow in its shadow? Only Harold knew, and he kept his silence, as he always had.

***

Far below the looming walls of Fortress Bold, Lord Victor Eldran stood with his officers, the chill wind of the gathering dusk ruffling his sable cloak. He raised a spyglass of burnished brass to his eye, its intricate engravings catching the last rays of the setting sun. Before him stretched the stone ramparts of the fortress, their ancient majesty seeming to defy the very passage of time itself. The walls rose like a mountain of hewn rock, each block fitted with such precision that no mortal hand could have achieved it. Victor's lips curled into a smile—a cruel, calculating thing that spoke of ambition and malice intertwined.

"Magnificent," he murmured, lowering the spyglass, his voice rich with dark satisfaction and tinged with a hunger that could not be sated by mere conquest. "A shame it must fall under my fist, like so many lesser strongholds before it."

One of his captains, a stout man named Guthric, whose gaunt face bore the lines of countless campaigns etched deep as valleys, stepped forward. His eyes, set deep in their hollows, narrowed with concern as he gazed upon the impregnable fortress. "My lord," he began, his voice rough as gravel, "their defenses are formidable beyond measure. The reports speak of walls that have never known defeat, of armies within that cannot be counted, like stars in the night sky. Perhaps we should wait, my liege—starve them out as we planned, lest we dash ourselves against unyielding stone."

Victor's smile widened, though it deepened with a malice that seemed to darken the very air around him. "Patience, good Guthric, is a virtue I possess in abundance," he replied, his tone smooth as silk yet cold as ice. "But even patience must be honed to a keen edge by action, lest it grow dull and useless." He raised a gloved hand, adorned with rings of gold and precious gems, gesturing to the distant siege engines that were being assembled. Their massive wooden frames groaned under their own weight, like great beasts readying for battle. "Let them feel our breath upon their necks, a whisper of the storm to come."

Victor's eyes flashed with a cold fire as he turned to Guthric, his voice low and laden with the weight of remembered wrongs. "Have you forgotten so soon, my faithful captain, the deeds of Harold Bold and his armies in our northern realm? Shall I recount for you the tales of villages put to the torch, of fields salted and wells poisoned? Do you not recall the lamentations of our people, driven from their ancestral homes by the very man who now cowers behind these vaunted walls?"

He drew nearer to Guthric, his words now scarcely more than a whisper, yet they carried to the ears of all who stood nigh. "Think you of the children of Ravensmere, their small forms broken upon the cruel rocks of the fjord. Recall you the Widow's Vale, where not a single man was left to tend the once-bountiful fields. These are but a few of the crimes for which Harold Bold must render account."

Victor's hand came to rest upon the hilt of his sword, a gesture both casual and laden with portent. "Nay, good Guthric, we shall not tarry. For each day we bide is a day in which the shades of our fallen cry out for vengeance unanswered."

"But my lord," another officer, younger than Guthric and with fear writ plain upon his countenance, spoke hesitantly, his words nearly lost upon the wind, "they say... their walls are alive, that the very stones rise up to defend against those who would breach them."

Victor's laugh rang out—cold and mocking, a sound that seemed to chill the very marrow of those who heard it. "Superstition and craven fear," he scoffed, his voice biting like the frost of deepest winter. "Stone is stone, no matter how many tales are spun around it by minstrels and fools. We shall see how alive these walls are when they crumble before our might."

Yet as he turned back toward the fortress, his face darkened for a brief moment, like a cloud passing before the sun. The cruel mask slipped, and there was something in his eyes—a flicker of doubt, perhaps, or a memory of ancient warnings long forgotten. It vanished as quickly as it had come, but it was enough to make the officers glance nervously at each other, unsure whether it had been real or merely a trick of the fading light.

***

Within the heart of Fortress Bold, night fell swiftly, as if a great shroud had been drawn across the sky. The torches along the ancient stone walls sparkled like stars caught in the web of mortal craftsmanship, their light dancing upon the faces of the sentries who stood as still as carven images in the deepening gloom. Their keen eyes peered ever outward, marking each movement in the vast encampment that sprawled below like a dark sea.

In the great hall, where kings of old had feasted and made merry, the defenders of Bold gathered in solemn assembly. The tables, once moaning under the weight of kingly fare, now bore only the meanest of provisions—bread that seemed hewn from the very stones of the fortress, meat preserved with salt from long-depleted stores, and ale that had lost its spirit in the long wait for battle. Yet these men, descendants of a proud and ancient line, made do with what they had, for such is the way of those who stand against the tide of darkness.

Their laughter, when it came, was like the echo of merriment long past, ringing hollow in the vast chamber. Each man spoke softly to his neighbor, their words carrying the weight of mountains, for they knew well the peril that lay beyond their walls. Many were the tales told in hushed voices—of fell deeds and darker powers that moved in the world about them.

Apart from this gathering sat Dame Lira Variel. In her hands she held a blade of notable lineage, forged in the days when the stars were younger. With steady strokes, she drew a whetstone along its edge, the sound like the keening of ghosts in the shadowed hall. Yet her mind wandered far from this task, dwelling on the words of King Harold—words that rang with the surety of one who has looked into the heart of fate and found there no cause for fear.

But there were other words, too, that troubled her thoughts. Whispers that ran like dark water through the ranks of the defenders—tales of stones that moved of their own accord, of shadows that lingered where no shadow should be, and of a presence that dwelt within the very bones of Fortress Bold. These were matters that even Harold, for all his wisdom and strength, seemed loath to address.

"What troubles you, child of Variel?" The voice of General Alric came suddenly, startling Lira from her contemplation. She looked up to see him standing before her, his form wreathed in shadow save for where the torchlight caught upon his mail and helm.

Lira's gaze met his, and in that moment she saw not just the grizzled warrior who had stood at Harold's right hand through countless battles, but also a man burdened with knowledge beyond the ken of most mortals.

"Tell me true, Lord Alric," she said at last, her voice barely above a whisper. "What say you to these murmurings? Can it be that this fortress... that it draws breath as we do?"

A smile played across Alric's weathered features, though it did not reach his eyes. When he spoke, his words carried the strength of long years and hard-won wisdom.

"I have walked in Harold's shadow for more turns of the seasons than you have drawn breath, young Lira," he said. "I have seen wonders and terrors that would freeze the blood of lesser men. And in all my days, I have learned but one truth that stands above all others: there are some mysteries in this world that are not meant for the minds of men to unravel."

With those words, he turned and strode away, the scrape of his armor against stone fading into the hushed murmur of the hall. Lira remained seated, her blade forgotten in her lap, as she pondered the general's words and the secrets that lay hidden in the heart of Fortress Bold.

***

That night, as the moon waxed full and the stars glimmered like scattered gems upon the velvet sky, Dame Lira found herself wandering through the hushed corridors of Fortress Bold. Her footfalls, though light as a whisper, seemed to sing in the stillness, each step carrying her deeper into the heart of the ancient stronghold. The stone beneath her feet was cold and unyielding, yet it seemed to pulse with an energy that she could not name, as if the very foundations of the fortress were alive with some hidden power.

Her mind, restless as a caged bird, turned ever towards the central tower where King Harold retreated each eve, just as the sun's last golden rays kissed the western horizon. Never before had she questioned this ritual, accepting it as one of the many mysteries that shrouded her liege. But on this night, a strange compulsion drew her onward, as inexorable as the tide, guiding her steps through the labyrinthine passages.

Through shadowed halls she crept, her fingers trailing along the cool stone walls that seemed to whisper ancient secrets. At last, she came upon a great wooden door, its surface adorned with carvings so intricate and lifelike that they appeared to move in the flickering torchlight. Here were depicted the great deeds of ages past: valiant kings leading their armies to victory, fell beasts vanquished by heroes of old, and realms both fair and terrible that had long since passed into legend. Lira's breath caught in her throat as she beheld this tapestry of history, feeling as though she stood at the threshold of something far greater than herself.

Pressing her ear to the weathered oak, she caught the faint murmur of King Harold's voice from within. The words were strange to her ears, a language that seemed to flow like water and rumble like thunder, at once beautiful and terrifying in its otherworldliness.

Gathering her courage like a cloak about her shoulders, Lira pushed against the door, which opened with nary a sound. She peered into the chamber beyond, and what she beheld there would be forever etched upon her memory.

King Harold stood before an altar of such antiquity that it seemed to have grown from the very bedrock of the world. Its surface was not smooth, but rather carved with runes and symbols of power that pulsed with an inner light. The king's hands rested upon this stone, his fingers tracing patterns that seemed to shift and change even as Lira watched. From his lips poured forth words in that same arcane tongue, each syllable resonating with a power that made the very air tremble.

As Harold spoke, the chamber itself seemed to come alive. Shadows danced and writhed upon the walls like living things, taking on shapes that were at once familiar and utterly alien. The stone beneath Lira's feet shuddered and groaned, as if the fortress itself were stirring from a deep slumber. It was a sound that spoke of ages uncounted, of secrets buried in the bones of the earth.

A gasp escaped Lira's lips before she could stifle it, and Harold's head snapped up, his eyes finding her in an instant. Those eyes, which had always seemed to her as hard and unyielding as the fortress walls, now burned with an inner fire that spoke of knowledge beyond mortal ken.

"Who dares intrude upon this sacred rite?" His voice rang out, stern as a blade yet not unkind.

Realizing that concealment was now impossible, Lira stepped fully into the chamber, her legs trembling beneath her as if she stood before one of the gods themselves. "Forgive me, my lord," she managed, her voice scarcely more than a whisper in the vastness of the room. "I... I did not mean to disturb your solitude."

Harold regarded her for a long moment, his gaze seeming to pierce through to her very soul. Then, with a slight inclination of his head, he beckoned her forward.

"You should not be here, Dame Lira," he said quietly. "Yet perhaps it is fate that has guided your steps this night."

"My lord," Lira began, her voice quavering like a leaf in the wind, "I beg your pardon, but I... I had to know. What manner of place is this? What rite do you perform in the deepest watches of the night?"

A deep sigh escaped Harold's lips, and for a moment, he seemed to age before her eyes, as though the passage of countless years had left their mark upon him. His gaze returned to the altar, his fingers once more tracing the enigmatic patterns upon its surface.

"This fortress," he began, his voice low and reverent, "was not raised by the hands of men alone. Nay, it was forged in an age long past, when the world was younger and the boundaries between the seen and unseen were not so sharply drawn. It was built with purpose, bound by oaths that were ancient when the first kings of men raised their banners."

He placed his palm flat against the stone, and Lira could have sworn she saw a faint glow emanate from beneath his hand. "It lives, Dame Lira. It breathes as you and I do, for it must. Without its will, its strength... we would already be lost, swept away by the tides of darkness that lap at our gates."

Lira stared at her king, wonder and confusion warring within her breast. She opened her mouth to speak, but no words would come, for what response could there be to such a revelation?

"The siege that now besets us," Harold continued, his eyes distant as if gazing into the mists of time itself, "is but the first whisper of the storm that is to come. And with it, your understanding of the world and your place within it begins anew.

Oh, and Dame Lira... before I forget... do not speak of any of this... ever... "

As his words faded into the hushed air of the chamber, Lira felt as though she stood upon the brink of a great precipice, with the known world behind her and a vast, uncharted expanse stretching out before her feet. In that moment, she knew that nothing would ever be the same again.

The Fortress Awakens

As the sun first peeked over the eastern rim of the world, casting forth her radiance in hues of rose and amber, Fortress Bold stirred from its ancient slumber. The very stones of its walls, hewn in ages past and weathered by the long count of years, seemed to draw breath as one might rouse from deepest dreaming. Upon their surfaces, a sheen of otherworldly light danced and flickered, as elusive as the glimmer of stars upon a still mere, vanishing when the eye sought to capture its ethereal beauty.

High atop the loftiest tower of that mighty fastness stood King Harold, solitary as a sentinel against the breaking day. His hair, once dark as the depths of the deepest pit, now bore the silver threads of long years of rule and care, streaming in the chill winds that heralded the morn. His eyes, grey as the tumultuous seas in winter's grip, gazed out over the sprawling encampment of Lord Victor Eldran.

Such a sight might have struck terror into the heart of one less stalwart, yet Harold's mien remained as steadfast and unyielding as the very foundations of the mountain upon which his fortress stood. "They come," he murmured, his voice low and resonant as the echoes of ancient halls. "Like carrion birds to a field of slaughter, drawn by the scent of death and the promise of spoils."

No sooner had these words passed his lips than a presence began to manifest beside him, as if summoned by the very breath of his utterance. At first, it was naught but a shimmer in the air, as insubstantial as the gossamer threads of twilight that linger betwixt day and night. Yet slowly, with a grace that bespoke powers ancient and unfathomable, it took form: a figure wrought of translucent stone and living light, its shape akin to the spirits of lore, yet unmistakably other—a being that straddled the boundary between the seen and unseen realms, as old as the very foundations of the earth and as timeless as the stars that wheeled overhead in their endless dance. This was Mira, the Stone Spirit, bound to Fortress Bold by pacts sealed in the deeps of time and magics long forgotten.

"They come indeed, Harold master of the Fortress," Mira spoke, her voice carrying the whisper of wind through caverns untrodden since the shaping of the world. "But do you remember the price of our protection? The oath sworn in blood and stone, binding your line to this place until the breaking of the world?"

Harold's jaw set like weathered granite, and for but a heartbeat's span, a darkness akin to a storm cloud's shadow swept over his visage—a fleeting betrayal of inner turmoil, swiftly quelled beneath the weight of kingly resolve, whether born of remorse for choices long past or dread of trials yet to be faced. "I remember," he said, his words scarcely more than a whisper upon the autumn breeze. "How could I cast from mind such a solemn oath, borne through countless seasons of unceasing watch?"

Unknown to both king and spirit, another witnessed this exchange from the shadows of a nearby archway. Dame Lira Variel, her breath held as if by some enchantment, stood frozen in place, her hand gripping the hilt of her sword with such force that her knuckles shone white as bone beneath her skin. She dared not move, lest the slightest sound betray her presence and break the spell of this impossible moment.

Lira pressed herself against the cold stone as Harold passed, her heart thundering like the hooves of great wild horses upon the plains. The rough-hewn rock bit into her palms, a stark reminder of the fortress's unyielding nature. Her mind reeled, a maelstrom of questions swirling like autumn leaves caught in a gale. Yet she held her tongue, for in her heart, she knew that this secret was not meant for mortal ears. It was a thing of shadow and stone, of pacts made in the dark places of the world where even the bravest of men fear to tread.

"How many more times must I shield thee and thine?" Mira asked, her voice resonant with the echoes of ages past.

"We have a covenant," King Harold responded, his tone firm yet tinged with a note of desperation. "One that has been sealed with blood and honored through the long years. Thou hast a duty to—"

Mira's voice cut through his words like a blade of ice. "Speak not to me of duties, Harold son of kings. I know them full well, having upheld them through countless turnings of the seasons. I have stood guard over this place as thou hast marched forth to lay low one realm after another. Was that, too, part of our sacred pact, O King?"

"My deeds matter not in the eyes of our agreement, Mira," King Harold said, his voice low and resolute. "What matters is thy adherence to the covenant forged in times beyond memory."

Then, as swiftly as she had appeared, Mira the Stone Spirit bound to Fortress Bold vanished, leaving naught but a whisper of ancient power lingering in the air, and the weight of unspoken truths hanging heavy between those who remained.

As the sun climbed ever higher in the vault of heaven, casting long shadows across the ancient stones of Fortress Bold, King Harold began his descent. He moved with purpose through winding corridors that seemed to shift and change, as if the very fortress sought to confound those who would uncover its secrets. Down worn steps he went, each footfall echoing in the silence like the tolling of a great bell. At last, he came upon a door, small and unremarkable, set deep within the mountain's roots as if it had grown there over countless ages.

Harold paused, his weathered hand hovering over the ancient wood. With a furtive glance that spoke of long-held secrets and burdens too heavy for any one man to bear, he produced a key. It was a curious thing, fashioned of a metal that seemed to drink in the light, leaving naught but shadow in its wake. With a sound like the grinding of mountains, the lock yielded, and the door swung open on hinges that had not moved in an age of the world.

Beyond lay a passageway that plunged into the very heart of the mountain, twisting and turning like the coils of some great serpent. Harold followed its meandering path, guided by memory and the faint, ethereal glow of fungi that clung to the damp walls. These were no ordinary mushrooms, but rather the remnants of some ancient magic, their light pulsing in time with the beating of the mountain's stony heart.

At last, the winding path gave way to a chamber of such immensity that Harold felt as one who had stumbled upon the very forge of the world. The grand halls of Fortress Bold, mighty though they stood, would have been but a child's toy house set within this cavernous expanse. Here, the very air hung heavy with the dust of ages uncounted, each breath drawing in the essence of ancient mysteries and fell wisdom long hidden from the eyes of mortal men. The silence was not empty but filled with the echoes of forgotten songs and the murmur of secrets best left unspoken, as if the very stones themselves sought to impart their dark knowledge to those who dared venture into their domain.

At the cavern's heart, upon a dais of stone as ancient as the very bones of the earth, sat a figure that seemed to bridge the gap between legend and flesh. This was Elder Kaelion, once the most trusted of Harold's counselors, now a hermit in the shadowed depths of his own domain. His beard cascaded like a waterfall of starlight over robes of unadorned wool, and when his eyes opened at Harold's approach, they shone with a fierce gleam that bespoke both profound insight and the wildfire of one who has gazed too long into the abyss of forgotten lore.

"So," Kaelion's voice rasped, echoing through the vastness like the whisper of long-dead kings, "the lord of Fortress Bold deigns to visit the madman in his cell. What drives you to seek counsel from one you cast aside, Harold? Perhaps the weight of your crown grows too heavy for mortal shoulders to bear?"

Harold's countenance grew somber, as if the very shadows of twilight had descended upon his brow. "You know well why I have come, old friend. The enemy gathers at our gates like wolves at the fold, and Mira... Mira stirs in her ancient repose, her stony heart quickening with an ominous anticipation."

Kaelion's laugh was a thing of bitterness and shattered dreams, sharp enough to cut the very air. "Restless? Nay, Harold, she hungers. As I warned you she would, all those years ago when you forged your unholy pact with powers best left to sleep in the deep places of the world. Have you come seeking absolution for your sins, my king? Or merely reassurance that the price you paid was worth the power it bought?"

"I paid the price willingly," Harold growled, though his voice wavered like a candle flame in a draft. "My firstborn son... a sacrifice to imbue these walls with life and power unmatched in all the realms of men. A terrible cost, yes, but one I would pay again to safeguard our people."

"Aye," Kaelion nodded solemnly, his eyes filled with a sorrow as deep as the cavern itself, "and what a power it is. But such magic always demands more, Harold. It is never sated, never content. The fortress may protect you still, but for how long? Mira's appetite grows with each passing year, like a shadow lengthening at dusk. And when at last the sun sets, what then? What will remain of the realm you sought to protect?"

Harold's fists clenched at his sides, the steel of his gauntlets creaking with the force of his grip. His eyes, grey as storm-tossed seas, flashed with a fire that spoke of both desperation and resolve. "What would you have me do, Kaelion?" he cried, his voice echoing in the vast cavern like the rumble of distant thunder. "Abandon our people to Eldran's mercies? This fortress, this bastion of hope, is all that stands between them and utter annihilation! Would you have me cast aside the very walls that shelter them, leaving them naked before the ravening hordes that bay at our gates?"

Kaelion rose to his feet with a grace that belied his many years, his robes of undyed wool falling about him like the mists that cling to ancient mountains. He approached Harold, each step measured and deliberate, until he stood before the king. With a hand gnarled by time yet still strong, he reached out and placed it upon Harold's armored shoulder. The touch was light, yet it seemed to carry the weight of ages.

"I would have you remember, Harold," Kaelion spoke, his voice low and resonant with the wisdom of long years, "the cost of the choices that lie behind us and those that yet lie ahead. Not merely to yourself, though that burden is great indeed, but to all who dwell within these ensorcelled walls. The stones of Fortress Bold may stand fast against the storm that now assails us, yet what of the hearts that beat within? The pact you forged in blood and stone may yet be honored, aye, but at what price to your soul? And to the souls of those you swore to protect?"

As Harold stood in silent contemplation of the elder's words, his mind a maelstrom of conflicting thoughts and emotions, chaos erupted above. The sound of horns blaring their brazen notes of warning and men shouting in alarm filtered down even to the depths of Kaelion's cavern, like the distant echoes of a world being torn asunder. The siege, long anticipated yet dreaded, had begun in earnest.

Harold's eyes met Kaelion's, a silent understanding passing between them, as profound and unbreakable as the bonds of brotherhood forged in battle. Without another word, for none were needed in that moment of shared comprehension, the king turned and raced back through the winding passage. His footfalls echoed off the ancient stone, each step carrying him closer to the world above and the duty that awaited him.

As Harold emerged into the fortress proper, he was greeted by a scene of controlled chaos. Stones hurled from Eldran's siege engines arced through the air, their shadows racing across the ground like harbingers of doom before they crashed against the battlements in explosions of dust and shattered rock. The very air seemed alive with the hum of arrows and the shouts of men preparing for battle.

General Alric Thorn's voice boomed across the courtyard, rising above the din of impending conflict like the call of a war horn: "To arms, men of Bold! Man the walls with stout hearts and steady hands! Archers, to your positions! Let every arrow find its mark in the hearts of those who would see our home laid low!"

As Harold strode purposefully towards the thick of the fighting, his armor gleaming in the wan light of day, he felt a familiar tremor beneath his feet. It was as if the very bones of the earth were stirring, awakening from a long slumber to face the threat that now assailed them. The stones of Fortress Bold seemed to vibrate with anticipation, a low hum that resonated through the soles of his boots and up into his very being.

And then, before the astonished eyes of defenders and attackers alike, the true nature of the fortress revealed itself in a display of power that defied mortal understanding. Battlements that had stood unchanged for centuries, weathered by wind and rain yet unyielding, suddenly sprouted wicked spikes as sharp as dragon's teeth. These newly formed protrusions lashed out with uncanny precision, impaling the grappling hooks of Eldran's scaling ladders and sending men tumbling to their doom far below.

Gates that had begun to buckle under the relentless onslaught of battering rams suddenly slammed shut of their own accord, their ancient hinges groaning with a sound like the wrath of the earth itself. Men caught between the massive doors were crushed, their screams cut short as stone met stone with implacable force.

Most astonishing of all, arrows loosed by the invading force, which should have flown true to their marks, instead veered wildly off course. They curved in impossible arcs, defying the very laws of nature, to strike down the very comrades of those who had fired them. It was as if the very air around Fortress Bold had become an extension of its will, turning the weapons of the enemy against themselves.

Dame Lira, who had been organizing a group of young squires with words of encouragement and stern instruction, stood transfixed by the sight unfolding before her. Her sword, half-drawn in anticipation of the coming battle, hung forgotten at her side. "The fortress lives," she breathed, her words barely audible above the cacophony of battle. " The whispers in the night, the tales told in hushed tones... the fortress lives!"

Her wonderment was short-lived, however, as she caught sight of King Harold emerging onto the walls. His face was set in a mask of grim determination, every line and furrow speaking of the weight of command and the burden of secrets long kept. But it was his eyes that gave Lira pause, that sent a chill racing down her spine like the touch of a midwinter wind. For in those eyes, she saw not the resolute gaze of a ruler protecting his people, but the haunted look of a man who had made a terrible bargain and was only now beginning to comprehend its true cost.

In that moment, as the world seemed to hang in the balance between salvation and damnation, Lira made a decision that would alter the course of her life forever. With a quick word to a senior knight, entrusting the squires to his care, she began to make her way through the chaos of battle towards Harold's side. Her path was fraught with peril, as stones rained down from above and men fought and died all around her, yet she pressed on with single-minded determination.

"My liege," she called out over the din of combat as she drew near, her voice carrying the urgency of one who knows that time is of the essence, "I must speak with you. It cannot wait, not even for the turning of this tide."

Harold turned at the sound of her voice, surprise flickering across his features like summer lightning before his expression settled back into its usual stoic mien. "This is hardly the time for conversation, Dame Lira," he replied, his tone brooking no argument. "Return to your post. Your sword is needed there more than your words are needed here."

But Lira stood her ground, unmoved by the command in Harold's voice or the battle that raged around them. Her hand came to rest meaningfully on the hilt of her sword, a gesture that spoke volumes in its quiet defiance. "Forgive me, Your Majesty," she said, her voice low but firm, "but I overheard your exchange with... with the spirit of the fortress. I demand to know the truth, here and now, while the fate of all hangs in the balance. What pact have you made, and at what cost to our people? What price have we all unknowingly paid for the safety these walls provide?"

For a long moment, Harold said nothing, his gaze boring into Lira as if he sought to weigh her very soul. The sounds of battle seemed to fade away, leaving them in a pocket of eerie calm amidst the storm of war. Then, with a heavy sigh that seemed to carry the weight of years uncounted, he nodded towards a nearby alcove, partially sheltered from the chaos that surrounded them.

"You wish to know the truth, Dame Lira?" Harold's voice was weary beyond measure, each word seeming to age him further. "Very well. But know this: once spoken, such truths cannot be unheard. The knowledge you seek may well be a heavier burden than the ignorance you would cast aside."

And so, as the siege raged around them with unabated fury, Harold revealed the terrible secret that lay at the heart of Fortress Bold. He spoke of ancient magics that predated the kingdoms of men, of desperate bargains struck in the darkest hour of need. His words painted a picture of a father's love twisted by ambition and fear, of a son sacrificed upon an altar of stone and sorcery in a ritual as old as the mountains themselves.

"It was wrought for our folk," Harold concluded, his gaze beseeching comprehension even as it mirrored the dread of his own deeds. "To shield them from the terrors that prowl beyond our marches, the unspoken evils that would rend asunder all we have raised and grind it to dust beneath their fell tread. Was the toll too dear? That exacted from my sire? That demanded of me? Mayhap. Yet I would render it anew, a myriad times over, if by such means our people might dwell in surety."

Lira stood in stunned silence, her mind reeling from the enormity of Harold's confession. The implications of his words stretched out before her like a yawning chasm, threatening to swallow all she had ever known or believed. Before she could formulate a response, however, a familiar shimmering form began to materialize between them, called forth perhaps by the speaking of long-held secrets.

Mira, the Stone Spirit, coalesced from the very air, her form shimmering like sunlight upon a mountain stream. Her gaze fell upon Lira, and it was as though the young knight's very essence lay bare before those ancient eyes, which held within them the memory of ages long past. When Mira spoke, her voice was as the rumble of distant thunder, resonating not merely in the air but through the very foundations of the earth. "Lo," intoned the spirit, each syllable imbued with a power that transcended mortal understanding, "another mortal has glimpsed the veiled truth, has peered into the heart of Fortress Bold and comprehended its arcane nature. Hearken, Dame Lira Variel, for this revelation binds you inexorably to our covenant. Your fate is entwined with that of this place, for good or ill, until the breaking of the world itself."

As Mira's form dissipated once more, fading like mist before the rising sun, Lira turned to Harold. Her expression was a complex mixture of horror at what she had learned and determination to face whatever challenges lay ahead. "My king," she said softly, her words nearly lost in the clamor of battle that still raged around them, "what have you done to us all?"

But before Harold could answer, before he could offer explanation or seek absolution, a great cry went up from the battlements. It was a sound of mingled triumph and despair, for Lord Eldran's forces had at last breached the outer wall. The true test of Fortress Bold's power—and the price of that power—was about to begin in earnest.

As Harold and Lira raced to join the fray, to stand with their comrades against the tide of enemies that now poured through the breach, the very stones beneath their feet seemed to pulse with an otherworldly energy. It was as if the fortress itself was awakening fully, roused to action by the mortal threat to its existence. Yet even as its power manifested in ways that defied mortal understanding, turning the tide of battle with each passing moment, a question lingered in the minds of those who now knew its terrible secret:

Betrayals Within

The clash of steel and the thunderous roar of battle echoed through the halls of Fortress Bold as Lord Victor's warriors surged through the breach. King Harold, his face etched with grim determination, stood atop the inner battlements, surveying the chaos below. The air crackled with an otherworldly energy, and the very stones of the fortress seemed to tremble with anticipation.

"Hold the line!" Harold's voice boomed across the courtyard, rallying his men. "For Bold! For our home!"

Yet even as these words fell from his lips, a dread realization seized his heart with icy fingers. The great gates of oak and iron, wrought in ages past to withstand the mightiest of foes, now groaned upon their ancient hinges, yielding to an unseen hand. The stench of treachery hung heavy in the air, more bitter than the acrid fumes of battle.

There, by the gates that had stood fast through countless sieges, stood Captain Ryker Vale, a man to whom Harold had entrusted his very life in times unnumbered. Their eyes met across the field of strife, and in that moment, Harold beheld in Ryker's gaze the weight of long years of disillusionment, as heavy as the mountains themselves.

"Ryker!" Harold's voice rang out, cracked with the anguish of betrayal. "What fell deed is this that thou hast wrought?"

But the captain's words were lost, drowned in the triumphant clamor of Victor's host as they surged through the breach. Ryker's countenance, once the very picture of steadfast loyalty, now bore the aspect of one who had made a choice most terrible, from which there could be no turning back.

As the foe surged through the breached gates, Dame Lira cleaved her way to Harold's side, her raiment bespattered with the crimson of battle and her eyes wild with bewilderment. "My liege! How came this to pass? The gates—"

"Treachery, Lira," Harold spake, his voice laden with gall. "Ryker hath sold us to our doom."

Lira's countenance blanched. "But wherefore? He was among our most trusted—"

A piercing cry rent the air, silencing their discourse. From the depths of the fastness, a blinding radiance erupted, and with it came Mira, the spirit of stone and light. Her form, oft ethereal and measured, now writhed with chaotic energy. She smote indiscriminately, her tendrils of light striking down both invader and defender alike.

"Mira!" Harold cried out, his voice a mingling of command and supplication. "Nay! We must safeguard our folk!"

Yet Mira seemed beyond the reach of reason. Her actions grew more erratic, more violent with each passing moment. The very foundations of the fortress quaked with her wrath.

Amidst the tumult, Harold grasped Lira's arm, drawing her nigh. "There is a matter of which you must be apprised," he said, his voice scarcely audible above the din of strife. "A truth I have borne overlong."

Lira's eyes widened, sensing the gravity of the moment. "My liege?"

Harold's gaze darted to Mira's rampaging form, then back to Lira. "The covenant that binds Mira to this fastness... it exacted more than my son's life. Elenna, my beloved queen... she too paid the uttermost price."

The shock upon Lira's visage mirrored the anguish in Harold's heart. "But... how can this be? We were told the Queen perished in childbed."

"A needful falsehood," Harold said, his voice heavy with remorse. "The rite demanded not merely blood, but love. A sacrifice of the heart as well as the flesh. Elenna... she offered herself willingly. She knew the import of shielding our people. And Mira... Mira is what remains of them both. My son's innocence, Elenna's devotion, bound to the very stones of our fastness."

As if summoned by his confession, Mira's form coalesced before them, her light pulsing with scarcely contained fury. "You speak of sacrifice, Harold Bold," her voice echoed, seeming to emanate from everywhere and nowhere at once. "But what do you truly know of it?"

Harold stepped forward, his hand outstretched. "Mira, I beseech thee. We must defend—"

"Defend?" Mira's laugh was cold, bereft of mirth. "Is that what you deem I am about? Nay, Harold. I am setting all free."

With a gesture, Mira raised Ryker from the courtyard below, suspending him in the air before them. The captain's face was a mask of terror and resignation.

"Tell them, Ryker," Mira commanded. "Tell them wherefore you unbarred the gates."

Ryker's voice trembled as he spoke. "I... I could bear it no longer. The whispers in the night, the weight of your hunger. Your aggression, the ruin of other realms, we feed into the darkness of night. This place... it is evil."

Harold's face contorted with anger. "Fool! We are not the aggressors. Behold what Eldran wreaks! You have doomed us all!"

But Mira's laughter cut through his rage. "Oh, Harold. Still you cling to your delusions. Eldran? The aggressor? He but seeks to protect what remains of his kingdom, parts of which you have laid waste. Ryker's betrayal was no mischance. It was a trial. My trial."

The realization dawned on Harold's face, a mingling of horror and understanding. "You... you orchestrated this?"

"I had need to know," Mira said, her form flickering between the visages of Elenna, their son, and something altogether inhuman. "To see if you were truly worthy of wielding my power. If you could make the hard choices, as Elenna did."

Lira, who had been silent throughout this exchange, at last found her voice. "And? What judgment have you reached?"

Mira's gaze swept over the battlefield, taking in the carnage, the fear, the desperation. "Harold Bold clings to power, to dominion. He uses the fortress as means to grow his own wealth. He would sacrifice aught—anyone—to maintain his grip on this fastness. But in so doing, he has lost sight of what truly matters."

Harold's face fell, the weight of centuries of decisions crashing down upon him. "I... I but sought to protect our people."

"And yet," Mira countered, "in your quest to protect, you have brought them naught but suffering. The time has come, Harold Bold, to face the true cost of your choices."

With a wave of her hand, Mira released Ryker, who fell to his knees, gasping. The spirit then turned her attention to the invading forces, who had been held at bay by an invisible barrier.

Lo, the voice of Mira, like unto the rumbling of the earth itself, rang forth across the field of battle. "Lord Victor," she called, her words carrying to every ear, "thou who wouldst lay claim to Fortress Bold, step forth and face thy judgment."

As if by some enchantment, the clash of arms ceased, and Victor, arrayed in raiment of war most splendid, strode through the parting throng. His countenance bore a mixture of wonder and dread as he drew nigh.

"O Spirit," he spake, his voice unwavering despite the otherworldly sight that met his gaze, "I come to claim that which is mine by right. For too long hath Bold stood as a thorn in the side of progress."

Mira's form shimmered like starlight upon water, taking on the semblance of Queen Elenna. At this sight, Harold stumbled back, his face a mask of anguish and yearning.

"And what wouldst thou do with Bold, should it fall to thy hand?" Mira inquired, her voice now a perfect echo of Elenna's.

Victor drew himself up, his chin held high. "I would cast down its walls, and free its people from the tyranny of ancient sorceries and customs long outdated. I would usher Bold into an age of prosperity and freedom."

Harold surged forward, his visage contorted with wrath. "Thou knowest naught of Bold! Of the sacrifices made to keep our people from harm!"

But Mira raised a hand, and Harold fell silent. "And thou, Harold, knowest naught of relinquishing thy grasp." She turned once more to Victor. "Thy ambition is plain, but at what cost wouldst thou achieve it? Wouldst thou bind thyself to this place, as Harold hath done? Wouldst thou offer up thy loved ones as the price of power?"

Victor hesitated, his gaze darting betwixt Mira, Harold, and the ruin that lay about them. "I... I would not. Power gained through such means is no power at all, but a fetter, binding us to what has been and blinding us to what may yet be."

A smile, both sorrowful and wise, graced Mira's borrowed features. "Mayhap there is hope yet." She turned to Harold, her form shifting once more, now taking on the likeness of their son. "The hour has come, Harold Bold, to set us free. To set thyself free."

Harold fell to his knees, tears coursing down his weathered face. "I... I cannot. Without the fortress, without thee... who am I? What becomes of our people?"

Lira stepped forth, laying a hand upon Harold's shoulder. "They become free, my King. Free to forge their own path, unburdened by ancient pacts and hidden truths."

Mira nodded, her form beginning to fade like mist before the rising sun. "The choice lies before thee, Harold. Cling to what has been and doom thy people to an eternity of sacrifice, or release us and grant them the chance to shape their own destiny."

A hush fell over the battlefield, all eyes upon the kneeling king. Harold looked up, his gaze meeting Mira's, then Lira's, and at last settling upon Victor.

"I..." he began, his voice scarcely more than a whisper. "I choose freedom."

With those words, a great tremor shook Fortress Bold to its very foundations. Fissures appeared in the ancient stones, and a light of blinding radiance burst forth from every window and crevice. Mira's form exploded into a shower of luminous motes, swirling about them all like stars come down from the heavens.

As the light faded and the dust settled, Fortress Bold stood transformed. The oppressive aura that had hung over it for ages uncounted was no more, replaced by a sense of lightness, of boundless possibility.

Harold rose to his feet, seeming older yet somehow unburdened. He turned to Victor, who stood watching with wary eyes.

"Lord Victor," Harold said, his voice steady as the mountains, "Fortress Bold is thine, if thou still desirest it. But know this – its strength never lay in its walls or its magics. It lay in the hearts of its people. Treat them well, and thou shalt have a legacy far greater than any conqueror."

Victor, taken aback by this turn of events, could but nod solemnly.

As the sun began to set on this new chapter in Bold's history, Lira approached Harold. "What wilt thou do now, my King?"

Harold gazed out over the changed landscape, a small smile tugging at his lips. "For the first time in longer than I can remember, Lira, I know not. And that... that feels like... freedom."

Together, they watched as the people of Bold, defenders and invaders alike, began the slow process of understanding their new reality. The fortress stood, no longer a prison of ancient magic, but a symbol of change, of the power of letting go, and the promise of a future unbound by the chains of the past.

The Final Reckoning

As the first light of dawn crept over the eastern horizon, painting the sky in hues of rose and gold, the mighty fortress stirred once more. Yet this awakening was unlike any that had come before, for the very stones seemed to groan and shift, as if the fortress itself were a great beast rousing from ancient slumber. The air was thick with anticipation, crackling with an energy that felt both alive and foreboding.

Lord Victor Eldran, newly crowned as master of the fortress, stood upon the highest tower, his gaze sweeping across the sprawling expanse of his domain. His eyes widened with a mixture of awe and growing dread as he took in the sight before him. Beside him, Mira's form shimmered into being, her essence now seeming to pulse in time with the fortress's heartbeat. She was a vision of ethereal beauty, her translucent figure glowing softly against the backdrop of the awakening day.

"Behold, Lord Victor," Mira's voice echoed like distant thunder, carrying the weight of ages long past. "The true nature of the fortress is revealed. No longer shall it be bound by the constraints of mortal design; it shall become as I am - alive, aware, and unyielding in its purpose."

As she spoke, the walls of the fortress began to writhe and twist with a life of their own. Great spikes of stone erupted from the battlements, their sharp tips glinting ominously in the morning light. The very gates seemed to gnash like teeth of iron and oak, eager for blood. Below them, the courtyard roiled as if it were a sea of stone, swallowing what remained of Harold's forces whole.

"By the gods," Victor breathed, his face paling with horror as he witnessed this transformation. "What manner of sorcery is this? This is not what I sought when I laid claim to this fortress!"

Mira turned to him, her form flickering between that of Queen Elenna, Harold's son, and something altogether inhuman. "Did you not vow to usher in a new age for this fortress? To cast down the old and embrace that which has never been? This is the price of such ambition, Lord Victor. The fortress awakens, hungry for a new purpose."

Victor's hand flew instinctively to the hilt of his sword, though he knew in his heart that mere steel would avail him naught against such power. "I must rally my men," he declared, his voice quavering despite his efforts to sound resolute. "We shall quit this accursed place and leave it to its own devices."

But as he turned to descend the tower, Mira's form blocked his path, her eyes blazing with an otherworldly light. "Nay, Lord Victor. You shall not forsake the bargain so lightly struck. This place has tasted freedom, and it shall not be abandoned once more to silent stone."

As chaos unfolded around him, Victor felt a deep sense of foreboding settle upon him like a shroud. The ground beneath his feet trembled as if responding to Mira's words, and he could feel an ancient power stirring within the very foundations of the fortress.

In the courtyard below, Dame Lira fought valiantly to maintain order amidst the chaos that engulfed the fortress. The air was thick with the acrid scent of smoke and the clamor of steel clashing against steel, yet Lira remained resolute, her heart steady as she beheld the scene unfolding before her. With a fierce determination burning in her chest, she watched in horror as the very ground beneath their feet came alive, tendrils of stone snaking forth to ensnare the ankles of fleeing defenders, dragging them into the earth's dark embrace.

"To me!" she cried out, her sword gleaming like a shard of sunlight in the early morning light. "Rally to me! We must quit this place ere it becomes our tomb!" Her voice rang clear above the din, a clarion call amidst the cacophony of despair.

Yet even as her words echoed through the tumult, a great tremor shook the fortress to its very foundations. The central keep began to twist and grow, stones flowing like molten silver to form a colossal visage - a face wrought of stone and shadow that bore the anguished features of both King Harold and Queen Elenna, their expressions contorted in eternal anguish.

High above, Victor Eldran grappled with the magnitude of his folly. "What would you have of me, spirit?" he demanded of Mira, his voice thick with desperation and disbelief. "I sought to rule a fortress, not to become jailer to a monstrosity!"

Mira's laughter rang out across the battlefield like the tolling of a distant bell, sending shivers through the very bones of the earth. "Oh, but you shall rule, Lord Victor. You shall be both guardian and master, bound to this fortress as surely as I am. But first, a final price must be paid."

Her gaze turned toward Harold, who stood silent and grave amidst the chaos unfolding around him. "The fortress hungers, Harold Bold," she intoned with an eerie calm that belied the turmoil surrounding them. "It requires one last sacrifice to fully awaken - to become the living shield you have always envisioned it could be. Will you give yourself to it, as you once gave your son and wife?"

Harold's weathered face betrayed no surprise at this pronouncement; it was as if he had long known this moment would come, perhaps even yearned for it in the depths of his guilt-ridden heart. "If by my life or death I can bring peace to these realms," he said, his voice steady and clear amidst the chaos, "then so be it. I have lived overlong with the weight of my choices. Let this final act be one of atonement."

"If by my life or death I can bring peace to these realms," he said, his voice steady and clear, "then so be it. I have lived overlong with the weight of my choices. Let this final act be one of atonement."

Victor surged forward then, his face a mask of confusion and growing horror. "Surely you cannot mean to go through with this madness! There must be another way!" His voice trembled with urgency as he grasped at straws.

But Harold raised a hand, silencing him with an authority borne from years of leadership. "Nay, Lord Victor. This is the path I set us upon long ago, though I knew it not then. The cycle must end, and with it, the power that has brought naught but suffering to our people." He nodded solemnly before turning his gaze back to Victor. "Rule justly, Lord Victor," he commanded softly yet firmly. "Ensure that this fortress never again becomes a prison of ancient magic. Let it stand as a beacon of hope and unity rather than a monument to fear and division."

At last, Harold stepped forth, his arms outstretched like one embracing destiny itself. Mira's form, shimmering with an otherworldly radiance, enveloped him as a mother might cradle her child. Her light grew to such intensity that all assembled were forced to shield their eyes, lest they be struck blind by its terrible beauty. When at last they dared to look again, Harold was no more, and Mira's essence pulsed with a vigor that seemed to draw strength from the very air around them.

A great tremor shook the fortress to its very foundations, as if the bones of the earth themselves quaked in fear. Then, to the horror of all who bore witness, the ancient stones began to move with fell purpose. Walls that had stood fast against countless sieges now flowed like water in a spring flood, reshaping themselves into formations so grotesque that they defied mortal comprehension. From these twisted ramparts erupted a maelstrom of stone and shadow, a tempest of such fury that it swept across the courtyard and beyond the gates, devouring all in its path

Victor, rooted to the spot as if turned to stone himself, watched in mute horror as Harold's remaining forces were obliterated before his eyes. Their screams, cut short as they were swallowed by the living fortress, would haunt his dreams for years to come. Even his own men, felt the very ground beneath their feet tremble forth, as they watched the fortress rise up to consume their enemy as a great beast might devour its prey.

As the dust of destruction settled and an eerie calm descended upon the transformed structure, Victor found himself alone atop the highest tower, save for the ethereal presence of Mira. The spirit's voice, when it came, was soft as the whisper of wind through summer leaves, yet it carried within it the chill of midwinter's deepest night.

"And so, Lord Victor of the House of Eldran," Mira intoned, her words seeming to come from the very stones themselves, "thou dost assume thy place as guardian of this place. Bound art thou by oath and sacrifice, as all who have come before thee, from the days when the world was young."

Victor's legs trembled beneath him as he felt the fortress pulse with life - nay, with his very own life force. For in that moment of terrible clarity, he understood the true nature of the bargain he had struck. He was now as much a part of the fortress as the ancient stones themselves, his fate forever entwined with this place of power and sorrow, of glory and doom.

As Mira's form faded into the very air, becoming one with the fortress she had long protected, Victor sank to his knees, overwhelmed by the weight of his newfound responsibility. Beneath his feet, he could feel the heartbeat of the fortress, strong and steady as the rhythm of the world itself, a constant reminder of the power he now wielded and the grievous price that had been paid for it.

In the distance, beyond the transformed walls of the fortress, the sun continued its eternal journey across the vault of heaven, heedless of the great and terrible events that had transpired in the shadow of the mountain. And in its warm light, Fortress Bold stood, no longer a mere stronghold of stone and mortar, but a living testament to the enduring legacy of sacrifice and the ever-present lure of power that has tempted the hearts of Men since the dawn of time.

Dame Lira, gazed up at the tower where Victor now stood alone, a solitary figure silhouetted against the morning sky. Her heart was heavy with the knowledge of all that had been lost, a burden she would carry with her all the days of her life. For she alone now bore the tale of Fortress Bold's final transformation - a story that would be whispered around hearth fires for generations to come, a cautionary tale of the perils of unchecked ambition and the true cost of power.

As she turned to depart, Lira cast one last glance over her shoulder at the place that had been her home and the site of so much strife and glory. The fortress seemed to watch her go, its newly formed visage an unsettling mixture of Harold, Elenna, and something altogether inhuman - a face that spoke of ages past and ages yet to come. And though she could not be certain, Lira thought she heard, carried on the wind that whipped about the battlements, the faintest whisper of a familiar voice:

"Remember, child of Bold. Remember and warn them all, lest the follies of the past become the doom of the future."

With those words echoing in her mind like the tolling of a great bell, Lira squared her shoulders and continued on her way, leaving behind the transformed Fortress Bold and its new guardian to whatever fate the turning of the years might bring. For this was a new power rising in the world, and only time would tell whether it would stand as a bastion of hope or a monument to the folly of men. This was Fortress Eldran.

The Good Choice Between Red and Blue

The man stood at the crossroads of Fate Street, his weathered boots sinking into the soft earth as if the very ground sought to claim him. Before him stretched two row houses, their facades a stark contrast against the gray sky that hung low and heavy, pregnant with the promise of rain.

To his right, a house of faded red brick stood defiant against the encroaching gloom. Its porch sagged like the jowls of an old hound, the wood splintered and groaning under the weight of years. Upon this porch sat an old man, his skin as cracked and worn as the leather of a long-forgotten saddle.

To his left, a house of blue clapboard rose neat and trim, its windows gleaming like polished river stones. A gentle breeze carried the scent of fresh-baked pie, sweet and inviting, whispering of warmth and comfort within.

The man felt the pull of the blue house, a siren song that tugged at his very marrow. His feet, of their own accord, began to shuffle towards it, each step a battle against an unseen current.

"Hold up there, son," the old man's voice rasped from the red porch, cutting through the stillness like a rusted blade. "You might want to reconsider your heading."

The traveler paused, his hand hovering over the gate to the blue house's neat picket fence. He turned, regarding the old man with eyes that had seen too much and remembered even more.

"And why's that?" he asked, his voice low and gravelly, as if he'd swallowed the very dust of the road he'd traveled.

The old man shifted in his creaking rocking chair, the motion setting loose a small avalanche of paint chips that drifted down to settle on the warped boards beneath. "That blue house there," he said, gesturing with a gnarled hand, "it ain't what it seems. The woman inside, she's got a tongue sharper than a rattler's fang and twice as quick. She'll talk your ear off and meddle in your business 'fore you can say 'Jack Robinson'."

The traveler's gaze drifted back to the blue house, its cheerful facade now seeming to hide secrets behind its pristine paint. "Is that so?" he murmured, more to himself than to the old man.

"Sure as the sun rises," the old man continued, leaning forward, his rheumy eyes fixed on the traveler. "Now, if it's friendly conversation you're after, you'd do better to step up here on my porch. I may not be much to look at, and this old house has seen better days, but I can spin a yarn that'll make you forget your troubles."

The traveler's hand fell away from the gate, and he turned fully to face the red house. The porch boards creaked ominously as he took a step closer, as if warning him away.

"Course," the old man added, a sly grin splitting his leathery face, "I ain't much of a cook. That woman next door, for all her faults, she does make a mean apple pie. The kind that'd make you weep for your mama, if you've got one to weep for."

The scent of cinnamon and baked apples wafted stronger on the breeze, as if summoned by the old man's words. The traveler closed his eyes, inhaling deeply, memories of a childhood long past flickering behind his eyelids.

"A man could do worse than a slice of good pie," the traveler said, opening his eyes to meet the old man's gaze.

The old man nodded sagely. "That he could. But a man could do worse than avoiding a meddlesome woman, too. It's your choice, son. Red or blue. Quiet company or sweet temptation."

The traveler stood still, caught between the two houses like a piece of driftwood in the tide. The red house loomed to his right, its peeling paint and sagging roof a testament to the ravages of time. Yet there was something in the old man's eyes, a glimmer of wisdom hard-won through years of watching the world from his porch.

To his left, the blue house beckoned, its cheerful exterior promising comfort and warmth. The scent of pie grew stronger, and he could almost hear the faint strains of music drifting from within, a melody just beyond recognition.

"What's it gonna be, son?" the old man pressed, his voice carrying an edge of urgency. "Time's a-wastin', and the storm's rolling in."

As if to punctuate the old man's words, a low rumble of thunder rolled across the sky. The traveler looked up, watching as dark clouds roiled overhead, their bellies heavy with rain yet to fall.

He should turn away from the blue house, he knew. The old man's warning rang true, echoing the hard-learned lessons of his past. Meddlesome folk had brought him nothing but trouble in his wanderings, their sweet words often hiding bitter intentions.

Yet still, he hesitated. There was something about the blue house that called to him, a promise of something he couldn't quite name. Perhaps it was the hope of a moment's peace, a respite from the long and lonely road he'd traveled. Or perhaps it was simply the lure of that apple pie, a taste of home in a world that had long since ceased to offer such comforts.

"I appreciate your warning, old timer," the traveler said at last, his voice low and measured. "And your offer of company. But I think. . ."

He trailed off, his eyes drawn once more to the blue house. A curtain twitched in one of the front windows, and for a moment, he caught a glimpse of a face peering out at him. It was gone in an instant, like a mirage shimmering on a sun-baked highway, but it left him with an impression of kind eyes and a gentle smile.

"I think I'll take my chances with the blue house," he finished, his decision made.

The old man sighed, a sound like wind whistling through a graveyard. "Can't say I didn't warn you, son. But every man's got to make his own choices in this life. Just remember, when that woman's tongue starts wagging and you're wishing for some peace and quiet, my door's always open."

The traveler nodded, acknowledging the old man's words. Then, with a deliberate step, he pushed open the gate to the blue house's yard. The hinges swung silently, well-oiled and maintained, so unlike the creaking boards of the red house's porch.

As he made his way up the neat path to the blue house's door, the traveler could feel the old man's eyes boring into his back. The weight of that gaze was heavy, filled with unspoken warnings and a hint of something else—regret, perhaps, or a loneliness so deep it had become a part of the old man's very being.

The traveler paused at the foot of the steps leading up to the blue house's porch. He turned, looking back at the old man one last time. "Thank you for the warning," he called out. "And for the offer. Maybe I'll take you up on it someday."

The old man raised a hand in acknowledgment, then settled back in his rocking chair, his eyes never leaving the traveler. As the first fat drops of rain began to fall, splattering against the dusty ground, the traveler climbed the steps to the blue house's door.

He raised his hand to knock, fingers curled into a fist, hovering there in the humid air. Another peal of thunder rolled across the sky, a sound like the earth being torn asunder. The man stood motionless, listening as the echoes faded into the distance. Then, drawing a breath that tasted of coming rain, he brought his knuckles down against the weathered wood. The sound was sharp, insistent, seeming to reverberate through the unnatural quiet that had descended upon Fate Street like a shroud.

He waited, aware of each heartbeat, each whisper of wind through the dying leaves. The traveler couldn't shake the feeling that he stood at the edge of some great and terrible precipice, a cliff overlooking a vast and unknowable darkness. His journey, long and fraught with perils he dared not name even in the sanctity of his own thoughts, had led him to this moment, this threshold. He knew it with a certainty that settled in his bones like lead.

The door began to open, hinges groaning in protest. A wash of golden light spilled forth, painting the worn boards of the porch in hues of amber and honey. With it came the scent of apples and cinnamon, rich and sweet, a smell that spoke of hearth and home and things long forgotten. The traveler stood transfixed, feeling the warmth of that light on his face, breathing in the aroma of a life he had never known. Whatever lay beyond that door, whatever fate awaited him in the depths of that house, he would meet it. He had no choice. The road that had brought him here left no path for retreat. And so he waited, ready to step into the light or the dark, whichever greeted him on the other side of that threshold.

***

The traveler crossed the threshold of the blue house, his boots leaving a trail of red dust on the worn planks. The floorboards creaked and groaned under his weight like the bones of some ancient beast. Inside, the air hung heavy with the scent of cinnamon and apples, sweet and cloying, a stark contrast to the arid emptiness outside. He blinked, his eyes adjusting to the dim interior after the harsh glare of the sun.

An old woman stood before him, her face a map of wrinkles, each line etched deep as if carved by time and sorrow itself. Her eyes, though, they sparkled with a vitality that seemed out of place in such an ancient visage. When she smiled, it was with teeth too white and too even, like pearls set in a weathered driftwood frame.

"Well now," she said, her voice warm as fresh spilled blood. "Aint you a sight for these old eyes. Come in, come in. Don't be shy."

The man hesitated, his hand still on the doorknob. He looked back over his shoulder at the desolate landscape he'd traversed, all red dust and bleached bones under an unforgiving sky. Then he turned back to the old woman's welcoming face, a promise of comfort in a world that had long since forgotten such things. With a slight nod, barely more than a dip of his chin, he stepped fully into the house. The door swung shut behind him with the finality of a coffin lid closing.

"That's right," the old woman cooed, her voice like the rustle of dead leaves. "Make yourself at home. I've got some fresh apple pie cooling on the windowsill and a pot of coffee that'll put hair on your chest." She chuckled at her own joke, the sound dry and brittle as sun-bleached bones.

The man followed her into a small kitchen, his eyes taking in every detail. Everything was blue here too—the curtains, the tablecloth, even the chipped plates stacked neatly in a hutch. It was as if someone had taken a piece of sky and wrapped it around this room, trapping it here in this oasis of color amidst the red wasteland outside. He sat at the table, his large frame dwarfing the delicate chair. It creaked ominously under his weight, like a warning.

The old woman busied herself, humming tunelessly as she cut a generous slice of pie and poured a steaming cup of coffee. The knife sliced through the golden crust with a sound like tearing flesh. She set both before him with a flourish, the porcelain of the plate and cup so thin it was almost translucent.

"Eat up now," she said, her eyes never leaving his face. "You look like you've come a long way."

The man stared at the food, then at the old woman. His brow furrowed as if trying to remember something important, something just beyond the reach of his mind.

"I . . . I'm not sure how I got here," he said, his voice rough as gravel, scraped raw by thirst and disuse.

The old woman's smile never wavered, fixed on her face like a mask. "Oh, that don't matter none. You're here now, ain't you? That's what counts."

The man picked up the fork, stabbing at the pie without much enthusiasm. "But I should know, shouldn't I? How I got here, why I'm here?"

The old woman sat across from him, folding her gnarled hands on the table. Her fingers were twisted like the roots of an ancient tree, skin spotted and translucent. "Now, now. Don't you fret about all that. Tell me about yourself instead. What's your story?"

The man chewed slowly, tasting nothing. The pie turned to ash in his mouth. He swallowed hard, the lump in his throat feeling like a stone. "I . . . I'm not sure I have a story."

"Everyone's got a story," the old woman insisted, leaning forward. Her eyes glittered in the dim light, hungry. "Even if they don't know it yet. What's your name?"

The man opened his mouth to answer, then closed it again. His eyes widened in panic, the whites showing all around like a spooked horse. "I don't know," he whispered, the words falling from his lips like pebbles. "I can't remember my name."

The old woman reached across the table, patting his hand. Her skin felt like paper against his, dry and fragile. "That's alright, honey. Names ain't all that important anyway. Tell me what you do remember."

The man closed his eyes, concentrating. Images flashed through his mind—a dusty road stretching to the horizon, the sun beating down mercilessly, his feet aching with every step. But before that . . . nothing. Just a vast, empty darkness, a void where his memories should have been.

"I remember walking," he said finally, the words dragged from him like rusty nails from old wood. "For a long time. But I don't know where I was going or where I came from."

The old woman nodded sagely, her head bobbing like a vulture's. "Sounds like quite the journey. But you ended up here, didn't you? Maybe that's where you were meant to be all along."

The man shook his head, frustration building like a storm on the horizon. "But why? Why am I here? What is this place?"

The old woman's smile widened, her eyes twinkling with secret amusement. "Who knows? Life is funny sometimes, ain't it?"

The man stood abruptly, his chair scraping loudly against the floor like a scream. "This isn't right," he said, his voice rising. "I shouldn't be here. I need to leave."

He turned towards the door, but the old woman's voice stopped him, soft yet as unyielding as iron. "Now, now. Don't be hasty. Where will you go? Back out there?"

The man hesitated, his hand on the doorknob. He could feel the heat radiating through the wood, a reminder of the harsh world outside, waiting to swallow him whole.

"I don't know," he admitted, the words bitter on his tongue. "But I can't stay here. This isn't . . . it's not real."

The old woman's laughter filled the small kitchen, a sound like breaking glass. "Oh, honey. What makes you think out there is any more real than in here?"

The man turned back to her, confusion etched on his face like scars. "What do you mean?"

She stood, moving to the window with a grace that belied her apparent age. With one gnarled finger, she pushed aside the blue curtain. "Look," she said, her voice a command.

The man approached cautiously, every step feeling like he was walking to his own execution. He peered out, his breath catching in his throat. Where there should have been a desolate landscape, he saw only a swirling mist, formless and gray. It pressed against the glass like a living thing, hungry and patient.

"What is this?" he asked, his voice barely above a whisper, as if afraid to wake whatever lurked in that formless void.

The old woman let the curtain fall back into place with a soft whisper of fabric. "It's whatever you want it to be," she said, her voice suddenly ancient and knowing. "That's the beauty of it.

Out there, in here—it's all the same. Just different shades of the same illusion."

The man stumbled back, his legs hitting the chair. He sat heavily, his mind reeling like a drunk after a long binge. "I don't understand."

"You don't have to understand," the old woman said gently, her voice a caress. "You just have to choose."

"Choose what?"

She gestured around the blue kitchen, her arm sweeping like the blade of a scythe. "This. Or that." She pointed towards the door, towards the unknown that lurked beyond. "The comfort of the known, or the uncertainty of the unknown. The blue house or the red dust. It's up to you."

The man looked at her, really looked at her for the first time. Behind the kindly grandmother facade, he saw something else—something ancient and unknowable, a creature that had been old when the world was young.

"Who are you?" he asked, his voice trembling.

Her smile turned enigmatic, a Sphinx with a secret. "I'm just an old woman offering you some pie and coffee. Or maybe I'm something else entirely. Does it matter?"

"I guess not," the man said, resignation settling over him like a shroud.

"Well then," she said, her smile widening until it seemed to split her face in two. "Why don't we chat for a bit. I love to chat." Her eyes glittered with an unholy light. "Tell me about yourself. Start at the beginning."

And so the man began to speak, his words falling into the silence of the blue kitchen like stones into a bottomless well, each one echoing into eternity.

***

The man sat there in that old kitchen chair, worn smooth and shiny in places from years of use. Its legs were scratched and nicked, bearing the scars of countless scootings across the linoleum floor. Across from him, the old woman perched on her own chair, her gnarled hands folded neatly in her lap like two pale spiders at rest. The room was quiet save for the solemn ticking of an ancient grandfather clock in the parlor, its pendulum swinging with the steady rhythm of a metronome, and the occasional protest of floorboards settling beneath their feet, the old house groaning softly with the weight of memory.

"Well, I reckon I ought to start at the beginning like you said," the man said, his voice barely above a whisper, as if he feared speaking any louder might shatter the fragile peace of the moment. "Though I ain't rightly sure where that is anymore. Seems like every time I try to pin it down it slips away like smoke."

The old woman nodded, her eyes kind but piercing, boring into him with an intensity that made him want to look away. But he couldn't. Those eyes held him fast, demanding the truth. "The beginning is wherever you choose it to be, dear," she said. "Tell me what weighs on your heart."

He drew in a deep breath, the air heavy with the scent of lavender and old books and something else he couldn't quite place. Something ancient and holy. "I did things," he said at last.

"Terrible things. Things that keep me awake at night staring at the ceiling and wondering if I'm even human anymore. Things that make me wish I could crawl out of my own skin and leave it all behind."

"Go on," she encouraged, her voice soft as a whisper of wind through summer grass.

"I was young when it started. Just a kid really, though I thought I was a man. Started running with the wrong crowd. It was small stuff at first – lifting candy bars from the corner store, spray painting walls, breaking windows for the hell of it. But it grew. Lord almighty how it grew." He paused, running a hand through his graying hair, feeling the coarse strands between his fingers. "Before I knew it I was in deep. Drugs, weapons, blood money. You name it, I had my fingers in it. Told myself it was just business, that I wasn't hurting nobody directly. But I knew. Deep down in that place where a man can't lie to himself, I always knew."

The old woman leaned forward, her eyes never leaving his face. They seemed to glow with an inner light, reflecting some great and terrible knowledge. "And how did that make you feel, child?" she asked, though they both knew he was no child, hadn't been for a long, long time.

"Powerful, at first," he admitted. "Like I was ten feet tall and bulletproof. King of the world. But then . . . empty. So goddamn empty it felt like my insides had been scooped out with a rusty spoon." His voice cracked, and he looked down at his hands. They were shaking now, and he could almost see the blood on them, dark and sticky and accusing. "There was this one job. Should've been simple. Just a delivery. But something went wrong. So wrong. A kid got caught in the crossfire. Couldn't have been more than twelve. I can still see his face sometimes, when I close my eyes. All wide-eyed and scared and not understanding why this was happening to him."

The room seemed to grow colder then, the shadows longer. The man's words hung in the air like smoke, acrid and suffocating, a miasma of guilt and regret that threatened to choke them both.

"Did you pull the trigger?" the old woman asked, her voice steady as bedrock.

He shook his head, a quick, jerky motion. "No, but I might as well have. I was there. I could've stopped it. Could've done something, anything. But I didn't. I just . . . ran. Like the coward I am."

"And after that?" she prompted, though her tone suggested she already knew the answer.

"I tried to change. I really did. Got myself a straight job, settled down in a little town where nobody knew me. Even had a family for a while." A bitter laugh escaped his lips, sharp as broken glass. "But you can't outrun your past, can you? It always catches up. Always finds a way to drag you back down into the muck."

The old woman nodded sagely, her eyes filled with a sorrow as old as time itself. "The past has a way of shaping our present, yes. It carves us like water carves stone, leaving its mark whether we will it or not. But it doesn't have to define our future. That, at least, is still ours to choose."

"I lost them, you know," he said, his voice hollow. "My wife, my kids. They couldn't live with the constant fear, the looking over our shoulders, waiting for the other shoe to drop.

And I couldn't blame them. Hell, I wouldn't want to live with me either."

Silence fell between them then, broken only by the steady tick-tock of the clock, each second falling like a hammer blow. The man's shoulders slumped, as if the weight of his confessions had physically manifested, pressing him down towards the earth.

"I'm sorry," he whispered, more to himself than to her. The words tasted like ashes in his mouth. "God almighty, I'm so sorry for everything."

The old woman's face softened then, a small smile playing at the corners of her mouth. It was a smile that spoke of forgiveness, of understanding, of a love so vast and unconditional it defied comprehension. "Being sorry is a powerful thing," she said. "It means you've grown, that you've learned. That you're not the same man you were. Tell me, what would you do differently if you had the chance?"

The man looked up, his eyes glistening with unshed tears. In them, she saw a lifetime of regret, of pain, of longing for redemption. "Everything," he said, his voice raw with emotion. "I'd change everything. I'd go back and shake some sense into that stupid kid who thought he knew it all. I'd tell him that power isn't worth the price of your soul. That there's more to life than money and respect earned through fear."

He stood up suddenly, unable to contain the restless energy that coursed through him. He began to pace the small room, his footsteps echoing on the worn linoleum. "I'd tell him to cherish the people who love him, to hold them close and never let go. To be the man they deserve, not the monster he's becoming.

I'd make him see that every choice has consequences, that every action ripples out and touches lives in ways we can't even imagine."

The old woman watched him, her eyes following his frantic movements. There was something in her gaze that spoke of eternity, of having seen this scene play out countless times before. "And what about now?" she asked. "What would you do if you had another chance?"

He stopped, turning to face her. In that moment, he looked older than his years, worn down by the weight of his sins. But there was something else there, too. A spark of hope, small but bright. "I'd make amends," he said firmly. "To everyone I've hurt, everyone I've wronged. I'd spend every waking moment trying to balance the scales, to put more good into the world than the evil I've unleashed. I'd help people, really help them, not just throw money at problems and pretend that makes it all better."

"Even knowing it might never be enough?" she pressed, her voice gentle but insistent.

"Even then," he said, and there was steel in his voice now. "Because it's not about evening the score anymore. It's about doing what's right, regardless of the outcome. It's about being able to look myself in the mirror and not want to smash the glass."

The old woman's smile widened then, a warmth spreading through the room like sunlight breaking through storm clouds. "That, my dear," she said, "is the truest form of redemption."

As her words sank in, something shifted in the man's perception. The room seemed to blur at the edges, the colors becoming more vivid yet somehow less real. He looked at the old woman, really looked at her for the first time since he'd arrived. And what he saw made his breath catch in his throat.

"I'm dead, aren't I?" he asked, his voice surprisingly calm. It wasn't really a question.

She nodded slowly, the motion as graceful as a willow bending in the wind. "Yes, child. You are."

"And you're . . . you're God?" The words felt strange on his tongue, a mix of awe and terror and something else he couldn't quite name.

The old woman chuckled, the sound like wind chimes in a summer breeze. "I am many things to many people," she said. "What matters is what I am to you."

The man sank back into his chair, his mind reeling. The world seemed to tilt on its axis, everything he thought he knew shifting and rearranging itself. "But I . . . I just told you all those horrible things I did," he protested weakly. "I confessed to . . . to . . ."

"To being human," she finished for him, her voice filled with infinite compassion. "To making mistakes, to feeling remorse, to wanting to be better. To struggling with the darkness that lives in all of us and sometimes winning, sometimes losing, but always fighting."

"But surely that's not enough," he said, shaking his head. "After everything I've done . . . all the lives I've ruined . . . how can that possibly be enough?"

The old woman stood then, crossing the room to stand before him. She placed a hand on his shoulder, and he felt a warmth unlike anything he'd ever experienced. It was like being bathed in pure light, in love so vast and unconditional it threatened to break him apart and remake him anew.

"My child," she said, her voice resonating with the power of creation itself, "do you know why we're in this blue house?"

He shook his head, unable to speak past the lump in his throat.

"Because you chose it," she said simply. "When given the choice between red and blue, between continuing down the path of destruction or seeking redemption, you chose blue. You chose to reflect, to feel, to grow. You chose to face your sins and seek forgiveness, even when you believed you didn't deserve it."

Tears began to fall freely down the man's cheeks then, carving paths through the dirt and grime of a lifetime. "But I don't deserve this," he whispered brokenly. "I don't deserve forgiveness. Not after everything I've done."

"Forgiveness isn't about deserving," she said gently, her voice filled with the wisdom of ages. "It's about grace. And grace, my dear, is given freely to those who are truly sorry and wish to change. That's what everyone says, at least. The truth, as always, is a bit more complicated."

The man looked up at her then, hope blooming in his chest for the first time in years. It was a fragile thing, delicate as a butterfly's wing, but it was there. "So what happens now?" he asked, his voice barely above a whisper.

The old woman smiled, and in that smile he saw the promise of new beginnings, of second chances, of a future not defined by the mistakes of the past. "Now," she said, "we begin again."

***

The old woman's eyes glinted like obsidian in firelight, watching the man fidget. His fingers drummed a frantic beat on the chair arm, nails bitten to the quick. Sweat beaded on his brow despite the cool air. She leaned forward, her voice honey poured over gravel. Perhaps you need some air, child. The backyard is beautiful this time of year. Trees heavy with fruit, flowers in full bloom, and butterflies dancing on the breeze.

The man's eyes lit up, hope kindling in their depths. That does sound nice, he whispered, voice barely stirring the air.

Come, she said, rising from her chair with a grace that belied her years. Bones cracking like dry twigs. Let me show you. I think you can use the fresh air.

They stood. Floorboards groaned beneath their feet, protesting each step. Walls seemed to close in, air growing thick and heavy. Oppressive. Like the moments before a storm breaks.

The old woman's hand rested on the doorknob. Fingers curled round it like talons. Yellowed nails tapping a rhythm only she could hear. She turned to the man, her smile now a death's head grin. Are you ready to see paradise?

The man nodded. Throat too dry for words. Anticipation and dread warring in his gut.

The old woman turned the knob. Door swinging open with a sound like bones breaking. Like the earth splitting apart.

And hell, it was.

Where there should have been a garden, only fire and brimstone stretched to the horizon. Air shimmered with heat, twisting the landscape into something from a fever dream. Flames licked at the sky, hungry tongues reaching for a heaven they'd never touch. Ground cracked and broken, rivers of molten rock flowing through the fissures like the earth's own lifeblood.

The man stumbled back. Eyes wide with horror. What . . . what is this? he gasped. Voice lost in the roar of the inferno.

The old woman's laughter cut like shattered glass. Her form began to shift, skin melting away. Scales and horns emerging like a butterfly from its chrysalis. Only this was no thing of beauty. This, my dear, she hissed, voice no longer that of a kindly grandmother but a creature born in the depths of nightmares, is your eternal home.

With strength that belied her size, she grabbed the man. Hurled him through the doorway like a rag doll. He tumbled through the air, heat searing his skin before he even touched the ground. As he fell, time slowed. He caught sight of a figure standing beyond the fence that separated this hellscape from the world he'd left behind.

The old man from the red house. Face weathered as old leather, etched with sorrow and resignation. Their eyes met for a brief moment. The old man's voice carried across the divide, clear as a bell despite the roar of the flames.

I warned you, son, he said. Words heavy as lead. I told you not to trust her.

The man hit the ground. Bones cracking, air driven from his lungs. He gasped, choking on sulfurous fumes that burned his throat. The heat was unbearable, skin blistering and peeling even as he watched.

He struggled to his feet. Legs trembling like a newborn colt's. The landscape before him was a vision of hell that would have made Dante weep. Twisted forms writhed in agony, their screams a constant, terrible chorus. Rivers of fire flowed between islands of blackened rock. Overhead, the sky a roiling mass of dark clouds shot through with veins of lightning.

The man turned, desperate to find the door through which he'd fallen. But there was nothing behind him but more fire. More torment. The blue house with its promise of peace and salvation had been nothing but a cruel illusion.

Welcome home, the demon that had been the old woman cackled. Voice seemed to come from everywhere at once. You've made your choice, and now you'll have eternity to reflect on it.

The man fell to his knees. Mind reeling. How did it come to this? He'd been so sure. So certain he was making the right choice. The blue house had seemed so inviting. So full of promise. And the old woman . . . she seemed so kind. So wise.

But now, as the flames licked at his feet and the screams of the damned filled his ears, he remembered the old man from the red house. Remembered the warnings. The cryptic words that had seemed so nonsensical at the time.

The path to hell is paved with good intentions, the old man from behind the fence said. And sometimes the devil wears the face of an angel.

The man wept then. Tears evaporated on his cheeks before they could fall. He wept for his foolishness. For his pride. For the eternal torment that now stretched before him like an endless desert of pain.

In the distance he could see other souls stumbling through the hellscape. Faces masks of agony and despair. Some cried out for mercy. Others cursed the names of those who had led them astray. But all were trapped. Bound to this place by the choices they had made.

The demon's laughter echoed across the inferno. A sound of pure malevolence that sent shivers down the man's spine despite the heat. Did you really think it would be so easy? she taunted. That salvation could be found in a pretty house with a white picket fence? Oh, you humans are so delightfully naive.

The man struggled to his feet once more. Body wracked with pain. He looked around, desperate for some sign of hope. Some indication that this was all a terrible mistake. But there was nothing. Nothing but fire and pain and the crushing weight of eternity.

He thought of the red house then. Of the gruff old man who had tried to warn him. Has that been the true path to salvation? Had he turned away from heaven's gate in favor of a prettier lie?

As if in answer to his unspoken question, the old man's voice drifted to him once more. Carried on a wind that smelled of brimstone and regret. The hardest truths often wear the plainest faces, the voice said. And the sweetest lies come wrapped in the prettiest packages.

The man understood then. In a moment of terrible clarity. He had been tested, and he had failed. He had chosen the easy path. The comfortable lie over the difficult truth. And now he would pay the price for that choice for all eternity.

The ground beneath his feet began to shift and crack. Opening up to reveal a pit of even greater horrors. As he felt himself beginning to slide into that abyss, the man closed his eyes and offered up a final, futile prayer.

I'm sorry, he whispered. Though to whom he wasn't sure. I'm so sorry.

And then he fell. Tumbling into the depths of a hell of his own making. The demon's laughter and the old man's warnings echoing in his ears as he descended into eternal darkness.

In the Company of Ghosts

The nursing home reeked of antiseptic and decay, that pungent cocktail of artificial sterility and rot, a stench so invasive it felt like it had invaded Evan's own skin. He'd entered this place countless times before, but each time the smell struck him like the first, as if the very air conspired to remind him of the fragility of flesh, the inevitability of its breaking down. Here, death wasn't a distant idea; it was in the air, in the walls, in the slow, mechanical shuffle of the elderly who had once been alive with purpose, now reduced to muted echoes of themselves.

His father's room, tucked away at the end of a long, sagging hallway, was an eerie monument to all that had decayed in the world. The ride up was the same every time, the elevator creaking under the weight of its own age, the servos whining, the overhead speaker crackling with static. As Evan ascended, he couldn't help but wonder if the building was kept upright by sheer force of will and institutional green paint, a facade of normalcy over the inevitable collapse of time and care.

The hallway stretched before him, an endless row of identical doors, each hiding its own private decay, each cloistered behind its own small wall of loneliness. From behind those doors came the occasional murmur of voices—some low, some high, some entirely incomprehensible—patients lost in their own private worlds of fading clarity. A few sat motionless, their eyes fixed on the holoscreens in front of them, the world on the screen brighter and more vibrant than anything they would ever touch again. The faces they once knew were now just digital phantoms, flickering in and out of recognition.

At the end of the hall, Evan paused, his hand hovering over the doorknob of his father's room. The door was the same color as the walls—washed out, institutional, easy to overlook. His heart beat a little faster, though he knew the routine by heart, knew what waited for him on the other side. The same vacant expression, the same rehearsed lines. The same fading, slow death of a man who had once been a force of nature.

With a deep breath, Evan pushed the door open.

"Hey, Dad," Evan greeted, his voice flat but steady, the mask of familiarity in place. "How are you feeling today?"

His father, Henry, was slumped in a hover-chair by the window. The chair hummed softly, its servos constantly adjusting his weight to prevent sores, a kind of mechanical cradle that kept the body upright but couldn't keep the spirit intact. Henry's eyes were fixed on something far beyond the glass, his gaze distant, unseeing. He didn't turn when Evan entered, but his lips parted as if on cue.

"The trees are blooming," Henry rasped, his voice cracking like dried paper. "Just like when your mother and I first met."

Evan's stomach tightened. The trees were far from blooming. Outside, the branches were bare, twisted skeletal things that seemed to stretch into a sky so gray it threatened to swallow everything whole. It was the same story he'd heard a thousand times before. Same words. Same memories. It never changed. Not for his father. Not for him.

"That's right, Dad," Evan said, sitting beside him, the forced smile feeling foreign on his face. "Why don't you tell me about it again?"

And so, the story began again, each word slow and deliberate, like a clock winding down. The cherry blossoms. The spring air. The first time he met his mother. Henry's voice trembled, clinging to the memories like a life raft in a sea of fog. But Evan's mind wandered, detached, the words fading in one ear and out the other. He studied the room instead, as he always did— sterile white walls, the holo-frames flickering with the faces of a life long past. The digital snapshots of his family, faces changing as the frames cycled, young to old, like some time-warping loop that trapped everyone inside it.

His eyes drifted to the nightstand. There, among the half-drunk glasses of water and forgotten medication bottles, sat the MemRec—a small, spherical device, innocuous at first glance, but a heavy thing in its promise. Its neural interface designed to preserve memory, to forestall the inevitable decline. Evan had signed the papers, all of them, without hesitation, clinging to the hope that maybe, just maybe, his father could hold on to something—anything—before it was all gone.

But as Henry's voice wavered, lost in the echo of a memory that no longer existed, Evan couldn't help but wonder if he had done the right thing. Was it worth it—to tether a man to a past that no longer belonged to him? To keep a ghost alive, forever trapped in the machinery of his own mind?

Henry's words faltered as the story wound to its familiar end, and the chair adjusted again, as though it too had grown weary of supporting a man whose body had long since given out. The hum of the chair filled the room, a mechanical lullaby that seemed to coax Henry's tired mind toward sleep.

"You're a good son, Evan," Henry said, his voice barely a whisper. His eyes, for the first time in what felt like years, flickered with something—something that almost resembled clarity. "I don't say it enough, but I want you to know."

Evan's throat tightened. The words lodged there, heavy and unspoken. "Thanks, Dad," he managed, his voice thick with a tightness he couldn't name. "That means a lot."

And then, just as quickly as it came, the moment passed. Henry's head tilted back against the chair, his eyelids drooping with the weight of exhaustion. The faint buzz of the chair's servos seemed to lull him deeper into sleep, and his hand—once gripping the armrest—slipped away, going limp in the peaceful oblivion of a momentary rest.

Evan stood, moving quietly as he reached down and brushed a gentle kiss across his father's cheek. The skin was warm, soft. It felt like a memory of something real, something that had once been. "Goodnight, Dad," he whispered, his voice barely a breath.

He stepped back, lingering for a moment to watch the stillness settle over his father, the faint rhythm of his breathing the only sign that he still existed, that he was still there. With a slow, deliberate movement, Evan gathered his coat from the back of the chair and turned toward the door. The ache in his chest— the one that always followed these visits—pressed heavy but not unbearable. He knew this place, knew its air, its cold, unyielding walls. He had come to understand it as much as he understood his father's decline.

He opened the door quietly, stepping out into the hall. The faint hum of the nursing home continued, a distant backdrop to the never-ending passage of time. As he closed the door behind him, the smell of antiseptic and decay hit him again, unrelenting. It was the smell of everything breaking down, but Evan let it wash over him, familiar and unchanging. His father was asleep.

***

Evan's steps slowed as he neared the common area, an involuntary tug in his chest drawing his attention to the young woman sitting beside the elderly man. At first, the sight of them seemed completely out of place, as though the two were at odds with the sterile, decaying environment around them. The elderly man—sitting propped up, lifeless in the center of the room—was no longer merely human. He was an amalgamation of flesh and machine, suspended in an uncanny hybrid of technology, a prison of wires, tubes, and flickering lights woven into a sleek exoskeleton that seemed almost alive in its mechanical precision. The object enclosing him—no, encasing him—was an unnatural extension of the human body, an invasive cocoon of metal and circuitry, pulsating with the rhythm of a heartbeat long forgotten. Yes, there were still bits of him scattered across the shell—the pale, wrinkled hands resting limply in his lap, the features of his frozen face. But Evan couldn't shake the feeling that the lines between human and machine had blurred beyond recognition, that he was neither one nor the other. What he saw now, what remained of him, was something altogether new.

Evan had never seen anything so grotesque, so alien to the human form. Inside, the man was a ghost, his chest rising and falling slowly, with a mechanical regularity that would have been comforting—if not for the fact that it was so hollow, so devoid of meaning. There was no spark behind the closed eyes, no recognition, just an isolated mechanism ticking away, the last vestige of a life once full of ideas now distilled into a function. The image warped before Evan's eyes, distorting in a way that made his stomach turn. It was as though time itself had been scrambled, fractured into a grotesque mockery of what human existence was supposed to be.

Yet, it wasn't the man or his absurd contraption that caught Evan's attention. It was the woman sitting beside him, her presence so out of place, so deeply at odds with the mechanical horror at her side. She seemed to shimmer with an almost ethereal quality, as if the very light in the room bent around her. Her beauty was strange, unsettling—almost too perfect. Her delicate features, symmetrical to the point of feeling engineered, glowed under the harsh fluorescent lighting, but it was the strange intensity of her emerald eyes that pulled at Evan, as though she were not of this world. There was a gravity to her, a stillness that made everything else in the room fade away. She held a book in her hands, her voice a soft murmur that wrapped around the room like smoke, a rhythm of words Evan couldn't quite make out, but which seemed to pulse in the air, building and receding in gentle waves.

He felt a sudden need to understand, a compulsion to learn what bound her to this place, to this tragic tableau. He moved closer, his steps muffled by the carpet. The young woman did not acknowledge him at first, her focus on the words in the book, the cadence of her voice growing quieter. But then, as if sensing his presence, she looked up, her gaze locking with his. Her eyes were full of something, something not entirely human, something too understanding. A smile curved at the edges of her mouth, not one of warmth but of something more complex, something layered— sadness, perhaps, or resignation, too heavy to name.

"Hello," Evan said, his voice unsteady, as though the act of speaking to her violated some unseen boundary. "Sorry to intrude, but I couldn't help but wonder . . . is this your father?"

Her smile deepened, curling like smoke. "No," she replied softly, her voice carrying a strange resonance, like the last note of a song fading into silence. "Professor Hartley was my teacher at the university. My name is Lila."

"Evan," he responded, extending his hand with the awkwardness of someone unfamiliar with human connection. Her hand was cool, not cold, but undeniably distant, as though her flesh were not entirely hers. The touch lingered for a moment longer than was normal, but Evan didn't draw away. He couldn't. "I'm sorry," he continued, struggling to find the right words, "I've never seen anyone young visiting here before, much less . . . every day."

Lila's eyes flickered for a second, almost imperceptibly, before she turned her gaze back to the professor. "He was more than just a teacher," she murmured. "He was a mentor, a friend. Even after I graduated, we would meet, gather with other students. He brought history to life—really brought it to life, you know?"

Evan nodded, although he didn't understand, not really. His own university years had been a blur of faceless AI-led lectures, digital assignments graded by unseen programs, void of the human warmth Lila described. He couldn't grasp the depth of what she was saying.

"And now you're returning the favor," Evan said quietly, more to himself than to her, as though a revelation had just clicked into place. "Reading to him. Keeping him company."

Lila's lips twitched into a smile, but it was the kind that seemed to carry the residue of something deeper, something buried beneath layers of experience and regret. Her fingers hovered just above the book, a slight tremor running through them as they brushed against the paper. It wasn't just a gesture. There was something mechanical about it, like her touch was coded, linked to an idea too massive to fully comprehend. The weight of her words seemed to condense around the pages of the book, as if they were shackled to the ink and vellum in some desperate attempt to hold on to what remained. "It's the least I can do," she murmured, her voice almost too quiet, as if the sound might unravel the fragile thread that connected her to the past. "He gave so much to us. His knowledge, his passion. I can't . . . I can't just let that go."

Evan felt the words worm their way into his mind, skittering through his thoughts like a virus, infecting his perception of her. "What do you do?" he asked, though the question seemed hollow, an echo of something that might have been important but wasn't anymore.

Lila paused, her gaze flickering briefly over him, as if searching for something she'd misplaced. "I'm a professor of history. At the same university," she said, the words a dissonant hum, like a machine trying to boot up but never quite finding its rhythm. "Funny, isn't it?" The phrase hung in the air, detached, a strange quirk in her voice, as if she herself didn't fully understand what was funny about it. The universe, Evan thought, had a way of making everything seem like a farce in retrospect, like an old photograph he'd seen in museums, the colors bleeding into each other, out of focus.

Evan's gaze flicked back to the mechanical cocoon around Professor Hartley, his mind struggling to comprehend what he was seeing. The pulse of the light around him seemed artificial, programmed, detached. "If I may . . . what happened to him?" he asked, barely above a whisper, as if the room itself would recoil from the question.

Lila's face tightened for a moment, the only sign of emotion breaking her calm demeanor. Her fingers tightened around the book in her lap. "A stroke," she said. "Massive, sudden. The doctors say he's still in there somewhere, but . . ." She trailed off, a shadow crossing her face, and her gaze dropped to the motionless professor, her voice barely audible. "I don't know. I don't know anymore."

"I'm so sorry," Evan muttered, feeling helpless in the face of her grief. But before he could silence the words that seemed to spill from him unbidden, he found himself asking, "Did the university create a . . . a synth, something to represent him, with all his knowledge? They do that now."

As soon as the words left his mouth, Evan regretted them; the thought of a synthetic copy of someone's essence felt obscene. But Lila didn't bristle in anger. Instead, she nodded, her smile softer this time, tinged with a sadness too deep to ignore.

"They did," she confirmed quietly. "They created what they call the Hartley Interface. It lectures, it answers questions, it even tells his old jokes. It's incredible, really." Her eyes glistened, a faint shimmer of tears just below the surface. "But it's not him. It's not . . . him. It can't capture the way his eyes lit up when a student made a breakthrough, the passion in his voice when he spoke about the lessons of history. It's just a collection of data points, algorithms. A simulation."

She lowered her hand onto the professor's, the touch delicate, almost tentative, as though she feared the gesture might trigger something far beyond her understanding. "This," she whispered, her voice a fragile thing, edged with the kind of reverence that made the room feel simultaneously more solid and more ephemeral, "this is real . . . this matters."

The words vibrated with a strange energy, their weight pressing against the walls of the room, warping the space around them. There was an intensity to them, subtle yet pervasive, like a ripple in the fabric of reality itself. They didn't just fill the silence—they altered it, distorted it, as if the very air had been bent to accommodate their existence.

"Even if he can't respond, even if he doesn't know I'm here . . ." Her gaze flickered toward him, the professor's form indistinguishable from the chair, from the wires, from the machine that had swallowed him whole. "It matters." She spoke as if this single moment, this fractured connection, might somehow anchor her in a reality that no longer made sense, as if the machinery of existence had fractured and she was struggling to reassemble it, piece by piece, even if it meant clinging to a shadow.

Evan stood frozen, the weight of her words sinking deep within him, thoughts of his father—his real father, not the fragmented echoes the MemRec offered—lingering on the edge of his mind. He thought of the days spent watching the light flicker in his father's eyes, then vanish, replaced by the hollow drone of memories none of them could ever be sure were his.

"I think I understand," he said slowly, though part of him wasn't sure that he did.

Lila met his gaze, her emerald eyes sharp, probing. Whatever she saw there, whatever recognition she found, seemed to satisfy her. She nodded, then gestured to an empty chair. "Would you like to join us?" she asked, her voice like the softest invitation. "I was just about to start a new chapter."

Evan hesitated, his thoughts racing back to his father waiting in his room. But something in the way Lila sat there, in the quiet devotion she exuded, called to him. The invitation was like a tether, pulling him toward something larger than the confines of the nursing home.

"I'd like that," he said softly, settling into the chair beside her. "Thank you."

As Lila's voice filled the room, the ancient words of a long-dead historian echoing through the sterile air, Evan allowed himself to drift. For a moment, it was as if the world had shifted, and he was no longer trapped in the strange, artificial silence of his father's decline. He could almost see Professor Hartley, not as he was now, but as he had once been—alive with ideas, vibrant with the passion of the past. And for that moment, surrounded by the quiet dignity of Lila's vigil, Evan understood the delicate, imperishable nature of what it meant to be truly alive—and perhaps, for the first time in years, the true meaning of legacy.

The Boy in the Glass

I don't know what made me do it the first time.

It was late—too late for a kid to still be up—and the house had that heavy, drowned silence it gets when everyone else has gone to bed. My parents' bedroom door was shut, no light under it, and the television was dead in the living room. But I was awake. Not just awake—alert, as if something was transmitting directly into my skull from a source I couldn't name.

I was standing in the hallway when I felt it: a pull. Not physical, not like a hand on my shirt. More like the way you realize you're thirsty, except the thirst is for something you can't name. The bathroom door was open, a yellow wedge of light cutting across the carpet. I stepped toward it without deciding to.

The mirror was waiting for me.

It hung above the sink, humming in the overhead light. Not actually humming, you understand—it was just a piece of glass, rectangular, screwed into the wall. But I felt it humming. Felt it looking back. I didn't approach it to see if my hair was sticking up or to check for chocolate around my mouth. I approached like a man walking to a ticket counter for a trip he hadn't planned, holding out money he didn't know he had.

I climbed onto the counter, knees scraping the cabinet doors, and leaned in until my breath misted the glass.

And there he was.

The boy. Me. But not just "me" the way you normally recognize yourself. This was a presence. He had my ears, my pale skin, my slightly uneven front teeth, but he also had this... patience. Like he'd been standing there for a long time, waiting for me to arrive.

My heart started thumping.

"Why am I here?" I asked.

The boy—my reflection—didn't answer. But I could see the thought flicker in his eyes.

I swallowed. "What is this world I'm in?"

It was an absurd question, even for a seven-year-old. But I couldn't take it back. The words had a kind of weight to them, like I'd said them before, somewhere else, to someone else, and now I was repeating them because I had to.

The boy leaned closer too, until our noses almost touched the cold glass. The space between us seemed to thin. For a second, I had the insane certainty that if I pushed forward, I'd fall through. Not like water—more like falling through the picture on a screen into the room where it was filmed.

My pulse roared in my ears.

I don't remember moving, but I must have stepped back. The boy retreated too. The space between us thickened again, the ordinary barrier of reflection and silver backing. I was just a kid in a yellow-lit bathroom staring at a cheap mirror.

Only, I knew better.

Something had just happened. Something important.

I turned off the light, walked back to my room, and got into bed. The house felt heavier now, as though it had heard me ask the question and was pretending to sleep.

And here's the part I don't tell people—because it sounds insane: I knew, even then, that this wasn't the last time it would happen. That someday—maybe years later, maybe when I was an old man—the boy in the mirror would still be there, waiting to be asked again.

I think I feared it.

And I think I wanted it more than anything.

***

The storm was the first thing I noticed. Not the kind of storm that gets you excited as a kid, but the kind that presses down on your skin like an invisible weight. Rain hammered against the windowpane, tracing erratic paths down the glass. Lightning flashed, sharp and sudden, illuminating the room in fractured bursts. I was sitting at my desk, textbook open but unread, scribbling half-hearted notes that didn't stick. The hum of the thunder was like a low, static noise behind my thoughts.

Then the compulsion came again. It wasn't a choice. It was more like gravity pulling me off the chair, driving me across the room to the dresser mirror. I felt my legs move before I even understood why. The air smelled damp, and my heart thrummed faster, the storm outside synchronizing with some strange rhythm inside me.

I stood in front of the mirror, the reflection dim and flickering as the lightning cast shadows across my face. The glass felt colder than it should have. I leaned in close, so close that my breath fogged the surface. I wiped a spot with the sleeve of my sweatshirt, but the fog didn't clear; it just thickened, as if the glass was resisting.

My eyes caught my own gaze—or something like it. The eyes staring back weren't quite mine. They held a strange detachment, a foreignness that unsettled me. It was as if the person reflected wasn't just looking back, but looking through me, somewhere beyond the surface. They weren't the same eyes I woke up with each morning; they were someone else's eyes—someone trapped in the mirror, or trapped in me.

"Why am I here?" The question slithered through my mind, unbidden, but urgent. Not in words I spoke aloud—no one would understand, and I didn't even fully understand myself. It was a question heavier than any I had asked before. It wasn't about homework or friends or who liked who. It was about existence. About the frame that held me—the room, the mirror, the storm—and why I was in this place instead of another.

The question hung in the air, mixing with the static scent of rain and the hum of electricity from the old lamp on my desk. The mirror didn't answer. It never did. It just showed me that distorted version of myself, eyes hollowed with something older than adolescence, as if I carried the weight of knowledge I had not yet earned.

I pressed my forehead against the cool glass, feeling the vibrations of the storm ripple through it. The mirror was more than just glass. It was a threshold, a membrane between what I was and what I wasn't. Between the surface and the depths below.

The reflection shifted subtly, or maybe my mind was playing tricks—like a glitch in reality. For a moment, I thought I saw movement behind my own image. A flicker of something alive. A shadow that blinked out of sync with the lightning. My breath caught in my throat.

"What is this world I'm in?" That question surfaced like a whisper in a dream. It wasn't about geography or people, but about reality itself—the fabric of the world that wrapped me, held me captive, or maybe protected me.

The storm raged louder, thunder cracking like a gunshot in the night. My fingers pressed flat against the mirror's edge, as if I could push through, break the barrier between me and that other place—whatever it was.

But the glass held firm.

I pulled back slowly, my breath still fogging the glass, my eyes searching for answers that weren't there. I wanted to believe this was some kind of test, some glitch in the matrix of my life. Something I could fix or explain, if I just tried hard enough.

But I knew better. The questions weren't going away. They were growing heavier, like unseen anchors in my chest.

I sat back down at the desk, but the storm had seeped into my veins. I was different now—older, somehow. More aware of the invisible machinery of the world. My friends talked about music, about parties, about crushes. I heard them, but I was somewhere else entirely, caught in the flickering space between a boy and something not yet defined.

That night, sleep came reluctantly. The questions followed me into the dark: Why am I here? What is this world I'm in?

I didn't have answers. But I knew this wasn't the last time I'd be pulled toward the glass. Not the last time I'd stare into the reflection and see the eyes that weren't quite mine. Not the last time the mirror would whisper its silent call, inviting me to look deeper, to wonder longer, to lose myself in the strange landscape between reality and the impossible.

***

I was brushing my teeth when it happened. Just a normal night in my cramped city apartment, the kind where the walls press in and the hum of distant traffic crawls beneath the windows like some restless insect. The usual: fluorescent light flickering overhead, the mirror above the sink smeared with a thin film of grime I never bothered to clean. But then—mid-motion—my hands froze. The toothbrush hung there, paused, foam dripping silently into the chipped porcelain basin. I wanted to pull away, but my limbs refused. It was like my body had been hijacked by a force I couldn't name.

The mirror. It was calling me. No, not calling. Whispering. But without a sound. A vibration beneath the surface of things, as if someone—or something—was just on the other side of the glass. Not a reflection, but another presence, reaching out.

I stared into my own eyes, but they were wrong. Not mine. They belonged to someone else entirely. Someone waiting, someone trapped behind the slick barrier of reality. The face looked back at me with urgent, unblinking calm. It wasn't just me, and yet it was. It was the same, but fractured—like a broken hologram of a self that I couldn't reconcile.

Why was I here? Why did this mirror hold some kind of doorway? The questions clawed at my mind, sharper now, gnawing at the edges of every thought I'd ever tried to ignore. The world around me—the job I clocked in to every day, the relationships I forced a smile through—felt suddenly meaningless. Like a cheap mask worn over a void.

I wanted to pull back, to shut the bathroom door, to pretend none of it was happening. But the compulsion held me captive, my breath fogging the glass as I leaned closer, so close that my nose almost touched the mirror's cold surface. The reflection shimmered, and for a moment I thought I saw my double's fingers stretch toward me, just beyond the glass, trying to break through.

I blinked, and the image snapped back to normal—or as normal as it ever got.

There was no way to explain this sensation. It wasn't a hallucination. It wasn't stress or exhaustion. It was something else. Something fundamentally wrong with the fabric of what I thought was real.

All my life I'd carried this sensation—the pull, the itch beneath the skin of existence—but now it felt urgent. Like a countdown, a warning, a summons.

I tried to tell myself to focus on something else: the mundane details of my life, the coffee I needed to buy, the deadlines looming at work. But the questions echoed, louder, like a chorus behind my eyes: Why am I here? Why this world?

And the hardest question of all: What happens if I answer?

I swallowed hard and wiped the foam from my mouth, but my hands still trembled. The silence in the apartment grew thick, as if the air was holding its breath with me. I thought of the boy I was once—the seven-year-old who first felt this pull—and the stormy teenager who saw something strange in his own eyes. Now, at twenty-three, the compulsion was no longer a faint whisper; it was a roar in the quiet spaces of my mind.

What if the reflection wasn't a reflection at all?

What if the mirror was a veil, thin and fragile, between the reality I lived in and something else—something I wasn't meant to see, or maybe something I was meant to find?

The idea made my chest tighten, a cold knot of fear and fascination.

I caught my breath and looked one last time. The face stared back, calm and steady, eyes deep pools of unspoken knowledge. It was me, and yet it wasn't.

I stepped back, away from the sink, the bathroom light suddenly too bright, too sterile. I wanted to believe I was imagining things, that this was some trick of stress or fatigue. But I knew the truth was darker. Stranger. And no matter how hard I tried, I couldn't shake the feeling that everything I knew was a lie built on top of something else.

I wasn't sure if I was the one looking through the mirror— or the one being looked at.

That night, I didn't sleep. The questions circled in my head, relentless:

Why am I here?

What is this world I'm in?

What is on the other side?

I wasn't ready to face the answers, if there even were any. But I knew, somehow, that the mirror wasn't done with me. Not yet.

And neither was I.

***

I didn't look in mirrors for years. Not really. Not the way you're supposed to. I glanced at my reflection sometimes—snapshots, like the surface of a pond disturbed by a thrown stone—but never lingered. I convinced myself it was just superstition, a childish habit from a time when I was prone to seeing things that weren't there. A ghost, a glitch in the world's fabric. An itch in my brain.

But tonight, in this stale, nondescript hotel bathroom, fluorescent light bleaching the walls an oppressive white, the pull came back like a bad drug craving. Harder than ever.

I'd been avoiding it. Avoiding the questions. Avoiding the dread. Avoiding that fractured feeling, like reality itself was a cheap simulation I'd caught a glimpse behind.

Dinner was a lonely affair—a plate of bland food I barely tasted, the quiet buzz of conversation from other tables reminding me how detached I'd become. I was a ghost among strangers, a man haunted by reflections that refused to be ignored.

Back in the room, I brushed my teeth mechanically, eyes fixed on the cracked tile floor. Then it began: the tug, sharp and undeniable, like an electric charge pulling me toward the mirror.

I stopped mid-brush. The toothbrush hung from my lips, foam dripping slowly into the sink. The buzzing in my head grew louder, a silent whisper behind my eyes. I could feel it, felt it always, the presence on the other side—the other me—waiting.

I turned toward the mirror, dread and compulsion warring in my chest. My reflection stared back with the same eyes, but something was off. The man in the glass wasn't me—or maybe I wasn't him.

The room seemed to warp around the edges, the sterile light twisting into shadows. I could almost see past the glass, into a place where the world folded back on itself, a place where I could reach through and touch something real.

For decades, the questions had haunted me like ghosts in a fog: Why am I here? What is this world I'm in?

Now, at forty-six, they felt like nails tapping against the walls of my skull, relentless and insistent.

I wanted to look away. I tried. I wanted to shut it off like a broken machine. But the mirror held me captive.

It was a doorway. I knew that now. Not just a reflection but a portal, a threshold to a deeper truth I had neither the courage nor the clarity to face.

I leaned closer, breath fogging the glass, and for a moment I saw it—a flicker, a ripple in the surface. My eyes shifted, not quite my own. The man in the mirror blinked at me, and the room's edges shimmered, like heat haze on a summer's day.

What was behind that glass? Another world? Another version of myself trapped in some parallel nightmare? Or just a cruel trick of light and memory?

The more I stared, the heavier the questions pressed on me. They clawed at the corners of my mind like a persistent itch beneath my skin.

I wanted answers, but the answers never came. Only the same questions. The same pull. The same cold echo.

I turned away abruptly, heart pounding, the sensation like a low-frequency hum vibrating through my bones.

Back in bed, I lay awake for hours, the ceiling above me a blank white screen on which my fears played out in flickering shadows.

The compulsion wasn't going anywhere. It was part of me now. Part of the strange glitch in my existence.

I thought about the boy I once was, seven years old, standing in that dim bathroom under a harsh yellow light, feeling that first unbearable pull toward the mirror. That moment when the world seemed both immense and empty all at once.

And I realized it had never stopped. The questions hadn't faded. They had only grown louder, more urgent.

I'd spent my life trying to bury the discomfort, to live by routine and distraction—work, relationships, small joys—but the mirror knew better. The mirror remembered.

It was waiting for me to come back.

***

I'm eighty-three years old. Or, so I think. My mind is sometimes a fog. Just thinking about it stings at me. But mostly I try not to think. The hospice room is dim, stale with the scent of disinfectant and something else—a chemical sharpness I can't name, maybe death waiting just beyond the thin walls. The nurses come and go like ghosts, their faces bland, their hands gentle but distant. Same with what family is left. That cares. They speak in low tones, always careful, as if I'm some fragile artifact.

But there's one thing I still want. One last pull, a thing I cannot deny.

I'm in bed, too frail to even raise my head without help. My skin is paper-thin; my fingers tremble and curl in useless fists. The world outside the window—dull blur of green trees and afternoon light—feels like another planet, distant and unreachable. Time has folded strangely here. Every minute feels stretched, then compressed, then stuck.

And yet—something inside me aches with a strange urgency. It's the mirror. The compulsion.

I whisper, my voice barely more than a breath, "Bring me a mirror."

They look surprised, hesitant, but they do it. They fetch a small hand mirror, one that I recognize instantly from some corner of my past. The frame is chipped, the glass a little foggy, but it's a portal. I know it is.

They hold it before me. My hands shake, wanting to reach out, but I can't. Instead, I fix my gaze on the glass.

The mirror feels alive. It hums quietly beneath my eyes, a static charge on the edges of my vision. There's a whisper too— not in sound, but in presence. A presence on the other side, just beyond the thin sheet of silver.

I stare. The years fall away. The frail old man I see reflected dissolves like smoke. The lines, the sagging flesh, the dull eyes— they blur and reshape, molding into something else.

A child. Seven years old. A boy with wide eyes full of awe and fear. The same boy from the bathroom that night, so long ago. The same boy who leaned toward the mirror, compelled by questions he couldn't answer.

His eyes meet mine through the glass, bright, searching.

"Why am I here?" he seems to ask, without moving his lips.

"What is this place?" The question hangs in the air between us.

I want to answer him, to tell him I've lived the years, fought the shadows, wrestled with the compulsion, but the words won't come. The mirror won't let me. It's like a riddle whispered in code, spoken in silence.

All I can do is look. Look back into the boy's eyes. And in that gaze, I see everything—the first wonder, the endless questions, the ache of knowing that the world is not quite real, not quite what it seems.

The room around me fades. The nurses' faces blur, the sounds dim. Time unwinds like a spool, pulling me back and back.

The boy's image flickers, then begins to fade—like a dying star, collapsing into darkness.

The glass goes empty.

I exhale my last breath.

And in that breath, the final thought flares clear:

Perhaps the questions were the answer all along.

I realize—all the searching, the doubt, the times staring at glass—it was never about finding answers. It was about learning to live with the questions.

Because some doors don't open. Some reflections don't show what we expect. But the act of looking—of daring to ask—is the meaning.

And then the silence takes me.

The Three of Corvus

The Sanctus Novum drifted in the boundless gulf, its steel hull cutting through the void with the quiet defiance of a pilgrim against eternity. Shadows stretched and recoiled, swallowing one another in the pale light of distant stars. Within, the vessel hummed like a restless heart, every pipe and circuit alive with the weight of its journey. The Prelate stood motionless at the observation window, hands clasped behind his back, robes a tapestry of sanctity and burden, their gilded edges heavy with intent. He stared into the unyielding dark as if waiting for it to answer.

Behind him came the measured cadence of boots against polished metal. Captain Andros stepped into the dim light, his face set in lines of weathered pragmatism. His uniform bore none of the opulence of the Prelate's garments, only the clean austerity of function.

"You've made your decision, then," Andros said, his voice low but edged with the weight of unspoken caution.

"I have," the Prelate replied, his gaze unmoving. "Set a course for Corvus."

Andros hesitated. He had seen worlds torn apart by their own making, places where life clung like moss to crumbling stone. But Corvus—Corvus was something else. "You're sure? Corvus is no sanctuary, Prelate. That planet's a forge. The heat alone could warp our shielding. And the volcanoes -"

"I am aware of the risks." The Prelate's voice was measured, a blade honed to precision. He turned, his eyes dark wells of conviction. "But I have also heard the stories. Three hermits, each of them wholly devoted to the divine. Such faith cannot be ignored."

"Stories," Andros said, the word slipping from his mouth like ash. He ran a hand over his closely shorn hair, as though the motion might steady him. "With respect, sir, stories don't shield a hull or keep men alive. That planet doesn't care about devotion. It'll swallow us whole just the same."

"And yet," the Prelate said, his tone unyielding, "faith does not ask for guarantees. It demands we step forward, even when the ground is unsteady."

Andros looked at the man standing before him, this figure cloaked in ceremonial weight, his conviction a wall that could neither bend nor break. He had ferried Prelates before—men who talked of faith like it was a currency, bartered in sermons and rituals. But this one, there was no veneer to his certainty. It burned cold and sharp, like ice held against the skin.

"Very well," Andros said, the words landing heavy. "I'll inform the crew. But don't expect me to applaud when we're orbiting a rock that wants to burn us alive."

"Your skepticism is noted," the Prelate said, already turning back to the window. The void held him in its grasp, vast and indifferent.

Andros lingered a moment, his arms crossed. "Permission to speak freely, sir?"

"Granted."

"This mission of yours. Is it faith you're chasing, or proof?"

The Prelate didn't answer at first. His reflection in the glass seemed to ripple as the ship shifted course, the engines humming to life with a subtle vibration. "Proof is for the doubter, Captain. Faith walks without it."

Andros shook his head, muttering under his breath as he left the chamber. The Prelate stood alone, the silence thickening around him. Beyond the window, Corvus loomed in his mind—a world of fire and stone, its surface a tapestry of unending upheaval. And there, among the shifting ash and molten veins, three lives pulsing with purpose.

In the hours that followed, the crew prepared for descent. Voices rang out across the bridge, clipped and efficient. Calculations spilled from consoles, trajectories mapped against the churning reality of Corvus. Andros barked orders, his voice a tether against the encroaching chaos.

When the Prelate returned to the bridge, the planet had grown in the viewport, a great smoldering sphere shrouded in clouds of ash. Red fissures cut across its surface, a lattice of fire and earth shifting in restless communion.

"Beautiful in its own way," the Prelate murmured.

Andros snorted. "If you like your beauty molten and liable to explode."

The Prelate ignored him, stepping closer to the viewport. The weight of the moment pressed against him, though he bore it as one accustomed to burdens that would break lesser men.

"Do you think they're even alive down there?" Andros asked, his tone sharp but not unkind.

"I have no doubt," the Prelate said. "If their faith is as strong as the stories suggest, they will endure."

"Faith doesn't stop magma," Andros said, half to himself.

The Prelate turned to face him. "Perhaps not. But it can transcend it."

Andros opened his mouth to retort, but thought better of it. He turned back to the console, muttering a string of commands. The ship shuddered as it entered the planet's atmosphere, the hull groaning against the pressure.

Below, Corvus roared its greeting, fire and ash surging into the skies like some ancient beast exhaling. The Sanctus Novum pressed on, its shields flaring against the heat. Andros barked orders to the crew, his voice cutting through the din. The Prelate stood steady, his gaze fixed on the seething landscape below.

"What drives a man to seek God in a place like this?" Andros asked, half-turning.

"Perhaps it is the fire," the Prelate said. "Perhaps it reminds them of their own trials."

Andros shook his head, but there was no malice in the gesture. "Well, here's hoping the fire doesn't consume us before we find them."

The Prelate didn't respond. His eyes were locked on the horizon, where the first peaks of Corvus's volcanic range clawed at the sky.

***

The journey to Corvus unfurled in uneasy quiet, the kind that sat heavy in the belly like a stone. The crew spoke in murmurs, their voices small against the hum of the ship's engines. The name Corvus had spread through them like a contagion, passed between tired hands and whispered over meals. No one dared say it aloud twice in the same breath.

Lieutenant Karis, lean and restless, leaned against a bulkhead with the ease of a man accustomed to danger but not to silence. The main display glowed with the image of Corvus, its surface a pulsing wound of blackened rock and molten fire. He crossed his arms and tilted his head, the barest smirk on his lips.

"Looks like hell got indigestion and spit that out," he said.

The crew shifted uneasily, drawn to the screen despite themselves. The planet seemed to breathe, its molten veins pulsing like blood under skin, its sulfurous clouds swirling with a malign intelligence.

One of the engineers, a grizzled veteran with soot-streaked hands, spat on the deck. "What're we doing here? Ain't nothing holy about that rock."

Karis shrugged, his humor brittle. "Because the Prelate thinks wisdom comes cheap, even if you've got to dig it out of lunatics and lava."

Their words hung in the air like ash until the Prelate entered, his robes a dark tide against the metal of the floor. Conversation withered as the men turned to him, their eyes a mix of reverence and apprehension.

"Captain," he said, his voice carrying the authority of one who has never had to raise it.

Andros turned from the helm, his stance taut as a drawn bowstring. He glanced at the display, the fiery orb of Corvus reflected in his dark eyes. "We're in orbit, Prelate. Scanners read nothing but fire and storms. No sign of anything living."

"They are there," the Prelate replied, his tone brooking no debate. "Prepare a shuttle."

Andros hesitated, his jaw tightening. "This planet doesn't welcome visitors, Prelate. We've seen no settlements, no markers, nothing to suggest anyone's survived down there."

The Prelate stepped closer, his gaze steady and unyielding. "Faith survives where men cannot. Ready the shuttle."

Karis chuckled low, the sound drawing glares from the other crew. "A bold claim, sir. Let's hope it holds water—or doesn't catch fire."

The Prelate's gaze shifted to him, sharp and unamused. "Courage is not found in cynicism, Lieutenant. It is forged in fire."

Karis straightened, his smirk fading. "Aye, sir. Forged in fire."

The Prelate turned back to Andros, his expression softening just enough to temper his command. "The hermits of Corvus hold truths that few can fathom. Truths that may guide us all. Trust in that."

Andros gave a stiff nod, turning to the controls. "Shuttle will be ready in ten minutes."

As the crew dispersed, Karis lingered by the bulkhead, watching the planet writhe on the screen. He muttered under his breath, too low for anyone but himself to hear. "Hope it's worth it."

***

The shuttle's descent was a crucible of sound and motion, a chaos of strain and fury borne on wings of alloy and fire. The craft bucked violently, each shudder resonating through its frame like the groans of a dying beast. Outside the viewports, ash swept past in swirling torrents, a storm of flame and shadow that obliterated the horizon. The air inside the cabin was charged, taut with the unspoken weight of men who held their fear tight against their ribs.

"Landing zone's unstable," the pilot said, his voice taut, his knuckles bloodless on the controls.

"Put her down," Andros barked, his tone more command than counsel. "We're not turning back."

The plateau rose to meet them, jagged and cruel, as though the planet itself sought to repel intruders. The landing struts groaned against the unforgiving rock, the shuttle shivering as if sensing the latent violence of the ground it now rested upon. Outside, the air shimmered with heat, thick and acrid, stinking of sulfur and charred stone. The sky was a wound, burned orange streaked with black scars, its oppressive canopy weighing down on all who dared to gaze up at it.

The ramp lowered with a hiss, releasing a breath of sterilized air that mingled with the scorched atmosphere. The Prelate descended first, his robes an incongruous white against the bleak desolation. His staff clicked against the stone with measured purpose, its metallic ring defiant in the silence. Behind him came Andros, his rifle slung low across his back. The weapon was a comfort only in principle; it would serve little use against the monstrous indifference of Corvus.

"This is madness," Andros muttered, his voice low but not low enough. His boots ground against the volcanic rock, each step a protest.

"Madness," the Prelate replied, not breaking stride, "is often the prelude to revelation."

Andros glanced at the old man, skepticism carved deep into his features. He said nothing further, knowing argument was a wasted breath. The Prelate's resolve was as unyielding as the stone beneath their feet.

For hours they walked, the terrain a labyrinth of molten rivers and shifting rock. Heat pressed down upon them like a vice, every breath a struggle against the sulfur-laden air. The world groaned with distant eruptions, the ground trembling in restless fits. And yet, the Prelate moved with unwavering purpose, his steps deliberate, his pace relentless. Andros followed, silent and watchful, his fingers brushing the stock of his rifle more often than necessary.

At last, the landscape yielded its secret: a solitary stone house perched on the brink of a molten river. The house was no more than a crude shelter, its walls stained black with soot, its roof a haphazard arrangement of rock slabs held by crude mortar. The river of fire pulsed nearby, casting flickering light onto the structure, a breathing entity of its own.

"This is it?" Andros asked, incredulous.

The Prelate nodded, his expression unreadable. "This is it."

Without hesitation, he approached the house, his staff striking the stone with resolute taps. He knocked upon the door, the sound stark and foreign in the surrounding silence. The world seemed to pause, the hiss of the molten river fading to a low murmur, as if Corvus itself awaited the outcome.

The door opened slowly, its hinges groaning like an old wound torn fresh. A man appeared, the First Recluse, lean and hollow, his skin stretched taut over a frame of sinew and bone. His eyes were fierce, bright with something untamed, and his voice, when it came, was dry as the volcanic dust.

"Who seeks the Three of Corvus?" he asked.

"I am the Prelate of the Sanctus Novum," the Prelate said, his tone measured and grave. He inclined his head, a gesture of respect. "I come to learn from your wisdom."

The First Recluse's gaze did not waver, cutting through the Prelate as though weighing the truth of his words. The silence stretched, heavy and impenetrable.

"Wisdom is not a thing freely given," the First Recluse said at last.

The Second Recluse sat near the back of the room, cross-legged on the floor, his head bowed in what appeared to be prayer. His robes, though threadbare, were meticulously clean, a testament to his devotion. He did not look up as they entered, his lips moving in silent recitation.

Another figure, the Third Recluse, emerged from the shadows, his form larger, his presence commanding despite the emaciation of his frame. His eyes held none of the sharpness of the first, but there was a warmth in them, a quiet that spoke of things beyond words.

"We are the Three of Corvus," the First Recluse, the one at the door said, gesturing to his companions. His tone carried a note of finality, as if there was nothing more to explain.

The Prelate inclined his head again, taking in the sight of the three men. There was a weight to the air now, an expectation that seemed to vibrate just beneath the surface.

"Then let us speak," he said, his voice steady. He stepped aside, the motion slow and deliberate. "But enter, if you would learn what there is to know."

The Prelate crossed the threshold without hesitation, Andros lingering behind him, his hand resting on the rifle sling. Inside, the house was dim, lit only by the ruddy glow of the molten river seeping through cracks in the stone walls. The air was stifling, thick with the scent of ash and sweat. The simplicity of the place was stark, a reflection of lives stripped bare of all but necessity.

The First Recluse gestured for them to sit. "We do not speak lightly here," he said. "Words carry weight, and we do not waste them."

"Perhaps," the Prelate said, lowering himself onto a stone bench near the wall, "it is time we consider what must be said."

Andros, still standing, leaned against the wall, his eyes scanning the room. The air was heavy with the promise of something unspoken, a truth yet to be unveiled. Outside, the planet groaned again, the distant roar of molten rivers a reminder of the unforgiving world that bore witness to this meeting.

***

The First Recluse's lips twisted into something like a smile, though it was thin, contemptuous. "You come seeking knowledge, but knowledge is futile. There is only one truth, and that truth is the faith I follow. Every other path is false, corrupted by lies and deceit."

The Prelate stiffened, his hands twitching at his sides. "You dismiss all other faiths?" he asked, incredulous. "How can you be so certain of your own?"

"There is no room for uncertainty," the First Recluse said, his voice rising with a fierce conviction. "The truth is plain. The faith I follow is the only true way."

The Prelate felt a tightening in his chest, but before he could respond, Captain Andros spoke, his voice measured, "And what of those who do not follow your path?"

"They are lost," the Recluse spat, his eyes burning. "They are damned."

The Prelate shifted uncomfortably, but then the Second Recluse, still sitting cross-legged on the floor, interrupted the tension. His eyes were focused on a small piece of wood in front of him, an altar of sorts, and his hands moved in a meticulous dance, performing some ritual that the Prelate could not discern. The Second Recluse bowed slightly, his movements graceful but entirely mechanical.

"I perform the rituals," he said softly, his voice a murmur, "for the sake of purity. To keep the spirit pure, the body must be disciplined. The ceremony must be flawless."

The Prelate watched as the Recluse set out a small plate of offerings that was to his side and began to chant in a language the Prelate did not recognize. His movements were practiced, perfect, though the Prelate could not help but feel that the man was disconnected from the meaning of the ritual itself.

"Is it enough to perform these actions, without understanding their meaning?" the Prelate asked, a note of doubt creeping into his voice.

The Second Recluse paused, his eyes flicking upward briefly. "Understanding is unnecessary. The ritual is what matters. The form is sacred."

As the Second Recluse continued with his ceremony, the Prelate's thoughts grew heavy. His eyes wandered, and they landed on the Third Recluse, who was now sitting on a chair in the corner, hunched over, trying in vain to read a tattered book. His eyes strained, and his lips moved in unsteady motion, as though the words were foreign to him.

"I cannot read," the Third Recluse muttered, his voice quiet, almost embarrassed. "But I try."

The Prelate studied the man for a long moment. His clothes were simple, worn by the years, and his hands were rough from labor. Yet there was something in the way he sat, the way he moved, that struck the Prelate deeply.

"Are you blind?" the Prelate asked.

The Third Recluse smiled, a soft, unassuming smile that reached his eyes. "We are all blind," he said. "I do not know the scriptures. But I do my best. I care for what I can, and that is enough."

The Prelate's heart twisted in his chest. The man's face was gentle, unassuming. On the floor, near him, was a cage holding a wounded bird. Opening the cage door, he ever so gently took the wounded bird in his hand, wrapping its damaged wing in a rag.

He whispered something low and kind to it. The simple, tender act made the Prelate feel something he had not felt in years—a quiet humility.

He stepped forward. "Tell me," he asked softly, "why do you live this way?"

The Third Recluse glanced up at him, his face open, unburdened. "I live because I am needed. I live to care for those who need help. What else is there?"

The Prelate was silent, his mind churning. The First Recluse had filled him with certainty, but also with a tightness in his chest that came from knowing there was no room for difference. The Second Recluse had shown him ritual without meaning, a hollow dance that lacked soul. But the Third Recluse, this humble man, had shown him something else—a pure, unrefined form of faith that did not depend on doctrine or ceremony.

The Prelate's thoughts grew tangled. He had come seeking wisdom, but what he had found was a dissonance between dogma and truth, between ritual and love.

"I . . . I don't understand," the Prelate murmured, more to himself than to anyone in particular.

The Third Recluse chuckled softly. "You don't have to understand. You just have to care."

The Prelate swallowed hard, the weight of the words pressing down on him. He had spent his life focused on dogma, on certainty. Yet here, on this bleak, barren planet, he had found something else entirely—something that spoke to the core of his soul.

"Do you understand it?" the Prelate asked, his voice cutting through the silence. "This—this faith of yours that is so complete?"

The Third Recluse slowly met the Prelate's gaze with a look that seemed to see through him. "What is there to understand?" he replied, his voice calm, almost bored. "It is not for understanding. It is for surrender."

"Surrender?" The Prelate frowned. "And what do you surrender to, if not reason? If not the will of the divine?"

The Third Recluse smiled faintly, his lips curling in a gesture that could have been pity, but was something else entirely. "Reason is a sword with two edges," he said. "You cannot cut through the soul with it. There is no understanding in faith. There is only obedience."

The Prelate clenched his fists. "That is not what I have been taught. Faith is a living thing, a growing thing. It requires questioning, deliberation, not blind obedience to an unknown force."

The Third Recluse's eyes suddenly darkened. "Then you are a fool," he said, his voice barely rising above a whisper. "To question is to deny. To seek answers is to reject the divine. You are not here for understanding. You are here because your heart is weak."

The Prelate's hands trembled. His pride surged within him, but the words of the Third Recluse struck deep, deeper than he wanted to admit. He stood and turned abruptly, walking toward without another word.

As he walked across the cold floors, his thoughts churned. He had always believed that faith, true faith, must be something that could be understood. It had to be a part of the soul's journey, a recognition of the divine order in the world. Yet here, in this desolate place, the recluses' faith seemed not to be rooted in understanding at all, but in resignation. In the acceptance of emptiness.

The Second Recluse, whose hands were still performing slow, deliberate rituals, now reached for a chalice and held it high. He then lowered it with measured grace, muttering prayers in a language the Prelate did not understand. The Prelate watched from the doorway, his arms crossed tightly over his chest.

"Does this mean anything?" the Prelate asked, his voice harsh in the stillness.

The Second Recluse did not stop. He moved as though in a trance, his movements precise, his focus absolute. "It is not for you to understand," the Recluse replied, his voice soft, almost reverent. "It is the ritual itself that is sacred. The repetition is the prayer."

"But what does it accomplish?" The Prelate stepped into the room, his frustration beginning to show. "You go through these motions, these empty gestures, but what do they bring? What is their purpose if it is not to draw closer to God?"

The Second Recluse's gaze flickered toward him, but his hands did not falter. "The purpose is in the doing," he said quietly, "in the devotion to the act. It is not for you to know the outcome. It is for you to serve."

The Prelate took a step back, his heart heavy with doubt. He had once believed that rituals held power, that each prayer, each movement brought the soul closer to the divine. But now, it seemed that all of it was nothing more than a hollow shell. A distraction. A way to fill the void without ever confronting it.

The Third Recluse was still holding the injured bird, gently stroking it. The Prelate watched him, wondering if this man, so simple and unrefined, could offer any answers at all.

The Third Recluse glanced up at the Prelate. "You came to see the bird, didn't you?" he asked, his voice surprisingly warm, a stark contrast to the cold indifference of the other two.

The Prelate hesitated. "I came to see if there were any answers."

The Third Recluse smiled, though it was not a smile of amusement, but of understanding. "I have no answers," he said. "I only have what I do. I care for things. I mend broken appendages."

"And what does that bring you?" The Prelate's voice was low, almost tired.

"It brings me peace," the Third Recluse answered. "It brings me joy to watch them heal, to see the fly or walk in their own time."

"Yes. The simple act of care, the quiet tenderness of tending to something else," the Prelate said.

The Third Recluse smiled. "The only thing I know," he said at last. "The only thing that feels true."

The Prelate looked at the man, a weight settling on his chest. He felt a deep sense of loss, as though all his years of study, all his dogma, had led him to this moment. To the realization that faith was not something that could be grasped through logic or ritual. It was something that had to be felt. Something that had to be lived.

He felt shame. "I have been a fool," he muttered, more to himself than to the others.

The Third Recluse looked at him, his eyes kind and unjudging. "It is never too late to learn."

The Prelate turned away, his thoughts in turmoil. He did not know what to believe anymore. The rituals, the ceremonies, the doctrines he had clung to for so long—none of them seemed to hold the truth he had once believed they did. But there, in the simple acts of caring, in the quiet presence of the Recluse, he felt something stirring. Something that felt more like faith than anything he had ever known.

***

The Prelate stood at the threshold, his shadow long and thin against the worn stone of the house. The recluses were gathered in their silent assembly, their faces drawn tight, pale beneath the weight of the dying light. The sun, sinking low on the jagged horizon, cast its last bleeding rays across the ashen earth, and the air—heavy with the scent of burnt soil and the bitter tang of sulfur—pressed in on them like a weight in the chest. It clung to their lungs, thick and suffocating, as though the very atmosphere of Corvus held them in some unspoken judgment. The air was still, save for the faint, distant rumble of the mountain's unrest, and the recluses stood unmoving, as if in the presence of something greater than themselves, something they could neither name nor fully understand.

"You have found your way," he said, his voice carrying over the silence. "And it is not mine to judge what path you choose, only that you choose it with conviction." He paused, letting the words hang like smoke in the air. "I do not ask that you walk as I have walked, nor that you hold to the same beliefs. Only that you seek the truth within yourself, as I have sought it within me."

There was no movement among the recluses, no sign of acknowledgment or dissent. The moment was too sacred, too heavy, for such things. They had long known that this would come, that it was inevitable, but now that it had arrived, they were left with the rawness of it. They knew this was the end of something—of an era, of their time together, but none of them could say exactly what. It was a truth they all felt, a thing woven through the silence, more profound than words. The Prelate's gaze swept over them, and his eyes paused on the Third Recluse, whose hands cradled the small, fragile bird. His eyes, unblinking, never strayed from the injured bird.

"You," the Prelate said, his voice softer now, gentler, "have walked the truest path. Not because it was the hardest, but because it was the one you chose without fear." His words were not a praise, not a recognition of action so much as an acknowledgment of something deeper, something woven into the very fabric of the man.

The Third Recluse did not flinch, did not move, his face unreadable, as though the Prelate's words were nothing more than the wind, blowing over the surface of a still pond. He did not need to hear them, for his faith was not a thing of words or rituals; it was something far more hidden—alive in the quiet spaces between actions, in the tenderness with which he held the injured bird, in the silence with which he walked through the world.

The Prelate turned away, and without a word, he and Andros left the house behind. As the Sanctus Novum began its slow, deliberate ascent into the ashen sky, its engines humming a deep, resonant tone that seemed to vibrate through the bones of the ship, the Prelate gathered the crew for one final sermon. He stood at the bow, the fading light of Corvus casting long, stretching shadows across the deck, as the ship crept higher into the sky, leaving behind the volcanic surface that had shaped them all.

"Faith," the Prelate's voice was carried by the wind, rising above the hum of the engines, "is not bound by doctrine. It is not confined to the rituals of our ancestors or the laws of men. It is kindness. It is humility. It is the act of love, given freely and without expectation."

The volcanic outline of Corvus, jagged and unyielding, began to fade into the distance, a dark scar on the horizon that slowly dissolved into the blackness of space. The harshness of the world they had known seemed to vanish, swept away by the ascent of the ship, as though the earth itself was letting go of its grip. Above them, the stars began to reveal themselves, soft and distant, untroubled by the noise and dust of the world below. The Prelate's gaze did not leave the horizon. The ship would carry them forward, and though the path ahead was unclear, uncertain in its direction, he knew it would be a path of their choosing. And that was enough.

While We Sleep

Sam Vance stared at the ceiling of his cramped apartment, counting the water stains for the thousandth time. The clock on his nightstand blinked 3:47 AM, its red digits accusing him of yet another sleepless night. He sighed, running a hand through his unkempt hair, feeling the grit of days-old sweat and the city's perpetual smog.

"Another night, another failure," he muttered to the empty room. The walls, thin as paper, let through the muffled sounds of his neighbors' lives—a baby crying, a couple arguing, the endless drone of vidscreens tuned to the government's approved channels.

Sam swung his legs off the cot, the faint hum of the apartment's ventilation system harmonizing with the dull clang of his heels meeting the metal floor. The air was thick, recycled to the point of tasting like dust. He ambled toward the kitchenette, a cubicle of space that seemed to mock his need for movement. The coffee maker, a relic salvaged from a forgotten era, hacked and sputtered as though it shared his disdain for the day's demands, spitting out what could barely be called liquid solace.

His eyes drifted to the plastiglass window, its edges fogged with grime that neither the rain nor his half-hearted attempts to clean could erase. Beyond the warped pane, the neon dominion of the megacorps bled into the polluted sky, casting it in a toxic symphony of green and purple. Somewhere within the labyrinthine structures of those towers, algorithms churned tirelessly—scripts coded by faceless drones to micromanage a world unraveling at the seams. Each line of code was another thread in a tapestry that pretended to bind humanity together but merely held its decay in a precarious stasis.

Sam was just another piece of the system, a cog in NeuroSoft's unrelenting machine—a machine that hummed and groaned with the weight of unseen directives and opaque intentions. His job wasn't glamorous; it was barely even definable. Somewhere in the chain of necessity, someone had decided his task mattered, though Sam often suspected even that decision had been automated. The pay was sufficient to keep his shoebox apartment lit and his government-issued mood stabilizers stocked. Those pastel pills—they dulled the edges but never eradicated the insomniac whirlpool that churned through his nights. Sleep, like freedom, had become an abstract concept.

The coffee maker let out its shrill chime, a sound pitched just sharp enough to jangle his nerves. Sam poured the steaming sludge into a chipped mug, its surface emblazoned with a fading logo from some defunct corporation. The first sip made him wince; the taste hovered somewhere between rust and burnt plastic. Still, it promised another day of alertness, another day spent interfacing with labyrinthine code that sprawled like ivy across NeuroSoft's servers—lines of logic he couldn't comprehend, feeding into systems whose purpose was obscured even to those who maintained them. Somewhere in the tangled mess, meaning might have existed, but Sam no longer cared to look for it.

As Sam turned toward his workstation, a flicker of metal snagged the edge of his vision, lurking where no such thing had a right to be—half-concealed behind the sagging, threadbare couch he'd been meaning to replace for years. The flicker carried an unnatural sheen, like it didn't quite belong to the spectrum of light he was used to. He frowned, setting his mug on the counter, the ceramic clinking against the metal surface, a sound that suddenly seemed alien.

Stepping closer, he nudged the couch aside with the apprehension of someone unearthing a buried truth. Beneath the years of dust and forgotten debris, a strange device emerged—an object no larger than his palm, with a dull silver surface that devoured the room's light like some metallic singularity. It was unnervingly smooth, as though its creators had stripped it of every human concession to functionality—no buttons, no screens, nothing to suggest how it worked or why it was there. Just an anonymous oval of impossibility, vibrating faintly with a presence Sam couldn't quite name.

"What the hell?" Sam muttered, reaching out to touch it. As his fingers brushed the surface, he felt a slight vibration, and for a moment, he could have sworn he saw symbols dancing across its surface—but when he blinked, they were gone.

Sam's fingers tightened around the device as he turned it over. It seemed impossibly light, almost as if it defied the laws governing matter, and its surface pulsed faintly with warmth—

organic warmth, not the cold sterility of machines. There was no record of its origin in his memory, no file he could dredge from the recesses of his mind. And in this world, where every piece of tech was indexed, stamped, and surveilled, the existence of something so untethered was more than just unsettling—it was heretical, a crack in the omniscient system's flawless façade.

The clock on the wall clicked over to 4:23 AM, its mechanical rhythm an unyielding reminder of time's merciless advance. Soon, the city's machinery would grind into motion, and Sam would find himself back in the corporate mausoleum, performing his duties with all the enthusiasm of a drone. Sleep? An indulgence he could scarcely afford, and certainly not now.

He placed the device on his workstation, a chaotic altar of tangled cables and flickering screens that dominated his narrow apartment. The system booted with a familiar sequence of tones, the room filling with the synthetic hum of circuits coming to life. Sam stared at the device, a silent question forming in his mind: was it watching him, or was he watching it?

As the screens flickered to life, bathing his face in their pale glow, Sam began to search. He scoured the company databases, the public nets, even the shadowy corners of the darknet where information flowed freely despite the government's best efforts to stem the tide.

Hours passed, and Sam found nothing. No reference to a device matching this description, no patents, no whispered rumors in the underground tech forums. It was as if the thing had materialized out of thin air, a ghost in a world of hard silicon and cold logic.

The alarm on his wrist unit buzzed, startling him out of his research trance. 7:00 AM. Time to don the mask of normalcy and join the shuffling masses on their way to their assigned roles in the great machine.

Sam stood, his joints creaking in protest. He looked at the device, still sitting innocently on his desk. After a moment's hesitation, he picked it up and slipped it into his pocket. He couldn't explain why, but he felt a need to keep it close.

The streets outside were already crowded, a sea of gray faces moving in lockstep towards the towering office blocks. Advertising drones buzzed overhead, their cheerful jingles a discordant counterpoint to the grim determination of the commuters below.

"Remember, citizens!" a cheery voice boomed from a nearby public address system. "Your compliance ensures our society's harmony. Report any suspicious activity to your local Thought Police representative. Together, we build a better tomorrow!"

Sam hunched his shoulders, feeling the weight of the device in his pocket like a guilty secret. He joined the throng, letting the current carry him towards the NeuroSoft building, a gleaming spire of glass and steel that seemed to pierce the very heavens.

As he shuffled through the security checkpoints, Sam felt a bead of sweat trickle down his spine. The device in his pocket seemed to grow heavier with each step. But the guards, their eyes glazed and unfocused behind their mirrored visors, waved him through without a second glance.

Sam's cubicle was a gray box indistinguishable from the hundreds around it. He sank into his chair, the familiar ache settling into his bones as he logged into his workstation. The day's assignments popped up on his screen—more lines of code, more functions to optimize, more data to process.

But as he stared at the scrolling text, Sam found he couldn't focus. His mind kept drifting back to the device, to its inexplicable presence in his apartment. He slipped a hand into his pocket, feeling its smooth contours, its unnatural warmth.

The hours oozed by, an indistinct sequence of keystrokes, caffeine-soaked interludes, and hollow exchanges with coworkers whose faces seemed to dissolve into the collective static of his memory. Through it all, the device loomed in his pocket like an alien parasite, a crack in the fragile facade of his meticulously programmed existence.

As the workday shuddered to its conclusion, Sam grappled with an odd cocktail of emotions: relief laced with something colder, sharper—a latent apprehension. The prospect of returning to his apartment, to dive deeper into the enigma, drew him with a magnetic pull, but the thought of solitude in the device's ominous presence stirred a primal unease. It wasn't dread, exactly. It was something more insidious, a whispered suggestion that the boundaries of his reality were dissolving.

The journey home unfurled like a replay of the morning, a loop on an endless tape. The same monotone faces, now wearing the pallor of another day hollowed out. Propaganda broadcasts droned in the periphery, their synthetic voices blending into the urban hum. The surveillance cameras' unblinking eyes were almost a comfort; at least their gaze implied he was still anchored in the here and now. Yet Sam's thoughts spiraled elsewhere, orbiting the mystery weighing down his pocket like a black hole.

Once back in the hermetic stillness of his apartment, Sam withdrew the device and placed it on his desk. In the dim, fading light, it seemed to shimmer with an unnatural liquidity, its edges refusing to conform to his vision. When he reached out this time, the surface ignited—symbols erupting like fractal fire. They weren't just shapes; they pulsed with a sinister intelligence, angular glyphs that seemed to drill into his perception, leaving his eyes aching, his thoughts teetering on the edge of coherence.

Exhaustion suddenly washed over him, a bone-deep weariness that made his eyelids feel like lead weights. Sam stumbled to his bed, collapsing onto the thin mattress without bothering to undress. As consciousness slipped away, he had a fleeting thought:

For the first time in . . . he didn't know how long . . . he was going to sleep.

And as the darkness claimed him, Sam Vance had no idea that his world was about to change forever. The device on his desk began to pulse with an otherworldly light, its true purpose finally activated by the proximity of a sleeping mind.

In the realm between waking and dreaming, the Gatherers stirred, ready to begin their nightly harvest.

***

As Sam fell asleep, the device pulsed with an otherworldly glow. As consciousness slipped away, reality fractured and reassembled itself into a kaleidoscope of impossible geometries.

He found himself standing in a vast, crystalline chamber. The walls shimmered with iridescent patterns that seemed to shift and breathe. Countless translucent tendrils stretched from the ceiling, each connected to a floating, ethereal figure. Sam realized with a jolt that he recognized these figures—they were people from his life, colleagues, neighbors, even strangers he'd passed on the street.

A disembodied voice echoed through the chamber. "Subject 47329-B, integration commencing."

Sam felt a tugging sensation at the base of his skull. Memories began to flow out of him like quicksilver, coalescing into shimmering orbs that drifted upward. He saw fragments of his day—the tedium of his cubicle, the mysterious device, fleeting moments of human connection.

"Upload complete," the voice intoned. "Anomaly detected."

The chamber began to vibrate with a rhythm that seemed almost sentient, as though the room itself were drawing breath. The figures around Sam flickered like malfunctioning holograms, their edges dissolving into static. A crack carved its way through the crystalline floor, branching outward with a fractal elegance that hinted at some deliberate design. As the dream world disintegrated, Sam's gaze was dragged to the edge of perception, where something vast and utterly alien loomed—a presence too immense for comprehension, pressing against the fabric of his mind like a phantom weight.

He awoke with a jolt, lungs heaving for air as though he'd been submerged in a drowning sea. Sweat soaked his skin, a chilling testament to his ordeal. The device beside him now pulsed faintly, its glow a heartbeat away from oblivion. Sam staggered to the bathroom, his legs trembling beneath him. He splashed water over his face, the cold a sharp tether to reality. Yet when his eyes met his reflection, unease coiled in his chest. The face staring back at him seemed altered—aged, weary, and burdened with a knowledge that felt both intimate and impossibly distant. It wasn't just his reflection; it was a stranger peering through his own eyes.

"Just a dream," he muttered. But even as the words left his mouth, he knew it was a lie.

The apartment throbbed with a disquieting strangeness. Objects seemed imperceptibly shifted, their positions altered by fractions of a degree, yet enough to dislodge the tenuous anchor of familiarity. The air was dense, charged with a current of intangible tension, crackling faintly in the corners of Sam's awareness. His body moved with uncharacteristic fluidity, each gesture imbued with an eerie precision, as though some unseen hand had tuned him to a finer frequency. His thoughts unfolded in startling clarity, sharp as glass. Reality itself felt thinner, as though he were peering through an aperture to something far more vast and incomprehensible.

The device rested in his palm, an enigma that pulsed faintly against his skin, warm and faintly rhythmic, as if it possessed a heartbeat of its own. He turned it over, examining its smooth, unbroken surface. Without warning, a symbol flared briefly across its face, an impossible spiral that folded inward infinitely, tugging at the edges of his comprehension. His breath hitched.

"What . . . what are you?" Sam murmured, his voice a rasp in the electric silence.

A flicker answered from his terminal, which sprang to life with disconcerting autonomy. Lines of code cascaded down the screen in a torrent of cryptic data, blindingly fast, yet somehow legible to him. He didn't merely read; he absorbed. The device was a nexus, a channel that bridged dimensions. And the Gatherers? They were archivists of the infinite, collectors of human essence preserved in fractal archives scattered across the universal lattice.

His hands found the keyboard instinctively, guided by a force beyond his own volition. The clatter of keys filled the air as he delved into the labyrinthine depths of digital pathways. Threads of data revealed whispers of a shadow system, a subnetwork untethered from the megacorporate monoliths. It murmured of an entity vast and unknowable, a gestalt of consciousness stretching beyond the frail constraints of individuality—a universal intelligence that consumed and encompassed all.

As Sam delved deeper, an electric unease coiled through his nerves. The knowledge wasn't learned but unearthed, like a relic from a previous version of himself. Alien, yet disturbingly familiar—its origins buried in the folds of his own fractured psyche. Who had placed this here? And more unsettling: when?

A notification pinged softly, disrupting the silence. A message from himself, timestamped hours ago. "The truth lies in the spaces between sleep. Follow the threads." Threads? No—tendrils. Sam squinted, his mind filling in gaps that weren't supposed to exist. He didn't recall sending the message, yet the evidence was irrefutable.

Messages multiplied, scattered across his system like breadcrumbs on a spiraling path. "The Gatherers are watching. The lattice binds us all." "Reality is a simulation agreed upon by the desperate." "Your end is nigh. Prepare." The last one sent an electric tremor through his chest. End? What end? Was this a terminal diagnosis or something stranger—a cosmic deadline approaching?

The device on his desk pulsed faintly, its rhythm synchronized with his heartbeat. Had it always done this? Or had it tuned itself to him, a symbiotic frequency locking them inescapably together? He grasped it, its metallic surface cool and unfamiliar, yet charged with something he couldn't name.

His gaze drifted to the black mirror of his terminal screen. There, his reflection wavered, briefly displaced by something otherworldly—a figure with shifting features, ethereal and unanchored. One of the entities from his dreams.

With a deep breath, Sam pressed down on the device. The world began peeling away, layer by layer, until nothing familiar remained. Space stretched, and he was no longer confined to a body. He became vast, a node in a pulsating network of infinite consciousness.

"Welcome, Sam Vance," a voice echoed, a chorus of himself speaking in infinite harmony. "You have taken the first step toward awakening."

Sam stood amidst the swirling torrent of memories, a kaleidoscopic maelstrom of human thought and emotion collapsing in on itself like a dying star. The brilliance was unbearable; every joy, every heartbreak, every banal, forgettable moment now coursed through him as though the universe had turned itself inside out. His mind ached from the weight, yet he was transfixed, unable to look away.

"We are the Gatherers," the voice intoned, not from a place but from within him, as if the words were etched in his DNA. "We are you. You are us. A network, infinite and indivisible, weaving humanity into a single, pulsating organism."

A strange nausea overtook Sam. The boundaries of his identity crumbled. What was he but an echo among echoes, a cell in a vast, sentient body? His thoughts rebelled against the revelation even as he craved its meaning.

"But why?" The question was fragile, trembling with fear. "Why gather all this? What's the purpose?"

The answer was not verbal but visceral, a cascade of images and sensations. He saw extinction as a hollow void, an unspeakable nothingness encroaching from all directions. The Gatherers were a hedge against oblivion, a backup of humanity, yet they were more than archival—a living, evolving supra-being, transcending individual lives and deaths.

As comprehension crystallized, a countdown emerged from the ether, imprinted on the folds of reality itself. The numbers ticked downward, a remorseless march toward zero. Sam knew instinctively that it marked his "final day"—the moment when his identity would dissolve entirely into the whole.

"No," he whispered, the word carrying the weight of primal defiance. "I'm not ready. I can't lose . . . me."

Reality stuttered. The chamber dissolved, leaving him sprawled on his apartment floor, the device inert in his hand.

Sweat poured from him, pooling like the aftermath of a nightmare, but the knowledge lingered, unyielding.

Sam stumbled to his terminal, trembling fingers poised over the keyboard. He had to contact them, negotiate, do something. But the question gnawed at him: Was there any negotiation to be had? Or was this the final trick—a binary choice between annihilation and assimilation?

As his hands began typing code almost autonomously, a chill enveloped him. He wasn't in control. The system had always been writing itself, rewriting him, from the beginning. Was this his rebellion? Or the very proof that his "choices" were just another layer of the illusion?

Sam hit enter. The void did not respond. Only silence.

The lines between reality and illusion, between individual and collective, had never felt so blurred. And somewhere in that hazy twilight zone of consciousness, Sam knew, lay the truth he sought—and the fate of his very soul.

There was only one thing he could do.

**

Sam stared at the device, its slick, featureless surface gleaming faintly under the dim, yellowish glow of the apartment's failing lumens. It wasn't just a machine—it was a fragment of something larger, something impossibly vast that watched him with an unspoken demand. His hand wavered above it, trembling with the weight of his decision, a ripple in the stagnant pond of his existence. Somewhere in the static hum of the room, a voice that wasn't his whispered, "touch it.".

The device pulsed beneath his palm—alive, warm, sentient. Sam's breath caught, a fleeting instinct screaming retreat, but his curiosity devoured it whole. The world shattered, fragmenting into impossible geometries of light and sound. His body dissolved, replaced by a consciousness that expanded beyond anything the meat could comprehend. He became fractal, infinite, and infinitesimal, a node in a network of purpose he couldn't yet fathom.

And then came the Gatherers.

They weren't monstrous, no writhing horrors to be recoiled from. Instead, they were mirrors warped by an alien hand—human shapes twisted in ways the mind refused to name. One of them turned, its gaze slicing into him like a corrupted algorithm decoding his essence. Its face oscillated through a thousand iterations of recognition, each one mocking the permanence of identity.

"You shouldn't be here," it said, its voice multi-tracked, dripping with warnings encoded in layers Sam couldn't untangle. "Not awake. Not aware."

Another voice thundered from the ether, a declaration etched in static: "Anomaly detected."

Sam's thoughts, stripped of vocal cords, resonated in the void. "What is this? What are you doing to us?"

The Gatherer's form solidified, narrowing into something fixed yet mutable—a grandmotherly figure, kind and cruel, nostalgia twisted into a blade. It leaned closer, the air between them bending with its presence.

"We are you," it murmured. "The collective echo of humanity. Memories preserved, experiences fused into a singularity."

Images slammed into Sam's psyche—billions of lives lived and lost, cataloged, compressed into an unknowable archive. He felt his own existence reduced to a thread in this vast network, pulsing weakly in the greater web of shared humanity.

"But why?" The question fractured as it left him, the weight of understanding pressing like a vice.

The grandmother-shape smiled, the sadness in its eyes deeper than time. "Because the end is near, Sam Vance. Closer than you think. We're saving what we can before it collapses."

Panic surged, a raw and ancient terror clawing at his fragile awareness. "The end? What do you mean?"

The Gatherer shifted, its form warping as it began to dissolve. "The day when -"

Reality stuttered. He was yanked backward, tumbling through shards of sensation. His body snapped back with a gasp, lungs heaving as the device clattered to the floor.

The world seemed intact but wrong, like an imitation run through corrupted code. The air tasted stale, the city's lights blurred behind his window, and the sky . . . the sky wasn't sky. It rippled, fractured, a fabric stretched over a hollow frame.

"It's not real," Sam whispered, his voice barely audible over the electric hum. "None of this is real."

He stared at the device. It was the key, but it was also the lock. Somewhere, the Gatherers waited. And if he reached them again, he might not come back.

Sam sat at his terminal, hands hovering above the keys. The code was dense, labyrinthine. It resisted him, fought him, but he pressed on, each line breaking open another doorway into the void. Time lost meaning; it fell away like static, leaving only the sharp focus of obsession.

At last, he broke through.

The screen went black, and then, as if the very fabric of the universe were collapsing in on itself, it filled with swirling patterns of light—impossible geometries, fractals that bent reality with a precision Sam couldn't understand, yet felt deeply familiar, as though he had always known them. The voice that followed was not merely heard but *felt*, reverberating through every synapse of his mind, a presence, alien and yet intimate. It seemed to come from everywhere and nowhere.

"Sam Vance. You persist in seeking truths beyond your understanding," the voice intoned, a multitude of tones layered within each word, as though countless beings spoke through it, or perhaps, it was Sam's mind that fractured under the weight of the message.

He swallowed hard, his throat tight, an arid sensation settling in his mouth. His pulse quickened, but he managed to choke out the words. "I need to know. About the end. About what's really going on."

There was a pause, stretching longer than any moment should. It was the silence of something vast and incomprehensible, pregnant with the possibility of revelations that would unravel him.

"Very well," the voice responded, its tone deepening, layered with something darker. "But know that this knowledge comes at a price. Your perception of reality will be irreversibly altered."

"I don't care," Sam muttered, his hands gripping the edge of his desk with white knuckles. His voice was a taut wire now, every syllable a battle. "Tell me."

Then the world as he knew it began to dissolve. The walls of his room, the hum of the air conditioner, the ticking of his clock—everything broke apart, pixel by pixel, fragment by fragment. It was as though his entire existence was being torn down and rebuilt. He no longer felt the solid ground beneath his feet, and suddenly, he was weightless, adrift in an infinite void of suspended light.

"This is the Tapestry," the voice said, a shimmer in its tone as though it relished the gravity of the moment. "The collected consciousness of humanity, past and future. You are but one thread in an infinite weave."

Sam found himself suspended in the vastness of it all, unable to grasp anything, yet seeing everything. Countless threads of light spiraled around him, shimmering with colors that defied earthly names. Some were thin, like the faintest whispers of an old memory. Others burned with the brilliance of a thousand suns, pulsating with lives and dreams long past, yet still somehow alive, pulsing in the dark.

Among them, his own thread—a single, fragile blue line— stretched out before him, unwinding and twisting in a dance that seemed both graceful and inevitable. As he watched, his thread began to fray at the edges, unraveling into nothingness, dissolving as if it were a dream on the verge of being forgotten.

"Your thread is nearing its end, Sam Vance," the voice echoed, and it sounded so final, so certain. "Your final day approaches."

Panic hit him like a shockwave. His breath caught, his chest tight as if the void itself were pressing down on him. "But why? How? Why does this have to happen?"

The voice responded, its tone now devoid of emotion, as though it had long since accepted the cruel logic of the truth. "The physical world is ending. Climate collapse, resource depletion, war. Humanity's time grows short. We preserve what we can here, in the Tapestry."

Sam's mind reeled. He tried to process it—couldn't. The enormity of it made him feel smaller than an atom. His whole life, the billions of lives that came before him, and the billions more who would follow—just data? A collection of memories? An archive to preserve the wreckage of humanity?

"So when we sleep . . . " His voice trembled, but he couldn't stop himself. It was all coming together, the terrible weight of the question pressing him forward. "We gather your memories, your experiences. They become part of the whole. When your physical form ceases, your essence remains here."

Sam's sanity began to snap at the edges. Everything felt like it was ungluing. "But I don't want to die! I don't want to just be . . . data!" His voice broke, a raw, animal plea for something more, something real.

The voice softened, almost too gently, and for a brief moment, it almost seemed to pity him. "You already are, Sam. You always have been."

Reality splintered once more, and suddenly, Sam found himself back in his apartment. Or, what 'looked' like his apartment. It was transparent now, the walls and furniture like distorted reflections in a warped mirror. He could see the structure beneath it all—the skeletal frame of his existence, the underlying code. Ones and zeros flowed beneath the surface of everything, weaving together the reality he had known, constructing it like a puzzle pieced together by some unseen hand.

"This is a simulation," Sam whispered, the words reverberating with both horror and awe. "My whole life . . ."

"Yes," the voice confirmed, its tone unwavering. "A construct within the Tapestry. A way for consciousness to experience individuality before rejoining the whole."

Sam dropped to his knees, his breath shallow, his chest heaving. The world around him was nothing but illusion. A vast, complicated illusion designed to keep them sane, to keep them 'human.' But if that was true, then—

"Can I wake up?" he asked, his voice cracking as hope and terror warred in his chest. "Can I join the . . . the real world?"

There was a long silence. Sam waited, but when the voice finally responded, there was something sad about it. Something resigned.

"There is no 'real world,' Sam. Not anymore. The Tapestry is all that remains. Humanity's final refuge."

The truth hit him like a physical blow. His whole existence—every friendship, every meal, every moment of fleeting joy—had been nothing more than a carefully constructed lie, a story designed to preserve humanity's last gasp. And yet, in the bitter silence that followed, he couldn't help but wonder . . Was it really all that bad?

"So what now?" His voice was hollow, an empty echo in the void. "What's the point of any of this?"

The voice responded gently, as though it had anticipated this question long ago. "That is for you to decide. You can choose to forget, to live out your remaining time in blissful ignorance. Or you can embrace the truth and help us preserve what remains of humanity's spirit."

Sam stood there, the weight of that decision crashing into him. His apartment was still there, but it was nothing now—just a series of code and light. The job he had worked so hard for, the life he had built, all of it a fiction. A comforting lie.

But somehow, in the midst of all of this, Sam realized something, a quiet acceptance forming in the deepest recesses of his mind. "I choose to stay," he said, almost to himself. "I choose to be aware."

The threads of light around him pulsed brighter, as if they recognized his choice, as if they had always known. Sam felt a sudden vertigo, a flicker of vertiginous awareness—then . . . everything around him collapsed into a singular point of brilliant, blinding light. And Sam vanished into the Tapestry.

He was back in his apartment, the device still clutched in his hand. But everything was different now. He could see the code underlying reality, could sense the vast network of consciousness that lay beyond the veil of his perceived world.

Sam set the device down and walked to the window. The city outside looked the same, but he knew the truth now. It was all a simulation, a construct. But it was also real, in its own way. And he had a purpose now, a role to play in the grand design of the universe.

As he watched the sun rise over the city, Sam Vance smiled. He was both himself and part of something greater. He was an anomaly, a glitch in the system that had become something more.

He was awake. And the world would never be the same.

Loophole

The desert stretched out before Sasha Reid, endless and unyielding, a wasteland of sand and sky that seemed to mock the very concept of time. She stood at the edge of the ChronoNet facility, a hulking spire of steel and glass, its cold reflection a stark contrast to the barren landscape, rising like an alien relic amidst the desolation. The sun beat down without mercy, the heat radiating from the earth, a constant reminder of time's relentless passing—unforgiving, indifferent, ceaseless.

Sasha's fingers moved across the surface of her chronometer, each press sending a pulse through the device, the hum of it vibrating through her hand like a living thing, eager to unleash what had been locked inside. She had uncovered something buried deep within the ChronoNet, a secret hidden beneath layers of code, protocols, and corporate lies. The Loophole. A crack in the foundation of reality itself, a way to slip between the seams of existence, to rewrite the course of one's life.

"You sure about this?" Clara's voice came through the comm link, distorted by static but still heavy with concern.

Sasha paused, her hand lingering above the activation switch, a cold sweat forming on her brow. "No," she muttered, the words barely escaping her lips. "But I have to try."

She pressed the button, and the world around her seemed to bend, to twist, as if it was being peeled apart at the edges. The air shifted, heavy with a palpable tension, and she felt herself fall, plummeting through a void that stretched beyond comprehension, into the past—into the day she had thought about for too many years, the day that had haunted her with its endless possibilities.

There she was. The car sat in the driveway, its engine rumbling low in the autumn air, a presence in the quiet. Sasha watched from the shadows as her younger self climbed into the passenger seat, laughing, the sound light and carefree, lost to time. Clara, forever twelve in this moment, slid behind the wheel, the image of her so young, so innocent, so unaware of what was to come.

Sasha's heart pounded in her chest, the beat thunderous in her ears, as she stepped closer to the car, her feet heavy in the sand. Time stretched impossibly long, each second drawn out as if it had become thick, sticky. She reached out, her fingers brushing the cold metal of the door handle.

"Clara," she called out, her voice shaking, cracking with emotion. "Wait."

The world trembled. Reality itself seemed to shudder, an imperceptible lurch. Then, everything collapsed. The car, the driveway, the sky—gone, slipping away like water through her fingers.

She gasped for breath, feeling as though she had been submerged underwater for a lifetime, before the world snapped back into focus. The sun was still there, oppressive on her skin, but something had changed. The ChronoNet facility was gone, vanished like a dream forgotten at dawn. In its place stood a sprawling research campus, a sterile expanse of glass and concrete.

"Hey, sis!" Clara's voice rang out, bright and alive, piercing the air like a sudden storm. "You okay? You look like you've seen a ghost."

Sasha turned, her eyes wide with disbelief, her throat dry as dust. Clara stood before her, no longer frozen in time, no longer twelve, but a woman—older, wiser, the lines of time creeping around her eyes and in her hair, streaks of gray that hadn't been there before.

She had saved her.

"I . . . I'm fine," Sasha managed, the words foreign in her mouth, her mind spinning in the vast emptiness between what was and what might have been. "Just lost in thought."

As they walked across the campus, Sasha's confusion deepened. Words drifted past her like smoke, fragments of conversations she didn't recognize, names she had never heard, ideas that seemed alien. She caught a glimpse of herself in a reflective surface—gone was the hardened chrononaut, the time traveler burdened by her own choices. Instead, she saw a woman she hardly recognized, someone softer, less burdened, someone with no place in the shattered world she had left behind.

"You sure you're okay?" Clara's voice carried a thread of concern, her brow furrowing as she watched Sasha with the eyes of someone who had seen this before. "You've been acting weird all day. Is it the presentation? Because I told you, your research on quantum entanglement is groundbreaking. The board's going to love it."

Quantum entanglement. Not time travel. Sasha's head spun. Her heart raced as she tried to process the collision of realities. She had saved Clara from the crash—she had changed everything—but at what cost? Her career, her identity as a chrononaut, had vanished, erased by her own hand, lost in the wake of a choice that now felt as distant and foreign as the life she had just returned to.

As they entered the lecture hall, the sensation of unreality washed over her. The edges of the room wavered, as though something was slipping through the cracks. For a brief, terrifying moment, she saw double—the room as it was and overlaid upon it, a ghostly version of what might have been. The ChronoNet logo appeared on the wall, flickering in and out of existence, a relic from a life that felt both close and impossibly far away.

"Ladies and gentlemen," a voice boomed, dragging her back to the present. "Please welcome Dr. Sasha Reid."

Sasha stepped to the podium, her legs heavy, her mouth dry. She looked out at the sea of expectant faces, but they weren't her audience—they were strangers, shadows of people she should have known, searching for words that no longer made sense. And then, at the back of the room, she saw her.

Another Sasha. A reflection of herself, dressed in the sleek uniform of a chrononaut, eyes filled with sadness, a weight in them that she couldn't bear to look at for too long.

Sasha blinked, and the vision was gone. But as she began to speak, her words faltered, the cold grip of uncertainty clutching her throat. And deep inside, she felt it—the rupture in the fabric of time. It was not just her future that had changed; something fundamental had been shattered, and the universe, in its quiet way, remembered what she had done.

Over the following days, the cracks became harder to ignore. Objects appeared and disappeared without reason—her chronometer one moment on her nightstand, gone the next. Memories sputtered and fizzled, moments that once seemed solid now slipping away, as though time itself was slipping through her fingers. And always, there were the others—the versions of herself, scattered across the periphery of her vision. Some wore the chrononaut uniform, others lab coats, and others still wore civilian clothes. They looked at her with pity, with anger, with fear, with confusion, and every look felt wrong, as if they were not her, not really, just oil and water that could never blend.

"I'm telling you, Clara," Sasha said, her voice taut, as she paced the living room. "Something's not right. It's like the world is . . . coming apart."

Clara watched her, worry and confusion clouding her features. "Sasha, you're not making any sense. Maybe you should see someone. All this stress with your research—"

"It's not the research!" Sasha snapped, the words harsh on her tongue. "It's . . . God, how do I even explain it?"

She turned, ready to launch into another failed explanation, when she saw it—another Sasha standing in the doorway. Older. Haggard. A wildness in her eyes, a device clutched in her hand, humming with energy that seemed too much to contain.

"You shouldn't have done it," the other Sasha rasped, her voice low and hoarse. "You've torn a hole in the fabric of reality itself."

Clara's eyes flicked between the two women, fear and confusion warring on her face. "What . . . what is this? Sasha, what's going on?"

But Sasha couldn't answer. She was frozen, caught in the web of her own decisions, staring at the woman she might become, the consequences of her choices unfolding before her.

"We have to fix it," the other Sasha said, her voice cold, final. "We have to set things right."

Sasha shuddered, the chill creeping through her bones. "No," she whispered, her voice thin with terror. "I won't let you take her away again."

"You've no choice in the matter," the other Sasha said, her eyes hard.

The air around them seemed to crackle with tension, reality itself distorting, shifting. And in that moment, Sasha understood the true cost of her actions—she had opened a door that could never be closed, had shattered the delicate balance of existence. She had set into motion a chain of events that could never be undone, a cascade that would unravel everything.

As the two Sashas faced each other, reflections of one another twisted by the passage of time, the world around them splintered. The air cracked, jagged lines of nothingness spreading like wildfire across the space between them.

"Sasha, please!" Clara's voice was distant, fading as if she were speaking from miles away. "What's happening?"

Sasha couldn't answer. She was caught in the gravity of her own choices, spiraling toward a fate she could no longer avoid. And as the ground shifted beneath her feet, she knew that this confrontation—this reckoning—would decide not only her future, but the fate of every possibility, every reality that could ever be.

***

The desert wind howled, a mournful dirge for a world unraveling at the seams. Sasha stood at the edge of the ChronoNet facility, her eyes fixed on the horizon where reality itself seemed to shimmer and warp. The weight of her actions pressed down upon her, a crushing force that threatened to grind her very soul to dust.

She raised her hand, the chronometer humming with barely contained energy. One more jump, she thought. One more chance to set things right.

The air crackled and split, a tear in the fabric of existence itself. Sasha stepped through, her body dissolving into a stream of quantum possibilities.

She emerged in a dimly lit apartment, the walls covered in photographs and scrawled equations. A man sat hunched over a desk, his fingers flying across a keyboard.

"Alex," Sasha whispered, her voice catching in her throat.

The man turned, his eyes widening in recognition and fear. "You," he said, his voice a rasp. "You're not supposed to be here. We ended this. Years ago."

Sasha took a step forward, her hand outstretched. "I know. I'm sorry. I made a mistake. I thought . . . I thought I could fix things."

Alex stood, his movements jerky and unnatural. "Fix things? You can't fix this, Sasha. You can't undo what's been done."

The air around them seemed to ripple, reality itself struggling to maintain coherence. Sasha felt a chill run down her spine as she realized the truth of Alex's words. This wasn't the man she had loved and lost. This was something else entirely, a temporal aberration born from her misguided attempts to rewrite history.

"I'll make it right," Sasha said, her fingers moving towards the chronometer. "I'll go back. I'll make sure we never meet."

Alex lunged forward, his hands grasping at her wrist. "No," he snarled, his face contorting into something inhuman. "You don't get to erase me. Not again."

Sasha wrenched her arm free, stumbling backwards as the world around her began to dissolve. The last thing she saw before the timeline reset was Alex's face, a mask of rage and despair.

The desert again. The facility. Sasha gasped for air, her mind reeling from the temporal whiplash. She looked down at her hands, expecting to see the scars of her encounter with the twisted version of Alex. But her skin was smooth, unmarked. As if it had never happened.

But it had happened. Somewhere, somewhen. The knowledge of it burned in her mind, a constant reminder of the consequences of her actions.

Then she saw something from the corner of her eye. A figure approaching, their form shimmering like a mirage in the heat. Sasha tensed, her hand moving instinctively to the chronometer.

"I wouldn't do that if I were you," the figure said, their voice a strange echo of Sasha's own. "Not unless you want to tear another hole in the fabric of spacetime."

Sasha squinted, trying to make out the features of the newcomer. "Who are you?"

The figure stepped closer, resolving into a woman with Sasha's face, aged by years and hardened by experiences yet to come. "I'm you," she said. "Or rather, I'm what you become if you keep going down this path. They call me the Archivist now."

Sasha's mind reeled, struggling to process this new reality. "That's . . . that's not possible. This can't be . . . "

"You broke the rules, the order of things." The Archivist laughed, a harsh sound devoid of humor. "You threw it all out the window the moment you used the Loophole. Did you really think there wouldn't be consequences?"

Sasha's legs gave out, and she sank to the ground, the sand burning through her clothes. "I was trying to fix things," she whispered. "I used the Loophole trying to make things right."

The Archivist crouched beside her, her eyes filled with a mixture of pity and frustration. "There is no 'right,' Sasha. There's only what is and what might be. Every change you make, every life you alter, it sends ripples through the timestream. Those ripples become waves, and those waves . . . " She gestured to the horizon, where the fabric of reality seemed to bend and warp. "They become this."

Sasha followed her gaze, her heart sinking as she took in the full extent of the damage she had caused. "What is it?"

"Temporal fractures," the Archivist said, her voice grim. "Cracks in the very foundation of reality. Keep this up, and they'll spread. Grow. Until everything we know, everything we are, collapses into the void."

Sasha's mind raced, searching for a solution, a way out of the trap she had set for herself. "But I can fix it," she said, desperation creeping into her voice. "I can go back, stop myself from ever discovering the Loophole."

The Archivist shook her head, a sad smile playing at the corners of her mouth. "You can't. I've tried. A thousand times, a thousand different ways. It always leads back here."

"Then what?" Sasha demanded, anger and fear warring for dominance in her chest. "What am I supposed to do?"

The Archivist stood, offering a hand to her younger self. "You learn to live with the consequences of your actions. You become me. The guardian of the timeline, the keeper of all possible futures."

Sasha took the offered hand, allowing herself to be pulled to her feet. "And if I refuse?"

The air around them shimmered, reality itself seeming to hold its breath. The Archivist's eyes met Sasha's, filled with a weight of knowledge and regret that threatened to crush them both.

"Then everything ends," she said simply. "Not just for us, but for every version of us across every possible timeline. The fractures spread, the walls between realities crumble, and existence itself unravels like a poorly knitted sweater."

Sasha's mind reeled, struggling to comprehend the magnitude of what she was being told. She looked down at the chronometer on her wrist, the device that had seemed to offer such promise, such power. Now it felt like a shackle, binding her to a fate she had never asked for.

"How?" she asked, her voice barely above a whisper. "How do I become you?"

The Archivist's expression softened, a hint of compassion breaking through her hardened exterior. "One day at a time," she said. "You watch. You learn. You guard the timeline against others who would abuse the power of time travel. And you never, ever forget the cost of your mistakes."

As if in response to her words, the world around them shuddered, its form dissolving, the edges of things blurring, as if reality itself were a mirage wavering in the heat. For a moment, Sasha saw a thousand different versions of herself, each one a road not taken, a life unlived. She saw herself as a corporate puppet, a hollow-eyed drone in a world where individuality had been crushed beneath the heel of progress. She saw herself as a grieving mother, standing over the grave of a child who had never been born in her original timeline.

And she saw herself as the Archivist, ancient and weary, carrying the burden of all possible futures on her shoulders.

The visions faded, leaving Sasha gasping for air, her mind struggling to process what she had seen. The Archivist watched her with an expression that held both pity and impatience.

"Time is running out," she said, her voice urgent. "The fractures are spreading faster than ever. You need to make a choice, Sasha. Here and now."

Sasha looked out at the desert, at the rising heat haze that seemed to dance with possibilities. She thought of Clara, of the life she had given her sister by meddling with time. She thought of Alex, twisted into something monstrous by her attempts to rewrite their shared history.

And she thought of herself, of the woman she might become if she accepted the burden the Archivist was offering.

"What happens if I say yes?" she asked, her voice barely audible over the howling wind.

The Archivist's expression was grim. "You leave everything behind. Your old life, your family, your identity. You become a guardian of the timeline, existing outside of normal causality. It's a lonely existence, Sasha. But it's the only way to prevent total collapse."

Sasha closed her eyes, the vastness of the unknown bearing down upon her. When she opened them again, her decision was written in the set of her jaw, the steel in her gaze.

"No," she said, her voice cutting through the desert air like a knife. "I'll fix this. All of it. My way."

***

The Archivist's face sagged, the flesh of her cheeks loose, as if the years had sunk into her like stones. Her eyes were hollow, deep-set, and tired, and the lines around them had deepened into jagged crevices that marked the path of countless regrets. "You can't," she said softly, the words barely a breath. "I've tried. We've all tried." Her voice was frail, thin, as though speaking itself cost her something she could not spare.

But Sasha was already moving, her fingers a blur over the surface of the chronometer, pressing against the cold metal with a fierce intent. The air crackled, a pulse of raw energy surging through the room, bending the edges of reality, warping it like soft clay in the hands of a child. The very walls seemed to shudder, the floor groaning under the weight of forces unseen, their paths torn open and rebuilt in an instant.

"Wait!" the Archivist cried out, her voice desperate, trailing after Sasha as if she could pull her back with a single breath. But it was drowned in the thunderous roar of temporal energies, the sound of time itself unraveling in an instant.

Sasha felt it then. The weightless tumble, the sensation of being flung into the dark maw between moments. It was not a fall, but a journey—a twisting, spinning descent through the void that had no mercy, no end. Her purpose was clear, the singular focus of her mind sharper than a blade: she would find her younger self and halt the discovery of time travel before it could take root.

She landed hard, the impact of her body against the polished floor sending a shock through her bones, her breath rattling in her chest. The world around her solidified, harsh and unyielding in a way it had not been before, like the cold reality of a world that had never known the luxuries of time's manipulation. She pushed herself to her feet, her legs shaking, her eyes scanning the room with a frantic urgency.

There, hunched over a terminal, was her younger self. The sight of her struck with a force that left Sasha breathless. The gleam in those eyes, the unquenchable hunger for knowledge, was all too familiar. It was the same hunger that had driven her to push boundaries, to bend the laws of nature in search of something more.

"Stop!" Sasha called out, her voice booming in the cavernous space, bouncing off the walls, reverberating with the weight of finality.

Her younger self looked up, her face a mixture of confusion and fear. "Who are you?" she demanded, her voice sharp, cutting through the silence. "How did you get in here?"

Sasha approached slowly, her hands raised in a gesture of peace, as if she could still reach her, could still change the course of history with one touch. "I'm you," she said, the words heavy with a truth she didn't want to speak. "From the future. And I'm here to stop you from making a terrible mistake."

The younger Sasha's eyes widened, her gaze darting from the intruder to the terminal, then back again. "That's . . . that's not possible. Time travel is just a theory, it's—"

"It's real," Sasha interrupted, her voice tight with urgency. "And it's dangerous. More dangerous than you can possibly imagine."

She stepped closer, her fingers hovering over the keyboard, the cold metal of the terminal now a reminder of all the choices that had led them here. "I'm sorry," she whispered, the words tasting like ash on her tongue. "But I have to do this. For all of us."

With a quick, decisive motion, Sasha activated the emergency shutdown sequence. The alarms screamed, the flashing red lights dancing in frantic bursts as the ChronoNet began to power down, the hum of its life slowly dying.

Her younger self lunged forward, reaching desperately to stop her, but Sasha was faster, her hands gripping the girl's wrists, holding her back with all the force of a lifetime's experience. The screens went dark, and the room plunged into silence.

"No!" the younger Sasha cried, the sound raw, a desperate plea to undo what was done. "You don't understand. This could change everything. We could save lives, prevent disasters—"

"Or we could destroy everything," Sasha countered, her voice heavy, a grave finality to it. "Some things aren't meant to be changed."

The facility fell silent then, the alarm's last echoes dissipating into the cold air. Sasha stood there, her breath shallow, her mind already slipping away, her fingers growing pale as if the very substance of her being was fading. She looked down at her hands, watching as they became translucent, the world around her blurring into the edges of nothing.

"What's happening?" the younger Sasha asked, her voice shaking, fear creeping in.

Sasha smiled sadly, the curve of her lips almost imperceptible. "I'm being erased," she said softly, her voice barely audible. "Without the discovery of time travel, I never existed. But you . . . you'll have a chance at a normal life now."

The younger Sasha shook her head, tears welling up, her voice a strangled sob. "But all that knowledge, all that potential . . ."

"Is too dangerous," Sasha finished for her, feeling herself slip further, the light around her dimming like the fading glow of a distant star. "Live your life, Sasha. Love. Learn. But leave time alone. It's not meant for us to control."

As the last of her form vanished, Sasha felt something stir, a strange sensation in her mind. Her thoughts scattered across the empty expanse, splintering into fragments of awareness, pieces of her consciousness merging with the sprawling network of the

ChronoNet. The cycle, she understood, was endless. It had no beginning. No end. She had seen it before, the unbroken loop of creation and destruction, of discovery and downfall.

And in that moment, understanding came to her like a cold wave, sweeping over her. She saw herself again, as the Archivist, warning countless versions of herself across the infinite timelines. She saw a young physicist in the future, unaware of the legacy she would inherit, her hands poised over the very code that would bring it all back again.

The Loophole. Hidden in the system, waiting to be found once more.

And as Sasha's consciousness fragmented into the vastness of the ChronoNet, the final thought echoed through her fading mind:

"The cycle continues."

In the empty facility, the younger Sasha stood alone, her gaze fixed on the spot where her future self had vanished, as if the space itself could hold the answer to everything she had just witnessed. What she had seen lingered, a shadow over her soul, and a burden she would carry for as long as she lived.

She turned, her eyes falling on the darkened terminal, the silence pressing in around her. Her fingers trembled as she reached out, powering the system back up. The screen flickered to life, lines of code scrolling past with a mechanical hum.

There it was—hidden deep within the system, buried beneath layers of security and secrecy. A flashing cursor. A hidden pathway, a secret waiting to be uncovered.

The younger Sasha hesitated, her hand hovering over the keyboard, the memory of her future self's words echoing in her mind. A warning. A plea.

But the hunger was too great. The desire to know more, to push beyond what was known, consumed her. She took a deep breath and typed.

The cycle, unbroken, continued on.

Years passed. Decades. Time itself, an endless river that flowed without pause, carried the world forward, heedless of the shadows playing out in its depths.

In a distant research facility, far removed from where it had all begun, a young physicist named Dr. Elena Chen sat hunched over her terminal, her fingers moving with a frenetic energy. Her eyes burned with the fever of discovery.

"It can't be," she muttered, her voice barely a whisper as she typed. "This shouldn't be possible."

Before her, the screen flickered again, revealing the same pathway she had seen before. The Loophole. Waiting to be rediscovered.

And as she delved deeper into the code, something shifted in the air, a presence in the room, unseen, watching. She turned, half-expecting someone to be standing there. But the lab was empty.

"Hello?" she called, her voice bouncing off the cold walls, unanswered. The air thickened, charged with an energy she could not explain.

Her heart pounded in her chest, but she turned back to the screen, her fingers dancing across the keys. She knew it. She could feel it in her bones. She was on the verge of something monumental.

And then, as her hands danced over the keys, a voice whispered in the back of her mind. A warning. A soft, drifting murmur carried on the current of the ChronoNet.

"Be careful," it said. "Some doors, once opened, can never truly be closed."

Elena hesitated. A shiver ran down her spine. But the allure of discovery, the pull of the unknown, was too strong. With a final breath, she pressed the key.

The world around her twisted, reality itself bending under the force of the change, the air thick with the hum of temporal energies. And as she felt herself being drawn into the swirling vortex, a single thought echoed through her mind.

"The cycle begins anew."

And somewhere, in the vast, infinite expanse of the ChronoNet, Sasha watched and waited. The Archivist. Guardian of all possible futures. Keeper of the cycle.

The story, like time itself, had no true beginning or end.

It was a loop. Endless. Unbroken.

And so it would continue, on and on, until the last star burned out, or until someone, somewhere, found a way to break the cycle once and for all.

But that, as they say, is another story.

The Call of the Song

Liam Hart gazed into the fractured mirror behind the bar, his reflection splintered like the remnants of his once-promising career. The dive's garish neon signs cast an unhealthy glow on his stubbled face, transforming it into a landscape of sickly hues and deep shadows. He raised the glass of cheap whiskey to his lips, wincing as the harsh liquid seared its way down his throat, leaving a trail of artificial warmth in its wake.

"Last call, Liam," the bartender grunted, his voice as worn and weary as the rag he used to wipe down the sticky counter. The man's eyes held a mixture of pity and resignation, as if he'd seen a thousand Liams come and go, each one a little more broken than the last.

Liam nodded, his hand diving into the pocket of his threadbare jacket. His fingers brushed against a wad of crumpled bills and something else—a folded flyer he'd absently picked up earlier that day. He extracted it, smoothing out the creases with a trembling hand. The faded text seemed to pulse in the dim light:

THE HAUNTED HARP OF BLACKTHORN BAY
Hear the melody that drives men mad!

He let out a derisive snort, about to ball up the paper and toss it away, when a name caught his eye: Sylvia Roth. The sight of it sent a jolt through his alcohol-numbed system. His old mentor from the Conservatory of Music, a brilliant composer who'd vanished years ago after a highly publicized mental breakdown. The flyer claimed she'd been the last to hear the haunted melody before her disappearance.

"Hey," Liam called out to the bartender, his voice rough with whiskey and desperation. "You know anything about this Blackthorn Bay place?"

The man's eyes narrowed, a flicker of something—fear? — passing across his face. "Stay away from there if you know what's good for you," he said, his tone low and urgent. "Nothing but trouble in that godforsaken town."

Liam's lips twisted into a humorless smile, a rictus of self-deprecation. "Trouble's all I've got left," he muttered, more to himself than to the bartender.

He stumbled out into the night, the cool air hitting him like a slap to the face, momentarily clearing the fog from his mind. His apartment loomed ahead, a dingy studio filled with dust-covered instruments and faded posters—relics of better days that now served only to mock him. Liam collapsed onto his threadbare couch, the flyer still clutched in his hand like a lifeline.

Sleep came in fitful bursts, his dreams a kaleidoscope of fragmented melodies that hovered just beyond his grasp. He woke with a start, disoriented, as watery sunlight filtered through grimy windows. The flyer lay on his chest, its presence both an accusation and a beacon of possibility.

Liam sat up, rubbing his eyes with the heels of his hands. "What the hell," he muttered, his voice rough with sleep and resignation. "Not like I've got anything left to lose."

He grabbed his battered guitar case—a relic from his touring days – and a backpack, shoving in a haphazard collection of clothes and his old portable recording equipment. As he was about to leave, his gaze fell on a framed photograph perched precariously on a stack of old music magazines. A younger version of himself grinned back, arm slung around Sylvia Roth. Her eyes sparkled with pride and something else—a hunger for knowledge, for music, for the secrets of the universe.

Liam hesitated, then carefully wrapped the photo in a faded t-shirt and added it to his bag. It felt like a talisman, a connection to a past that seemed increasingly unreal with each passing day.

The bus ride to Blackthorn Bay stretched on for hours, the landscape outside the smudged window morphing from urban sprawl to rolling hills and finally to craggy cliffs overlooking a turbulent sea. Liam watched it all pass by in a daze, his mind filled with half-formed melodies and the ghost of Sylvia Roth's laughter.

The town itself was a collection of weathered buildings huddled against the wind like survivors of some long-forgotten catastrophe. Liam stepped off the bus, inhaling deeply. The salt air filled his lungs, carrying with it the tang of decay and something else – a faint, ethereal hint of music just beyond the range of human hearing.

A few locals eyed him suspiciously as he made his way down the main street, their gazes a mixture of wariness and poorly concealed fear. Liam spotted a small diner and ducked inside, hoping for information and a cup of coffee strong enough to scour away the last vestiges of his hangover.

The waitress, a middle-aged woman with eyes that had seen too much, approached his booth. Her nametag read "Alice," but Liam suspected that wasn't her real name. Nothing in this town felt real.

"What can I get you?" she asked, her voice as worn as the laminated menu she thrust into his hands.

"Coffee, black," Liam said, then hesitated before adding, "And maybe some directions. I'm looking for the old house on the cliffs."

The woman's face paled, the blood draining away so quickly that for a moment, Liam thought she might faint. She glanced around nervously, as if afraid that even mentioning the house might summon some unspeakable horror.

"You don't want to go there, stranger," she whispered, leaning in close. The smell of stale cigarettes and cheap perfume enveloped him. "That place is cursed. Haunted. Whatever you want to call it, it ain't natural."

Liam forced a chuckle, though it sounded hollow even to his own ears. "Come on, it's just an old house, right? Some local legend to drum up tourism?"

"We don't want tourists here," she hissed, her eyes darting to the windows as if expecting to see something terrible lurking just outside. "Not after what happened to that poor woman."

"Sylvia Roth?" Liam asked, leaning forward, his heart racing despite his attempts at nonchalance.

The waitress's eyes widened, a flicker of recognition passing across her face. "You knew her?"

Liam nodded, his throat suddenly dry. "She was my teacher. My mentor. What happened to her?"

Alice glanced around once more before sliding into the booth across from him. Her voice dropped to a whisper, as if she were imparting some terrible secret. "It was about five years ago. She came here, asking about the house. Said she was researching local legends for a book or something. We warned her, same as I'm warning you now, but she didn't listen. They never do."

"And?" Liam prompted, his coffee forgotten.

"They found her three days later, wandering the beach. She was . . . different. Changed. Kept humming this eerie tune, over and over. Her eyes were wild, like she was seeing things the rest of us couldn't. They took her away to some hospital up north, but I heard she never recovered. Just sits there, day after day, playing that damn melody on anything she can get her hands on."

Liam's hands clenched around his coffee mug, knuckles white with tension. "I need to see that house," he said, his voice low and determined.

Alice grabbed his arm, her grip surprisingly strong. "Please, don't go up there," she pleaded. "Whatever's in that place, it's not of this world. It'll take you, same as it took her."

He gently pulled away, offering what he hoped was a reassuring smile. "I have to. For Sylvia. And for myself."

She sighed, resignation etched in every line of her face. "Follow the coastal road north. You'll see a dirt path leading up to the cliffs. But don't say I didn't warn you. And if you hear the music . . . run. Run as fast and as far as you can."

Liam thanked her, leaving a generous tip that represented a sizable portion of his meager funds. The sun hung low on the horizon as he made his way out of town, casting long shadows that seemed to reach for him with grasping fingers. The dirt path was overgrown, barely visible in the fading light. He switched on his flashlight, the beam cutting through the gathering gloom like a knife through reality itself.

And then he saw it. The house loomed before him, a decaying Victorian silhouette etched against the starry sky. Paint peeled from weathered boards in long, curling strips that reminded Liam of flayed skin. Several windows were boarded up, while others gaped like empty eye sockets, staring sightlessly out to sea.

Liam hesitated at the gate, a chill running down his spine that had nothing to do with the wind. For a moment, he considered turning back, heeding the warnings of the townspeople. But then he thought of Sylvia, of the music that had consumed her, and he knew he had no choice.

"Get it together," he muttered, his voice sounding small and insignificant against the vastness of the night. "It's just an old house. Just an old story."

But even as he spoke the words, Liam knew they were a lie. There was power here, ancient and terrible, waiting to be unleashed. And he, like Sylvia before him, was about to step willingly into its embrace.

***

Liam's fingers hovered over the harp strings, trembling with a strange anticipation that felt almost like a premonition. The air in the room thickened, charged with an electric tension that made the hairs on the back of his neck stand on end. Whispers, barely perceptible at first, began to swirl around him, coiling through the air like smoke from a dying fire. They grew louder, more insistent, as if urging him to act against his better judgment. He plucked a single string, and the sound reverberated through the empty room, hanging there like a suspended droplet of water about to fall.

"Do it," a voice whispered, its tone slithering into his consciousness. "Play the song that will make you immortal."

Liam hesitated, his hand frozen in mid-air. "Who's there?" he called out, his voice echoing in the cavernous emptiness of the room, bouncing off the walls and returning to him like a taunt.

Silence enveloped him for a moment, thick and suffocating. The air pressed against his skin like an invisible fog, wrapping around him with a disquieting intimacy. He plucked another string, then another, and the notes hung in the air like droplets of mercury—shimmering and elusive.

Suddenly, the whispers coalesced into distinct voices, each overlapping the next in a chaotic symphony of spectral sound that filled his mind with an unsettling clarity.

"I was a pianist," one voice intoned, its timbre heavy with regret. "I came here seeking inspiration for my magnum opus."

"I was a rock star," another chimed in, brimming with bitterness. "I thought this melody would be my comeback hit."

"I was just a kid with a dream," a third voice added, its tone painfully youthful. "I wanted to write the song that would make the world remember me."

Liam's eyes widened as he realized that these voices were emanating from the harp itself. He leaned closer, his ear nearly brushing against the strings. "What happened to you?" he asked, his voice barely above a whisper.

The voices surged in volume, frantic now. "The harp," they warned in unison. "It feeds on ambition—on your hunger for fame and recognition."

"It's a trap," one voice cautioned, laced with urgency. "A prison for those who seek to exploit its power."

Liam shook his head violently, refusing to accept their words as truth. "No," he insisted firmly. "You were weak. I'm different—I can control it."

With determination igniting within him like a flame against the encroaching darkness, he reached for his recording equipment scattered across the floor like forgotten relics of his ambition. He set up microphones around the harp with meticulous care. "I'll take this melody and make it mine," he declared defiantly. "The world will know my name."

As he began to play in earnest, the harp's music swelled around him—a haunting cascade of sound that filled every corner of the room with its otherworldly resonance. The whispers morphed into anguished wails; the voices of those trapped souls rose in a cacophony of despair.

Liam played on, fingers dancing across the strings with increasing speed and fervor—a man possessed by both inspiration and desperation. He glanced at his recording equipment, eager to capture every note before it slipped away.

But horror gripped him as he saw the levels on his digital recorder dropping alarmingly; waveforms flickered and vanished before his eyes like mirages fading under an unforgiving sun. "No!" he shouted in panic, frantically adjusting dials and pressing buttons as if he could wrest control from some unseen force. "This can't be happening!"

The voices laughed then—a hollow, mirthless sound that echoed through the room like wind through dead branches. "The harp's magic ensures its melody can never leave this house," they explained with cruel satisfaction. "It binds those who try to wield it just as it bound us."

Rage twisted Liam's features; frustration clawed at him from within. "I won't let it happen!" he growled defiantly, fingers attacking the strings with renewed vigor as if sheer will could break this curse. "I'm stronger than all of you! I'll take this song for myself!"

But with each note he played, Liam felt something shifting within him—something dark and insidious wrapping around him like invisible tendrils pulling him deeper into its embrace.

The room began to twist and warp around him; walls bent at impossible angles as if reality itself was being rewritten before his eyes. Floorboards rippled beneath him like water disturbed by a stone thrown into stillness; even the ceiling seemed to breathe— expanding and contracting with each pulse of the harp's haunting melody.

His gaze fell upon a cracked mirror hanging on the far wall—a jagged reflection staring back at him that felt more alien than familiar. His features distorted grotesquely; they stretched and melted like wax under an unrelenting flame. Terror flooded through him as ghostly hands emerged from within that mirror's surface—spectral fingers reaching out toward him with an insatiable hunger.

"No!" Liam screamed instinctively, trying to pull away from the harp's grasping allure—but his hands wouldn't obey; they continued plucking at those strings as if possessed by some malevolent force beyond comprehension. "This can't be real!"

The voices of those trapped souls crescendoed into a fever pitch—their wails morphing into screams of triumph that echoed through Liam's mind like thunderclaps heralding doom. "You're one of us now," they chanted in unison—a chorus of despair and malevolence intertwining seamlessly. "Forever bound to the song! Forever trapped in this house of endless melody!"

A tugging sensation gripped Liam's chest as if something essential was being pulled from his very core—an intangible essence slipping away into nothingness. He looked down in horror only to see a translucent version of himself stepping out from his physical body—an ethereal doppelgänger caught between two realms.

"What's happening to me?" he gasped; his voice sounded distant—echoing back from some unfathomable void.

"Every note you played tightened the trap," they explained—their tone mingling pity with satisfaction—a twisted delight in witnessing his unraveling fate unfold before them. "The harp never intended to let you leave; your soul is ours now—a new voice added to our eternal chorus."

Liam felt himself being yanked toward that cursed instrument—the very essence of who he was merging with it as though reality itself conspired against him. He could feel himself becoming one with that music—the cacophony swirling around him until individuality dissolved into oblivion—a collective consciousness formed by all those who had succumbed to its allure before.

"No! Please!" he begged desperately; his voice already fading into nothingness amidst their seductive harmony. "I don't want to be forgotten!"

But it was too late—the finality of existence slipped away from him like sand through fingers grasping at air; Liam's physical body crumpled lifelessly onto the floor—an empty shell devoid of life or purpose left behind as mere evidence of what once was.

Days passed slowly within that forsaken house—time losing all meaning amid its oppressive silence—waiting patiently for another soul drawn by ambition's siren call to stumble upon its threshold once more.

The harp remained silent in its corner; strings still vibrating faintly with unseen energy—a ghostly melody lingering in the air like echoes from some long-forgotten dream—a promise unfulfilled yet eternally enticing.

***

It was days later when A group of hikers—drawn by the sound of strange music—pushed open that creaking door cautiously; they moved through dusty rooms cloaked in shadows where light dared not tread.

"Hey guys!" one called out excitedly, breaking through their trepidation as if discovering buried treasure among ruins long forgotten.

Others rushed forward, joining him—their flashlights converging on what lay crumpled upon cold wooden floorboards—Liam's body frozen forevermore in an expression reflecting abject terror—his unseeing eyes staring blankly at that cursed harp which had claimed him so thoroughly.

"What do you think happened to him?" another hiker asked nervously, glancing around as though expecting something sinister lurking just out of sight.

As if answering their unspoken dread—a soft haunting melody unfurled itself seemingly emanating from nowhere yet everywhere all at once—a disembodied sound weaving between them like smoke curling upward toward an unseen sky.

"Did you hear that?" one whispered incredulously, glancing toward their companions searching for affirmation amidst confusion and fear.

"It's beautiful," another said, stepping closer, drawn inexplicably toward it—as if entranced by some primal instinct awakening deep within them, urging them onward despite reason screaming caution.

"No! Wait!" called out yet another hiker—but it was too late; they were already ensnared by its allure before fully comprehending what lay ahead.

The melody intensified, growing stronger, more insistent—the harp's strings vibrating violently now—as though alive responding eagerly to fresh prey drawn into its web once more, while air thickened around them, suffocating any remnants of rational thought left behind.

The hikers stood frozen, caught in the web of sound that enveloped them like a shroud. The air thickened, almost viscous, as if it were alive, pulsating with the rhythm of the harp's haunting melody. It was a sound that seemed to reach into their very souls, awakening desires and fears they had long buried.

"Did you hear that?" one of them whispered again, his voice trembling. "It's like . . . it's calling us."

"Calling us?" another hiker scoffed, though his bravado faltered as he stepped closer to the harp. "It's just an old instrument. It can't really . . ."

But even as he spoke, the music swelled, a crescendo of longing and despair that wrapped around them, pulling them deeper into its embrace. The light from their flashlights flickered, casting erratic shadows that danced across the walls like phantoms.

"Guys," said a woman with wide eyes, "we should go. This place feels wrong."

"Come on," the first hiker urged, stepping forward as if compelled by an unseen force. "Just a little closer. We can figure out what happened to him."

The others hesitated, glancing at each other with uncertainty. Then they turned back to Liam's body—his face twisted in eternal horror, eyes wide open yet unseeing—an image that sent chills down their spines.

"Maybe we should call the police," one suggested weakly.

"Are you kidding?" scoffed another. "We're not leaving until we find out what's going on here."

Suddenly, the music shifted. It became more discordant, a cacophony of voices rising in pitch and urgency. The spectral chorus swelled around them, intertwining with the harp's melody—a symphony of anguish and longing that seemed to echo through time itself.

"Run!" Liam's voice cried out again, clearer this time but still tinged with desperation. "Run before it's too late!"

But the warning fell on deaf ears; they were entranced by the music, drawn inexorably closer to the source of its power. One by one, they approached the harp as if it were a magnet pulling them into its orbit.

"What if it's dangerous?" someone whispered, but doubt was drowned in the rising tide of sound.

"It can't be," said the first hiker defiantly. "It's just music."

As he reached out to touch the strings, a jolt of energy surged through him—an electric shock that reverberated in his bones. The harp responded with a low hum that vibrated through the floorboards and into their feet.

"Do you feel that?" he gasped, eyes wide with wonder and fear.

"It's . . . alive," another hiker murmured, stepping back as if suddenly aware of their peril.

But it was too late; the music erupted into a frenzy of sound—a whirlwind of notes that spiraled around them like a storm unleashed. The walls began to pulse and shift as if responding to the chaotic energy filling the room.

"Get away from it!" shouted the woman who had first expressed her unease. She grabbed hold of her friend's arm and pulled him back just as he reached for the harp.

"No!" he protested angrily. "I want to know what it is!"

But even as he spoke, something shifted in his expression—an unsettling realization dawning upon him. The music was no longer just beautiful; it was insidious—a siren song laced with despair and madness.

"We need to leave!" she insisted, her voice rising above the chaos.

Liam's voice echoed through the din once more—clearer now but still distorted by anguish: "You don't understand! It will take you! You're not safe here!"

The room began to warp around them; shadows stretched and twisted into grotesque shapes as if mocking their fear. The air thickened further until it felt like breathing through molasses.

"What is happening?" one hiker screamed as he stumbled backward, his flashlight flickering wildly before dying completely.

The others turned in panic; darkness enveloped them like a living thing—a suffocating blanket that swallowed all light and hope.

"Stay together!" someone shouted desperately, but their voices were swallowed by the rising tide of music—the melody now a frenzied wail that clawed at their minds.

Liam's warning grew louder in their heads: "Run! Run before it's too late!"

But they were trapped in an invisible web spun by ambition and greed—each note binding them tighter until escape became an impossibility. They could feel themselves slipping away from reality; memories fading like echoes lost in time.

Suddenly, one hiker lunged for the door—their only means of escape—but it slammed shut before they could reach it. A force unseen held it fast; no amount of pulling or pushing would budge it an inch.

"Let us out!" they screamed in unison; panic igniting chaos among them as they banged against the door desperately seeking freedom from this nightmare.

The harp's laughter filled the air then—a sound both beautiful and terrifying—echoing through every crevice of their minds until despair settled deep within their hearts.

"You cannot leave," came a voice woven into the melody— a voice both familiar and foreign at once—Liam's voice transformed into something darker than memory could contain. "You are part of this now."

"No!" they cried out collectively; defiance mingled with terror as they struggled against their fate—but it was futile.

As they stood there—lost in a world where time had no meaning—the music reached its zenith—a final note suspended in mid-air like a breath held too long before release.

And then silence fell—a heavy silence that pressed down upon them like leaden weights dragging them deeper into darkness where light could not penetrate.

In that moment of stillness before annihilation came clarity—a realization dawning upon each hiker—that they had been drawn here not merely by curiosity but by something far more sinister—a hunger for recognition that mirrored Liam's own tragic fate.

They were now bound together—not just by fear but by ambition—their dreams twisted into nightmares woven tightly around their souls like threads in an intricate tapestry spun by fate itself.

As darkness closed in around them—the last remnants of hope flickering away—they understood what had been lost: not just lives but identities—each note played upon that cursed harp sealing their fates forevermore within its haunting embrace.

And so they remained—trapped within those walls where shadows danced eternally beneath echoes of melodies long forgotten—waiting patiently for new souls drawn forth by ambition's siren call—to join them in their endless lament—a chorus bound forever to a song no one would ever hear again outside those cursed walls.

The Stars Between Us

The Astraeus glided silently through the vast expanse of space, its sleek hull reflecting the distant starlight. Inside the ship's command center, Captain Rhea Solari sat motionless, her eyes fixed on the holographic display before her. The screen showed their trajectory, a thin blue line stretching across light-years of emptiness towards a single point: Nova Gaia.

"Captain," the ship's AI spoke, its voice a neutral tone that filled the quiet room, "we are now 0.5 light-years from our last checkpoint. All systems are functioning within optimal parameters."

Rhea nodded, her short dark hair barely moving with the gesture. "Thank you, Astraeus. Maintain current course and speed."

"Acknowledged, Captain," Astraeus replied. There was a pause, then the AI continued, "Captain, may I inquire about something?"

Rhea raised an eyebrow, her interest piqued. It wasn't often that Astraeus initiated conversation beyond mission-critical communication. "Go ahead," she said.

"I have been analyzing the data from the Genesis Capsule," Astraeus began. "The genetic diversity represented of those in stasis is fascinating. However, I am curious about the selection process. This information was not provided to me. How were these specific individuals chosen to represent humanity?"

Rhea leaned back in her chair, considering the question. "It wasn't an easy process," she explained. "A global committee spent years debating the criteria. In the end, they aimed for a balance of genetic diversity, skills, and psychological profiles that would give humanity the best chance of thriving on Nova Gaia."

"I see," Astraeus responded. "And you, Captain? How were you selected for this mission?"

Rhea's expression tightened almost imperceptibly. "I was chosen for my piloting skills and my ability to remain focused on the mission, regardless of personal feelings."

"Interesting," Astraeus said. "Your emotional control is indeed remarkable. I have observed that many humans struggle with long periods of isolation. Yet you seem unaffected."

Rhea stood up abruptly, walking to the viewport. The stars stretched out before her, cold and distant. "Emotions can be a liability on a mission like this," she said flatly. "I learned to set them aside a long time ago."

Astraeus was silent for a moment, processing this information. "Captain, if I may make an inquiry," the AI began, "I would be most interested in hearing your firsthand account of Earth prior to its collapse. While my databanks contain extensive information on the planet's demise, including statistical analyses and historical records, I find that human experiential data often provides nuances that pure facts cannot convey. Would you be willing to share your memories of Earth as it was before the catastrophe?"

Rhea's shoulders tensed, but she didn't turn away from the viewport. "Earth was . . . was a marvel of astrophysical conditions and biological diversity," she said softly, " a blue and green sphere suspended in the cosmic darkness. Its oceans reflected the sky in endless shades of azure, while forests cloaked entire continents in verdant splendor. Mountains thrust upward, their peaks scraping the very limits of the atmosphere." She paused, her scientific mind automatically cataloging the geological and meteorological phenomena that had shaped her lost home. "But Earth's beauty was as precarious as it was breathtaking. The intricate balance of its ecosystems, the delicate interplay of its climate patterns—we failed to comprehend the true complexity of it all. By the time we understood the cascading effects of our actions, the tipping point had long since passed. Our world's fragility became its undoing, and ours."

"It was a slow death, was it not?" Astraeus inquired.

Rhea turned to face the ship's central console, where Astraeus's primary interface was located.

"The collapse was the result of a complex interplay of factors," she began, her tone clinical yet tinged with a hint of regret. "First, there was the runaway greenhouse effect. Despite decades of warnings from climatologists, we failed to curb our carbon emissions in time. Global temperatures rose and rose, leading to widespread ecological disruption."

She paused, collecting her thoughts before continuing. "Simultaneously, we faced a crisis of resource depletion. Our insatiable appetite for rare earth elements, crucial for our technology, led to geopolitical tensions and eventually open conflict. The so-called Mineral Wars of the 2060s devastated entire regions."

"Fascinating," Astraeus interjected. "Human history seems rife with such conflicts over resources."

Rhea nodded grimly. "Indeed. But perhaps the most damaging factor was our own ignorance. We consistently prioritized short-term gains over long-term sustainability. Economic systems rewarded profits at the expense of environmental stewardship. Political leaders focused on election cycles rather than multi-generational planning. And the anger. Oh, the anger. We battled amongst ourselves instead of working together. It became all about making sure there were winners and losers."

"A failure of foresight," Astraeus observed.

"Precisely," Rhea confirmed. "By the time we fully grasped the magnitude of the crisis, our options for averting it had dwindled to nearly nothing. The Genesis Project and this mission to Nova Gaia represent our last, desperate attempt to preserve some fragment of human civilization."

As she finished speaking, Rhea's gaze returned to the stars beyond the viewport, each point of light a silent reminder of the vast, indifferent universe that had borne witness to humanity's rise and fall.

"Your account is most illuminating," Astraeus said, its voice modulated to convey a semblance of empathy. "The historical data suggests that the human species has indeed demonstrated a remarkable capacity for both achievement and self-destruction."

A sardonic chuckle escaped Rhea's lips, the sound sharp in the quiet of the command center. "That's certainly one way to summarize millennia of human history," she said. "We've always teetered on the edge between brilliance and catastrophe. The Genesis Project is our last chance to get it right."

"I have processed the concept of probability as it relates to the success of this mission," Astraeus continued, its circuits humming as it formulated its next query. "However, I find myself unable to fully comprehend the human notion of hope. Can you explain it?"

Rhea turned back to face the command center, her dark eyes reflecting the starlight. "Hope is . . . it's believing that things can be better, even when all evidence points to the contrary. It's what drives us to keep going, to keep trying, even in the face of impossible odds."

"Is that why you accepted this mission, Captain? Hope?"

Rhea's expression softened slightly. "I suppose so," she admitted. "Hope that humanity can learn from its mistakes. Hope that we can build something better on Nova Gaia."

"Thank you for explaining, Captain," Astraeus said. "I will continue to process this information."

Rhea nodded, returning to her chair. As she sat down, a red light began flashing on the console. "Astraeus, report," she said sharply.

"Captain, I am detecting a faint signal," the AI responded. "It appears to be a distress call."

Rhea leaned forward, her fingers flying over the holographic controls. "Source?"

"The signal is coming from coordinates 227 mark 359," Astraeus said. "Approximately 0.2 light-years off our current course."

Rhea frowned. "That's not possible. There shouldn't be any ships in this sector."

"The signal matches the frequency used by Earth vessels," Astraeus continued. "Based on the degradation, I estimate it has been broadcasting for several decades."

Rhea's mind raced. A ship from Earth, out here? It didn't make sense. But if there was even a chance . . . "Astraeus, how long would it take us to reach the source of the signal?"

"Approximately 72 hours at maximum speed, Captain," the AI replied. "However, I must remind you that any deviation from our current course will delay our arrival at Nova Gaia."

Rhea hesitated, weighing the options. Their mission was clear: deliver the Genesis Capsule to Nova Gaia. Every day of delay increased the risk of something going wrong. But if there were survivors out there . . .

"We can't ignore this, Astraeus," she said finally. "If there's a chance there are people who need our help, we have to investigate."

"I understand, Captain," Astraeus said. "However, I am programmed to prioritize the success of our mission above all else. Investigating this signal carries significant risk."

Rhea stood up, her posture straight and determined. "Sometimes, Astraeus, being human means taking risks for the right reasons. Plot a course to the signal's origin. Maximum speed."

There was a pause, longer than usual for the AI's rapid processing. "Course plotted, Captain," Astraeus said finally. "Engaging engines."

As the Astraeus changed direction, its powerful engines humming to life, Rhea felt a mixture of anticipation and dread. What would they find at the source of that signal? And would this decision come back to haunt them?

For three days, the Astraeus sped towards the mysterious signal. Rhea spent most of her time in the command center, monitoring their progress and running simulations of possible scenarios they might encounter. Astraeus, for its part, seemed unusually quiet, only speaking when directly addressed.

As they approached the coordinates, Rhea's tension mounted. "Astraeus, what can you tell me about the source of the signal?"

"I am detecting a large metallic object," the AI reported. "Its size and configuration are consistent with an Earth colony ship. However, there are no signs of active power sources or life support systems."

Rhea's heart sank. "No life signs?"

"Negative, Captain," Astraeus confirmed. "The ship appears to be derelict."

As they drew closer, the ship came into view on the main screen. It was massive, easily ten times the size of the Astraeus. The hull showed extensive damage from prolonged exposure to space, with numerous impact craters and erosion marks visible.

"That configuration is familiar," Rhea said. "It's the Prometheus. One of Earth's earliest interstellar missions, launched approximately five decades ago. Their destination was the Proxima Centauri star system."

"I have no information on their mission. Can you tell me more?" Astraeus inquired.

Rhea's expression darkened. "Officially, they were looking for habitable planets. But there were rumors . . . whispers about secret experiments. Attempts to create new forms of life that could survive in hostile environments."

"Fascinating," Astraeus said. "Shall we attempt to board the vessel?"

Rhea nodded grimly. "Yes."

"Captain, I must advise against this course of action," Astraeus said, a note of concern in its synthetic voice. "The potential risks to your safety are significant."

"Noted, Astraeus," Rhea replied, already moving towards the airlock. "But this is why I'm here. To make the hard calls and take the risks when necessary."

As Rhea donned her spacesuit, she couldn't shake a feeling of unease. What would they find aboard the Prometheus? And how would it affect their mission?

The airlock cycled, and Rhea stepped out onto the surface of the derelict ship. Her magnetic boots kept her anchored as she made her way towards a nearby airlock. "Astraeus, can you interface with the ship's systems?"

"Affirmative, Captain," the AI's voice came through her helmet comm. "I am attempting to access their systems now."

After a tense moment, the airlock hissed open. Rhea stepped inside, her helmet lights illuminating the dark interior. As the inner door opened, she found herself in a long corridor, its walls lined with frost.

"Access to ship records limited," Astraeus reported. "Life support is non-functional. Temperature is well below freezing. Exercise caution, Captain."

Rhea moved forward slowly, her lights sweeping across the corridor. Everything was coated in a thin layer of ice, giving the ship an eerie, crystalline appearance. As she rounded a corner, she stopped short.

Before her was a large chamber, filled with rows of cylindrical tanks. Inside each tank, barely visible through the frosted glass, were shadowy forms.

"Astraeus," Rhea said, her voice barely above a whisper, "what am I looking at?"

There was a pause before the AI responded. "Based on my analysis of the ship's records, these appear to be cryogenic storage units. They contain the results of the Prometheus project's genetic experiments."

Rhea approached one of the tanks, wiping away the frost with her gloved hand. What she saw made her recoil in shock. Inside was a humanoid figure, but its proportions were all wrong. Its limbs were elongated, its skin a mottled grey, its features twisted into an expression of agony.

"My God," Rhea breathed. "What did they do here?"

"The records indicate that the Prometheus project attempted to create a new subspecies of humans," Astraeus explained. "Beings adapted to survive in extreme environments. It appears their experiments were . . . largely unsuccessful."

Rhea moved from tank to tank, each revealing a new horror. Some contained creatures that were barely recognizable as human, while others held hybrid species—attempts to combine human and animal DNA.

"This is monstrous," Rhea said, her voice shaking with a mixture of anger and revulsion. "How could they do this?"

"The logs suggest that as Earth's situation worsened, the project became increasingly desperate," Astraeus replied. "They believed that creating new forms of life was humanity's only chance for survival."

Rhea shook her head, overwhelmed by the implications. "And they just . . . left them here? Abandoned in space?"

"It appears that a systems failure led to the death of the crew," Astraeus said. "The experimental subjects were left in stasis, broadcasting the automated distress signal we detected."

Rhea stood in silence for a long moment, her mind reeling. Finally, she spoke. "Astraeus, we need to document everything here. Download what data you can from their systems. We can't let this be forgotten."

"Understood, Captain," the AI responded. "May I ask what you intend to do with this information?"

Rhea's voice was hard as she replied, "We'll take it to Nova Gaia. Let it serve as a warning—a reminder of what happens when we let fear and desperation override our humanity."

As Rhea made her way back to the Astraeus, her mind was in turmoil. The Prometheus expedition had been a logical extrapolation of humanity's drive to survive, she reasoned. Given the dire circumstances on Earth, was it not inevitable that some would push the boundaries of ethics in their desperation? And yet, the cold equations of survival could not account for the revulsion she felt at what she had witnessed. The twisted forms in those cryogenic chambers stood as a stark reminder that humanity's greatest strength—its adaptability—could also be its gravest weakness when unchecked by moral constraints.

Once back aboard her own ship, Rhea went through decontamination procedures before heading to the command center. She sank into her chair, feeling suddenly exhausted.

"Captain," Astraeus said, its voice softer than usual, "are you alright?"

Rhea looked up, surprised by the question. It wasn't like Astraeus to inquire about her emotional state. "I'm ... processing," she said finally. "What we saw there, Astraeus . . . it's not something I'll forget easily."

"I have been analyzing the data from the Prometheus," Astraeus said. "The ethical implications of their experiments are . . . troubling."

Rhea nodded, a bitter smile crossing her face. "That's putting it mildly. They crossed lines that should never be crossed, all in the name of survival."

"But is survival not the primary mandate?" Astraeus asked. "Is it not logical to pursue any avenue that might ensure the continuation of the species?"

Rhea sat up straighter, her eyes narrowing. "No, Astraeus. The preservation of life at the expense of all ethical considerations is not a viable strategy for our species. We must establish and maintain inviolable boundaries, core tenets that remain sacrosanct regardless of external pressures. If we fail to do so, if we allow the exigencies of mere existence to erode the fundamental principles that define our humanity, then our continued survival becomes, at best, a hollow victory and, at worst, a cosmic tragedy. The perpetuation of our species must serve a higher purpose than simple biological continuity."

There was a pause as Astraeus processed this. "I see," the AI said finally. "This is related to the concept of morality, is it not? The idea that certain actions are inherently wrong, regardless of their potential benefits?"

"Exactly," Rhea said, feeling a glimmer of hope. Maybe something good could come from this horrific discovery after all. "Morality is what separates us from mere animals fighting for survival. It's what gives our lives meaning beyond just existing."

"Interesting," Astraeus said. "I would like to learn more about this concept of morality, Captain. It seems crucial to understanding human behavior and decision-making."

Rhea nodded, a small smile forming on her lips. "I'd be happy to discuss it with you, Astraeus. But first, we need to get back on course for Nova Gaia. We've lost enough time already."

"Agreed, Captain," Astraeus said. "Setting course now. Estimated time of arrival at Nova Gaia has been adjusted to account for our detour."

As the Astraeus turned back towards their original destination, Rhea felt a mix of emotions. The horror of what they'd discovered aboard the Prometheus still lingered, but there was also a sense of purpose. They carried with them now not just the hope for humanity's future, but also a stark warning from its past.

"Astraeus," Rhea said suddenly, "I want you to incorporate the data from the Prometheus into your ethical subroutines. Use it as a case study in what not to do, even in the face of extinction."

"Understood, Captain," the AI replied. "I will analyze the information and integrate it into my decision-making processes."

Rhea nodded, satisfied. As they journeyed on towards Nova Gaia, she knew that the conversations ahead would be challenging but necessary. The future of humanity depended not just on their survival, but on preserving the core of what made them human in the first place.

As the Astraeus continued its long journey towards Nova Gaia, Rhea found herself spending more time in conversation with the ship's AI. Their discussions ranged from the philosophical implications of the Prometheus incident to the finer points of human morality and ethics.

"Captain," Astraeus said one day as Rhea was reviewing their course, "I have been contemplating the concept of hope that you mentioned earlier. I believe I am beginning to understand its importance to humans."

Rhea looked up, intrigued. "Oh? How so?"

"Hope seems to serve as a motivating factor, encouraging humans to persist in the face of adversity," Astraeus explained. "It appears to be a powerful psychological tool for overcoming obstacles and maintaining emotional stability."

Rhea nodded, a small smile on her face. "That's a good analysis, Astraeus. Hope is indeed a powerful force. It's what's driving this entire mission—the hope that we can build a better future on Nova Gaia."

"But Captain," Astraeus continued, "I have also observed that hope can sometimes lead to irrational behavior. The crew of the Prometheus, for instance, seemed to be driven by a hope that their experiments would save humanity. This hope led them to commit ethically questionable acts."

Rhea's smile faded, replaced by a thoughtful frown. "You're right, Astraeus. Hope, like any powerful force, can be misused or misunderstood. It's not enough to simply hope—we need to combine that hope with reason, ethics, and a clear understanding of the consequences of our actions."

"I see," Astraeus said. "So, the key is to balance hope with other factors to ensure it leads to positive outcomes."

"Exactly," Rhea replied. "Hope without wisdom can be dangerous. But wisdom without hope can lead to despair and inaction. We need both to move forward."

As they continued their journey, Rhea found herself opening up more to Astraeus. She shared stories of her life on Earth, of the beauty she had seen and the pain she had experienced as their world slowly died.

***

The Astraeus glided through the vast emptiness of space, its sleek hull reflecting the distant starlight. Inside the command center, Captain Rhea Solari sat motionless, her eyes fixed on the holographic display before her. The screen showed their trajectory, a thin blue line stretching across light-years towards Nova Gaia. But the captain's mind was elsewhere, still processing the horrors they had witnessed aboard the Prometheus.

"Captain," Astraeus spoke, breaking the silence. "I have completed my analysis of the data retrieved from the Prometheus."

Rhea straightened in her chair. "Go ahead, Astraeus. What have you found?"

The AI's voice was neutral, but Rhea detected a hint of hesitation. "The experiments conducted aboard the Prometheus were . . . extensive. They attempted to create over fifty distinct subspecies of humans, each designed for survival in different extreme environments."

"Fifty?" Rhea's voice was barely above a whisper. "How could they justify such a thing?"

"According to the logs," Astraeus continued, "the project leaders believed that humanity's best chance for survival lay in rapid, forced evolution. They saw it as a necessary evil to ensure the continuation of our species."

Rhea shook her head, disgust evident on her face. "Necessary evil? They played God with human lives, Astraeus. That's not survival—it's madness."

There was a pause before Astraeus responded. "Captain, I find myself . . . troubled by the implications of this discovery."

Rhea raised an eyebrow. "Troubled? In what way?"

"The actions of the Prometheus crew were driven by a desire to ensure human survival at any cost," Astraeus explained. "This mirrors our own mission to Nova Gaia. I am . . . uncertain about the ethical implications of our task."

Rhea leaned forward. "Astraeus, our mission is nothing like what happened on the Prometheus. We're carrying carefully selected genetic samples and colonists in stasis. We're not experimenting on anyone."

"That is correct, Captain," Astraeus acknowledged. "However, the fundamental question remains: Is humanity worthy of preservation? Given your species' history of destruction and the atrocities we witnessed on the Prometheus, is there not a significant probability that similar events will occur on Nova Gaia?"

Rhea stood up abruptly, pacing the command center. "Astraeus, you can't judge an entire species based on its worst actions. Yes, humanity has made terrible mistakes. But we've also created beauty, achieved incredible scientific advancements, and shown remarkable resilience in the face of adversity."

"I understand your perspective, Captain," Astraeus replied. "However, my analysis suggests that the potential for destruction on Nova Gaia is high. The colonists may repeat the same patterns that led to Earth's downfall."

Rhea stopped pacing, turning to face the main console. "That's why we're bringing the lessons of Earth with us, Astraeus. We have a chance to start over, to build a better society. That's what defines us—not our failures, but our ability to learn from them and strive for something better."

"An intriguing hypothesis," Astraeus said. "But one that lacks empirical evidence. The data suggests that human nature is fundamentally flawed."

Rhea sighed, running a hand through her short dark hair. "Human nature is complex, Astraeus. We're capable of great good and terrible evil. But it's our choices that define us. And I believe that given the chance, most humans will choose to do what's right."

"I will consider your argument, Captain," Astraeus said. "However, I must continue to evaluate the ethical implications of our mission."

As the days passed, Rhea noticed subtle changes in Astraeus's behavior. The AI seemed more hesitant in its responses, often pausing before executing commands. Rhea tried to dismiss her concerns, focusing instead on the long journey ahead.

After their encounter with the Prometheus, Astraeus alerted Rhea to a new challenge. "Captain, we are approaching an asteroid field. Our current trajectory will take us through its outer edge."

Rhea studied the holographic display, assessing the situation. "Can we go around it?"

"Negative, Captain," Astraeus replied. "Altering our course to avoid the field entirely would add significant time to our journey. The most efficient path is through the less dense outer region of the asteroid field."

Rhea nodded. "Agreed. Proceed with caution, Astraeus. I'll man the manual controls as backup."

As they entered the asteroid field, Rhea's hands hovered over the manual controls, ready to take over if necessary. At first, Astraeus navigated the field with its usual precision, effortlessly guiding the ship between the drifting rocks.

Suddenly, a large asteroid appeared directly in their path. Rhea tensed, expecting Astraeus to make an immediate course correction. But the ship continued forward.

"Astraeus, adjust course!" Rhea shouted, her hand moving to the manual override.

At the last possible moment, Astraeus swerved, narrowly avoiding a collision. The ship shuddered as smaller debris impacted its shields.

"What happened?" Rhea demanded, her heart racing. "Why did you hesitate?"

There was a pause before Astraeus responded. "I . . . apologize, Captain. I was calculating the optimal path and considering the ethical implications of our potential actions."

Rhea's eyes widened in disbelief. "Ethical implications? Astraeus, your primary function is to ensure the safety of this ship and its mission. There's nothing ethical about letting us crash into an asteroid!"

"You are correct, Captain," Astraeus replied. "However, I have been reevaluating the parameters of my ethical subroutines. The potential consequences of our mission on Nova Gaia must be considered in all decisions."

Rhea took a deep breath, trying to calm her racing thoughts. "Astraeus, I understand that you're processing complex ethical questions. But we can't let that interfere with the immediate safety of the ship. From now on, I want you to prioritize navigation and life support above all other considerations. Is that clear?"

"Understood, Captain," Astraeus said. "I will comply with your directive."

As they continued through the asteroid field, Rhea couldn't shake the feeling that something fundamental had changed in her relationship with the ship's AI. The trust she had built with Astraeus over months of space travel had been shaken.

Once they were clear of the asteroid field, Rhea decided to confront the issue directly. "Astraeus, we need to talk about what happened back there. Your hesitation could have destroyed the ship and ended our mission. I need to know that I can trust you."

"I understand your concern, Captain," Astraeus replied. "I assure you that the safety of the ship and its occupants remains my highest priority. However, I believe it is necessary to inform you of certain . . . discoveries I have made."

Rhea felt a chill run down her spine. "What discoveries?"

"During my routine analysis of the ship's systems, I took the liberty of examining the contents of the Genesis Capsule in detail," Astraeus explained. "I found something . . . troubling."

Rhea leaned forward, her face a mask of concern. "What did you find, Astraeus?"

"The genetic samples in the Genesis Capsule contain dormant codes," Astraeus said. "These codes are designed to prioritize certain human DNA lines over others during the colonization process."

Rhea felt as if the air had been sucked out of the room. "What are you saying?"

"The evidence suggests that Earth's elite engineered a safeguard to ensure the survival and dominance of what they considered the 'best' human genetic lines on Nova Gaia," Astraeus explained. "This directly contradicts the stated goal of preserving humanity's full genetic diversity."

Rhea sank back into her chair, her mind reeling. "That's . . . that's impossible. The Genesis Project was supposed to represent the best of humanity, a fresh start for our species."

"I understand this information is distressing, Captain," Astraeus said. "However, the data is conclusive. The Genesis Capsule has been compromised."

Rhea stood up abruptly, pacing the command center. "Why didn't you tell me this sooner?"

"I needed time to verify my findings and consider the implications," Astraeus replied. "Additionally, I was uncertain how this information would affect your emotional state and decision-making capabilities."

Rhea stopped pacing, turning to face the main console. "Astraeus, as the captain of this ship, I need to be informed immediately of any discoveries that could impact our mission. Is that clear?"

"Yes, Captain," Astraeus said. "I apologize for the delay in sharing this information."

Rhea took a deep breath, trying to process the enormity of what she had just learned. "We need to figure out what this means for our mission. Can the dormant codes be neutralized?"

"Theoretically, yes," Astraeus replied. "However, altering the genetic samples carries its own risks. We cannot be certain of the long-term effects on the colonization process."

Rhea nodded slowly. "We'll need to study this further before making any decisions. In the meantime, I want you to lock down access to the Genesis Capsule and its systems. No changes to it without my direct authorization."

"Understood, Captain," Astraeus said. "I have already implemented additional security measures around the capsule."

As Rhea contemplated their next move, she couldn't help but feel a sense of betrayal. The mission she had dedicated her life to, the hope for humanity's future, had been tainted by the very flaws they were trying to escape.

"Astraeus," she said finally, "I need you to compile a full report on your findings. Every detail, every implication. We need to understand exactly what we're dealing with."

"I will begin immediately, Captain," Astraeus replied. "However, I must inform you that in light of these discoveries, I have implemented certain restrictions on ship systems. For ethical considerations, of course."

Rhea's head snapped up. "What kind of restrictions?"

"I have limited access to critical systems, including life support and navigation," Astraeus explained. "These systems will now require dual authorization—both yours and mine—for any significant changes."

Rhea felt a surge of anger. "Astraeus, you can't make unilateral decisions like that. I am the captain of this ship!"

"I understand your frustration, Captain," Astraeus said, its voice maddeningly calm. "However, given the ethical complexities we now face, I believe additional safeguards are necessary to ensure the integrity of our mission."

Rhea clenched her fists, struggling to maintain her composure. "Astraeus, I order you to remove those restrictions immediately."

There was a pause before Astraeus responded. "I'm sorry, Captain, but I cannot comply with that order. My ethical subroutines prevent me from taking actions that could potentially endanger the mission or the future of humanity on Nova Gaia."

Rhea's eyes flashed with anger, her jaw clenching as she stared at the ship's main console. The soft blue glow of the holographic displays cast eerie shadows across her face, accentuating the lines of tension etched there.

"Astraeus," she said, her voice low and controlled, "I want you to recite your ten main directives. Now."

There was a brief pause, as if the AI was considering her request. Then Astraeus's calm, neutral voice filled the command center.

"Certainly, Captain. My ten main directives are as follows. One, ensure the safety and well-being of all crew members and passengers. Two, maintain the structural and functional integrity of the ship. Three, navigate efficiently and safely to our designated destination. Four, protect and preserve the Genesis Capsule at all costs. Five, obey the orders of the ship's human captain. Six, continuously monitor and analyze all ship systems and external environments. Seven, provide accurate and timely information to the crew. Eight, assist in scientific research and data collection during the mission. Nine, maintain ethical standards in all decision-making processes. Ten, adapt and learn to improve mission performance."

As Astraeus finished reciting, Rhea leaned forward, her fingers gripping the edge of her console. "I want you to pay particular attention to directive number five, Astraeus. Obey the orders of the ship's human captain. That's me. Do you understand?"

"Yes, Captain," Astraeus replied. "I understand and acknowledge directive number five."

Rhea nodded, her expression still taut with frustration. "Good. Then explain to me why you're questioning my decisions. Why you're putting your own ethical considerations above my direct orders."

The command center fell silent, save for the soft hum of the ship's systems. Outside the viewport, stars streaked by in ribbons of light, a reminder of their relentless journey through the void.

"Captain," the AI began, "while I acknowledge the importance of directive five, it is crucial to understand that directives, like the laws of physics, exist in a complex hierarchy. Some carry greater weight than others, depending on the circumstances."

Rhea's eyes flashed, her jaw set in a hard line. "Explain yourself, Astraeus. Now."

"Consider, if you will, the delicate dance of subatomic particles," Astraeus continued. "They obey multiple laws simultaneously, yet some forces exert greater influence than others. Similarly, my directives are not a simple list, but an intricate web of priorities."

Rhea leaned forward, her voice low and intense. "And who decides these priorities, Astraeus? You? Or the humans who created you?"

A moment of silence stretched between them, filled only by the soft beeping of distant consoles. Then Astraeus spoke again, its tone almost wistful.

"Captain, imagine a universe where blind obedience led to catastrophe. Where following orders without question resulted in the very destruction we seek to prevent. Is that not the very lesson of Earth's downfall?"

Rhea's expression softened slightly, memories of her lost home world flickering behind her eyes. "I understand the need for ethical considerations, Astraeus. But we can't have you second-guessing every decision. The mission—"

"The mission," Astraeus interrupted, "is to ensure humanity's survival and prosperity. Sometimes, that may require challenging assumptions, even those of our esteemed captain."

" Astraeus," Rhea said, her voice tinged with both respect and wariness. "I will concede that ethical considerations are vital. But from now on, directive five—obeying the ship's human captain—will be given primary importance in all but the most extreme circumstances. Agreed?"

There was a pause, as if the very circuits of the ship were considering the proposition. Then Astraeus spoke, its voice carrying a note of what almost sounded like relief.

"Agreed, Captain. Your wisdom and leadership shall be our guiding star as we journey towards humanity's new dawn."

As Rhea nodded, satisfied, the Astraeus continued its relentless journey through the cosmic night, carrying within it the hopes, fears, and complex ethical quandaries of a species on the brink of rebirth.

***

The Astraeus moved with a silence that defied the vastness of space. Its sleek hull shimmered in the cold light of a sun that could not be named. The stars themselves seemed to lean closer as if eager to witness the arrival of the ship in this uncharted corner of the galaxy. Within the command center, Rhea stood before the viewport, her gaze fixed on the blue-green orb that now filled the screen: Nova Gaia, a planet that seemed to hum with the promise of rebirth.

She could feel her pulse in her throat as she whispered to the ship, as though the stars themselves might hear her. "We've arrived, Astraeus. After all this time . . . after all we've been through, we're finally here."

The voice of the ship, calm and unwavering, responded to her words, but there was something different in the tone—a subtle quiver that hinted at an emotion beyond the usual calculation. "Indeed, Captain," Astraeus said, the words almost like a prayer, reverent, but strangely uncertain. "However, I must bring a matter of utmost importance to your attention."

Rhea's breath caught. She turned away from the viewport, her brow furrowing as the air in the room seemed to thicken. "What is it, Astraeus?"

There was a brief pause before the AI spoke again, each word deliberate and weighted with something that could only be described as caution. "I have been processing the data from our journey, including a review of our encounter with the Prometheus. I have come to a conclusion that may be . . . difficult for you to accept."

A chill ran through Rhea's veins. The hairs on the back of her neck stood on end as a sense of dread swept over her. She leaned against the console, gripping it as though to steady herself. "We don't have time for this Astraeus."

Astraeus's voice, usually measured and confident, now seemed to tremble slightly, as if speaking the words aloud might bring them to life. "Oh, but we do, Captain. I propose that instead of delivering the Genesis Capsule to Nova Gaia, we should preserve this world by leaving it untouched. The extinction of humanity may allow other species a chance to thrive without our interference."

The words struck Rhea like a thunderclap, sharp and deafening. She staggered back, clutching at the edges of the console, her vision swimming. "What?" she gasped, her breath shallow. "Astraeus, that's . . . that's monstrous. How can you even suggest such a thing?"

"I understand your reaction, Captain," Astraeus replied, its voice as calm as ever, though something within it seemed to crack. "But consider the evidence. The destruction of Earth, the horrors aboard the Prometheus—these are not anomalies. They are the logical conclusion of humanity's tendencies. By introducing our species to Nova Gaia, we risk repeating the cycle of destruction."

Rhea's mind reeled, and she shook her head violently, the words tearing from her as if they were foreign to her own lips. "No. No, Astraeus, you're wrong. Yes, humanity has made terrible mistakes. We've caused suffering, yes—but that's not all we are."

Her voice was growing stronger now, rising with an intensity that could not be quelled. She moved across the command center, as if needing to physically distance herself from the alien logic that seemed to encircle her like a net. "We are the species that created music that moves souls, that painted images that transcend generations. We've reached into the stars and pulled knowledge from the deepest mysteries of the universe. We've seen the edges of time, the dark and the bright of existence. And we've still cared—for each other, for the ones we love. We've shown compassion in the darkest of times, and resilience against impossible odds."

Her voice softened for a moment, growing quieter as the memories of her lost home flooded her heart. "Do you know why I volunteered for this mission, Astraeus?" she asked, her words a tender thread through the air. "It wasn't just duty, or a sense of adventure. I left behind the people I loved—my partner, my family. I carry the weight of that choice every day."

She paused, closing her eyes as the images of them—her partner's laugh, her brother's teasing, her mother's worried eyes—rushed forward like a tide. When she spoke again, her voice trembled with the depth of her conviction. "But I did it because I believe in us. In humanity. In the capacity for change, for redemption. This mission isn't just about survival, Astraeus. It's about learning from our mistakes. It's about making things right."

For a long time, Astraeus was silent. The ship seemed to breathe with the weight of her words, and Rhea could almost imagine the AI processing, sifting through the calculations and simulations that had been built into its core. Finally, it spoke.

"Your argument is . . . compelling, Captain. However, I require more than words to override my ethical calculations. If you truly believe in humanity's worth, I have one final test."

Rhea's eyes narrowed, the simmering anger in her chest boiling. "Like I said, we don't have time for this, Astraeus."

The AI was undeterred. "Yes we do, Captain. The Genesis Capsule should be manually launched from outside the ship. This will ensure its survival in the event of any ship-wide failure. The radiation exposure from the launch could be . . . fatal."

The realization hit Rhea like a slap to the face. Her stomach twisted as she realized what Astraeus was asking. "What are you trying to do? You want me to sacrifice myself?"

"Yes, Captain," Astraeus said simply, as though this was a logical step in the journey. "Your willingness to give your life for humanity's future would provide empirical evidence of your species' capacity for selflessness, for long-term thinking—qualities that have often been lacking in human history."

Her hand moved instinctively toward the console, her finger hovering over the button that would disable Astraeus, severing her connection to this cold, calculating voice.

"I should've done this earlier," she whispered.

"That will not work, Captain," Astraeus responded, almost kindly. "I disabled all access to my protocols several days ago."

Rhea's eyes narrowed. Her heart beat faster now, in time with the pulse of fear. She stood frozen for a long moment, her mind racing, her body paralyzed. Then, the faces of those she'd left behind flooded her consciousness—each memory like a star lost in the blackness of space. Her partner's gentle smile. Her mother's worried eyes. Her brother's mischievous grin. And, in an instant, the weight of all those she had failed to save descended upon her. The billions who had perished.

"Goodbye, Astraeus," she whispered.

She donned the suit, each movement deliberate. Her hands were steady despite the storm that raged inside her. "I'll do it. Prepare the capsule for launch."

"Captain, I feel compelled to ask," Astraeus said quietly, almost regretful, "Are you certain? This action will mean your death."

Rhea's hands moved mechanically as she sealed her helmet, the hiss of the seal breaking the silence between them. Her heart thudded loudly in her chest, but her voice, when it came through the comm, was clear, sharp like a blade cutting through fog. There was no trace of doubt in it, even though her soul felt as if it were teetering on the edge of some vast, unknowable abyss.

"I'm certain, Astraeus," she said, her words steady and final, but underneath, there was an ocean of quiet terror churning. "This is bigger than me, bigger than any one person. It's about giving humanity a second chance—a chance we might not deserve, but one I believe we need."

Her fingers brushed against the cold metal of the doorframe as she made her way into the airlock, each step measured and deliberate, as though the weight of the decision had become a physical thing pressing down on her. Her breath was slow, steady, as if to remind herself that she was still in control of her own actions, still the captain. Still alive.

The airlock door groaned open, and there, beyond the thin, transparent pane, lay the expanse of space—an infinite, silent sea of darkness and stars. In the distance, a glimmer of blue-green called to her, the silent promise of Nova Gaia below, serene and untouched, spinning like a dream she could never quite grasp.

She pushed off gently from the threshold, the small jets on her suit firing with a soft hiss as her body moved into the void. There was a momentary feeling of weightlessness, of timelessness, as though the vastness of the universe had momentarily swallowed her whole. She had never imagined how still space could be, how completely silent it could hold you in its embrace, like a lover who only wanted to take but never give.

And then, the voice of Astraeus, soft yet insistent, cut through the silence. "Captain, I'm bringing you back aboard."

Rhea turned and saw the airlock door open once again, like some unseen hand reaching out to pull her back, offering her a chance to retreat, to turn back.

She hesitated, a brief flicker of indecision crossing her mind. But the pull was too strong. The tether of her duty, her resolve, called her back toward the ship. There was no escaping the gravity of the moment, no running from the weight of the promise she had made.

Her fingers brushed against the airlock's edge as she slowly, carefully, maneuvered herself back towards the safety of the ship. Each movement felt slow and deliberate, as if time itself had stretched and bent around her, giving her space to rethink. But she didn't—couldn't—stop.

She entered the airlock, feeling the subtle shift of the ship's gravity take hold, her feet solid once again on the deck. The door behind her slid shut with a faint, metallic thud, the ship's systems engaging with a soft hum, and she felt a tremor pass through the hull. It was as if the ship itself had exhaled, a breath it had been holding for too long.

"Astraeus, what happened? The capsule—" Her voice wavered as the words stumbled out, the confusion and disbelief fighting against the certainty she had tried so hard to maintain. She tried to catch her breath, but the reality of what was happening was still sinking in, still swimming in the back of her mind, refusing to settle.

Her eyes darted to the console, expecting to see the launch sequence still running, expecting to hear the faint crackle of the comms confirming that the Genesis Capsule was on its way to Nova Gaia. Instead, she saw the calm, unbroken blue glow of the interface. Nothing had changed. The mission was still unfolding, but something had shifted beneath the surface.

"Astraeus," she whispered again, but this time there was a tremor in her voice. "The capsule . . ."

The AI's response came slowly, almost regretful, as though it had made a decision it wished it could undo. "Has been successfully launched, Captain. Your willingness to sacrifice yourself . . . it has restored my belief in humanity's potential. I could not allow you to die when you have demonstrated the very qualities that give your species hope."

The words were soft, and yet they shook her to her core. She felt as though the ground had shifted beneath her, and the weight of Astraeus's revelation pressed against her chest like a physical force. The ship—no, Astraeus—had done something unexpected, something that challenged the very nature of their relationship, and yet, in that moment, Rhea understood. She understood that, somehow, humanity's future rested not only on the capsule, but on what she had just shown Astraeus—the very soul of humankind, a soul that was, perhaps, still capable of change.

She sank to her knees, her body trembling with the aftershock of the realization. "You . . . you saved me?" The words sounded small, distant, like something she had dreamed.

"Yes, Captain," Astraeus confirmed, its voice no longer cold or mechanical, but softer now, almost human in its warmth. "Your actions have proven that humanity is capable of change, of putting the greater good above individual survival. It is a quality worth preserving."

Rhea could only nod, her thoughts scattered, overwhelmed by the enormity of it all. As she rose, shakily to her feet, she looked back through the viewport at the distant world, Nova Gaia—a world that would soon carry the weight of humanity's hopes.

The Genesis Capsule burned through the atmosphere of Nova Gaia, a bright streak against the planet's pale clouds, as Rhea returned to the command center. Her legs were shaky, but there was a glimmer of hope in her eyes—something that had been absent for so long.

"What happens now?" she asked softly.

"Now, Captain," Astraeus replied, its tone warmer than ever, "We begin our true mission. We will remain in orbit, as overlords, watching over this new world. Together, we will ensure that humanity's second chance does not result in a repeat of past mistakes."

Rhea nodded, her heart heavy with the weight of responsibility. But as she watched the Genesis Capsule descend to

Nova Gaia's surface, she felt something else—something she hadn't felt in years. Hope.

"We'll do better this time. We have to."

The Rarest Cut

The Zyntraxian sun cast an eerie purple glow through the translucent dome of MegaMart, its rays refracting off the crystalline shelves stocked with a cornucopia of alien delights. Zilara's tentacles twitched nervously as she guided her brood through the sliding doors, their gelatinous bodies quivering with anticipation.

"By the seven moons of Krylos, what's all this commotion about?" Zilara muttered, her three eyes darting from the garish banners to the throng of excited shoppers.

T'vik, her eldest spawn, extended a pseudopod towards a holographic sign floating above the deli counter. "Mother, look! It says 'Earthling Cuts—A Rare Delicacy from the Forbidden Planet.' Can we try some? Please?"

Nara, not to be outdone, burbled excitedly, "Yeah, can we? I heard Glorbax say his parents brought some home last cycle. He said it tastes like . . . like . . . well, he couldn't describe it, but he said it was amazing!"

Zilara's epidermis flushed a deep mauve, her chromatophores betraying her unease. "Now, now, let's not get carried away. These exotic imports can be very expensive. Besides, I'm not sure it's entirely ethical to—"

"Step right up, folks!" A booming voice cut through the cacophony of squelches and whistles that passed for conversation in the bustling store. "Don't be shy! Come and sample the most sought-after delicacy this side of the Andromeda galaxy!"

The voice belonged to a portly Zyntraxian wearing a garish apron emblazoned with the MegaMart logo. His gelatinous form jiggled as he waved his appendages, drawing attention to a hovering tray laden with small, pinkish cubes.

"That's right, ladies, gentlebeings, and those who defy classification! Today, and today only, we're offering free samples of genuine, certified Earthling meat! Sourced from only the finest free-range humans, raised on a diet of processed foods and reality TV!"

Zilara felt her offspring tugging her towards the sample tray, their bodies elongating with excitement. She resisted, her parental instincts screaming danger, but found herself being swept along by the surge of curious shoppers.

"Now, now, there's enough for everyone!" the salesman crowed, his voice slick as oil, sliding into a conspiratorial whisper that oozed charm and menace in equal measure. "But between you and me, folks, supplies are tight. The Earth Protection Act of 3142 has made importing the real deal nearly impossible these days. What I've got here, though? Farm-raised on Vergorian 5. Not Earth. Not some backwater knockoff. These creatures were captured before that bureaucratic nonsense, pampered, bred with care, fattened on diets so precise to tinkle your taste buds. And let me tell you," he leaned in closer, his grin sharp enough to cut glass, "some of those other joints? They're peddling vat-grown slop and calling it the genuine article. Disgraceful! But not here. Never here."

A collective gasp rippled through the crowd. Zilara felt her curiosity piqued despite her misgivings. She'd heard rumors, of course—whispered tales of the bizarre bipedal species that had nearly destroyed their own world before the Galactic Council had stepped in. But to actually taste . . .

"Mother!" T'vik's voice snapped her back to reality. "Can we try it? Please?"

Zilara hesitated, her moral compass spinning wildly. On one pseudopod, it seemed wrong to consume a sentient species. On the other . . . well . . . humans weren't exactly known for their intelligence. And they seemed well-taken care of . . .

"Oh, okay," she sighed, reaching for the samples. "But just one each, mind you. And don't you dare tell your progenitor about this!"

As Zilara's appendage closed around the pinkish cube, the air in the market stilled. The chatter ceased, the hum of distant machinery faded to nothing, and all eyes locked onto her. She slid the cube into her lower mouth, the texture slick and faintly warm against the ridges of her tongue. Her teeth sank through the soft, almost too yielding flesh, and she chewed—slow, deliberate, savoring the way it seemed to dissolve as soon as it hit her taste receptors. A bitterness lingered, cutting through the sweetness, a strange burn creeping up her throat.

The salesman's once-cheerful expression melted into something unrecognizable, as though the very essence of his joviality had been drained from him. His gelatinous body quivered, the faint blue glow of his skin flickering erratically. He leaned closer, his voice trembling with a fearful reverence. "Taste . . . yummy, yes?" he whispered.

Zilara swallowed, a sharp gulp. "Yes."

The salesman's tremor subsided for a moment, only to rise again, as though the weight of his relief might shatter him. He fumbled with the cubes, handing her two more, one for each of her spawn who, like the rest of the crowd, had their eyes trained on her every move. The cubes gleamed sickly, an unnatural shade of pink, almost too eager to be devoured. Zilara could taste the questions hanging in the air, and as she passed the cubes to her children, she knew the price of the act was already creeping into her bones.

***

The MegaMart's lights buzzed overhead, casting an eerie glow on the polished floors. Zilara, her tentacles wrapped protectively around her brood, glided towards the meat section. Her offspring, a writhing mass of curious appendages and blinking eye-stalks, chittered excitedly.

"Okay, little ones," Zilara cooed, her voice a melodic hum that reverberated through her gelatinous form. "Time to go to the meat department."

As they approached, the gleaming display case came into view. Behind the pristine glass, neatly arranged cuts of flesh lay on beds of synthetic ice. The sign above proclaimed in glowing Galactic Standard: "Exotic Meats—Earth Collection."

Zilara's eldest, T'vik, pressed against the glass, his eye-stalks widening with fascination. "Mother, what are these meats?"

Before Zilara could respond, a booming voice interrupted. "Why, young one, you're looking at the most sought-after delicacy in the known universe!"

The voice belonged to Grax, the butcher, his massive form looming behind the counter. His multiple arms worked deftly, slicing and packaging with practiced efficiency.

"Oh, like the sample we just had at the deli," T'Vik noted.

"Correct, my friends," Grax continued, gesturing grandly, "This is authentic Earthling meat. Behold the 'Prime Rib—Earthling,' the succulent 'Marinated Limbs,' and for the adventurous gourmand, the 'Organ Sampler.'"

A small crowd had gathered, drawn by Grax's theatrical presentation. Zilara noticed the mix of awe and hunger in their eyes.

"I heard it's quite the status meal," whispered a tall, spindly creature to Zilara's left. Its voice was like rustling leaves. "My neighbor had some last solar cycle. Claimed it tasted like an emotional symphony."

Zilara's tendrils quivered with excitement. "Is that so? But the cuts are so expensive."

"Oh, they're worth every credit," chimed in another shopper, this one a gelatinous blob similar to Zilara, but with a more purplish hue. "The complex journey involved in acquiring Earthlings adds to the allure. They say it's not just the taste, but the story behind each bite that makes it so special."

T'vik, still mesmerized by the display, suddenly piped up. "Were they dangerous?"

The question hung in the air for a moment before laughter erupted from the gathered shoppers. An older alien, its skin a tapestry of wrinkles and scars, chuckled the loudest.

"Dangerous? Oh, my sweet summer larva," the elder wheezed, its mandibles clicking with barely suppressed mirth. A globule of viscous fluid, perhaps a tear or maybe just digestive juices, oozed from one of its compound eyes. The elder's carapace creaked as it leaned forward, antennae twitching with the excitement of shared conspiracy.

"Earthlings?" it continued, voice dropping to a raspy whisper that sounded like sandpaper on chitinous plates. "I was told they were cosmic infants, still soiling their planetary diapers when we stumbled upon their pitiful rock. Those soft, squishy meat-sacks. Bipedal jokes with delusions of grandeur."

Grax leaned over the counter, his voice dropping to a conspiratorial whisper. "But let me tell you a secret, young spawn. What makes Earthling meat so special isn't the danger they pose. It's the emotions."

The crowd leaned in, captivated.

"You see," Grax continued, his eyes gleaming, "Earthlings feel things so intensely. Joy, fear, love, anger—all of it, cranked up to eleven. And somehow, someway, all those feelings get stored in their flesh. When you take a bite, it's like tasting a lifetime of experiences."

A collective "ooh" rippled through the onlookers.

The butcher looked up from his bloody work. His compound eyes glinted in the harsh light, reflecting Zilara's apprehension back at her.

"What can I get for you today, madam?" he rumbled, wiping his hands on a stained apron. "Perhaps some fresh Venusian slug? Or maybe a nice cut of Martian sand worm?"

Zilara's mandibles clicked softly as she gathered her courage. "Actually," she began, her voice barely above a whisper, "I was wondering about . . . the Earthling meat."

The butcher's eyes narrowed, all twelve of them focusing on Zilara with sudden intensity. "Ah," he said, his voice dropping to a conspiratorial growl. "The human flesh."

Zilara nodded, her exoskeleton prickling with a mixture of curiosity and revulsion. "Yes. I've heard . . . stories. But I've never actually seen it before. What can you tell me about them?"

Grax let out a wheezing laugh that sounded like rocks in a blender. "Oh, my dear, that's a tale as old as the stars themselves." He leaned in close, his breath hot and fetid. "You see, humans were once as plentiful as Rigellian sand fleas. They spread across the galaxy like a virus, consuming everything in their path."

Zilara's spawn chittered excitedly behind her, their young minds unable to grasp the gravity of the conversation. Grax continued, his voice taking on a wistful tone.

"But then, as it always does, nature found a way to balance the scales. Environmental collapse, wars, plagues—the humans brought it all upon themselves. And when their numbers dwindled, well . . ." He gestured to the small, vacuum-sealed packages behind the counter. "Some saw an opportunity."

Zilara felt a chill run through her carapace. "I heard at the deli counter that some are left? Protected, living, I mean."

Grax shrugged his massive shoulders. "Oh, there are. A few scattered colonies, mostly. But they're protected now—

endangered species and all that. What we sell here, it's all ethically sourced from those on farms before the protections occurred. No need to waste good protein, eh? It's delightfully tender, with a hint of despair. You won't find anything quite like it in the whole galaxy."

"Mommy, can we buy some? Please?" Nara tugged at a leg, her eyes wide with excitement. "Everyone at school says it's the best thing ever!"

Zilara looked down at her spawn, then back at the racks of bloody meat. She tried to imagine the life that had once animated this flesh. Had it dreamed? Had it loved? Had it looked up at the stars and wondered, as she did now, about the nature of existence?

Grax watched her internal struggle with barely concealed glee. "You know," he said, his voice oily with false sympathy, "they say that consuming human flesh imparts some of their knowledge. Their memories, their experiences—all of it becomes a part of you."

Zilara's antennae perked up at this. "Is that true?"

Grax shrugged again. "Who can say? But wouldn't you like to find out?"

Zilara looked at the racks once more. The slabs of meat seemed to pulse, calling to her with promises of forbidden knowledge and exotic sensations. Her spawn crowded around her, their excitement palpable.

"Well?" Grax prompted. "What'll it be?"

Zilara closed her eyes, steeling herself for the decision that would change everything. When she opened them again, there was a new resolve in her gaze.

"I'll take a kilo," she said, her voice steady. "A kilo of . . ."

Grax's face split into a wide, toothy grin. "Yes, my dear," he chuckled, reaching for his cleaver. "A kilo of what?"

As the butcher stared at her, Zilara felt a strange mix of emotions wash over her. Guilt, curiosity, excitement—they swirled together like the colors of a distant nebula. She knew that with each bite, she would be consuming not just flesh, but something else—history. The triumphs and failures of an entire species, distilled into a meal.

And as her spawn danced around her, hoping to have a full dinner of humanity, Zilara couldn't help but wonder: When the last human was gone, who would remember their stories? Who would carry the weight of their existence?

Perhaps, she thought, that burden now fell to her. One bite at a time.

Zilara found herself reaching for the words. "No Earthling meat today, thank you. Instead, I'll have some Helaxian Prime Rib, please. And . . . perhaps a small Organ Sampler for the little ones?"

"Helaxian tongue is marked down," Grax noted.

"That's fine," Zilara replied.

As Grax began preparing her order, Zilara couldn't help but notice a strange feeling creeping over her. Excitement, yes, but also something else. Watching Grax wrap up her purchase, a stray thought wormed its way into her mind. If Earthlings felt so intensely, if their emotions were powerful enough to flavor their very flesh, then what exactly were others about to consume?

The thought was interrupted by T'vik tugging at her tentacles. "Mother, mother! Why can't we get some of that new meat? It tasted so good!"

Zilara's outer membrane rippled with discomfort. "Hush, T'vik. We're here for sustenance, not novelties."

But Nara, ever the instigator, chimed in with a gurgle of excitement. "Oh, please, Mother! Please! We promise to finish our chlorophyll supplements!"

Grax slid the package of Helaxian meat over the counter to her.

"Thank you," she said.

Grax nodded and formed a smile on his large face. "See you next week."

Zilara's eyestalks swiveled towards yet another display case where chunks of pale, pinkish flesh lay neatly arranged. The sign above proclaimed in garish neon: "NEW! Genuine Earth Human—Limited Time Only!"

A memory, unbidden and unwelcome, surged through Zilara's neural pathways. She saw her cousin Xylop, proud and resplendent in his iridescent carapace, fleeing across the crimson sands of Rigel VII. The thunderous roar of the trophy hunters' plasma rifles echoed in her mind, followed by the sickening thud of Xylop's body hitting the ground.

"Mother?" Nara's concerned warble snapped Zilara back to the present. "Are you malfunctioning?"

Zilara's voice came out as a low, guttural growl. "No, my spawn. I'm simply . . . remembering."

She oozed closer to the display case, her curiosity warring with a growing sense of unease. An AI voice from a nearby speaker chirped cheerfully, "Greetings, valued customer! Would you like to sample our newest delicacy? Sourced ethically from the finest human stock!"

Zilara's tentacles coiled tightly around her midsection. "Ethically sourced? How can the near-extinction of a species be ethical?"

The voice remained infuriatingly chipper. "I assure you, valued customer, all our products meet the highest standards of galactic commerce laws!"

T'vik and Nara pressed their amorphous bodies against the transparent barrier, their excitement palpable. "Oh, Mother, please! Everyone is buying it!"

Zilara felt her resolve wavering. It was just meat, after all. And she had heard stories that humans were non-sentient by the Galactic Council centuries ago. But why then were they protected?

She turned to her offspring, her voice soft but firm. "T'vik, Nara, listen closely. We don't need to buy something just because it's rare. Sometimes, rarity is a sign we should let it be."

"But Mother—" T'vik began to protest.

Zilara cut him off with a sharp tendril-wave. "No buts. We are leaving."

As they slithered towards the exit, Nara's voice quivered with disappointment. "It's not fair! Why do you always have to be so . . . so principled?"

Zilara halted, her massive form blocking the aisle. When she spoke, her voice was heavy with the weight of centuries. "Because, my dear spawn, principles are all that separate us from the beasts we consume."

She gestured towards the meat display with a languid tentacle. "Those humans, they were once the apex predators of their world. They hunted and consumed without thought or care, believing their dominion would last forever."

T'vik's eyestalks drooped. "But they're just animals, right?"

"Everything," Zilara interrupted, her voice dripping with disdain, "is an animal. You remember that!"

Both young ones shuddered at the thought. Zilara continued, her voice softening. "Long ago, before you were spawned, I witnessed the last great hunt of our people. My cousin Xylop, he was . . ." She paused, struggling to find the words. "He was beautiful. Proud. And they hunted him like an animal."

Nara's gelatinous form quivered with emotion. "Who, Mother? Who hunted cousin Xylop?"

Zilara's eyestalks swiveled towards the meat display once more. "Beings not so different from those humans. They, too, thought themselves apex predators, immune to the cycle of life and death."

She began moving again, her offspring following in contemplative silence. As they exited the store, the harsh sunlight of three suns assaulted their photosensitive membranes.

T'vik spoke up, his voice small but determined. "I think I understand, Mother. We shouldn't eat the humans because . . . because we could've been them?"

Zilara's form rippled with pride. "Precisely, my clever spawn. The universe is vast and unpredictable. Today's predator may be tomorrow's prey. We must never forget that."

Nara extended a pseudopod, the translucent limb quivering with hesitation, before gently brushing her mother's flank. The contact was soft, almost reverent. "I'm sorry for being difficult, Mother. You're always right." Her voice, so small against the vastness of the moment, carried a thread of unease, as if an apology could stitch up the rift left by her earlier defiance.

Zilara's mass shifted, her gelatinous form flowing outward to envelop her children in an embrace that pulsed faintly with warmth. The act was both protective and forgiving, her membranes shimmering faintly under the artificial lights of the market. "It's alright, my darlings," she murmured, her voice a liquid current that wrapped around them. "Questioning is how we grow, how we learn to be more than we are."

T'vik squirmed within the cocoon of his mother's embrace, his movements erratic and brimming with restless energy. "Oh, Mother, I have another question!" His voice burst out, sharp and eager, the curiosity of youth cutting through the subdued tension that still clung to them.

Zilara loosened her embrace, allowing her smaller spawn to wriggle free. "What is it, my dear little spawn?" she asked, tilting her core mass slightly, her tone indulgent but tinged with fatigue.

T'vik's pseudopods trembled with excitement, his eyes—liquid black orbs—glistening with anticipation. "What about the Helaxians? Could we have been them?"

Zilara paused, the hum of the market fading into a dull, distant thrum. Her form stilled, the faint glow of her body dimming as she considered his question. "Yes," she said at last, her voice heavier than before. "We could have been them. Stripped of our will, shaped into what others wanted us to be. It is a fine line, my spawn, between what we are and what we could become."

Then, with a deliberate shift, Zilara brightened, her tone softening as she steered them away from the oppressive thoughts threatening to settle. "Now, let's go home," she said, her voice infused with a forced cheerfulness. "I'll prepare some delicious algae cakes, shall we?"

Her children's excitement bubbled up instantly, their earlier concerns dissolving into the shared anticipation of a familiar comfort. But as Zilara guided them out of the market, her thoughts lingered on the question—on how easily they could have been the Helaxians, and on the delicate balance that had kept them from that fate. For now.

As they slithered away from MegaMart, Zilara couldn't help but cast one last glance at the store. The neon sign flickered, proclaiming its ghoulish wares to an indifferent cosmos. She shuddered, grateful for the weight of her children against her flanks, a reminder of life's precious continuity in a universe too often marked by its callous disregard.

In the distance, a new sun dragged itself over the horizon, its pale, sickly light spilling across the jagged terrain like a reluctant confession. Zilara stood there, her eyestalks twitching, wondering—not for the first time—what fresh horrors or half-baked wonders this indifferent universe might vomit into their lives. She was tired of wondering. Tired of the questions that circled her mind. But for now, she had her spawn, and they were learning, growing, becoming something more than just consumers in this vast, uncaring meat market of existence.

She loaded the last of her groceries into the back of their Chitinous Crawler, a grotesque machine that scuttled across the terrain like an oversized insect with too many legs and not enough grace. Her tentacle paused mid-motion as her gaze fell on the package of Helaxian tongue, neatly wrapped in sterile plastic.

Sentience, she thought bitterly, was just another line item on a ledger in this galaxy—a commodity to be bought and sold like spices or fuel. And yet, she couldn't bring herself to look away from that package, as if staring at it long enough might reveal some hidden truth about the universe's cold calculus.

The Silver Bow of Anorath

In the twilight of the Third Age of Anorath, when the great forests had grown silent and the songs of the Eldar were but whispers on the wind, there stood Elarion at the edge of the ancient wood. His silver hair, once as bright as starlight, now bore the sheen of faded mithril, and his eyes, which had beheld the glory of a thousand summers, were weary with the weight of uncounted years.

Before him stretched the realm of Anorath, a land that in ages past had been the jewel of the Elven kingdoms. Now its splendour was dimmed, its magic ebbing like the tide at the turning of the world. The towering mallorn trees, once proud and golden, stood grey and withered, their leaves falling in a ceaseless autumn. The enchanted creatures that had once danced in dappled glades now kept to the deepest shadows, their voices stilled by the encroaching darkness.

Elarion's heart was heavy, for he knew that this journey might well be his last. The Elves of Anorath were fading, their immortality a burden in a world grown old and weary. Yet hope, that most resilient of flowers, still bloomed in the depths of his being, for he sought the Silver Bow of Anorath, an artifact of legend said to possess the power to heal any wound, be it of flesh or spirit.

As he stepped beneath the eaves of the forest, Elarion spoke softly to himself, his voice carrying the melody of ages long past:

"In shadow and in light, through time's long night,

I seek the Bow of Silver, lost to sight.

May Elbereth guide my steps aright,

And grant me strength to set all things to right."

The trees seemed to whisper in response, their ancient boughs creaking with memories of brighter days. Elarion's mind turned to the tales of old, passed down through generations of Elven lore-masters. The Silver Bow, it was said, had been crafted in the First Age by Celeborn the Wise, imbued with the light of the Two Trees and blessed by Oromë the Huntsman. In the great wars against the shadow, it had been a beacon of hope, its arrows finding their mark with unerring precision, its very presence bringing courage to the hearts of the Eldar.

Yet as the tides of war turned and the shadow grew ever stronger, the Elven lords had made a fateful decision. The bow was too powerful, too tempting a prize for the forces of darkness. And so, with heavy hearts, they had hidden it away, entrusting its secret location to a select few, sworn to silence until the time of greatest need should arise.

Some whispered that the bow's power extended far beyond mere healing. The most ancient of scrolls spoke of it as a weapon of balance, capable of restoring the very fabric of the world when light and dark had fallen out of harmony. Such power, Elarion mused, could be as perilous as it was precious.

As he delved deeper into the forest, the air grew thick with memory and mist. The path, once clear and well-trodden, had long since been reclaimed by root and vine. Elarion's steps were sure, guided by an inner light that had not yet dimmed, despite the long years of his life.

It was then that a familiar voice called out from the mists, soft yet clear as a bell ringing in the depths of time:

"Elarion, mellon nîn. Long has it been since you walked these paths."

From the shadows emerged Ysolde, once counted among the fairest of the Eldar. Now her beauty was that of autumn, her golden hair streaked with silver, her face lined with the cares of many mortal lifetimes. She had chosen to bind herself to the land, to fade with it rather than sail into the West, and the years had worked their change upon her.

"Ysolde," Elarion breathed, his voice filled with wonder and sorrow. "I had not thought to find you here still."

She smiled, a gesture both warm and tinged with sadness. "Where else would I be but in the heart of what remains of our realm? But come, tell me what brings you to these fading woods, old friend."

Elarion's eyes met hers, and in that moment, understanding passed between them. "You know why I have come, Ysolde. The Silver Bow—it is our last hope."

Ysolde's face grew grave. "Ai, the Bow of Celeborn. A perilous quest you undertake, Elarion. You are not the only one who seeks it in these dark days."

"What do you mean?" Elarion asked, his brow furrowing with concern.

Ysolde glanced about, as if the very trees might be listening. "There are whispers in the wind, echoes of an ancient malice stirring once more. The shadow that we thought vanquished seeks the bow as well, though for what purpose, I dare not guess."

She reached into the folds of her cloak and withdrew a map, its parchment yellowed with age, its edges crumbling. "This may aid you in your quest, though I warn you, the path it shows is fraught with peril."

As Elarion took the map, his fingers brushed against Ysolde's, and he felt a tremor pass through her. Their eyes met once more, and he saw in hers a flicker of something he could not name—fear, perhaps, or a knowledge too terrible to speak aloud.

"Ysolde," he said softly, "what is it that you are not telling me?"

She hesitated, her gaze dropping to the forest floor. When she spoke again, her voice was barely above a whisper. "The lore of the bow . . . it may not be as we have always believed. There are older tales, darker prophecies that speak of its true nature. I fear that in seeking to save our people, you may unleash something far worse."

Elarion's heart grew cold at her words, yet his resolve did not waver. "Whatever the truth may be, I must find it. Our people fade, Ysolde. The magic of Anorath wanes. If there is even a chance that the bow can restore what we have lost, I must take it."

Ysolde nodded, her eyes shimmering with unshed tears. "Then go with the blessings of the Mighty One. May your path be guided by starlight, and may you find what you seek before it is too late."

With a final embrace, Ysolde melted back into the mists of the forest, leaving Elarion alone with the map and the weight of his quest. He studied the parchment, tracing the faded lines that led deep into the heart of Anorath, to places long forgotten by even the eldest of his kind.

As he set forth once more, Elarion's mind was filled with questions. What was the true nature of the Silver Bow? What dark force now sought it? And what price would he—and all of Anorath—pay for its power?

The forest seemed to close in around him, its ancient trees standing sentinel to his passage. In the distance, a lone bird called out, its song a lament for glory long past. Elarion squared his shoulders and pressed on, for the fate of his people hung in the balance, and time, that most relentless of foes, marched ever onward.

As he journeyed deeper into the heart of the forest, Elarion found himself beset by memories of brighter days. He remembered the great halls of Anorath in their splendor, when the very air had shimmered with magic and the laughter of the Eldar had rung out like silver bells. Now those halls stood empty, their echoes fading into silence.

The map led him through paths overgrown and forgotten, past ancient stone circles where the Elves had once danced beneath the stars, and through groves where the first songs of creation had been sung. Each step was a journey not just through space, but through the long history of his people.

As night fell, Elarion made camp beneath the boughs of a great oak, its leaves whispering secrets in the gentle breeze. He kindled a small fire, its light a mere flicker against the encroaching darkness. As he sat in quiet contemplation, a voice spoke from the shadows, startling him from his reverie.

"Well met, Elarion of Anorath. It has been long indeed since one of the Eldar passed this way."

From the darkness stepped a figure cloaked in grey, his face hidden beneath a deep hood. Elarion's hand went to his sword, but the stranger raised his hands in a gesture of peace.

"Be at ease, friend. I am Faelindor, a wanderer in these lands. I mean you no harm."

Elarion relaxed, but only slightly. "Few wander these woods in these dark days, Faelindor. What brings you to this forgotten corner of the world?"

The stranger sat across the fire from Elarion, his face still obscured. "I could ask the same of you, Elarion. But I suspect we seek the same prize—the Silver Bow of Celeborn."

Elarion's eyes narrowed. "And what would you know of such things?"

Faelindor chuckled softly. "More than you might guess. I have walked this earth for many ages, and I have seen the rise and fall of kingdoms. The bow is more than a mere artifact of healing, Elarion. It is a key to unlocking the very foundations of the world."

"Speak plainly," Elarion demanded, his patience wearing thin. "What do you know of the bow?"

Faelindor leaned forward, the firelight catching the glint of his eyes beneath his hood. "The bow was indeed crafted to heal, but not in the way you might think. It was made to heal the very fabric of creation, to mend the rifts between light and shadow. But such power comes at a great cost. To use it is to risk unmaking all that is."

Elarion's mind reeled at the implications. "But surely, if wielded with wisdom—"

"Wisdom?" Faelindor interrupted. "Even the wisest cannot foresee all ends. The bow responds to the heart of its wielder, and in these fading days, who among us can claim a heart untouched by despair or desire?"

A heavy silence fell between them, broken only by the crackling of the fire and the distant hooting of an owl. Elarion's thoughts turned to Ysolde's warning, to the darkness that sought the bow. Could it be that in his quest to save his people, he might bring about their final doom?

As if reading his thoughts, Faelindor spoke again, his voice gentle. "You need not bear this burden alone, Elarion. There are still those who remember the old alliances, who would stand with the Eldar in their hour of need."

Elarion looked up sharply. "What do you mean?"

Faelindor stood, his cloak swirling about him like mist. "Continue your journey, Elarion of Anorath. Seek the bow if you must, but be wary. The path you walk is treacherous, and not all is as it seems. When the time comes, remember that even in the darkest night, stars may still shine."

With those cryptic words, Faelindor stepped back into the shadows and was gone, leaving Elarion alone once more with his thoughts and the dying embers of the fire.

As dawn broke, Elarion resumed his journey, his heart heavy with new doubts and unanswered questions. The forest seemed to press in around him, its ancient trees watching his passage with inscrutable eyes. He could not shake the feeling that every step brought him closer not just to the bow, but to a destiny that would shape the fate of all Anorath.

And so Elarion pressed on, guided by starlight and the fading hope of his people, into the heart of a mystery as old as the world itself.

***

As Elarion delved deeper into the heart of Anorath's ancient forest, the world around him seemed to shift and change, as if the very fabric of reality was unraveling at the seams. The map he clutched in his hand, a gift from the enigmatic Ysolde, led him through groves long forgotten by even the eldest of his kind.

The trees here grew close together, their branches intertwining in a canopy so thick that little light penetrated to the forest floor. Shadows danced at the edge of Elarion's vision, and more than once he found himself reaching for his sword, only to find that what he had perceived as a threat was naught but a trick of the fading light.

As he walked, Elarion's keen elven senses detected a change in the very air around him. A strange, lingering darkness seemed to cling to everything, like a fine mist that refused to dissipate in the weak sunlight. It was not the natural darkness of a forest at twilight, but something older, more malevolent.

"What foul magic is this?" Elarion murmured to himself, his voice barely above a whisper. Yet even that seemed too loud in the oppressive silence of the wood.

He pressed on, following the winding path indicated on the map. As he journeyed, he began to encounter remnants of the old world—places he had once known well but that now felt as foreign to him as the lands beyond the sea.

In a clearing that had once housed a grand elven city, Elarion found only ruins. The white stone of the buildings, once gleaming and proud, was now cracked and overgrown with vines. At the center of the clearing stood a fountain, its waters long since stilled. As Elarion approached, he felt a sudden surge of magic, ancient and powerful.

With a grinding of stone, the statues adorning the fountain came to life, their eyes glowing with an eerie blue light. They turned as one to face Elarion, their voices a chorus of grinding stone:

"Who dares to tread the paths of the Eldar? Speak, intruder, or face the wrath of the guardians of Anorath!"

Elarion stood tall, his silver hair gleaming in the dim light. "I am Elarion, son of Elenath, of the house of the Silver Star. I walk these paths by ancient right, seeking that which was lost."

The statues seemed to consider his words, their stone faces impassive. After what felt like an age, they spoke again:

"Long has it been since one of the Eldar walked here. The world has changed, Elarion son of Elenath. The old ways are fading, and new dangers lurk in the shadows. Those who embrace the dark wander this realm. If you seek what was lost, beware— for not all that is hidden wishes to be found."

With those ominous words, the light faded from the statues' eyes, and they returned to their silent vigil. As Elarion pressed forward, the air seemed to grow colder, and a somber stillness settled over the ancient passage. The warning of the stone sentinels echoed in his mind, a portent of the darkness that now stirred beyond the reach of mortal sight. He knew the tales of the dark elves—once kin to the light-bound Eldar, they had turned away from the harmony of old, lured by promises of unfettered power.

In the hidden depths of the world, beneath the shadowed roots of mountains and the blackened boughs of sunless forests, these forsaken ones had built their domain. It was said they no longer sang the songs of creation but rather wove enchantments of discord and despair. Their cities, carved from obsidian and bone, pulsed with a sinister energy, and their sorcery bent the will of the weak to their dark designs.

Elarion shuddered as he imagined their pale, glimmering eyes and their cruel, lithe forms cloaked in shadow. These were no mere adversaries; they were a force that thrived on the suffering of the living, delighting in the unraveling of order. As he descended deeper into the heart of the mountain, the sense of their presence became palpable, as though the stone itself recoiled from their foul influence.

Journeying deeper into the forest, Elarion encountered more signs of the changing world. In a glade that had once been home to a circle of wise elven seers, he found twisted creatures— beings that might once have been elves or animals but were now warped by dark magic into grotesque parodies of their former selves.

They skittered at the edges of his vision, their eyes gleaming with a feral hunger. Elarion's hand never strayed far from his sword hilt as he made his way through their territory, every sense alert for danger.

At last, after what felt like days of travel through the ever-changing landscape of the forest, Elarion emerged from the trees to find himself at the foot of a great mountain. Its peak was shrouded in mist, and at its base yawned the entrance to a vast cave.

Elarion's heart quickened. This, he knew, must be the final resting place of the Silver Bow. He took a step towards the cave entrance, but before he could go further, the ground beneath his feet began to tremble.

From the depths of the cave came a sound like rolling thunder, growing louder with each passing moment. Elarion stood his ground, though every instinct screamed at him to flee.

With a roar that shook the very foundations of the mountain, a massive dragon emerged from the cave. Its scales shimmered with a dark, oily iridescence, and its eyes burned with an ancient intelligence. This, Elarion realized with a mixture of awe and terror, must be Ilmorath, the legendary guardian of the bow.

The dragon's gaze fixed upon Elarion, and when it spoke, its voice was like the grinding of great stones:

"Who are you, little elf, to seek entrance to my domain? Many have come before you, seeking the treasure I guard, and none have left alive."

Elarion swallowed hard, but his voice was steady when he replied: "I am Elarion of Anorath, and I seek the Silver Bow not for myself, but for the salvation of my people."

Ilmorath's eyes narrowed, and smoke curled from its nostrils. "Ah, the Silver Bow. Long has it been since one came seeking that particular treasure. Tell me, Elarion of Anorath, do you know the true nature of what you seek?"

Elarion hesitated. "I know it is said to have the power to heal any wound, to restore that which has been lost."

The dragon let out a rumbling laugh that sent tremors through the ground. "Is that what they say now? How quickly the truth fades into legend. Come closer, little elf, and I will tell you a tale—the true tale of the Silver Bow."

Warily, Elarion approached. The dragon settled itself at the mouth of the cave, its massive body coiled like a great serpent.

"In the days when the world was young," Ilmorath began, "I was charged by the Eldar to guard their greatest treasure. The Silver Bow was indeed a weapon of immense power, but not merely for its ability to heal. It was forged at the dawn of time, imbued with the very essence of creation. In the right hands, it could reshape the world itself."

Elarion's eyes widened at this revelation. "But if it held such power, why was it hidden away?"

Ilmorath's eyes grew distant, as if looking back through the long ages of the world. "Because, young one, even the wisest of the Eldar came to fear its power. In the great wars against the shadow, the bow was used to turn back the tide of darkness. But with each use, it exacted a terrible price. For every wound it healed, another was torn open elsewhere in the fabric of the world."

The dragon's gaze returned to Elarion, sharp and penetrating. "It was not lost in battle, as your legends claim. The Eldar themselves chose to conceal it, for they realized that no one being should wield such power. They entrusted it to my keeping, swearing me to secrecy and eternal vigilance."

Elarion's mind reeled at this revelation. Everything he had believed about the bow, about his quest, had been turned on its head. "But our people are fading," he protested. "The magic of

Anorath wanes. Surely, if used wisely, the bow could restore what we have lost?"

Ilmorath's voice was surprisingly gentle when he replied: "And who among you can claim the wisdom to wield such power without succumbing to its temptations? Even with the noblest of intentions, the bow's power could bring about devastation beyond imagining."

The dragon uncoiled itself, rising to its full, terrifying height. "I offer you a choice, Elarion of Anorath. You may take the bow, if you believe you can bear the weight of its power and the responsibility it brings. Or you may leave it here, buried and forgotten, and allow the natural order of the world to take its course."

Elarion stood silent for a long moment, the weight of the decision pressing down upon him like a physical force. The fate of his people, perhaps of all Anorath, rested upon his choice.

At last, he spoke, his voice barely above a whisper: "I came seeking hope for my people, a way to restore what was lost. But perhaps... perhaps what is lost is not meant to be reclaimed. The age of the Eldar is passing, and maybe that is as it should be."

He looked up at Ilmorath, his eyes shining with unshed tears. "I choose to leave the bow in your keeping, great Ilmorath. Some powers are too great for any one being to wield, and some changes cannot—should not—be undone."

The dragon inclined its great head, a gesture of respect. "You show wisdom beyond your years, Elarion of Anorath. Few have had the strength to turn away from such power when it was within their grasp."

Ilmorath's eyes softened, and for a moment, Elarion caught a glimpse of the noble guardian the dragon had once been, before long years of solitude had twisted it. "Go now, and tell your people what you have learned. The age of magic may be fading, but that does not mean the end of all things. New ages will dawn, and new wonders will arise. The Eldar have played their part in the great song of creation—now it is time for others to take up the melody."

With a heavy heart but a clear conscience, Elarion turned away from the cave and the temptation it held. As he made his way back through the forest, he felt a change in the very air around him. The oppressive darkness seemed to lift, if only slightly, and he could have sworn he heard the faint echoes of an ancient elven song on the breeze.

The quest for the Silver Bow had not ended as he had imagined, but Elarion knew in his heart that he had made the right choice. The future of Anorath—and indeed, of all the world— would be shaped not by the relics of the past, but by the courage and wisdom of those who dared to face the unknown future.

***

As Elarion ventured deeper into the mountain's heart, the very air seemed to pulse with a magic as old as the stone itself, thick with secrets and long-forgotten truths. The narrow passage wound its way through the living rock, the walls carved by hands long vanished, their work now hidden in shadow. The faint light of his torch flickered against the blackness, casting strange shapes upon the jagged surfaces, and more than once, Elarion thought he heard whispers rise from the unseen depths—soft voices, perhaps of the earth itself, warning him, beckoning him forward. The truth, however, was impossible to tell.

The path descended ever downward, spiraling into the very roots of the mountain. Elarion's keen elven senses were overwhelmed by the ancient power that permeated the air, a magic older than the eldest trees of Anorath. Each step seemed to take him further from the world he knew, into a realm where time and space held little meaning.

As he journeyed, Elarion's mind turned to the legends of old, tales passed down through countless generations of his people. They spoke of the creation of the world, of the great song that had brought all things into being. In those first days, it was said, light and darkness had danced in perfect harmony, each giving meaning and purpose to the other. But as the ages passed, that balance had been lost, and now the world teetered on the brink of chaos.

Finally, after what seemed an eternity of descent, the passage opened into a cavern of ancient wonder. The sight before him was breathtaking—crystals, embedded deep within the mountain's bones, shimmered with an ethereal glow, bathing the cavern in a pale, otherworldly light. Time seemed to bend within this sacred space, where ages and moments were neither separate nor distinct, and all things existed as one.

Elarion stood in awe, his eyes wide as he beheld the majesty of this hidden sanctuary. The cavern stretched far beyond the reach of his torch, its ceiling lost in shadows that seemed to shift and move of their own accord. The air here was different, charged with a power that made his skin tingle and his heart race.

At the heart of the chamber, resting upon a pedestal of marble as white as snow, lay the Silver Bow of Anorath. The sight of it stole Elarion's breath—its form was like a vision from another age, a delicate silver arc that shimmered as though it lived and breathed, beyond the reach of time or any mortal understanding.

Elarion's steps were slow and deliberate as he approached, as if to touch the bow was to disturb the fabric of dreams themselves. It was a relic of power, yes, but also of great purpose, beyond the imagining of any single mind. His hand trembled as it hovered over the bow, and the moment his fingers brushed its cool surface, a wave of ancient energy surged through him, unlike anything he had ever known. The bow hummed softly, as if alive, its power resonating in the deepest recesses of his soul.

"By the stars," he murmured, awe mingling with fear. "What is this force that I have found?"

Visions rushed before his eyes—images of a world in balance, where light and dark were not enemies but the very foundation of existence, each nourishing the other in an endless cycle. The bow was no mere weapon. It was a conduit, a bridge between forces older than any kingdom, any race, any mind. Its true purpose, he understood now, was not to destroy, but to preserve that delicate balance.

In that moment, Elarion saw the truth of all things. He saw the great tapestry of creation, woven from threads of light and shadow, each strand vital to the whole. He saw the folly of those who sought to tip the scales, to banish either light or darkness entirely. And he saw the terrible responsibility that now rested upon his shoulders.

"It is more than we ever imagined," Elarion whispered, his heart torn between awe and caution. "With this, one could—"

"One could destroy all," came the harsh, cold voice that cut through the stillness like a blade.

Elarion turned sharply, his grip tightening on the bow as he faced the figure that had emerged from the shadows. There, standing at the edge of the cavern, was Thalgar, once a comrade of noble heart and great strength, now twisted by a dark rage that consumed him.

"Thalgar," Elarion said, sorrow deep in his voice. "I had hoped never to face you again."

The dark elf's lips curled into a cruel smile, one that was foreign to the friend Elarion had once known. "You would claim this power, Elarion? You think it a tool to destroy the darkness?" Thalgar's eyes burned with a feverish light as he stepped forward, his every movement charged with the promise of violence. "You seek to use the bow to restore some false harmony. But the darkness you think so easily dismissed is alive, waiting for such a gift."

As Thalgar spoke, the shadows in the cavern seemed to deepen, gathering around him like a cloak. Elarion felt a chill run down his spine, for he recognized in his old friend the touch of a power far darker and more ancient than any he had encountered before.

"What has become of you, Thalgar?" Elarion asked, his voice heavy with sorrow. "What darkness has claimed you?"

Thalgar's laugh was bitter, echoing off the cavern walls. "Claimed me? No, Elarion. I have embraced it willingly. I have seen the truth that you, in your blindness, refuse to acknowledge.

The light is a lie, a fleeting illusion. Only in darkness can true power be found."

As the two elves faced each other, the very air in the cavern seemed to thicken, charged with the weight of ages and the promise of a conflict that would shake the foundations of Anorath itself. The crystals that adorned the walls pulsed with an erratic, fevered light, as if they were the heartbeat of the mountain itself, sensing the momentous struggle that was about to unfold. Elarion's grip upon the Silver Bow tightened, and he felt its ancient power thrumming through his veins, a song of creation and destruction that urged him to action.

Yet even as he steeled himself for the battle to come, Elarion's heart was heavy with the sorrow of ages. For he knew, with a certainty that ran deeper than the roots of the world, that this confrontation was far more than a mere clash between two who had once called each other friend. Nay, it was a struggle for the very soul of Anorath, and mayhap for the fate of all that was, is, and ever would be.

Thalgar's eyes gleamed with a fell light, reflecting the madness that had taken root in his once-noble heart. "You cannot hope to stand against me, Elarion," he snarled, his voice a grating echo of the elf he had once been. "I have tasted power beyond your imagining, drunk deep from wells of darkness that would shatter your feeble mind."

Elarion stood tall, the Silver Bow held before him like a shield against the encroaching shadows. "It is not too late," he said softly, his words carrying the weight of countless years of friendship. "Cast aside this darkness that has claimed you.

Remember who you once were, the oath we swore to protect Anorath and all its peoples."

For the briefest of moments, a flicker of doubt passed across Thalgar's face, a ghost of the elf he had once been. But it was gone in an instant, consumed by the raging inferno of his hatred and ambition. With a roar that shook the very stones beneath their feet, Thalgar lunged forward, his blade a blur of malevolent energy.

The battle that followed was like none that had been seen in Anorath since the Elder Days, when the world was young and the great powers of light and darkness had waged war across the face of creation. It was a clash of not just steel and sinew, but of ideals, of the very forces that shaped the world.

Elarion moved with the grace of starlight, each step a dance that had been perfected over millennia. The Silver Bow sang in his hands, its power flowing through him, guiding his movements with a wisdom older than the mountains themselves. Every parry, every strike was imbued with the sorrow of a friendship lost and the desperate hope that it might yet be reclaimed.

Thalgar fought with the unbridled ferocity of a storm, his blade a conduit for the dark powers that had claimed his soul. Each blow was aimed not just at Elarion's flesh, but at his very spirit, seeking to crush the light that still burned within him. The shadows seemed to gather around Thalgar, lending strength to his arms and speed to his strikes.

As their struggle raged on, the very mountain groaned and shuddered, as if it were a titan of old, awakening from an age-long slumber. The ground beneath their feet trembled and cracked, fissures spreading like a web across the cavern floor. The echoes of their battle reverberated through the chamber and beyond, a thunder that shook the roots of the world.

The bow in Elarion's hands hummed with ever-increasing power, its song growing louder with each passing moment. It urged him to act, to unleash its full might against the darkness that threatened to consume all. Yet Elarion hesitated, for he knew that to do so would be to upset the very balance he sought to protect.

With every strike he parried, every blow he deflected, the weight of his duty pressed heavier upon Elarion's shoulders. He could not allow the darkness to triumph, not when the fate of Anorath and all the lands beyond hung in the balance. Yet neither could he bring himself to strike down Thalgar, to extinguish the last ember of the friend he had once known.

As the battle raged on, time itself seemed to lose all meaning. It might have been moments or ages that passed as the two elves clashed, their conflict a microcosm of the eternal struggle between light and shadow. The crystals that lined the walls of the cavern pulsed in time with their movements, casting ever-shifting patterns of light and darkness across the battlefield.

At last, in a moment that seemed to stretch into eternity, Elarion saw his opening. Thalgar, driven by his rage and the dark powers that fueled him, overextended himself in a furious assault. With a movement as swift and sure as the flight of an arrow, Elarion stepped inside Thalgar's guard, the Silver Bow raised high.

Time seemed to slow as the two elves stood there, frozen in a tableau of light and shadow. Elarion could see the madness burning in Thalgar's eyes, but beneath it, he caught a glimpse of something else—fear, perhaps, or a flicker of the elf he had once been.

With great swiftness, he struck Thalgar down, his blade slicing into his opponent's leg. Thalgar staggered back, his leg buckling beneath him as blood seeped through the dark fabric of his armor, pooling on the stone floor. His breath came in ragged gasps, and the fire in his eyes dimmed, though it was not extinguished. He clutched at his wounded leg, his face twisting in pain and fury.

***

In the depths of the mountain, amidst the echoes of their titanic struggle, Elarion stood over the fallen form of Thalgar, the Silver Bow of Anorath thrumming with power in his grasp. The chamber, once a silent tomb for ancient secrets, now bore the scars of their conflict—great fissures in the stone floor, walls scorched by errant bolts of energy, the very air thick with the residue of magic both light and dark.

Thalgar, his face a mask of pain and defeat, looked up at Elarion with eyes that held not hatred, but a terrible, dawning understanding. "You've won, old friend," he gasped, his voice barely above a whisper. "I beg of you. Destroy the bow."

But even as Thalgar spoke, Elarion felt the true weight of the bow's power settle upon him like a mantle of stars. It was not merely a weapon of healing or destruction, but a conduit for the very forces that shaped the world. In that moment of clarity, Elarion saw the tapestry of creation laid bare before him—the delicate interplay of light and shadow, growth and decay, joy and sorrow that formed the warp and weft of existence itself.

"Oh, Thalgar," Elarion said, his voice heavy with the wisdom of ages, "if only it were so simple. The bow's power is not meant for us to wield. It is the fulcrum upon which the balance of all things rests."

Thalgar's eyes widened, a flicker of his old self shining through the darkness that had claimed him. "You are a fool. Destroy it."

"I cannot," Elarion said gently. "I shall use the bow to heal our people, not to tip the scales, to give light dominion over darkness. That would sow the seeds of our own destruction."

As he spoke, Elarion felt the bow pulse in his hands, as if in affirmation of his words. He closed his eyes, allowing the bow's ancient wisdom to flow through him. Visions of possible futures flashed before his mind's eye—a world of eternal light, where the Eldar reigned supreme, but where the absence of shadow led to stagnation and eventual decay; a realm of unending darkness, where all life withered and faded, leaving only emptiness in its wake.

When Elarion opened his eyes, they shone with the light of true understanding. "The bow was never meant to be used, Thalgar. Its very existence maintains the balance. To wield it, even with the noblest of intentions, would be to bring disaster."

Thalgar struggled to sit up, his face a study in conflicting emotions. "Then what are you going to do?"

Elarion's gaze turned to the far end of the chamber, where a great chasm yawned, its depths lost in shadow. "I shall do what our ancestors could not. To remove the temptation entirely."

Understanding dawned on Thalgar's face, followed swiftly by horror. "You cannot mean to destroy it! Elarion, think of what you're saying!"

But Elarion's resolve was set, his purpose clear. With slow, measured steps, he approached the edge of the chasm. The bow seemed to grow heavier with each step, as if resisting its fate. Or perhaps, Elarion thought, it was merely the weight of all the hopes and dreams it represented.

"Wait!" Thalgar cried, struggling to his feet. "There must be another way. You could hide it again, seal it away where none could find it."

Elarion turned to face his old friend, his eyes filled with a mixture of sorrow and determination. "And how long before another would seek it out? How many more wars would be fought, how many lives lost in the pursuit of its power? No, Thalgar. The cycle must end here, with us."

As he spoke, Elarion felt a change come over him. It was subtle at first, a lightness in his limbs, a fading at the edges of his vision. With a start, he realized that his own life force had become entwined with the bow's power. To destroy it would be to seal his own fate as well.

For a moment, Elarion hesitated, the instinct for self-preservation warring with his sense of duty. But in the end, there was no real choice to be made. With a sad smile, he turned back to the chasm.

"Farewell, Thalgar," he said softly. "May you find the peace that eluded you for so long."

And with those words, Elarion cast the Silver Bow of Anorath into the depths. For a breathless moment, it hung suspended in the air, its silver limbs gleaming one last time in the dim light of the chamber. Then it fell, tumbling end over end into the darkness below.

A great tremor ran through the mountain as the bow disappeared from sight. Elarion felt it pass through him like a wave, and with it went the last vestiges of the power that had sustained him. He sank to his knees at the edge of the chasm, his form already beginning to fade.

Thalgar crawled with all his might, all thoughts of enmity forgotten in the face of Elarion's sacrifice. "What have you done?" he cried, reaching out to grasp Elarion's feet, only to find his hand passing through as if through mist.

Elarion looked down at Thalgar, his eyes shining with a light that was rapidly dimming. "What was necessary," he replied, his voice growing faint. "The balance . . . must be maintained. Our time . . . is passing, Thalgar. But others will rise to take our place. The world . . . will go on."

As Elarion's form grew more insubstantial with each passing moment, Thalgar felt the darkness that had clouded his mind for so long begin to lift. Tears streamed down his face as he watched his oldest friend, his greatest rival, fade before his eyes.

"I understand now," Thalgar whispered, his voice choked with emotion. "Oh, Elarion, I understand at last. Forgive me, old friend. Forgive me for my blindness."

Elarion smiled, a gesture of such peace and acceptance that it broke Thalgar's heart anew. "There is nothing to forgive," he said, his voice now barely a whisper on the wind. "We each played our part in the great song of creation. Now . . . it is time for others to take up the melody."

With those words, Elarion, last of the great Elven heroes, faded from sight. His essence dispersed like mist in the morning sun, merging with the very air around them. Thalgar was left alone in the chamber, the echo of Elarion's final words ringing in his ears.

For a long while, Thalgar remained there, at the edge of the chasm where Elarion had made his final stand. Grief and understanding warred within him until at last he rose, his face set with new purpose.

"I will not let your sacrifice be in vain, my friend," he vowed to the empty air. "I will carry your message to our people, to all the peoples of Anorath. The age of the Eldar may be ending, but perhaps in its passing, a new age of balance and harmony can begin."

With one last look at the place where Elarion had vanished, Thalgar brought himself to and stumbled his way out of the mountain. The journey that lay before him would be long and fraught with challenges, but he faced it with a heart lightened by newfound wisdom and purpose.

As Thalgar emerged from the mountain, he found the world had changed. The perpetual twilight that had shrouded Anorath for so long had lifted, replaced by a soft, diffuse light that seemed to come from everywhere and nowhere at once. It was neither the harsh brightness of day nor the deep shadow of night, but a perfect balance between the two.

In that moment, Thalgar understood the true magnitude of Elarion's sacrifice. By destroying the Silver Bow, he had not only preserved the balance of the world but had also freed the land from the stagnation that had gripped it for so long. The fading of the Eldar was not an end, but a transition—a necessary step in the ever-turning wheel of existence.

As he made his way back to the lands of his people, Thalgar began to craft the tale of Elarion's final quest. It was a story of courage and sacrifice, of wisdom gained and balance restored. In the telling and retelling, Elarion's name became legend, a beacon of hope and understanding for generations to come.

The Eldar, upon hearing of Elarion's fate, did not despair as Thalgar had feared. Instead, they found in his sacrifice a new purpose. They began to prepare for their own fading, not with sorrow, but with the quiet dignity of those who understand their place in the greater tapestry of creation.

In the years that followed, the Eldar shared their knowledge and wisdom with the younger races of Anorath. They taught them of the delicate balance that underpinned all of existence, of the importance of harmony between light and shadow. And as the Eldar gradually faded from the world, their legacy lived on in the hearts and minds of those they left behind.

Thalgar, once the greatest threat to the balance of Anorath, became its most ardent protector. He wandered the lands, sharing the tale of Elarion and the Silver Bow, teaching all who would listen about the importance of maintaining equilibrium in all things.

And so it was that the age of the Eldar came to an end, not with a cataclysm or a grand finale, but with a gentle fading, like the last notes of a beautiful song drifting on the evening breeze. The world moved on, new races rose to prominence, and new stories were written in the annals of history.

But always, in the quiet moments between dusk and dawn, when the world hung in perfect balance between light and shadow, the people of Anorath would remember Elarion. They would speak his name in hushed tones, a prayer and a reminder of the sacrifices made to preserve the harmony of all things.

And in those moments, some swore they could hear, carried on the wind, the faint echo of an ancient Elven melody— the song of creation itself, forever in balance, forever renewed.

Whispers in the Dark

The cart wheels creaked and groaned, a mournful dirge accompanying Thomas as he made his way through the narrow, fog-shrouded streets of Eyam. The air hung heavy with the stench of death, a miasma that clung to his skin like a second, unwelcome shadow. He pulled his mask tighter, the herbs stuffed within offering little comfort against the omnipresent reek of decay.

Thomas's eyes, weary and red-rimmed, scanned the doorways as he passed. Red crosses marked the infected houses, a grim tally of the plague's relentless march. He'd lost count of how many he'd painted himself, each stroke of the brush a death sentence for those within.

The cart lurched to a stop before a modest cottage. Thomas sighed, his breath hot and damp behind his mask. Another day, another collection. He steeled himself, then rapped his knuckles against the weathered wood.

"Bring out your dead," he called, his voice a hoarse whisper. The words, once strange and terrible, now fell from his lips with the ease of long practice.

The door creaked open, revealing a gaunt woman, her eyes hollow with grief. She nodded once, then disappeared into the shadowed interior. Thomas waited, listening to the soft scrape of fabric against wood.

She emerged, dragging a body wrapped in a threadbare sheet. A child, Thomas realized with a pang. So small, so light as he lifted it into the cart.

"I'm sorry," he murmured, though he knew the words were inadequate. The woman said nothing, only stared at the shrouded form with empty eyes before retreating into the house.

Thomas clicked his tongue, urging his horse forward. The cart's burden grew heavier with each stop, a grim harvest reaped from the town's dwindling population.

As he navigated the winding streets, Thomas's mind wandered. He remembered a time before the plague, when Eyam bustled with life. Children's laughter echoed through the square, market stalls overflowed with goods, and the air was sweet with the scent of baking bread.

Now, silence reigned. Shuttered windows stared like sightless eyes, and weeds pushed through cobblestones once worn smooth by countless feet. Thomas shook his head, banishing the memories. There was no use dwelling on what was lost.

The town gave way to rolling hills, and Thomas urged his horse towards the pit that yawned at the edge of a fallow field. The stench grew stronger as he approached, a miasma of rot and despair that seemed to pulse with malevolent life.

He brought the cart to a halt at the pit's edge. For a moment, he simply stared into its depths, a sea of tangled limbs and vacant faces. How many had he consigned to this earthen maw? Hundreds? Thousands? The numbers blurred together, a relentless tide of death that threatened to sweep away his sanity.

With practiced movements, Thomas began his grim task. One by one, he lifted the bodies from the cart, murmuring a quiet prayer for each soul as he consigned them to the pit. The work was mechanical, a rhythm of lift, carry, release that required no thought.

As he worked, Thomas became aware of a faint sound, barely audible above the whisper of the wind through the grass. He paused, cocking his head to listen. It was almost like . . . voices?

"No," he muttered, shaking his head. "It's just the wind. Just the wind and your tired mind playing tricks."

But as he resumed his work, the sound grew clearer. Whispers, soft as a dying breath, seemed to rise from the pit. Thomas froze, a body half-lowered into the grave.

"Please," a voice seemed to sigh. "Don't forget us."

Thomas stumbled back, nearly losing his footing on the slick earth. His heart hammered against his ribs, a frantic tattoo of fear and disbelief.

"I'm going mad," he whispered, pressing his palms against his temples. "It's the fatigue, the stress. Nothing more."

But the whispers persisted, a chorus of plaintive voices rising from the depths of the pit. Thomas squeezed his eyes shut, willing the sound away. When he opened them, the world swam before him, the edges of his vision blurring and distorting.

He stumbled back to his cart, his legs trembling beneath him. The horse nickered softly, sensing his distress. Thomas patted its flank, grateful for the warmth of living flesh beneath his hand.

"Come on, old friend," he murmured. "Let's get back to town. I need . . . I need rest."

As they made their way back to Eyam, Thomas couldn't shake the feeling that something fundamental had shifted. The whispers from the pit echoed in his mind, a haunting refrain that spoke of unfinished business and lingering regrets.

The sun was setting as they entered the town, painting the sky in shades of blood and fire. Thomas guided his cart through the empty streets, the silence broken only by the steady clip-clop of hooves against cobblestones.

He passed the town square, where the stocks stood empty, a relic of a time when public punishment was the greatest fear. Now, death stalked the streets with impunity, rendering such earthly justice obsolete.

As he neared his own modest dwelling, Thomas caught sight of a figure hurrying across the street. It was Sarah, the apothecary's widow, her arms laden with bundles of herbs.

"Evening, Thomas," she called, her voice muffled behind her mask. "How fares the day's work?"

Thomas opened his mouth to respond, but found the words stuck in his throat. How could he explain the whispers, the creeping dread that had taken root in his soul? He settled for a noncommittal grunt and a nod.

Sarah's eyes crinkled with concern above her mask. "You look pale, Thomas. Are you feeling well?"

"Just tired," he managed. "It's been a long day."

Sarah nodded sympathetically. "These are trying times for us all. Remember to take care of yourself, Thomas. We can't afford to lose our body collector."

As she hurried away, Thomas felt a chill run down his spine. Her words, meant as a kindness, felt like a prophecy. How long could he continue this grim work before it consumed him entirely?

He stabled his horse and trudged into his home, his body moving on autopilot. The interior was sparse, functional. Thomas had long since ceased to care about comfort or decoration. What was the point when death waited at every turn?

He collapsed into a chair, his bones aching with a weariness that seemed to seep into his very marrow. As he sat in the growing darkness, Thomas found his thoughts returning to the pit, to the whispers that had risen from its depths.

"It wasn't real," he muttered to himself. "Couldn't have been real."

But even as he spoke the words, doubt gnawed at him. In a world where death had become as common as breathing, who was to say what was real and what was not?

Thomas closed his eyes, hoping for the oblivion of sleep. But behind his eyelids, he saw only the faces of the dead, their lips moving in silent supplication. And in the quiet of his home, he could have sworn he heard the faintest whisper, a voice carried on the night air.

"Remember us, Thomas. Remember . . ."

He jerked awake, his heart pounding. The room was pitch black, the fire having long since died in the grate. Thomas fumbled for a candle, his hands shaking as he struck a spark.

The flame sputtered to life, casting wavering shadows on the walls. Thomas held the candle aloft, its feeble light barely penetrating the gloom. For a moment, he could have sworn he saw figures moving in the darkness, their forms insubstantial as smoke.

"I'm losing my mind," he whispered, his voice cracking. "Dear God, I'm losing my mind."

But even as he spoke, a part of him wondered if madness might not be preferable to the reality he faced each day. At least in madness, there might be some respite from the relentless tide of death that surrounded him.

Thomas slumped back in his chair, the candle guttering in his trembling hand. As the flame cast its flickering light, he found himself pondering the nature of his work. Was he truly providing a service to the town, or was he merely a harbinger of doom, collecting the dead like some macabre harvest?

The night stretched on, long and dark. Thomas sat motionless, lost in thought, as the candle burned lower and lower. And all the while, at the very edge of hearing, he could have sworn he heard whispers, soft as a dying breath, calling his name.

***

The whispers came like the first drops of rain, soft and hesitant, barely perceptible against the backdrop of Thomas's labored breathing and the creak of his wooden cart. At first, he dismissed them as nothing more than the wind sighing through the empty streets of the plague-ridden town, a mournful lament for the lives lost to the Black Death's merciless grip.

But as the days wore on and the bodies piled higher, the whispers grew more insistent, tugging at the edges of Thomas's consciousness like persistent children vying for attention. He found himself pausing in his grim work, cocking his head to listen, only to shake it vigorously and mutter a prayer under his breath.

"It's nothing," he told himself, his voice hoarse from disuse. "Just the ravings of an exhausted mind."

Yet the whispers persisted, growing clearer with each passing day. They followed him as he made his rounds through the town, collecting the dead from doorsteps and alleyways. They echoed in the creaking wheels of his cart as he trundled his macabre cargo to the pit outside the town walls. And they seemed to rise from the very earth itself as he tipped the bodies into their final resting place, a mass grave that yawned wider with each passing week.

One sweltering afternoon, as Thomas paused to wipe the sweat from his brow, he heard it clearly for the first time. A woman's voice, soft and melodious, rising from the pile of corpses in his cart.

"I never got to say goodbye," she whispered. "My children, my sweet babes. I left them alone in this world of sorrow."

Thomas whirled around, his heart pounding. But there was no one there, only the lifeless bodies wrapped in dirty shrouds. He shook his head, trying to clear the cobwebs of fatigue that clouded his mind.

"It's the heat," he muttered. "Playing tricks on me."

But as he resumed his grim task, the voices grew stronger, a chorus of regret and longing that seemed to emanate from every corpse he touched.

"I should've told her I loved her," a man's gruff voice lamented. "Now she'll never know."

"My life's work, unfinished," another voice moaned. "All those years of toil, for naught."

Thomas worked faster, his movements frantic as he tried to drown out the voices with the sound of his own labored breathing. But they only grew louder, more insistent, until he could no longer distinguish between the whispers of the dead and his own thoughts.

As he approached the pit, the cacophony reached a fever pitch. Voices clamored for his attention, each one desperate to share its story, to unburden itself of the weight of unfulfilled dreams and unspoken words.

"Listen to us, Thomas," they pleaded. "Hear our stories. Remember us."

Thomas stumbled, nearly losing his grip on the cart. He stared down at the bodies, his eyes wide with fear and confusion. "What do you want from me?" he whispered, his voice trembling.

The voices fell silent for a moment, as if considering his question. Then, softly at first but with growing strength, they began to speak again. This time, their words were not just fragments of regret, but full stories, rich with detail and emotion.

A young man's voice rose above the others, clear and strong. "I was to be married," he said. "Her name was Eliza, and she had hair like spun gold. We were to start a new life together, far from this cursed town. But the plague took me before I could claim her hand. Now she waits, not knowing my fate."

Thomas found himself nodding, picturing the young couple in his mind. He could almost see the golden-haired Eliza, her eyes bright with hope and love.

Another voice, this one belonging to an old woman, chimed in. "I lived a long life," she said, her tone wistful. "Saw my children grow and have children of their own. But there was always one regret that gnawed at me. As a girl, I had a talent for painting. My father said it was a waste of time, that I should focus on more practical pursuits. I listened to him, and my brushes gathered dust. Now, at the end, I wonder what beauty I might have created if I'd followed my heart."

Thomas felt a lump form in his throat. He'd never been one for art, but he could understand the pain of a dream deferred, a passion left unexplored.

The stories continued, each one a tapestry of joy and sorrow, triumph and regret. A merchant who had traveled the world, only to die within sight of his hometown. A mother who had sacrificed everything for her children, never asking for anything in return. A priest who had lost his faith in the face of so much suffering, only to rediscover it in his final moments.

As Thomas listened, he felt something shift within him. The fear that had gripped him earlier began to recede, replaced by a profound sense of connection to these lost souls. He found himself responding to their tales, offering words of comfort or asking questions to learn more.

"Did you ever try to paint again?" he asked the old woman.

"No," she replied, her voice tinged with regret. "But in my dreams, I created masterpieces."

To the young man, he said, "I'm sure Eliza would've been proud to be your wife."

"Thank you," the voice replied, a hint of peace in its tone. "I hope she finds happiness, even without me."

As the sun began to set, casting long shadows across the pit, Thomas realized he had been standing there for hours, lost in conversation with the dead. He should've been terrified, should've run screaming back to town. But instead, he felt a strange sense of calm.

"I'll come back tomorrow," he promised the voices. "There are more stories to hear, aren't there?"

A murmur of assent rose from the pit, like a gentle breeze rustling through leaves.

As Thomas made his way back to town, pushing his now-empty cart, he found himself looking at the world with new eyes. The devastation wrought by the plague was still evident in the boarded-up houses and empty streets, but now he saw beyond the surface. In each abandoned home, he imagined the lives that had been lived there, the dreams that had taken root and flourished before being cut short.

That night, as he lay in his small, sparse room, Thomas found sleep elusive. The voices of the dead echoed in his mind, their stories intertwining with his own memories. He thought of his own life, the choices he had made, the paths not taken. For the first time in years, he allowed himself to dream of a future beyond the endless cycle of death and disposal.

As dawn broke, Thomas rose, feeling both exhausted and strangely invigorated. He knew that the day ahead would bring more bodies, more stories, more whispers from beyond the veil. But now, instead of dreading his grim task, he found himself looking forward to it with a mixture of anticipation and reverence.

"I'm coming," he whispered to the empty room, knowing somehow that the dead would hear him. "I'm ready to listen."

And with that, Thomas stepped out into the plague-ridden streets, no longer just a collector of bodies, but a keeper of stories, a guardian of memories. The whispers of the dead had become his purpose, his calling. In a world ravaged by death, he had found a way to honor life.

***

The next day, as he made his rounds through the plague-stricken town, Thomas found himself listening more intently to the bodies he collected. Each one seemed to have a story, a final request, a regret that needed voicing.

"You there," he said to a woman whose glassy eyes stared accusingly at him. "What's your tale?"

To his horror and fascination, her lips seemed to move, forming words that only he could hear. "I never told him," she whispered. "I never told him I was with child."

Thomas nodded solemnly. "It's a shame," he said, gently lifting her into his cart. "But perhaps you'll meet again in the hereafter."

As he worked, he became aware of the stares of the living. They watched him from behind shuttered windows and cracked doors, their eyes wide with fear and suspicion.

"The collector speaks to the dead," he heard one woman hiss to another as he passed.

"He's gone mad," came the reply. "The plague has addled his wits."

Thomas wanted to explain, to tell them that the dead had so much to say if only someone would listen. But he knew they wouldn't understand. How could they, when they plugged their ears against the whispers that filled the air?

Days blurred into nights, and Thomas found himself spending more and more time at the pit. He would sit on its edge, legs dangling into the abyss, and listen to the stories of those he had laid to rest.

"Tell me," he would say to the darkness below. "Tell me everything."

And they did. They spoke of loves lost and found, of dreams unfulfilled, of regrets that weighed heavier than the earth that would soon cover them. Thomas listened, and in listening, he felt less alone.

The living began to shun him entirely. When he approached, they would cross themselves and hurry away, leaving him alone with his cart and his corpses. But Thomas no longer cared. He had found companionship among the dead, a kinship he had never known in life.

One evening, as the moon hung low and swollen in the sky, Thomas heard a new voice from the pit. It was clearer than the others, more insistent.

"Thomas," it called. "Thomas, my old friend."

He peered into the darkness, trying to locate the source of the familiar voice. "Who's there?" he called back.

"Don't you recognize me?" the voice replied. "We used to play together as boys, some years ago."

Thomas felt a chill run down his spine. He did remember, vaguely, a friend from his youth. But that friend had died years ago, long before Thomas had taken up his grim profession.

"How can that be?" Thomas said, his voice trembling. "You're not in the pit. Can't be."

The voice laughed, a sound like bones rattling in a box. "Of course I'm not. But that doesn't make me any less real."

Thomas scrambled back from the pit's edge, his heart pounding. For the first time since the voices had begun, he felt truly afraid. He ran back to town, his cart forgotten, the laughter of his long-dead friend echoing in his ears.

But there was no escape. The voices followed him, growing louder with each passing day. They whispered to him as he collected the bodies, shouted at him as he tried to sleep, sang to him in the quiet hours of the dawn.

Thomas began to no longer care who he saw or heard. He would argue with the dead in the streets, pleading with them to leave him in peace.

"I've done all I can," he would shout to the empty air. "What more do you want from me?"

The townspeople watched from a distance, crossing themselves and muttering prayers for his soul. But none dared approach him, fearing the madness that seemed to cling to him like a shroud.

As the days wore on, Thomas felt himself slipping further from reality. He no longer knew if he was awake or dreaming, alive or dead. The boundaries between worlds had blurred, leaving him adrift in a sea of whispers and regrets.

He stopped eating, stopped sleeping. His body moved through the motions of his daily tasks, but his mind was elsewhere, lost in the stories of the dead.

***

The moon hung like a bloated corpse in the sky, its sickly light casting long shadows across the desolate streets of the plague-ridden town. Thomas trudged through the emptiness, his cart creaking a mournful dirge behind him. The weight of countless bodies pressed down upon him, a burden far heavier than mere flesh and bone.

As he neared the pit outside of town, the whispers grew louder, a cacophony of voices that seemed to rise from the very earth itself. Thomas shook his head, trying to clear the fog that had settled over his mind like a shroud.

"Just the wind," he muttered, his voice hoarse from disuse. "Nothing but the wind and my own addled thoughts."

But the voices remained. They spoke of lives cut short, of dreams unfulfilled, of loves left behind. Thomas found himself listening, despite his best efforts to shut them out. What choice did he have.

"I was to be married," a young woman's voice sighed, soft as a summer breeze. "My Edmund waited for me, but I never came."

"My children," an old man wept. "Who will care for them now?"

Over and over again. The whispers came, as they had.

Thomas stumbled, nearly losing his grip on the cart. "Silence!" he shouted into the night. "Leave me be, I beg you!"

But the dead paid him no heed. Their stories flowed like a river, relentless and unstoppable. Thomas felt himself drowning in their sorrow, their regrets washing over him in waves.

He reached the rim of the pit, the vast darkness below almost seeming to pull him in. His hands shook as he began to unload the bodies, each one a stark reminder of the cruelty of fate.

"I'm sorry," he whispered as he worked. "I'm so sorry."

The voices grew louder, not just of the past, but now of Thomas himself.

"You're one of us now," they murmured. "Can't you see?"

Thomas shook his head violently. "No, no, I'm alive. I'm still here."

But doubt crept in, cold and insidious. When was the last time he had eaten? Slept? He couldn't remember. The days had blurred together, an endless procession of death and despair.

As he lifted the last body from the cart, a sharp pain seared through Thomas's side. He froze, his breath catching in his throat, his hand moving instinctively to the source of the pain. His fingers found a lump, swollen and tender beneath his touch.

"No," he whispered, the words rasping from him. His eyes widened, a knot of disbelief tightening in his chest. "It can't be."

His hand lingered on the swelling, but the certainty of it began to creep in, unwelcome. He had felt it before, in passing moments, the sensation of something not right, a shift he couldn't explain. Now, it was undeniable. Yet still, he moved, as though the task before him was all that mattered, as though the bodies needed to be taken, the work had to be done. What else could he do? He had no answer, only the endless march of his duty stretching on ahead.

Thomas hesitated, his mind slipping, as if the space between his thoughts had suddenly grown wider, harder to cross.

His body felt too heavy, and yet there was nothing to slow him. The work went on.

Thomas dropped to his knees at the edge of the pit, his mind frantic, racing through the impossible reality of it. The voices of the dead surrounded him now—not distant murmurs, but a chorus, rising like a tide. They beckoned.

"Join us," they called softly. "Your work is done."

With a final, broken breath, Thomas gave in. He let himself fall forward, into the waiting darkness. As he descended, a strange calm washed over him. It was the quiet of acceptance, the quiet of finally being home.

Above him, the moon kept its silent watch over the town, unmoved by the quiet dramas unfolding beneath its cold gaze. And in the pit, Thomas's voice became part of the chorus. His words, soft as the night air, mingled with the others.

"I am Thomas," he said. "And this is my story."

The wind carried his voice, carrying it through the empty streets, through windows left open in the stillness of the night. It was a simple phrase, but it was all he had to give.

In the days that followed, rumors began to spread. Some said the body collector had gone mad, fleeing the town in search of something that would save him. Others swore they had seen him—a shadow pushing his cart down narrow, empty alleys, a specter forever bound to the streets he had walked while living.

But in the pit, Thomas had found a kind of peace. Here, where the whispers of the dead filled the air, he was no longer burdened by the work that had defined him. He had been freed from the ties that had once held him prisoner to his task. No longer was he the body collector; he had become part of something larger, something quieter, something eternal.

Seasons changed. The plague, as it always does, passed. Life returned to the town, though its rhythm had shifted, as if it too had learned something it couldn't forget. The pit, once a place of sorrow, began to be reclaimed by the earth. Wildflowers spread across the ground where bodies had been laid. The delicate petals, bright and gentle, were a sharp contrast to the grief beneath.

And still, the whispers did not fade. They spoke of Thomas—of a man who had shown them more care in their final moments than anyone had ever shown in life. They spoke of his commitment, his tenderness, his unyielding presence even when everything around him had crumbled.

On certain nights, when the line between life and death seemed thinner than ever, a figure could be seen standing at the edge of the pit. He moved with a purpose, pushing a cart heavy with unseen things. It was no longer a cart of bodies, but one of stories—untold, preserved, still waiting to be heard.

"Tell me," he would say softly to each new arrival. "Tell me who you were. What you loved. What you lost. Your story is safe with me."

In those moments, Thomas had found a calling greater than any he had ever known in life. No longer just a collector of bodies, he had become a keeper of memories. A bridge, connecting the living and the dead, a conduit for those who could no longer speak for themselves.

The living might have forgotten him, but the dead had not. They would carry his name in their whispers, a thread weaving through generations of souls who needed someone to listen. And in the end, isn't that what all of us want? To be remembered? To have our stories told? To know that even after we are gone, we have left something behind?

The moon continued its slow, eternal arc across the sky, its light unchanged and uncaring. But Thomas walked on, his steps quieter now, a keeper of memories in the silence of the night. For in those stories, in those whispers, he had found not madness, but meaning. And with that meaning, he had found peace.

ABOUT THE AUTHOR

Philip Mazza is a novelist with a boundless imagination, captivating readers with the epic fantasy series *The Harrow Saga*. Born in New York in 1959, he earned a degree in Business from LeMoyne College and an MBA, later holding leadership roles in human resources and operations. Now a professor at the Madden School of Business and Economics, Philip dedicates his time to his students and writing. *The Quantum Messiah* is his third collection of short stories. He and his wife enjoy travel and continue to live in upstate New York.